MANIPULATION

Also by V.C. Kincade

Control
Dominance

Coming Soon

Revelation

Coming Up

Return
Obsession
Convergence
Reckoning

Manipulation

A Blackburn Erotic Thriller

V.C. Kincade

Northshore Noir Press

Cover design © Northshore Noir Press

Cover artwork: *The Quiet Ruin,* Susan Stevers, 2024.

Northshore Noir Press
Toronto, Canada
www.northshorenoir.com

ISBN: 978-1-998648-35-1

eBook ISBN: 978-1-998648-36-8

Contents

Chapter 1

Detective Victor Reeves parked his unmarked sedan at the curb of 74 Thyme Street. The engine ticked as it cooled in the thickening heat, each metallic click marking time against the morning's stillness. Three patrol cars sat in a row near the plain ranch house, their light bars dark, radios murmuring through half-open windows like distant conversation. An ambulance waited nearby. Its crew leaned against the back doors, their postures loose and resigned, already certain there was no one left to save. They'd tried.

The house sat low on its lot at the corner of Seventh. Vinyl siding bore the dull patina of sun and age. The front yard stretched more dirt than grass, patches of bare earth showing through like worn fabric. A chain-link gate hung open, one hinge twisted at an angle that suggested years of neglect. Reeves stepped over scattered gravel that crunched beneath his shoes and walked toward the porch.

Officers Zachariah Winters and Angela Camacho met him by the door. Winters stood tall, his gray hair cut military-close; Camacho, compact and steady, kept her hands folded at her belt in stillness.

"Detective," Winters said. "The neighbors called at six-twenty. One shot fired. We arrived and found John Dala on the steps." He nodded toward a spot by the doorway where the concrete bore a darker stain. "The gun was at his feet."

Reeves opened his notebook. The leather cover felt soft from years of handling, the gesture worn into muscle memory. "Did he cooperate?"

Camacho's glance was brief but telling. "He hasn't stopped talking since we got here. He said he shot his wife in the kitchen. Claims she deserved it over breakfast." She shrugged once, the gesture carrying volumes she didn't need to voice.

Yellow tape marked off the entrance, its bright warning stark against the faded siding. Further inside, the forensics team spoke in low, professional tones. Camera shutters punctuated the hush with mechanical precision.

"The victim?" Reeves asked.

"Rhyanne Scudamore," Winters replied after consulting his notes. "Forty-three years old. Shot once in the back of the head at close range."

Reeves climbed onto the porch. The boards flexed and groaned beneath his weight. The hallway inside felt narrow and airless. At its end, a strobe from a camera flickered against walls that had lost their color to time and indifference.

The kitchen felt cramped and heavy with trapped heat and a silence broken only by the careful movements of the forensics techs. On the floor beside a cold stove lay Rhyanne Scudamore face down, her dark hair spread in a wide arc across stained linoleum. The cast-iron skillet still held eggs, their edges hardened.

Blood had sprayed along the lower cabinets in a distinctive pattern. Most of it had already dried to brown in the morning warmth, the metallic scent mixing with burned food and old grease.

Marcus Webb looked up from his work when Reeves entered. "It's pretty clear-cut," he said. "Looks like a contact wound to the head. The thirty-eight revolver was still warm when we bagged it."

Reeves took in each detail. Routine procedure filtered everything through experience and restraint. The scene resembled dozens before it, yet it was never quite routine enough to ignore what lingered in the air when violence outlasted its cause.

Reeves studied the kitchen. Scudamore had faced the stove when she was shot, caught mid-task. The eggs in the pan showed one side browned too long, the other pale and untouched. Whatever mistake had happened here had cost her everything.

"Any signs of a struggle?"

"None." Webb's response carried professional detachment. "She never turned around. The shooter was close, maybe three feet. Quick."

Outside, Reeves watched Winters and Camacho guide John Dala into a patrol car. Dala looked unremarkable. He was soft around the middle, with pallid skin that spoke of too many hours indoors. His hands were cuffed behind his back, his expression flat but oddly satisfied, as if this outcome had been waiting all along.

"She couldn't cook eggs right," Dala muttered before the door closed with finality. "Twenty-three fucking years and she never got it right."

The car pulled away, tires crunching over loose asphalt. Reeves watched until it disappeared around the corner, then glanced at the crowd gathering down the block. Neighbors had been drawn out by sirens, their morning routines fractured by violence.

A woman approached the tape. She was silver-haired and drawn tight with worry. She wore a faded housecoat and slippers that had seen better days.

"Officer?" she called to Reeves. "I'm Lori Clattenberg. I live next door."

He met her at the line. From her porch she would have had a clear view of the Dala house. Every argument would have been audible through thin walls.

"I'm Detective Reeves. Did you see anything, Ms. Clattenberg?"

"I heard them," she said, arms folded tight against herself, though sweat already beaded on her forehead. "They fought every morning about breakfast, laundry, something small every time." Her voice carried the exhaustion of repeatedly witnessing another person's downfall.

"This morning?"

"It was worse." She kept her gaze fixed on the Dala house, as if it might reveal something new. "She was crying and begging him to stop yelling. Then I heard the shot." Her hand trembled as she pointed at the porch steps. "He came outside after. He just sat down and put the gun beside him like he was waiting for a bus."

Reeves wrote as she spoke, his pen moving steadily across the page.

"How long were they here?"

"Five years? Maybe six." She hesitated before adding, "He hit her before. Sometimes I called you people, but nothing came of it. She had always said she fell or walked into something." Clattenberg blinked hard against tears that threatened to spill. "I should have done more."

The cycle played itself out in Reeves' mind with depressing familiarity. Abuse, police calls, apologies, another incident. Until one day the pattern reached its inevitable end.

"You did what you could." He meant it simply. It was a truth learned too many times on this job. "We'll need your statement later at the station."

She nodded and made her way home, each step careful on the uneven lawn.

Reeves called over Field and Schiller and set them to canvassing for doorbell footage and witnesses on both sides of the street. It was the standard work that built cases one methodical step at a time. Unglamorous but necessary, constant as sunrise after violence breaks through suburban walls.

* * *

She'd hit him hard enough to break his nose and enjoyed it.

Detective Morgan Blackburn flexed her hand. Her suspension had been no surprise. She knew it would happen before she even slapped him. The tendons shift beneath her skin. Dawning sunlight flooded the kitchen, pooling across counters and glinting off the running faucet. She rinsed an apple under the stream, its surface gleaming bruised-red while cold water numbed her fingertips. The sharp scent of Empire mingled with Bach from the small speaker by the window: crisp, ordered notes threading through the room like silver wire.

Her grip tightened on the apple, pressure anchoring her in memory. Kendria Chaplin had found pleasure in rubbing a similar red apple between her legs, just as Blackburn had commanded. Her moans had been low and rough. Apple was their safe word, and to prevent Kendria from orgasming, Blackburn had knocked it from her grip, ending their session. Kendria had obeyed. Kendria had been hers.

Until she wasn't.

The memory dissolved as routine took over. Blackburn sliced the apple with deliberate movements. Sunlight caught droplets sliding across the fruit's skin, each action ordinary, a barrier against what waited beyond these walls.

Flash: Oak Street. Heat radiated from the pavement in waves. Banter cut short by screeching tires, a silver car bearing down with mechanical malevolence. Time fractured. Blackburn's arms grasped for Kendria too late; bodies torn apart by force and fate at an impossible speed. The aftermath: only noise. A stranger shouting slurs, chaos rising like steam from hot asphalt. Something twisted inside her. Not grief, but fury at losing what could have been hers. Her palm met flesh with a wet crack; the man's head snapped back, blood blooming bright across his upper lip.

It felt good.

Blackburn lay stretched on her leather couch, a demitasse balanced between her fingers, half an inch of espresso cooling bitterly in the bottom. The nearly empty plate sat on the table, moisture glistening where fruit had bled. On her lap, the latest copy of Rijksmuseum Bulletin.

Sunlight etched soft lines across the floor, catching her jaw still set, teeth pressing against words and anger she refused to release. The suspension sat heavy on her shoulders, an invisible weight that made her skin feel too tight. She'd never tolerated leashes.

Her phone rang, abruptly and insistently. Reeves' name lit the screen.

She answered with a clipped, "What."

"Where are you?" Reeves kept his tone flat, though traffic hummed in the background. He was not at the office. "We have a shooting at Seventh and Thyme."

Blackburn sipped the last of the espresso, bitterness coating her tongue. "Hayes suspended me. Turns out punching racists isn't part of my job description."

The line went quiet except for distant sirens. When Reeves spoke again, he sounded tired. "Yeah. I heard." He paused, letting silence fill what neither needed to say.

She exhaled heavily. "That clown made it personal. So did I," she said, voice low, words pared to bone. "You'll have to work it without me for now."

"But—"

"Just handle it, Reeves." She cut him off and ended the call.

The next call came minutes later: Chief Hayes. She let it ring until the screen went black, then reached for the TV remote and switched on New Dresden Today.

The anchor's voice blended into white noise: "Tonight at six, an exclusive from Brynn Cassidy that could shake New Dresden's foundation."

She clicked it off before the promo ended. Brynn was a damned fly. An annoying pest constantly rolling in shit.

She stayed motionless, sinking deeper into old leather that smelled faintly of conditioning oil as neighborhood sounds pressed in: a dog barking beyond her fence, a car door slamming two houses down with metallic finality.

A knock broke through. Three raps. She waited until the second round came, louder, insistent. Blackburn looked at her watch. Seven forty-two. She had been sitting here for less than ninety minutes, though it felt like forever.

With effort, she pushed up and crossed to the door. Each step slow and even, nothing in her movements wasted energy or betrayed urgency.

Through the frosted sidelight, she recognized Willow Adler's frame immediately. Heavy set, short, familiar. They'd been together, on and off, for more than two years. Right now: a forbidden 'on.' Disallowed by NDPD's policy on dating subordinates.

But Blackburn couldn't resist: Willow was an almost perfect subordinate.

Willow caught sight of Blackburn's silhouette and waved, holding up a paper bag, grease spots darkening its bottom corner.

Blackburn opened the door.

"Chief Hayes sent me," Willow said, eyes steady behind her glasses. "He's worried; you're not answering calls."

Blackburn shrugged. "Ignoring him."

Her phone started ringing again behind her, that same custom tone she had chosen specifically because it annoyed her. Hayes again. She ignored it just as easily.

Willow lifted the bag an inch higher. "Bagels. Nova lox."

A pause. Then Blackburn exhaled, tension easing from her shoulders.

"All right," she said, stepping aside with a nod toward the kitchen. "Come in."

Willow entered quietly, shoes left at the door, coat hung in its usual place. She moved to the kitchen, footsteps silent on the cool tile.

"They say you're suspended," she said, reaching for a butter knife as she opened a drawer with ease. Blackburn unpacked deli bagels, still warm and yeast-scented, and set cream cheese beside them.

"I am. I hit someone. It's online now. Viral." Cold. Factual. Blackburn nodded, watching Willow slice bagels and feed them into the toaster.

Willow took a seat across from her, peeled back the plastic on the Nova lox, its briny scent drifting through the air.

"Did you watch it?" Willow asked, pulling hot bagels free, steam curling upward.

"I didn't need to," Blackburn said, sliding her plate closer. "I was there."

Willow paused mid-preparation, glancing up. "The chief wants you at headquarters for a morning press conference." The words came fast, rehearsed.

"What's it about?" Blackburn's tone sharpened like a blade finding its edge.

"I don't know." Willow looked past her to her own plate.

"You do," Blackburn said.

Before Willow could answer, Blackburn's phone rang: Brynn Cassidy's number appeared on the screen. Blackburn wondered if it was time to get a new, unlisted phone number.

The phone was dark for just a moment when a new alert flashed; another call coming in. Blackburn answered.

"Good morning, Chief Hayes."

"Blackburn, I need you at headquarters for a press conference." His voice was taut, professional strain woven through each word.

"So," Willow said, "what's this about?"

Hayes hesitated just long enough for intent to show. "Clyde Mullen's attorney reached out. They'll drop any lawsuit if you apologize on camera."

Willow froze, bagel suspended midair at the word "apologize." She knew Blackburn well enough to know those words rarely left her lips, and never with honesty.

Blackburn registered Willow's reaction and responded with a dry wink. "What time do you want me there, chief?"

"8:45. Press conference at nine sharp."

"Understood." Blackburn ended the call, methodical as ever.

"You're not actually going to apologize," Willow said, skepticism threading through her voice.

Blackburn's mouth sharpened into something between a smile and a warning. "I'm going to make sure he remembers this morning for all the wrong reasons."

Willow's laugh broke the tension as she turned back to breakfast, still uncertain which 'he' Blackburn had in mind.

Blackburn stood, brushing crumbs from her hands to the plate. Then, at the doorway:

"We've got time for something quick."

She didn't wait for agreement. Willow loved the shower. Two crooked fingers beckoned once before she turned toward the bathroom.

Willow lingered in the doorway, fingers grazing her t-shirt's soft edge, watching Blackburn move through her morning routine. The bathroom's warm light cut soft lines across tile; the steady rush of water filled the silence with white noise. She liked the discipline that followed the surrender to her Lioness. Her toes tingled as she thought of what she might get.

Blackburn stepped under the shower, letting out a sharp breath as heat struck her skin like needles. She set the temperature just above comfort: a choice, not a mistake. The bite grounded her, a routine reminder that power belonged to her alone.

Steam thickened in slow spirals, blurring the mirror until only shapes remained. The spray beat a strict rhythm against tile: persistent, methodical, enough to mute thoughts of suspension and Hayes's ultimatum.

Willow peeled off her clothes with little care for order, dropping them by the door. She stepped into the steam, enveloped by warmth as she closed the distance between them.

Inside the shower's haze, their bodies found each other. Willow just within reach, hands working careful patterns over Blackburn's arms and along her spine. The touch was exacting, as she'd been taught. Pressure here, release there.

Blackburn angled against the cool tile. It shocked her heated skin, and she drew Willow closer. A slow pull at Willow's nipples earned an indistinct sound: pleasure acknowledged but not dramatized. Their mouths met in brief collisions more forceful than tender, tasting of salt and coffee.

Water slid over their skin in rivulets, disguising half-voiced needs. Willow's hand slipped between Blackburn's thighs; she worked in patient strokes, unhurried, letting Blackburn set the pace with only a word or tilt of hip.

"Harder," Blackburn murmured, voice pitched low against steam.

Willow answered with pressure and rhythm that made Blackburn's breath catch. Blackburn held Willow's arms as release built: a quiet struggle for composure rather than spectacle.

"You're beautiful," Willow said, voice low and reverent. The words settled in warm air, observation more than compliment. "So beautiful. I'm lucky to be yours."

Willow's fingers worked their magic and Blackburn let go, her body tense as pleasure surged through her like electricity. Her quiet gasp blended with the shower's muted rush. Water stripped away her tension for one brief minute.

She traced Willow's cheek with care, feeling the heat beneath her wet skin, then landed a hard, loud slap. "You're good," she said, water slipping down her back in warm trails. "You've learned so well."

"Thank you, Lioness." Willow's smile was swift and genuine. "I figured out what you like to see."

Blackburn tapped Willow's shoulder. Two quick touches, their silent cue. Willow slipped out, leaving Blackburn beneath the steady spray.

Willow wrapped herself in a towel that smelled of fabric softener, slid on her glasses, and watched Blackburn's outline behind fogged glass. The sting on her cheek was delicious. "What's your angle for the press conference?" she asked, toweling hair dry.

Blackburn tilted her head back into the stream before shutting off the water with a squeak of old pipes. "There were so many people with their phones out," she said as she stepped out and reached for a towel. "The truth is out there. And I will just speak to the truth."

In the bedroom, Blackburn dressed methodically: black suit crisp from the cleaner's, pale blue shirt smooth as water, collar pressed flat. She grabbed her Halperin compact and swept a light layer of powder across her face. She would be on camera.

"You look sharp," Willow said from the doorway.

"Do I look honest?" Blackburn asked, searching Willow's face for doubt.

Willow nodded once. She understood what was at stake.

Blackburn crossed the room and kissed her briefly, tasting toothpaste. "Let's go."

Chapter 2

Blackburn eased her sedan into the staff lot behind headquarters, hands steady on the wheel. Through her rearview mirror, she watched the crowd at the front entrance. Signs were raised, faces split between anger and support. Media strobes flared white-hot against morning shadows, fracturing the scene into jagged fragments. A line of uniformed officers held the perimeter.

"Circus." The word barely disturbed the silence. In her mirror, she caught Willow's compact car turning in. Blackburn tapped a slow rhythm on the steering wheel, leather warm beneath her fingers, tracking Willow's path as she parked and approached.

The back entrance was quiet. It was rough concrete walls and a card reader beside a plain metal door that smelled faintly of rust. Willow hesitated at the threshold, badge trembling in her grip before she swiped it. Blackburn noticed and let a crooked smile cross her lips. Willow knew *something* was about to happen. The lock clicked open, too loud in the monotonous echoes of the protesters.

Inside, LED light carved sharp edges down empty corridors. Their footsteps echoed over worn linoleum, Willow's quick steps chasing Blackburn's pace as they navigated ancillary hallways toward the press room. The air tasted stale, recycled.

The atmosphere shifted as they entered from the side. Voices rose in anticipation, cameras trained on the podium like weapons, every lens awaiting movement. Chief Hayes stood rigid, arms folded across his chest, jaw working silently. Beside him, a press officer shifted from foot to foot, uniform crisp beneath lights that made everyone squint.

Brynn Cassidy spotted Blackburn and started toward her, threading through the assembled reporters. Blackburn lifted a hand in a flat gesture: not now. Brynn stopped short but lingered nearby, close enough that Blackburn caught her perfume, something sharp and green.

Hayes met Blackburn's eye across the room and signaled her forward with a tilt of his chin. As she approached, Willow melted into the crowd, her presence absorbed by the shifting mass of press and public.

Blackburn nearly collided with Deputy Chief Kelsey McLaughlin. McLaughlin's mouth twitched in fleeting disdain before Blackburn continued past.

Hayes intercepted Blackburn before she reached the podium. His voice stayed low, his breath was foul. "Keep it simple. You apologize to Mullen and nothing more. He'll withdraw his complaint and forgo any future lawsuits. I've got the mayor breathing down my neck on this fiasco." His look made clear there would be no negotiation.

"Who is Mullen?"

"Clyde Mullen. The man you hit."

"Allegedly."

"Don't you dare, Blackburn," Hayes said as he covered his mouth. No one could read his lips. "Don't you fucking dare."

Blackburn scanned the room, taking in the agitation of the assembled press; pens clicking, phones glowing, shoulders hunched forward. "What about the protesters outside?"

Hayes kept his eyes ahead, a muscle ticking in his cheek. "Public Relations will deal with them. Stick to your statement."

"I haven't seen a copy."

A faint smile tugged at her lips as she shifted her attention to Brynn Cassidy in the crowd. Their eyes met across the press scrum; Blackburn mouthed, Found it? When the nosy reporter had approached her right after her suspension, Blackburn told the woman to find the real videos.

Brynn's answering nod was almost imperceptible. Blackburn's smile deepened, warmth spreading through her chest.

At 9:02 AM, the press liaison stepped to the podium, badge catching the light in sharp flashes. The room stilled as he cleared his throat; the sound amplified through speakers that hummed with static.

"Thank you for being here," he said, voice steady and unhurried. "Detective Morgan Blackburn will make a brief statement. Chief Hayes will then address the reporters."

Blackburn looked at Hayes and held her hands palms up: still no prepared statement.

Expectation thickened the air like humidity as Blackburn approached. Her movements were calm, a solid presence amid chaos. Cameras clicked in bursts, mechanical and hungry. A low murmur rippled through the reporters. Chief Hayes watched from the wings, expression unreadable but tense, hands clasped behind his back.

She adjusted the microphone, metal cold against her fingers, and let silence settle over the room before speaking, voice low but clear, posture composed.

"I address you as a detective and as an individual." She paused, eyes moving from face to face until they found Brynn again, steady and knowing.

"I acknowledge losing my composure. A lapse in professionalism for which I take full responsibility."

A ripple moved through the room like wind through wheat. Hayes shifted his weight; approval flickered across a few faces.

She continued, tone even, gaze unwavering. "But we need to be honest about what occurred."

The tension edged higher, discomfort passing through the crowd like electricity. They hadn't expected deviation from protocol this early. Only Brynn seemed unsurprised, leaning forward.

"A woman died in the street last night. Kendria Chaplin. An African American woman. She was struck by a car, and I reached her side before anyone else. While I was kneeling beside her, trying to offer something decent in the middle of that chaos, Clyde Mullen started filming. Then he started laughing."

She paused. The room tensed, the silence shifting as the memory settled between them like smoke. Some here had seen the Mullen's footage. Others knew there had been other cameras. Trained on him.

"He made a joke about her body. She wasn't even cold. A joke about her skin tone. It was ugly, and racist, and it doesn't bear repeating."

Her voice stayed even, each word as deliberate as stones dropped in water. She let them sit with it, let it work through their stomachs.

"I forgot at that moment that I wear a badge. I forgot about the fallout. The suspensions and press conferences and investigation and public fallout. All I saw was a man mocking the dead in front of me. And I reacted."

Hayes's jaw tightened; she could see the vein at his temple, knew he wanted her to stop, contain it. She kept going.

"There's a video circulating, one that makes me look like the villain. It went live before I'd even finished at the scene." She turned, eyes finding Brynn's and holding. "But there are other recordings and more witnesses. Those show what happened."

A shift at the edge of the crowd; someone with a phone raised, the screen's glow reflected in their glasses.

"I shouldn't have struck him. An officer is supposed to rise above any provocation." Her gaze swept the room. "But what does anyone do when someone desecrates the dead? When he taunts over a body that won't ever get up again? He said the only way he'd..."

Blackburn paused. Considered. The microphone picked up her breath. She pulled the trigger.

"The only way he'd touch an N-word was if she were dead." Her jaw set as she exhaled slowly, the words hanging in the air like an accusation. "I know what I did, and if I could do it over, if being better than human were possible, I wouldn't have hit him."

A pause. She leaned into the mic, letting the moment stretch until it nearly snapped.

"I'd have broken his fucking jaw."

Silence cut through the room like a blade. Hayes paled, color draining from his face. Blackburn wondered if she'd pushed it too far. Then... explosion. Reporters closed in, shouting over each other for position, voices crashing together.

Blackburn stepped away from the podium, a trace of satisfaction visible at the corner of her mouth. She passed Hayes without acknowledgment and moved into the corridor beyond, heels clicking a steady retreat. The questions would land wherever they landed.

At the podium, Chief Warren Hayes anchored himself with both hands, knuckles white under the press lights. Voices came fast and relentlessly, each one a direct hit. Sweat prickled on his scalp beneath the glare, trickled down his spine. His collar felt like a noose.

"Chief Hayes, were you aware of the unedited footage before Detective Blackburn's suspension?" A reporter pressed forward, microphone extended like an accusation.

"I'm not—"

"The unedited version clearly records Clyde Mullens making racist and sexist statements," someone shouted out.

Hayes drew himself upright, tasting copper. "No. I don't know anything about that."

Another voice rose, clearer than the rest: "Given what's come out, do you stand by your decision to suspend Detective Blackburn?"

"Yes. We follow procedure." His response was automatic, thin as paper. He heard it falter in his own ears.

A third question fired from the back: "If a Black man said that about a dead white woman, would he also be walking free?"

Chief Hayes cleared his throat, the sound rough. The question came from a protester, not a reporter. It didn't matter. All eyes were on him, waiting. "The department doesn't condone any form of hate speech or bigotry," he began, voice tense. "However, as a private citizen, Mr. Mullen's comments, while deeply offensive, fall outside the purview of our disciplinary actions."

He paused, scanning the room filled with reporters and onlookers, feeling their judgment like heat. "We understand the public's outrage and the pain these words have caused. While we can't take legal action against speech protected under the First Amendment, we are committed to fostering a community that stands against hate in all its forms."

Noise burst around him, disbelief cresting into open anger. He caught fragments: accusation disguised as inquiry, too many to answer at once. He raised his hands in a placating gesture but found no purchase.

A reporter in the front row spoke up, her voice calm but the question unyielding: "Was Detective Blackburn's response justified?"

Hayes didn't hesitate, though his tone had lost its edge. "No. It isn't acceptable for a detective to strike someone absent a direct threat." He steadied himself, choosing his words with care. "Suspect or otherwise. It was a mistake."

The press seized on the admission like blood in the water. Questions rose in quick succession.

"Detective Blackburn suggested the department cares more about image than truth. Is that accurate?" Another reporter, sharp and unrelenting.

"We do not," Hayes replied, jaw set. "She did not make that claim. This department stands by the truth and the law." But as the words left him, he felt uncertainty lurking beneath, an uncomfortable sense that Blackburn had maneuvered him into this position.

The press corps pressed harder. *Was the public trust compromised? Would every second of bodycam footage be made public? Did Blackburn's actions expose deeper divisions within the department?*

Hayes responded where he could, keeping his answers firm, but the room's mood shifted. Less outrage now, more appetite for a reckoning. He understood it would not be Blackburn's reckoning alone.

Chapter 3

Reeves worked methodically. He'd tried calling Blackburn, but she told him to handle it. So he did. He moved from door to door, notebook open, repeating his questions with patient persistence. The answers rarely changed. Neighbors had heard raised voices through walls too thin for secrets, but none claimed to have seen anything useful. A few recalled police showing up before. Arguments that ended in warnings, crying that led to restraining orders Rhyanne never enforced.

By noon, the forensics team had cleared out. The body was gone, leaving only tape and markers. The house sat hollow, its windows catching sunlight and reflecting nothing but glare. Reeves closed his notebook. The pages were now filled with similar stories. He walked to his car. This was a case with no ambiguity. It was open and shut. No tangled motives or weeks spent chasing digital breadcrumbs through server logs.

John Dala shot his wife over breakfast. He admitted it on the spot and provided every detail needed. Evidence aligned with the confession. The motive was painfully clear, the outcome already written. After months buried in cases filled with technical dead-ends and corporate lawyers, Reeves almost appreciated the brutal directness of it.

He drove away from Thyme Street without looking back, already outlining his report in his head. Sometimes a case wanted to be solved. Sometimes it just needed to be properly recorded.

He entered the Homicide Division, his coffee sending up wisps of steam into the afternoon air. The bullpen stretched before him in its familiar arrangement: orderly desks beneath LED lights that drained color from everything they touched. Cooper and Sinclair sat hunched at their stations, the steady click of keyboards marking time like a metronome in the unusual quiet.

The atmosphere had shifted today. What should have been the usual morning chaos of phones trilling and voices carrying across the room in overlapping conversations had been replaced by something subdued, almost reverential. Reeves set his coffee down on his desk. The ceramic met wood with a sound that echoed in the hush.

"Gentlemen," Reeves offered.

Cooper glanced up, fatigue etched into every line of his face. His shirt bore the telltale wrinkles of yesterday's wear, tie hanging loose like a surrender flag. "Did you see it?"

"See what?"

Sinclair swiveled toward them, abandoning his paperwork entirely. He wore the unsettled expression of someone caught between disbelief and deep concern. "Blackburn's press conference. Nine o'clock this morning."

A familiar tightness coiled in Reeves's gut. He had deliberately avoided watching, knowing Blackburn's choices rarely landed anywhere between disaster and genius. "I was at a scene. What happened?"

"She apologized," Cooper said, his voice stripped of all inflection.

"That's what Hayes wanted."

Sinclair cut in. "She apologized for hitting Clyde Mullen in the face." He hesitated only a moment before adding, "Said she should have broken his jaw instead."

Reeves's hand stopped halfway through lifting his coffee. Steam curled between them in the silence.

"She said that? Out loud?"

Cooper nodded once. "Walked out right after she said it. Press cameras rolling, Hayes was frozen behind her like a statue."

Sinclair shook his head ruefully. "She looked straight into those cameras before she left. Then she just walked out without another word."

That was why she was so terse on the phone. Reeves had watched Blackburn orchestrate her risks before, had seen her push when others would pull back. But this wasn't calculated; it felt raw, exposed.

Sinclair broke the silence first, pulling out his worn leather wallet. "I'll bet a hundred she's back inside of a week."

Cooper shook his head without turning from his monitor. "Not interested."

"It's easy money," Sinclair pressed. "The shortest suspension so far is for a uni who fell asleep. A week, I think. I say she comes back faster."

Cooper didn't respond.

Reeves crossed to the case board mounted along one wall. Columns split by each detective's name showed red ink for active cases and black for closed files. He picked up a red marker and wrote SCUDAMORE beneath his own column, pressing harder than necessary so the letters bled dark into the whiteboard's surface, joining the ghosts of cases past.

His desk waited in a back corner. The battered surface was crowded with coffee-stained mugs and unread newspapers. Dawson had not canceled his subscription. The chair complained with a familiar squeak as he sat down. "Blackburn never goes down easy," he said, his voice low and certain. He pressed his palm against the cool metal scanner of the file locker, which opened with a sharp click. He pulled out the files from last night, their edges still crisp and sharp against his fingertips, and dropped them onto his desk with a soft thud.

Sinclair tried again: "You think I'm wrong? You think she'll be back sooner?"

"I think she's out for longer." Reeves opened his email and scrolled through overnight case logs. "She told every camera she had considered aggravated assault and didn't regret it. There's no way Hayes can smooth that over with a couple of days off."

The air in the bullpen felt heavy with unspoken knowledge. No one addressed it directly. Blackburn's record was common currency among them: the broken rules, the cases closed, the lines she redrew when no one else dared. But now the fallout had gone public. Viral. The kind that didn't get quietly swept aside.

Cooper kept his eyes fixed on his monitor, fingers tracing a restless pattern beside his keyboard. "You hear what Mullen said after? Called her a 'dyke bitch who can't handle real police work.'"

Sinclair stiffened in his chair. "Was that into a mic?"

"Microphones were still rolling." Cooper's expression flattened into something hard. "He should be grateful all she did was slap him the first time."

"He's risking a lawsuit from her."

"For dyke bitch?" Sinclair asked with a frown.

"For not being able to handle real police work," Reeves said with a grin.

Blackburn wasn't known for losing control. Her force made statements; it was never reckless. Two incidents with Mullen meant something had shifted beneath the surface. A calculation altered, an impulse trusted one time too many.

He poked his desktop, made it beep in protest. "Let's get back to work. We've got enough on our plates." He dialed the coroner's office, the numbers automatic after years of repetition.

"Morgue, Janet speaking."

"Detective Reeves with NDPD. I'm looking for preliminary findings on Rhyanne Scudamore."

"One minute." Papers shuffled. Keys clacked with efficient speed in the background. "Found her file. Single gunshot wound to the head at close range. It appears to be a thirty-eight. Dr. Martinez will do the full autopsy by Thursday but we pulled a bullet from her brain. Finding is homicide."

Reeves scribbled notes in his tight handwriting on a yellow legal pad already half-filled. "Time of death?"

"The preliminary estimate is between six and six-thirty this morning based on liver temperature and early rigor."

He thanked her and hung up. At his terminal, he logged into the state database and entered Rhyanne's information. The screen blinked before bringing up her driver's license photo. A woman stared forward with weary eyes and tension etched around her mouth. Her hair was pulled back severely from her face. There was no sign she had made any effort beyond the minimum required.

The address matched Thyme Street. The emergency contact listed was Heather Katt, mother, living out in the Westbrook suburbs.

Sinclair eyed both of them, searching for a consensus he wouldn't find. "Think she'll keep working from home? Unofficially?"

"With Blackburn?" Cooper's reply held no humor. "She'll make contact when she wants to. A suspension won't stop her." He paused, letting that settle into the quiet. "Only question is whether we pick up."

Reeves sipped his coffee, now gone cold, thinking of how many times he had watched Blackburn run interviews from the side of a hospital bed or dictate strategy from in front of some half-lit motel room miles from any precinct. Procedures meant little to her. A suspension would shift her tactics, not shut her down.

"When she calls, and she will," Reeves said, keeping his voice even, "we handle it on our terms. For now, we do things by the book." He looked at each detective. "Hayes will be watching every move for weeks. We don't give him reasons to be concerned."

Sinclair spun lightly in his chair, still adjusting to the absence. "We're flying solo."

"We're still detectives," Cooper said.

"With or without Blackburn," Reeves finished, though he felt the hollow echo in those words more than he would admit out loud. He rested his hand on the phone receiver for a moment before lifting it. Two decades on the job hadn't made these calls easier. There was no script for telling someone their daughter was dead. No words could soften the blow or make sense of the senseless.

He dialed and listened to the hollow ring.

"Hello?" The voice was older and already wary. Something in its careful restraint signaled a history of dreaded calls.

"Mrs. Katt, this is Detective Victor Reeves with New Dresden Police. I'm calling about your daughter, Rhyanne Scudamore."

Silence stretched taut as wire. When she answered, her voice had shrunk to almost nothing. "What happened?"

"I'm sorry to tell you that your daughter was found dead this morning. She was shot at her home. Her husband, John Dala, is in custody."

A sharp exhale followed. It was neither sob nor gasp, just air forced out as her world restructured itself in an instant. "God. Oh God. I told her this would happen. I begged her to leave him."

Reeves waited, holding the phone steady as she wept quietly on the other end. He didn't interrupt with platitudes or false comfort that would ring hollow. Cooper's eyes flickered up quickly, a sign of sympathy, before he put his head down again.

"Mrs. Katt, I know this is difficult, but I need to ask a few questions. Can you describe your daughter's relationship with Mr. Dala?"

"He was violent," she said, her voice rough and stripped of pretense. "He hit her all the time. She had visited with bruises or black eyes and made up stories about falling down stairs or walking into doors. After a while, I stopped pretending to believe her."

"Did she ever try to leave him?"

"She tried a few times over the years. She always went back. He had promised to change and swore he needed her. I think she was terrified of what he had do if she really left." There was a pause while she gathered herself. "Was it quick? Did she suffer?"

Reeves spoke gently but honestly. "It was very quick."

He couldn't know exactly what Rhyanne had experienced in those final moments, but Mrs. Katt deserved whatever small mercy certainty could offer.

They spoke for another ten minutes while Reeves collected background details and explained the next steps. The autopsy, release of remains, required paperwork that would transform grief into procedure. Heather agreed to come to the station the next day.

He ended the call and sat still for a moment, staring at the phone as if it might ring again with different news. The bullpen gradually returned to its routine; phones trilled, keys clicked in familiar rhythms, information moved from screen to screen and mind to mind. But each sound felt somehow diminished, half an echo of its usual energy.

He turned back to his computer and began typing his report. Time of discovery, responding officers, suspect's statement, physical evidence collected. Facts organized in plain language that reduced a life to standard procedure.

The system confirmed John Dala had been booked and was being held without bail pending arraignment on three charges. First-degree murder, domestic violence resulting in death, unlawful discharge of a firearm within city limits. The DA's office would review it for formal prosecution.

Reeves picked up the phone again and called the district attorney's office. He waited while the receptionist patched him through to ADA Melanie Bowman.

"What do you have for me, Detective?"

"Domestic homicide, straightforward as they come. The husband shot his wife at breakfast and confessed on scene. Multiple neighbors heard him admit it. Long history of domestic calls."

"Priors?"

Reeves checked Dala's arrest record on his screen. "Three domestic assault arrests in five years. Each time the same result. Fines, probation, anger management that he never completed."

"Classic escalation," Bowman said, her tone flat with familiar exhaustion. "Send me everything when you're done. We'll charge Murder One and see if he wants to deal."

Reeves made the last call to the county jail to arrange a formal interview. No surprise when the desk sergeant called back twenty minutes later.

"The suspect declines interview," the sergeant said. "He's demanding a lawyer. He wants a public defender."

Reeves logged it and pushed away from his desk. The chair protested again. The case would move as expected now. Arrest, booking, lawyer, arraignment, plea negotiations. Dala would likely plead down to second degree and accept fifteen to twenty years behind bars. He would emerge old and alone.

Late afternoon shadows crept across the squad room floor as the day wore on. Reeves scanned the board again. SCUDAMORE was written in fresh red under his name.

Clear lines. Fast resolution. Nothing was left hanging in uncertainty.

The system would handle the rest.

* * *

Reeves opened Kendria Chaplin's file again. The photos were stark and impersonal under the harsh strip lights above his desk. Another death by an autonomous vehicle on Oak Street. Another event that circled something larger and unfinished.

He picked up his phone and dialed Marilyn Chaplin's number, feeling how far they had slipped from certainty without their anchor in place, and wondering if that gap was exactly where trouble began.

* * *

Cooper drew the Jenna Langston file to the center of his desk. Photographs fanned out before him, each image a silent record: a young woman captured at the edge of routine, moments before it ended. He studied her face briefly, letting the details settle into memory. Zhang had been arrested, but there was so much work to do to support a conviction. It had been the chief's call, and he did none of the work.

"I'm looking at Jenna Langston again," he said. His voice cut through the steady hum of the bullpen. "I'll re-interview Swiatek and Keys on their no-driver statements. Focus on timing and distance. Distinguish what they actually recall from what fits the story."

Sinclair's attention flicked up from his monitor. "Are they changing their tune?"

"They reconstruct what makes sense." Cooper opened his notebook, the pages crisp beneath his fingers. His handwriting was measured, his questions precise. "Keys was sixty feet ahead, in his truck, distracted. Swiatek had line of sight but was riding through traffic dodging cars when he saw it and gave chase. I want them to walk me through it again, moment by moment."

Returning to standard procedure felt steadier than chasing hunches or theorizing motives. Blackburn's absence meant working in sequence: interviews, evidence, process of elimination. Slower, but less prone to error.

He scanned his notes for Marla Sutton's number and circled it with his pen. "We need to speak to Jenna's friend again. Marla Sutton. See if Jenna mentioned anyone watching her, or anything unusual."

Reeves spoke without looking up. "Didn't we ask already?"

"Blackburn did a while back. She prioritized other lines." He let that stand; no reason to bring up Blackburn's personal connection to the victim. "Sometimes people only remember what matters after they're asked more than once."

He dialed Willow's extension from memory. Two rings before she picked up, her tone clear and efficient.

"Willow Adler."

"Willow, it's Riley Cooper. I need your analysis on possible remote access to Zhang's car. How soon can you have it?"

A beat of silence passed before she replied. "Which angle? Signal interference, GPS drift, or acceleration patterns?"

"All three," Cooper answered so confidently it was like he knew what any of that entailed. "Focus on anything that points to outside control first. We're missing an explanation of how someone operated that car with the doors sealed."

"The doors should have unlocked after impact," Willow said crisply. Faint keyboard clicks underscored her words. "Safety protocol triggers release ten seconds post-collision for emergency response."

"But that didn't happen."

"No," she agreed quietly. "It didn't." More typing filled the pause. "I'll send you my initial findings by the end of the day."

She hesitated only briefly before adding, "There's another issue. The cameras tracking the vehicle's approach went offline minutes before impact. Not a glitch or power loss."

Cooper's gaze sharpened on the window as he processed this extra layer. "Deliberate?"

"Yes," Willow said. "Whoever did it targeted specific feeds at precise times that coincided with the car." Her voice held steady authority tinged with unease. "I'm still checking the visual anomalies leading up to impact. Artifacts I haven't seen from standard system errors."

Cooper nodded once, alone with the incremental shift as investigation moved forward by inches rather than leaps.

Reeves had stopped pretending to work. He listened openly now, arms crossed, attention fixed. Cooper caught his eye and nodded. They both understood: Jenna Langston's death showed planning, technical skill, clear intent.

"How long until we get the footage report?" Cooper asked.

"Tomorrow morning," Willow replied. "Tonight, if I stay late."

"Don't skip dinner. Morning's fine." Cooper ended the call. He opened his browser and typed: vehicle access emergency protocols.

"What are you after?" Sinclair rolled his chair over, notebook in hand.

"I want to know how someone could operate a car if the doors won't open." Cooper scanned through manufacturer specs, safety bulletins, emergency procedures. The Raider Straight Line was engineered with redundancy: sensors, auto-rescue features, manual releases tucked out of sight.

"Here." He pointed to the screen. "Emergency release behind the rear plate. Manual override for all locks, opens every door at once. Intended for fire or crash rescues."

"They'd need the right code," Sinclair said.

"Or standard responder gear." Cooper kept reading, the screen's glow harsh against tired eyes. "Universal override devices exist. Part of fire department kits for these cars."

"Can the device control the car itself?" Sinclair asked, leaning across his desk.

"Just the doors. Can you imagine?" Cooper laughed.

They sat with that information for a moment. Whoever did this knew the system intimately, or had access to specialized tools. Not something an amateur picks up overnight.

"Any update on finding the Chaplin car?" Sinclair asked.

"Nothing yet," Cooper replied. "It's probably tucked in a garage by now. Bodywork, new paint, maybe even a new registration if someone's thorough."

Sinclair opened his notebook, methodical in his movements. "How many shops work on Raider Straight Lines? Proprietary tech. Only a handful can do it legally."

Cooper nodded. "Start there. Authorized service centers first, then check independents who buy parts under the table. Look for recent jobs: collision damage, paint work, anything major."

Sinclair began tapping out calls immediately. "I'll see who's touched one of these in the last week."

The bullpen felt different without Blackburn's presence. Less rigid but also less certain. With her gone, they were shifting into something closer to real teamwork than hierarchy by default. Cooper found himself moving into leadership out of necessity, not preference; he had always followed orders well enough, leaving strategy to others.

"We need regular check-ins," Cooper said quietly but firmly. "Share progress, flag overlaps before we waste time."

"Daily wrap-ups?" Reeves offered.

"End of each day," Cooper agreed. "We compare notes and coordinate next steps." He closed Jenna Langston's file but left his own notes ready for edits. "And if anyone hears from Blackburn, official or otherwise, we bring it here first before acting."

They nodded, each knowing the reprieve wouldn't last. Blackburn's reputation for control was well-deserved.

Cooper returned to his desk, eyes tracking through technical manuals and incident reports. He combed through networks and safety protocols, searching for the flaw that let someone weaponize an autonomous vehicle. The task was familiar and repetitive; progress demanded patience. If a weakness existed, he intended to find it.

Answers hid in the mundane details. They only needed to spot them.

Chapter 4

Cooper arrived early, letting himself into the bullpen with a clatter of keys against glass. The midweek morning sun edged across the floor in hard lines, illuminating silent rows of desks. He filled the coffee machine with reluctance. Measured grounds, water, button pressed. Then waited as it sputtered to life, filling the air with its bitter promise.

The quiet held less tension than before, replaced by a dull acceptance of their changed circumstances. Without Blackburn at the helm, their work would proceed by procedure rather than sparks of intuition. He was grateful that there were no new cases, but he still had old ones.

Cooper stared at the screen until the numbers blurred at its edges, white text swimming against the harsh blue background. The forensics report had arrived twenty minutes ago, but he'd read the same paragraph four times, his mind catching on the implications like fabric on a nail. *The questioned fibers are consistent. 97.3% probability.* The words should have felt like victory. Instead, they settled in his chest with the weight of inevitability.

He pushed back from his desk, the chair's wheels catching on the worn carpet. Around him, the empty bullpen hummed with its usual white noise. Ventilation. The groan of water in the pipes, the perpetual drip of the broken coffee machine that no one had bothered to fix. The LED lights above cast everything in institutional gray that made even the living look half-dead.

Cooper's coffee had gone cold. He'd been putting off this moment, telling himself he needed to review everything one more time. But the truth was simpler and harder to admit: he'd been hoping the evidence would somehow rearrange itself, offer a different story than the one taking shape in his hands.

Lewis Discart. Twenty years of practicing medicine on fabricated credentials, twenty years of patients who'd trusted him with their lives. As a student intern, his daughter had discovered the lie buried in digitized records, and now she was dead. The mathematics of it was elegant in its brutality.

He reached for his phone before he could stop himself, muscle memory overriding protocol. His fingers found Blackburn's contact, thumb hovering over the call button. She was suspended. Officially, he shouldn't even be thinking about her. But the knowledge felt hollow in his chest, incomplete without her voice cutting through the uncertainty.

The phone rang once. Twice.

"Cooper." Her voice carried its familiar authority, undiminished by suspension or distance.

"Boss, I—" He caught himself, the word slipping out before he could think. "Sorry. I know you're not supposed to be involved, but the fiber analysis came back on the Discart case."

Silence stretched between them, long enough for Cooper to wonder if she'd hung up. When she spoke again, her tone had shifted to something more careful, more calculating.

"What does it say?"

Cooper glanced around the bullpen, checking if anyone was listening. He laughed. He was alone. The coast was clear, but Cooper still lowered his voice.

"Ninety-seven point three percent match on the hoodie fibers," he said, feeling the familiar rush of validation that came with her attention. "The purple one from Discart's closet. Monica was digitizing medical records when she found her father's secret: twenty years of fake credentials. I have written confirmation that the California licensing board has no record of him."

"Physical evidence?" Her voice carried an intensity he'd learned to recognize, the one that meant she was building something in her mind.

"Surveillance footage shows someone in that hoodie near the alley the night she died. Discart claims he was home, but his security system was disabled. Wife's alibi can't confirm he was at home because she was asleep."

"Anything else? What about the university transcripts?"

"I don't have confirmation from Wood Creek University that he ever attended." Cooper felt his shoulders tense, anticipating her displeasure.

"You don't need them." The certainty in her voice cut through his doubt like a blade. "You have motive, opportunity, and physical evidence. The fibers seal it."

Cooper found himself nodding even though she couldn't see him, his body responding to her authority across the distance. "We move for the warrant?"

"Yes." A pause. "Cooper?"

"Yeah?"

"Get your warrant. Good job. And Cooper?" Her voice softened just enough to remind him of the line they'd both just crossed. "This conversation didn't happen."

The line went dead, leaving Cooper staring at his phone. Around him, the bullpen continued its mundane rhythm, oblivious to the fact that he'd just reminded himself why Blackburn remained the gravitational center of their world, suspension or not. Even in exile, she could make him feel more capable, more certain, than anyone else ever had.

He gathered the files, feeling their weight differently now. The evidence hadn't changed, but her voice in his ear had transformed uncertainty into purpose. As he typed up the warrant, Cooper tried not to think too hard about what it meant that his first instinct had been to call someone who wasn't supposed to exist in his professional life anymore.

But he couldn't shake the feeling that she'd been waiting for his call, that somewhere in her house, she was orchestrating their moves even from the shadows. The thought should have troubled him more than it did.

Sinclair arrived not long after, looking sharper than usual. His suit showed fresh creases; his hair still held traces of dampness from a recent shower. "Coffee ready?"

"Just finished," Cooper said.

Sinclair poured a mug. His favorite, chipped along the rim but still declaring him "World's Okayest Detective." "I spent last night calling auto shops," he said. "Three places in town see Raider Straight Lines regularly. I'll check them out today."

Reeves arrived next. His shirt wasn't tucked right, and dark circles ringed his eyes. The product of too many hours reviewing case notes alone. With Blackburn gone, Reeves's thoroughness had only deepened.

"Another late one?" Cooper asked.

"Couldn't sleep." Reeves fixed his coffee with mechanical precision. Two sugars stirred exactly twelve times. "Two deaths by autonomous vehicles in under a week isn't a coincidence. What if…"

"No fucking way is this a serial killer," Cooper said. "Don't even say it."

"Maybe we're dealing with a copycat?" Sinclair offered. "We have Zhang in custody."

"That's bullshit and you know it. I'm surprised he isn't out yet. Just because he *owned* the car doesn't make him the driver," Reeves said, shaking his head. "The chief should never have arrested him."

Cooper quickly got on the phone to the prosecutor's office while the others chatted over coffee. It felt provisional.

"We need to figure out if these victims were chosen or just unlucky," Reeves said. He sipped coffee that lived up to its bitter strength. "Jenna worked data entry. A private life by any standard. Kendria sold candles and advocated sustainability." He paused to consider it further. "Neither seems like an obvious target."

"Unless the risk came from somewhere else," Sinclair said. His voice barely carried across the break room.

"I'm heading out to get a warrant," Cooper said as he grabbed his paper from the printer.

"Great! Who is it?"

Footsteps echoed in the hallway. The three detectives looked up as Willow approached. Hesitant, almost wary. She held a manila folder against her chest, eyes shifting to the empty corridor behind her.

"Morning, Willow," Cooper called.

She stopped in the doorway, holding her ground but not entering. Her glasses caught the overhead light, masking her expression. "Good morning. I have something for you." She lifted the folder. "Written instructions."

Cooper watched her, then glanced at Reeves and Sinclair. He placed his files with care. "Who are they from?"

"Detective Blackburn," Willow said. Her voice had dropped to something subdued. "She asked me to bring these in today."

Sinclair gave a short laugh. "Suspended two days and she's still running the show."

"When did she hand those to you?" Reeves asked.

Willow shifted her weight from foot to foot. "Last night." She opened the folder to display three white envelopes, each marked in Blackburn's careful script. "She wanted them on your desks, exactly as labeled."

Cooper gestured for them. "I'll take them from here."

"She said you'd need to read them where she left them," Willow replied, holding tight to the folder.

Sinclair muttered, "She doesn't know how to stop."

Reeves motioned with his chin. "Go ahead, Willow. Put them out for us."

Willow nodded and stepped into the bullpen. They watched her move from desk to desk, placing each envelope with precise care before returning to the doorway.

"Anything else?" she asked quietly.

"That's all," Cooper said.

Willow retreated, happy to head to the basement, footsteps fading down the hall.

Cooper nodded silently toward her. "Whatever, I'm out of here," he said as he followed Willow out.

The two men lingered in silence, eyes drawn to their desks where Blackburn's notes now waited. A silent reminder that she remained involved despite her absence.

"Ten bucks says it's another file re-org," Sinclair said.

"Twenty she's found connections we missed," Reeves replied.

"Should we wait for Cooper?" Sinclair asked.

"What are you, five?" Sinclair said, picking up his envelope. He looked at it, looked at Cooper's, and set it down. He laughed to himself. "It just feels wrong to do it without him."

"Plus, good excuse to do nothing at all," Sinclair laughed.

Cooper was back within two hours. He had obtained the warrant for Lewis Discart and, along with uniformed officers, had arrested his suspect. He was on a high.

"We arrested him just before he went into surgery," Cooper said. "Patient wasn't happy, but the guy had no medical license. I was basically saving a life," he said as he erased Discart in red and wrote the name in black on the whiteboard.

"Congrats, my man," Sinclair said. "You ready to open the envelopes?"

Cooper looked around. "You guys waited? Uh, no, I have to make a couple of calls first. About the arrest," he said, flopping down at his desk.

"Lewis Discart is in custody," he reported, the words carrying a finality that surprised him with its heaviness. "Invoked his right to counsel immediately. No interview opportunity."

Blackburn asked the obvious question: "Have you told his wife?"

"Should I bring her in?" Cooper found himself hoping she'd say no, though he couldn't articulate why. Maybe it was the memory of Mrs. Discart's voice when she'd called looking for her daughter, the way fear had crept into her words as the days stretched on without answers.

"Notify her of the arrest. In person. Like any victim's mother." Blackburn's tone gentled, revealing a compassion that she rarely showed but always felt. "Remind her about Victim Services. She'll need support."

Cooper nodded, understanding that this too was part of the job: not just catching the guilty, but acknowledging the wreckage left behind. Mrs. Discart would wake up tomorrow to a world where her husband of twenty-five years was a stranger, where every memory of their life together would be tainted by the knowledge of what he'd been capable of.

As he hung up, Cooper caught his reflection again in the glass, and for a moment, he wondered how well any of them knew the people closest to them.

"The mystery envelopes?" Sinclair asked, waiving his in the air.

Cooper rolled his eyes and snatched his off the desk. He broke the seal first and drew out a single page of crisp handwriting:

Cooper: What if someone doesn't need the codes? Look into quantum computing capabilities. A portable quantum computer in the back of a van. Think the size of a police surveillance van, full of a computer. Does it exist? They could break the panel's encryption or brute-force the codes faster than the car's security could detect the attempts. Check if any local universities, tech companies, or government contractors have quantum computing resources. Our killer might not need inside knowledge—they might just need better technology than we assumed possible.

—B

Cooper read through the note twice, feeling the paper's weight between his fingers. It was like she had listened to yesterday's discussion. Across the bullpen, Sinclair and Reeves did the same with their notes, eyes narrowed in concentration. Sinclair's mouth hardened with a mix of reluctant respect and irritation. Reeves just nodded, absorbing Blackburn's instructions without comment.

"Well?" Cooper said.

Sinclair tapped his paper against the edge of the table. "I got directed microwave technology, whatever the fuck that is."

"Microwave? For cooking?"

"Don't know. It says 'a focused microwave emitter could superheat the lithium cells from outside the vehicle. Check research facilities or defense contractors in the area.' Sounds more like a Willow thing to me."

Cooper laughed and folded his note. "If she gave this stuff to us, just imagine what Willow got. Reeves, what have you got?"

Reeves slid his note into his pocket. "Maybe Willow gave her these ideas. The boss thinks there's a connection we missed between the victims. She wants warrants for their phones. Wants me to check their encrypted mesh network logs. See if the phones spent any length of time together."

Cooper set his own note aside, folding his hands. "She's right," he said.

"About what?" Sinclair asked.

"All of it." He nodded at their notes. "These are good steps. We should have gotten there sooner."

Reeves glanced away, lips pressed tight. "Doesn't mean I like getting assignments from someone on suspension."

"No," Cooper said. "But we'll do it, anyway."

Sinclair flattened his note with care, the paper crackling. "Hate admitting she's ahead of us, and she isn't even working."

"The boss won't stay on the sidelines for long," Cooper replied, standing up. "I have to go talk to Cindy Discart."

"Not calling her?" Sinclair said as he carefully folded the paper.

"No. This one has to be in person," Cooper said as he headed out. Sinclair made one last fold, and threw his paper airplane toward Cooper's back.

"I have to go too," Reeves said as he eyed the clock. "I have an interview."

"Who?"

"Scudamore's neighbor," he said, heading into the hallway.

* * *

The interview room felt oppressively small. Harsh LED strips overhead cast everything in an unforgiving institutional light. Reeves sat opposite Mrs. Clayton. She was a woman well into her seventies. Her hands clutched a worn leather purse, fingers working the clasp with nervous energy.

She lived at 67 Thyme Street, directly across from the Dala house. She had a front-row seat to every argument that echoed down their quiet block.

"Thank you for coming in," Reeves said, turning to a fresh page in his legal pad. The margins were already crowded with notes. Another file building inexorably toward trial.

Mrs. Clayton adjusted her glasses, eyes sharp behind thick lenses despite her age and the dated tortoiseshell clips holding back steel-gray hair. Her dress carried the mixed scent of rose water and mothballs.

"I should have called before," she began softly. Guilt colored every word. "We all saw it coming. Nobody wanted to get involved."

Reeves waited, pen poised.

"Tell me about Monday morning," he said.

She nodded tightly, gathering herself. "They started before six. Him shouting. He was always so loud you could hear every word. It was about something she did wrong." She dabbed at her eyes with a tissue pulled from her purse but kept going. "This time it was the eggs. He called her useless, stupid, and worthless. The same things he always said."

Reeves wrote quickly, capturing not just facts but the pattern. A record of escalation that would matter in court.

The details mattered more than anything in these cases. Anger repeated and reinforced until it finally exploded on an ordinary morning with nothing left to contain it.

"Did you hear Mrs. Scudamore say anything?"

"She was crying. Begging him to stop." Mrs. Clayton's tone flattened, each detail delivered with grim precision. "She said she would make new eggs, that she was sorry. He just kept shouting." She hesitated, fingers tightening on her purse. "Then it got quiet for maybe half a minute. I almost thought it was over. Then I heard the gun go off."

Reeves knew that violence had its own acoustics. Yelling could fade into background noise, like traffic or barking dogs. People learned to filter that out. Gunshots always cut through, demanded attention, changed everything.

"What did you see next?"

"Everything went silent." Mrs. Clayton's hands twisted the purse strap. "Maybe two minutes later, John came out the front door. He walked slowly and calmly, just sat down on the steps and set the gun next to him. He waited there, like he had all the time in the world."

After she left, promising she would be available to testify if needed, Reeves returned to his desk and pulled up John Dala's record on the department system. The screen loaded a list of offenses that traced a predictable trajectory. More frequent, more violent, consequences that never quite matched the crime.

Cooper dialed the Raider Straight Line security office, scanning his list for follow-up contacts.

At his desk, Reeves switched back, spreading out the Chaplin file. Photos arranged beside witness statements in careful rows. Kendria's license photo looked back at him: composed and hopeful, better suited to a storefront window than a homicide report. Reeves had started conversations like this before. Too many times. And each one carved something out of him.

He checked the preliminary details: Next of kin was Marilyn Chaplin, age seventeen; no spouse listed; parents not listed. No clear sign of extended family yet. In past cases, grief often erased important names. Siblings who rarely called, distant relatives turned relevant by tragedy, friends who had filled parental roles without official titles. The aftermath narrowed everyone's focus; detectives were left to fill in what families forgot to mention.

10:30 AM. Late enough that he wouldn't be waking anyone, early enough that he might reach them before routine swallowed grief whole.

He dialed Marilyn Chaplin using a number pulled from school records.

Four rings passed before she answered. Voice steady and direct.

"This is Marilyn Chaplin."

He registered the formality; few teenagers answered phones this way. She sounded like someone managing a problem rather than a child facing loss.

"Ms. Chaplin," he said evenly, "this is Detective Victor Reeves with New Dresden Police. I'm calling about your mother."

A pause stretched between them. A breath controlled.

"Yes," she said. "I was expecting your call."

"I want to express my condolences for your loss. I know this is a difficult time."

"Thank you." The reply was flat, more routine than heartfelt. "When can we meet? I have information relevant to your investigation."

Reeves paused, the phone warm against his ear. Most families needed reassurance before they could share details. Grief and shock clouded everything. Marilyn Chaplin treated it like another item on her schedule.

"I'm available whenever you are," he said. "Would you prefer to come to the station, or should I come to your home?"

"Home is better. My transportation's unreliable, and I need to coordinate with the funeral director this week." She hesitated, voice thinning for just a moment. "Thursday afternoon works. Nine o'clock?"

"Thursday at ten in the morning. I'll need your address."

She gave it, along with clear directions. Efficient, practical, as if she had done this before. Reeves made notes, surprised by her composure under pressure that left most people scrambling.

"Ms. Chaplin, is there anyone else in the family I should contact? Relatives, close friends. Anyone who might know something useful?"

"I'll email you a list," she said immediately. "Phone numbers and brief descriptions of their relationship with my mother. Do you want anything specific?"

Reeves felt himself trying to keep pace with her efficiency. "Anyone who spoke with her recently. Business associates, confidants."

"Understood. You'll have it within an hour."

"I appreciate your help. And again, I'm sorry."

"Detective Reeves?" Her tone sliced through the apology; controlled, cold, effective. Blackburn's style if he had ever heard it. "I know you're sorry. Everyone is. But that solves nothing. Find who killed my mother. That's what matters."

She ended the call before he could answer.

Reeves set down the phone and considered the conversation: seventeen years old and already handling crisis logistics better than most adults. Either Kendria Chaplin had raised her well, or life had forced maturity early.

His computer chimed. A new email from Marilyn Chaplin with the list she had promised:

Robert and Anastasia Chaplin—maternal grandparents, retired, live in Phoenix; limited contact for several years due to disagreements over lifestyle.

Frank Daley—mother's ex-boyfriend; relationship ended two years ago; incarcerated at Millfield Correctional Facility (shoplifting from her store).

Sandra Williams—mother's close friend since college; local; regular contact; owns yoga studio on Elm Street.

Marcus Williams (no relation)—candle materials supplier; professional connection only; may know about financial issues.

Each entry included phone numbers, addresses where possible, and Marilyn's assessment of their relevance. A report far more precise than most family records.

Reeves printed the email and crossed to Cooper's desk, paper still warm from the printer.

"Chaplin case contacts just came in," he said. "One stands out: ex-boyfriend. He's currently locked up."

Cooper paused mid-call with Raider Straight Line. He covered the mouthpiece with his palm. "What's the angle?"

"Frank Daley. Shoplifting, from Coconut Glass Candles. The only question is whether he could reach anyone outside. If he held a grudge against Kendria."

Cooper's mouth twitched. "Shoplifting seems small-time for payback." He glanced at the file. "Kendria's business was steady. Daley steals from her. Why?"

"Run him through the system. Associates, contacts, anyone with technical expertise to pull off an auto hack."

Cooper nodded once. "Give me an hour," he said, then spoke into the phone again, voice flat and patient for the corporate rep on the line.

Reeves returned to his desk and mapped out follow-ups. He would call Kendria's parents in unless something pointed to a deeper lead. Sandra Williams, Kendria's closest friend. He would need to see her in person. Marcus Williams might know about business stress or threats.

Across the bullpen, Sinclair raised his head. "Anyone grabbed Mills since Dawson went on leave?"

Reeves didn't look up from his notes. "Not that I've heard."

Sinclair's face hardened, jaw tight. "Five-year-old victim, case stalling out while we shuffle paperwork. Feels wrong."

"Case needs an assigned detective," Reeves replied firmly. "You jump in without assignment, you screw up evidence and risk losing everything in court."

Sinclair tapped his pen too hard against the desk, the sound sharp in the quiet. "So it sits there?"

"We do this by the book. Talk to Hayes if you want in; let him reassign officially." Reeves kept his tone even. "Shortcuts blow cases apart. Mills deserves more than that."

The bullpen went quiet for a moment, tension threading between old desks and flickering monitors. They all knew Reeves was right: procedural mistakes cost more trials than thin evidence ever would. But bureaucracy had its own way of killing investigations bit by bit.

Reeves dialed Sandra Williams, searching for any detail that would crack things open. A word, a memory tucked away in routine conversation. Anything that could explain how someone turned a car into a weapon.

He settled into the work: asking questions no one wanted to ask, listening for things no one else heard. Progress was slow and unremarkable but method built results.

They would solve this through careful investigation or not at all.

They owed it to the victims to do nothing less.

* * *

Wednesday afternoon settled over the bullpen like dust: heavy, quiet, unhurried. The morning's rush had subsided into routine. Calls returned. Reports filed. Leads sifted with the steadiness that came when adrenaline gave way to process.

Reeves read the report. Three years back was the first arrest for domestic assault. Rhyanne had called 911 after Dala left her with a black eye during an argument about overdue bills. Officers noted visible injuries but she declined to press charges. He was released in twenty-four hours.

Eighteen months later came another charge, same category. This time Rhyanne spent the night at St. Mary's with a concussion. Dala had pushed her down the stairs. She lied at first and claimed she fell while carrying laundry. But an observant nurse convinced her to speak with police. Dala pleaded down, paid a fine, got probation.

Eight months ago, neighbors called when they heard Rhyanne screaming for help. Officers found her with bruising around her throat and a split lip. Dala claimed she had attacked him first, and he had only defended himself. Without clear evidence to contradict him, he got another plea deal. Extended probation and anger management classes he attended twice before stopping.

The pattern was depressingly typical. Escalating violence met with minimal consequences. A victim who had stopped believing anyone would truly help. Reeves saw this cycle repeatedly. The system offered second chances, but men like Dala used them as permission slips.

He called Zurich National Bank, where Rhyanne cleaned offices on the overnight shift. Patricia Brooks answered. Her voice was professionally pleasant but tired underneath.

"She was dependable," Brooks said when asked about Rhyanne. "Never late or called in sick without good reason. She was quiet but always did quality work." A pause as she considered Reeves' question about trouble at home. "She had bruises sometimes and always had explanations. She walked into doors, fell down stairs, the usual stories. But we all knew what it meant." Another heavy silence.

"She wasn't due in until Thursday night so when she didn't show yesterday, I didn't think much of it then. Now I wish I had checked on her."

There was guilt everywhere except where it belonged.

Reeves thanked Brooks and ended the call before dialing the forensics lab.

"Ballistics, Rodriguez speaking."

"Detective Reeves, NDPD. I need confirmation on evidence from the Scudamore case. You should have a thirty-eight revolver from the scene."

Keyboard clicks filtered through the line. "Flood & Charles Model 38, five-shot revolver. Registered to John Dala, purchased three years ago at Riverside Gun Shop. We test-fired it this morning. The bullet recovered from the victim matches the gun perfectly. No doubt about it."

Dala's purchase history filled in its own disturbing gaps. He had bought the weapon six months after his first domestic violence charge, around the same time he had started court-mandated anger management. Rather than learning to manage his temper, he had prepared for its inevitable eruption.

The public defender's office confirmed Carol Right would represent Dala. Reeves knew her by reputation. She was competent, unflappable, skilled at extracting whatever concessions she could for clients facing overwhelming evidence.

Right answered on the second ring. "My client isn't answering questions," she told Reeves without preamble. "We'll need time to review all the evidence before making any decisions."

"He already confessed," Reeves said. "Half the neighborhood heard him do it. The responding officers got it on record. Whatever mitigating circumstances you find won't change what happened."

"We'll see," she said evenly. "There are always factors. Mental health issues, past trauma, temporary emotional disturbance. Maybe this doesn't have to be Murder One."

The lines were already drawn. The prosecution was building maximum leverage for plea negotiations. The defense was probing for any foothold to reduce the penalty. At the center lay a dead woman neither side could bring back.

The rest of the afternoon dissolved into reports and file updates. The procedural steps that kept cases moving through the system. Reeves logged evidence with meticulous care, cross-checked witness statements for consistency, and flagged items for follow-up as needed. The facts arranged themselves into a grim but coherent narrative.

By end of shift, he had assembled what prosecutors needed. Solid forensics, credible witness statements, clearly established motive and opportunity. No gaps for reasonable doubt to creep through.

He studied SCUDAMORE in red across the case board. A visual reminder that tomorrow meant preparing everything for transfer to the District Attorney's office, shifting the investigation into prosecution's hands.

Evening light slanted through squad room windows. The city's lights began their nightly awakening beyond the glass. Somewhere across town, Heather Katt was making funeral arrangements for her daughter. Somewhere else, John Dala sat in a county jail cell, likely still justifying what he had done.

The process wouldn't restore Rhyanne Scudamore's life. It would hold her killer accountable and send a message that might reach someone else before it was too late.

That had to be enough.

Cooper leaned back, stretching sore shoulders after hours hunched over manuals and protocol sheets. The chair creaked beneath him. Across the room, Sinclair spun a pen idly while cross-checking invoices. Reeves typed up interview notes, his pace even and automatic. A rhythm shaped by years of repetition.

Sinclair broke the quiet first. "Anyone want to change their bet on when Blackburn's back?"

Reeves kept his eyes on the screen. "Still putting up a hundred?"

"Standing." Sinclair set his pen down and lifted his arms in a stretch. "One-week suspension. Says she'll walk in by next Wednesday. Might have to shave those odds."

Cooper's laugh was more exhale than sound. "Think it'll be sooner?"

"Pressure's building." Sinclair jerked his chin toward the wall-mounted TV cycling muted coverage of Kendria Chaplin's murder. Her photo lingered on screen beside headlines about autonomous vehicles and civic outrage. "Mayor wants answers. Press won't drop the serial killer angle."

Reeves didn't look up from his notes. "They'd rather have her solving than swinging at witnesses."

"Fair." Sinclair resumed spinning the pen, slower this time. "She gets results nobody else does."

Reeves spoke without glancing over. "Cooper, any updates on how access was locked down in the Raider?"

Cooper nodded once, focusing on his documentation. "According to Raider specifications, doors auto-unlock ten seconds after a major impact. Standard for trapped occupant rescue. The report I got indicated a zero point zero zero three percent failure rate. The doors should have opened."

"Didn't happen with Jenna," Sinclair said.

"No," Cooper agreed. He flipped a page, gaze narrowing on highlighted sections. "Doors stayed sealed. Windows wouldn't give. Eye witness said he pounded on the glass."

Reeves stopped typing, fingers hovering above the keys.

Sinclair asked, "No one tried the not-so-secret panel under the rear plate?"

"Owner customized," Cooper said, voice even. "No. You'd need internal access codes, deep knowledge of system architecture, maybe physical modification to core hardware."

He rubbed at tired eyes, the LED lights harsh after hours of scrolling through lines of code and engineering diagrams.

"This isn't joyriding or vandalism," he continued. "It's professional. Government or private sector level capabilities."

"Government? Jesus, the girl was in marketing," Reeves scoffed.

Cooper set his papers aside and looked at both men in turn.

"We're looking at someone with a defense contracting background or insider status at one of these firms," he said simply. "Someone with real resources and classified access."

Silence stretched for a moment as that landed. A shift in the investigation's scale neither welcome nor avoidable.

"Think the Feds will take it?"

Outside, rain began tapping at the windows. Steady, persistent as they contemplated what kind of enemy they might actually be hunting now.

"You know that's not our decision to make," Sinclair said, voice low.

"Maybe not," Cooper replied. "It's still on our desks until someone tells us differently." He reached for his phone. "I'll call the manufacturer. I want to know if they've had any security breaches or missing tech. Anything that might explain unauthorized access."

A hush fell over the bullpen as each detective returned to their tasks. Work that demanded patience and left little room for sentimentality. Cooper focused again on technical schematics, looking for ways an autonomous car might be turned into a weapon by design or manipulation. Sinclair uploaded images and cross-referenced data sets, intent on giving a name back to someone forgotten by nearly everyone else. Reeves entered interview summaries, building out the record that would later support prosecution in Jenna's case.

Beyond the windows, night spread across New Dresden: traffic moved in slow streams; businesses closed their doors; life continued with its usual indifference to violence and loss.

Cooper found some reassurance in that continuity. The city moving forward even as they cataloged its casualties.

They would solve these cases. Not quickly or easily. But by increments: interviews logged; leads chased; technical obstacles overcome through diligence rather than inspiration.

The investigation endured, patient as nightfall itself.

Chapter 5

By seven Thursday morning, Reeves was back at his desk with coffee that tasted of burned grounds and an empty squad room save for one detective finishing overnight reports. He spread out the Scudamore paperwork across his desk. Pages arranged in precise order, each one a piece of what remained to be done.

The case report demanded absolute accuracy. Every fact, every statement, and each piece of evidence needed to be documented with precision that would withstand scrutiny. Defense attorneys lived for inconsistencies. Reeves approached the work methodically, laying out the timeline first. Six o'clock, neighbors reported raised voices penetrating thin walls. Six-twenty, the sharp crack of a gunshot. Six twenty-two, John Dala emerged from the house and sat on the porch steps. Six twenty-five, first 911 call logged by dispatch. The sequence had to be bulletproof. Any gaps or contradictions would become leverage for the defense to exploit.

He included the crime scene photographs in clinical detail. Rhyanne's body crumpled beside the stove, untouched eggs congealing in their pan, blood spatter painting the kitchen cabinets in a grotesque pattern. The images were deliberately dispassionate. They showed measurements, angles, evidence markers. They captured violence stripped of drama but impossible to dismiss.

Next came the witness statements, each one reinforcing the others. Mrs. Clayton recounted the argument and fatal shot. Lori Clattenberg described years of escalating abuse. Officers Winters and Camacho recorded Dala's spontaneous confession at the scene. Each account interlocked with the others, building a version of events that left little room for alternative interpretation.

The ballistics section was brief but damning. Photos showed Dala's revolver alongside test-fired rounds. The rifling marks matched perfectly. The technical language was dry, but the conclusion was stark. This gun fired this bullet into this victim. No ambiguity existed.

By nine in the morning, Reeves had assembled sixty-three pages of documentation. Reports, images, analyses. The file was comprehensive enough to satisfy prosecution requirements and robust enough to withstand defense scrutiny. He uploaded it to the secure system and dialed ADA Melanie Bowman. He checked his watch. He still had time before the interview with Marilyn Chaplin.

She answered on the second ring. "Detective Reeves. Tell me you have something airtight."

"The full case file is uploaded for your review," he said. "Domestic homicide with multiple witnessed confessions and unassailable physical evidence."

"Music to my ears. What are you seeing for charges?"

He shifted in his chair, hearing it protest. "Murder One makes sense based on the premeditation angle. The pattern fits, plus he bought the weapon after his first domestic arrest. But I wanted your assessment before we lock it in."

"Walk me through your thinking."

"Dala purchased the revolver three years ago. Six months after his first DV charge," Reeves said, consulting his notes. "We've got documented escalation since then. Three prior arrests with increasing severity each time. Monday morning, he shot his wife in the back of the head during breakfast prep and immediately confessed. The weapon purchase suggests planning."

Bowman paused, likely reviewing her own files. "The defense will almost certainly argue sudden provocation or heat-of-passion. They'll angle for Murder Two or even voluntary manslaughter."

"That's my concern too," Reeves replied. "The victim's mother seems pragmatic about options. Do you want to consider offering Murder Two for a guaranteed guilty plea?"

It was a familiar calculation. Murder One meant potential life without parole but required proving premeditation beyond a reasonable doubt. Murder Two guaranteed at least twenty-five years but reduced risk of acquittal or jury sympathy for Dala.

"What's your read on the family's position?"

Reeves considered his conversation with Heather Katt. Grief had filled every word, but resignation too. She had seen this ending coming for years, powerless to prevent it. "The victim's mother wants meaningful consequences, but she's realistic. She understands her daughter isn't coming back. If we can guarantee substantial prison time and spare her a traumatic trial, I believe she would accept it."

"Let me review the file thoroughly and run it by my supervisor." Bowman's tone turned thoughtful. "The escalation pattern and weapon purchase timing might support Murder One, but Dala's profile could complicate things with a jury. He's middle-aged, steadily employed, no violent history outside the marriage. Juries sometimes struggle to see the pattern with domestic violence."

This wasn't news to Reeves. He had watched juries hesitate and even acquit because they couldn't reconcile someone who seemed respectable on paper with brutal acts committed behind closed doors. Certain crimes were too easy to rationalize away.

"If we offer Murder Two, what's the realistic sentence?"

"Given his priors and the aggravating factors, probably twenty to twenty-five years." The prosecutor spoke without emotion. "He'll have parole eligibility eventually, but with this record and these facts, it's unlikely he would see freedom before serving most of it."

Reeves jotted notes on his pad. Years, projected release dates, Dala's current age versus his age after two decades inside. At forty-five now, he would emerge at sixty-five. Old enough to pose less physical threat, young enough to live with his choices for years after.

"I'll touch base with the mother this afternoon about her position on a plea," Reeves said. "But let's proceed as if we're heading to trial. Better to maintain flexibility."

He ended the call and set about preparing evidence packages for the prosecutor's office. The weapon was sealed in a clear evidence bag, spent cartridge with chain-of-custody documentation, blood samples meticulously tagged by location, trace evidence of fibers and residue. Every transfer required signatures, timestamps, witness verification. Nothing could be left to chance.

This was the machinery of justice. Grinding forward through procedure and protocol. Each item served its purpose. Each step created an auditable trail. The system demanded perfect documentation.

Late afternoon shadows stretched across desks as Reeves reviewed everything one last time. Documentation complete and cross-referenced, physical evidence directly linked to Dala through multiple vectors, witness statements corroborating each other and the physical evidence. It was as strong a case as twenty years of experience could build.

Tomorrow would bring the formal transfer. Detective work yielded to prosecutorial process.

From here, the system would advance through its prescribed steps. Motions filed and argued, bargaining sessions in sterile conference rooms, evidence presented under oath before judge and jury. Resolution would come through negotiation or verdict. John Dala would answer for Monday morning's violence.

It would not resurrect Rhyanne Scudamore. It would not erase years of escalating harm, nor ease her mother's burden of grief. Yet it would establish a boundary. Violence carried consequences, and someone would be held accountable.

It was time to go. Hopefully, to hold another killer accountable.

* * *

Bach continued, relentless and composed, as Blackburn dried her hands on a towel and reached for her phone. After that barn burner of a press conference three days ago, her phone hadn't stopped.

The press prowled like hyenas, snarling and snapping, but Blackburn was the lioness, unyielding and ready to tear into any reporter foolish enough to come too close.

"Reeves," read the caller ID: duty breaking through whatever sanctuary remained in this kitchen.

She answered, voice even.

"Boss, I'm with Marilyn Chaplin. She would like—"

Another voice came on the line. Female this time, every word was clipped. "Detective Blackburn?"

Blackburn cleared her throat. "Yes."

"I've seen the video. The full recording from Oak Street." The speaker's tone never wavered; it was methodical, distilled to its core meaning without room for excess feeling. "Of my mother's death."

Blackburn closed her eyes briefly, a pulse beating at her temple as she pressed her palm to the cool marble countertop.

"I'm sorry you had to experience that." She added restrained emotion to her reply. It was a deeply layered habit.

A pause; then, calmly: "I didn't *have* to watch it. I chose to." Marilyn inhaled audibly before continuing, still measured, but there was something behind it all that refused to break through. "I wanted to thank you for what you did at the scene, for protecting my mother."

The compliment hung unanswered for a moment.

"Marilyn," Blackburn said at last, "I need to talk with you soon, but I can't right now." Her hand curled tighter around the edge of the counter until knuckles blanched white. "I've been suspended for that very action."

A longer silence followed, static riding over distance and grief alike.

Blackburn stared at nothing in particular and waited for what might come next from either end of the line or from herself, bracing against everything she could not control.

"I saw the news," Marilyn said, her voice carrying a calm gravity that made her seem older than seventeen. "You told them you wanted to break that man's jaw."

Blackburn didn't look up. "Mmm," she answered, neither confirming nor denying. Sunlight touched the stainless-steel knives standing in the polished chef's knife block on her counter.

"I want to know you'll be on the case." Marilyn's words were steady. "I respect the NDPD, and Detective Reeves. But my mother's death needs attention from someone who cares."

A notification pinged. Then another. A message from Chief Hayes flashing across Blackburn's phone, only to be quickly replaced by a BDSMessages notification. She had a clear preference for which one to answer.

"The Chief is calling," she said, fingers drumming once on the granite. "Detective Reeves will follow up. I expect we'll speak again soon."

"Goodbye, Detective," Reeves added, his tone clipped and formal before the line cut out.

Blackburn hesitated over Hayes's name for a moment, then answered with a flat, "Chief."

Morning light drew lines across Blackburn's kitchen as Hayes's voice came through, rough and urgent: "I need you in my office. Now."

Blackburn studied her nails. "Actually, I'm enjoying my suspension, though I have already worked off the clock."

Hayes's patience was gone. "Drop it, Blackburn. I want you in. Now."

She ended the call without responding, a small smile tightening her lips as she moved toward her bedroom.

The white shirt and charcoal suit were chosen with intention: nothing wasted, every detail sharp. A message that she had been home, not cowering in some back room waiting for Damocles's sword. In the mirror, she checked the fit: a single button left undone for effect, collar straightened with care. She considered her next move on how best to retake Kendria's case, then turned away from her own reflection.

* * *

The precinct lot was filling up by the time she arrived. Her steps echoed on the blacktop. Steady. Some officers greeted her with crisp salutes; others watched in silence, arms crossed and faces set.

She paused just long enough for them to feel her attention on their badges. A silent warning. Then she kept walking. Catching one skeptic off guard, she leaned in close enough for only him to hear:

"One-four-nine." Her voice was low; he covered his badge without thinking, bluster replaced by unease.

She carried that same energy into Chief Hayes's office. She kept her expression suppressed. Edward Bernicki from HR sat by the window, fidgeting as he hugged a folder against his chest under the LED glare. A stranger sat in front of the chief.

"Shut the door and sit," Hayes said without looking up, tapping fingers on his desk.

Blackburn greeted Edward by name as she took a seat, voice polite but distant, and settled into place, posture rigid and composed.

"Morgan Blackburn," she said, extending a hand out to the stranger.

"Averi Ward," he said, taking her hand. "Internal Affairs."

Blackburn nodded and sat. She glanced up at the ceiling tile with a water-stained shaped like a badge. It had been there for as long as she could remember.

Hayes leaned forward; his chair groaned in protest. "HR has an idea about how we handle this problem." He nodded at Bernicki but didn't wait for him to speak.

"I wasn't aware there was still a problem," Blackburn replied quietly.

"You're the problem," Hayes answered, though something softer moved under the surface of his words as he glanced at Ward. But he remained silent.

It was Bernicki's jaw that twitched. He glanced down at the policy binder. "Per department guidelines, assaulting a civilian triggers a suspension and pay forfeiture, as well as an internal investigation." He gestured quickly to Ward. "But there's no standard for how long the suspension lasts. Three days would satisfy policy. Detective Blackburn could be back on shift already."

Blackburn didn't smile. "Anyone ever get a three-day suspension before, Edward?"

Bernicki shuffled papers. "No. The shortest on record is five days unpaid, and that was for sleeping in uniform during a shift." He looked up, managing an awkward attempt at levity. "You break new ground, Detective."

She gave him a cool nod. She liked being the first. "A short, unpaid suspension? Where is the punishment?"

Hayes cut in, tone brisk. "Are you asking to be punished?"

Blackburn crossed one leg over the other, foot swinging as she considered her options. She let the hum of overhead lights fill the gap. With different people in the room, Blackburn would have burst out laughing. "I am asking to be seen to be punished. Public perception."

She turned to look at Ward. "When is it your turn?" Blackburn asked.

"Uh, oh, I—" was all Ward could spit out.

"Let me answer your questions. I was speaking with Ms. Chaplin when the vehicle struck her. I responded immediately to provide aid. She was dying in the street as Mr. Mullen began shouting at her. It's widely accepted that hearing is the last sense to go at the end of life, by the way. At no point did Mr. Mullen pose a physical threat to me. I could have ignored his outburst. I did call for backup. I understand our use of force policy, and I acknowledge my response wasn't fully in line with it. Is there something else?"

Ward hesitated, then asked, "Why didn't you detain him after the incident?"

Blackburn met Ward's eyes, then Hayes's, before returning her attention to Ward. "He hadn't committed a crime."

"Anything else?" Hayes asked Ward.

"I'd like a full—"

"You have the videos. This was your interview," Hayes said, cutting him off.

"Then let's make it work," she said as she glanced at her nails. "Fine me two weeks' worth of pay. And instead of putting my money into the city's black hole, have it donated to a local anti-violence group. We could use it as a show of good faith. chief, you said so at the press conference. We are dedicated to the community."

The idea landed cleanly. For a moment, no one spoke.

Then Hayes broke into a genuine smile, the lines around his eyes softening. "That's good," he whispered, almost to himself, then louder: "Actually, that's great." He turned toward Bernicki, an eagerness in his posture that was missing earlier. "Imagine the press. It sends a hell of a message: personal and professional accountability and commitment all in one headline."

Bernicki straightened in his chair, his sweater bunching at his elbows as he leaned in. "It hasn't been done before," he admitted, a trace of surprise coloring his tone. "But yes, sir, we can work with

Media Relations and Public Relations. Make it a good news story. I can draw up the forms before the end of the day."

Blackburn nodded once. "Send me notice of my fine, I'll send the check."

Bernicki smiled. "Perfect," he said, fidgeting with his stack of papers. His chair scraped loud against the tile as he stood.

"Wait, I..." Ward said. All eyes turned on him. And waited. And waited. He finally shook his head and looked at his notes.

"It's a win all around. I'm taking credit for the idea, you hear? It's good optics, keeps everyone happy," Hayes replied, barely glancing up as he scribbled some notes.

Blackburn watched as Ward left first, followed by Bernicki's retreat, the hem of his sweater snagging on the door before he slipped out. "Worth every cent just to see him so excited," she said dryly.

When the door latched shut, her tone shifted. Control wasn't just about holding back. It's about deciding when to let go. "We need to talk about Kendria Chaplin."

The office felt close and heavy, stagnant air lingering between them. Hayes rubbed one hand across his jaw, waiting.

"She wasn't random. I was interviewing her about Jenna Langston when she was killed," Blackburn said, voice low.

Hayes tapped a restless rhythm on his desk. "What? You think—?"

"Someone didn't want her talking," she said.

He frowned, shaking his head once. "We have Zhang in custody for Langston."

Blackburn's response was immediate: "You know that arrest won't hold. Zhang didn't do this."

"When were you going to tell me?" Hayes shot back. Frustration colored his words.

Blackburn kept her gaze steady. "You spoke over me when you suspended me. Sir. It's possible that whoever silenced Kendria is behind both deaths. We have to consider they may be linked." Her fingers drummed against the worn leather on the chair arm, a rhythm that filled the silence between them.

Hayes exhaled, his palm rasping across stubble and scalp. "What exactly did Chaplin tell you?"

"We didn't get far," Blackburn said, irritation threading through her restraint. It was technically true. Sort of. But it moved her narrative along, and she spoke with conviction. "She was hit before she could say much. Any progress tracing that vehicle?"

Hayes shook his head. "Nothing yet." He studied her face, searching. "What tells you this isn't just another AV incident? Malfunctions happen."

Blackburn held his stare. The air between them thickened. He shouldn't have signed off on Zhang's arrest, and now he was scrambling to justify it.

Finally, she shifted. The chair's leather protested beneath her. "The squad has been working on the case, chief. I don't know the details, they are not reporting to me at the moment. I need to talk to Marilyn Chaplin. Kendria's daughter. If anything seemed off lately. Phone calls, someone following her. I want to know."

Chief Hayes's expression remained fixed. "Your priority is the car. Assign your team. Get it done. I hate saying this," he said, reaching into his desk drawer. "It's good to have you back."

A gold shield and a black gun in its holster slipped toward her.

Blackburn rose with restraint. The office pressed close, recycled air coating her throat. One quick glance, cool and unreadable. Her fingers found cold metal.

"Understood," she said, clipping the badge to her waist. "My squad isn't known for idling." A pause, dry as chalk. The gun holster snapped into place. "Well, maybe Sinclair."

She slipped out, the controlled click of the door leaving Hayes alone with his unease.

*　*　*

Blackburn entered the bullpen, her heels marking a steady rhythm against worn linoleum. Cooper caught her arrival first, sandwich suspended midway to his mouth. Reeves and Sinclair drifted over, pulled by habit and obligation.

Cooper nodded in greeting. "Boss! You're back early. How'd you pull that off?"

"Charity has its uses," Blackburn said, shifting a stapler from Dawson's desk to give her space. Dawson was still on mental health leave, his desk serving as little more than a touchdown station. "Cash moves things along." Her tone sealed off further questions.

Sinclair's grin came automatically. "Good to have you back, boss. Place runs smoother with—"

"It's been less than a week." Her glance cut through his enthusiasm like cold steel. He fell silent, properly chastened. She offered a flicker of warmth, the briefest wink. "Did you win the bet?"

Sinclair laughed. "No one took it."

"Let's move," Blackburn said, voice controlled. "Find the car. If you haven't already, get security footage."

"Done," Sinclair said quickly. Blackburn held his gaze a beat longer before nodding.

"Do you have the license plate?"

"Not yet. But—"

"Get it." The order landed cleanly and directly. "Now."

She retreated to her office. It had been only a few days, but she had feared she would not see it again. Now, she looked at her kingdom through hooded eyes, like greeting a long-lost lover.

Blackburn sank into her chair. She quickly dialed and wedged the phone against her shoulder, and signed into her computer. The familiar ritual was almost orgasmic.

"Marilyn Chaplin? It's Detective Blackburn."

"I'm glad you called, detective. I'm ready to talk. About my mother."

Blackburn's spine straightened against her chair. "Go ahead."

"Not on the phone," Marilyn said. "I want to meet. At my mother's shop. Coconut Glass Candles."

Blackburn drew a breath, keeping it silent. "The shop?" Her tone remained neutral. The black leather table flashed in her mind's eye and her thighs clenched all on their own.

"There might be something on the security camera," Marilyn's voice dropped to barely above a whisper. "It's been on my mind. I need to find out."

The pen bit into Blackburn's palm. "You've looked at the footage?"

"No," Marilyn replied. "I haven't touched it. There's police tape on the door. I just remembered the camera above the front door."

"Does it record inside as well?" Blackburn asked gently but probing.

"Only the entrance and outside, I think."

"All right." Blackburn kept her voice level. "When do you want to meet?"

"In an hour?"

"I'll be there."

She ended the call and stood, her coat whispering against the chair back as she grabbed it. Her mind already calculated the minutes needed to reach the scene first.

She crossed the bullpen without breaking stride. "Reeves, grab your coat." She didn't check if he followed; his footsteps confirmed it.

In the car, Reeves's thumb scrolled across his phone's glowing screen. Blackburn drove efficiently, the city sliding past in elongated shadows. The days' fractures hung between them, splintered loyalties and hairline cracks in the chain of command. For now, neither acknowledged them. There would be time for that later.

The silence pressed against the windows until Blackburn spoke. "Your take on the slap, Reeves?" Her eyes tracked the road, knuckles pale against the steering wheel.

Reeves grinned, settling deeper into cracked vinyl. "Didn't think you had it in you, boss. But glad you did. The way his head snapped?" He gave a low whistle. "Hell of a move."

A smile ghosted across Blackburn's mouth.

She kept her tone arid. "It's not my first time putting someone back in their place."

Their laughter briefly lightened the car's atmosphere. It dissipated as Reeves cleared his throat. "Alright. So why am I coming along for this?"

Blackburn's glance flicked sideways, then away. "Figured you'd earned a break from desk duty."

He snorted. "Sure. But really?"

The pause stretched. "Bearing witness." Each word carefully placed.

Blackburn guided the car into a space down the street, the engine's tick-tick-tick counting down to silence.

They were early. Afternoon sun painted long shadows across glass and brick. Blackburn looked down the street. Inside the shop, everything waited in perfect stillness, an empty stage anticipating its players.

"I think Marilyn picked the store on purpose," Blackburn said, the seatbelt's click sharp in the quiet. "Not her house. Not the precinct."

Reeves considered this, fingers drumming his knee. "So you think she's got an agenda?"

"It's the crime scene. She needs babysitters to help her enter for the first time. If there's store security footage, if the cameras caught the car, caught her inside the car..." Blackburn pushed her door open, not waiting for him. The hot exhaust of a passing bus filled her lungs. She waved uselessly at the air to dispel the smell.

"It might be our most important piece of evidence." Reeves's door slammed with a metallic crack that echoed off the buildings.

"Don't slam the damned door, Reeves. Jesus."

"Sorry, boss."

"We're not just—"

"Can you spare some change? Just a couple bucks?"

The raspy voice sent Blackburn's hand to her holster. It was unlatched before she caught herself.

"I got a dollar," Reeves said as he reached into his front left pants pocket and withdrew a neatly folded dollar bill.

"Thanks," the man mumbled as he faded back into the shadows.

Blackburn stared at Reeves before slowly smiling. Of course he would.

"Let's go," she said as she turned toward the shop.

Their footsteps synchronized as they moved down the bustling street, shadows stretching before them. Blackburn looked up and down the street for a moment. No signs remained of where either woman had died.

"If Kendria's on those tapes, she might unravel," Reeves said.

Blackburn maintained her steady pace, keeping her voice controlled. "Something's off." She stepped from the curb toward the shop, Reeves's footsteps following close behind. "We're early, but look."

The police tape drooped across the entrance, yellow plastic rustling against the doorframe in the morning breeze. Blackburn's stride faltered for half a second. Through the smudged glass, movement caught her attention: a figure bent over the counter, hands working at something that shouldn't have been touched.

"Damn it." The words escaped her lips in a bare whisper. Her heels clicked against the asphalt in sharp rhythm as she broke into a jog, instinct overriding the burn in her calves.

"Marilyn!" The name cut through the air like a blade. The girl's head jerked up, eyes wide with panic. She stood paralyzed, trapped between moving and staying still.

Reeves rushed alongside her, his longer legs covering ground fast. Blackburn pushed harder, breath tight in her throat, refusing to fall behind, refusing to let this chance escape.

She reached the door just as Marilyn's finger hovered over the keyboard, the moment balanced on the edge of a single keystroke.

Chapter 6

The door of Coconut Glass Candles was open, allowing the soft notes of vanilla and sandalwood to mix with city smog. Sweet, earthy and poisonous. It was the scent that grief leaves behind. Marilyn Chaplin hunched over the computer behind the counter, her fingers striking keys with sharp precision.

"You shouldn't be in here." Blackburn's voice cut through the shop's quiet as she stepped over the threshold, Reeves close behind. The floorboards groaned beneath them, the sound bouncing off rows of candles that stood like small sentries, each bearing Kendria's careful price tags in her distinctive looped script.

Marilyn didn't look up from the screen. "It's my mother's shop."

"It's off limits." Blackburn moved closer, cataloguing the woman's locked shoulders, the micro-flinch at their approach. Monitor light carved shadows into Marilyn's face, aging her beyond her seventeen years. Since it was not a crime scene, Blackburn had no official control over who accessed it.

"Just transferring the security footage for you, Detective Blackburn," Marilyn said, her voice steady despite the tremor that chased her fingers across the keyboard. "The camera's pointed at the door, it covers some of the street."

She extracted the USB from the port. The click rang unnaturally loud in the hushed space. She handed it to Reeves but kept her eyes on Blackburn. A look that cut past accusation or suspicion to land somewhere sharper. Recognition perhaps, or something closer to revelation. It raised a prickle along Blackburn's neck.

Reeves pocketed the drive. Silence stretched taut between Marilyn and Blackburn. Marilyn's mouth became a hard, flat line, holding back more than words. Her glance lingered before she circled the counter.

Blackburn and Reeves stepped aside to let her pass.

Kendria's signature scents still saturated every corner. Marilyn's hand skimmed over waxed surfaces, fingertips grazing each neatly arranged candle. Every jar sat aligned on an invisible grid, proof of quiet intention.

Blackburn tracked her movements across the display. Marilyn stood squared off, blouse pressed smooth against shoulders, held rigid with effort. Professional presentation. But beneath, strain bled through in the set of her jaw, the careful distance she maintained. Blackburn filed each detail away, building her assessment piece by piece.

Reeves drifted between shelves, fingers hovering near candles and crystals before withdrawing. He studied the flyers tacked to the wall. He was background noise in human form.

Marilyn stopped at a tall pillar candle, vanilla rising sharp above the florals. Her eyes closed briefly. When they opened, any softness had vanished. Her voice came level and clear.

"What were you and my mother talking about?"

The question was delivered purposefully. Blackburn shifted her weight against the counter, projecting patience rather than authority. She met Marilyn's stare directly, offering a smile that touched only her mouth.

"When she died?"

"Yes. When she died."

"We spoke about Jenna Langston." Blackburn kept her tone neutral, each word deliberately placed. The half-truth settled between them like dust.

Skepticism flickered across Marilyn's features before disappearing behind a studied blankness. The corners of her mouth tightened almost imperceptibly. Blackburn observed the resistance forming behind that careful mask.

The detective let her gaze wander the room, maintaining her relaxed stance. She needed to let Marilyn know she was neither threatening nor threatened.

"Jenna Langston," Marilyn repeated softly.

"The woman in that autonomous car accident. It happened just down the street." Blackburn gave a single nod, holding Marilyn's gaze. "Your mother hadn't witnessed anything, at least nothing she realized at the time. She just wanted to help where she could. Though she had not mentioned the security footage, so thank you, Marilyn."

Another lie, delivered with ease. Blackburn let it rest between them, watching Marilyn process the fiction in silence. Better to leave her with a version of her mother that wouldn't raise questions. A small mercy, or perhaps a strategic one.

Marilyn's fingers found the rim of a candle jar, tracing its edge with mechanical precision. Each movement seemed considered, as if she was rationing her words. Blackburn could see the calculations behind her eyes.

"My mother always wanted to help." The statement came stripped of emotion. "She never knew when to leave things alone."

There, beneath the surface, resentment leaked through, faint but unmistakable. Blackburn filed it away, already weighing its implications. A daughter sharp enough to nurse grievances might be sharp enough to act on them.

"Didn't she?" Blackburn kept her voice low, curious, without sympathy. "Was there anything in particular she got involved with?"

Marilyn's eyes narrowed fractionally. Not quite hostile, but wary.

"It looked like you were holding hands with her," Marilyn said finally. Control wrapped tight around each word, but accusation bled through regardless. Blackburn felt rather than saw Reeves slow his wandering and tune in.

Blackburn held her ground, expression unchanged. She gave a nod. "Yes." Her tone revealed nothing. "We were praying for Jenna."

She let Marilyn absorb the answer. A subtle shudder passed through the girl's frame before she nodded. She was unsure if she wanted to be convinced. Reeves finally stopped moving long enough to risk drawing attention.

"That sounds like my mother," Marilyn said after a beat. Her gaze slid away, leaving unresolved tension hanging between them. Reeves moved again.

Blackburn tracked Marilyn's retreat deeper into the shop, watching fingers trail along shelves with unconscious familiarity. Doubt crept along the edges of her thoughts, persistent as smoke.

Smart kid. No. Smart young woman. One whose observations could give Hayes ammunition to pull Blackburn from the case if this wasn't played carefully.

Marilyn stopped at a votive display, her hand closing on a small brass key half-hidden behind the candles. She tossed it once, caught it smoothly. The first unstudied gesture she'd made.

"Your speech, at the press conference," Marilyn said without turning, voice pitched low but carrying clearly. "It was impressive."

Blackburn closed the distance with exacting steps, allowing a ghost of a smile. "I just told the truth."

"A threat of violence?" Marilyn asked.

Blackburn's attention caught on the key glinting between Marilyn's fingers. She kept her face neutral. "I was suspended." Matter-of-fact. "They're fining me and giving it to an anti-violence group."

"Really?" Reeves's skepticism rang clear.

Blackburn didn't waver. "Really. Two weeks' salary worth. The city will make a show of picking just the right charity."

"Is it much?" Marilyn asked.

Reeves gave a short, cynical laugh.

"No," Blackburn answered dryly, stepping closer to Marilyn. "It's discipline, not generosity."

The key rested in Marilyn's palm, its weight barely noticeable. Blackburn caught the moment of stillness and sharpened her tone, cutting through pretense.

"How well did you know your mother's life, personal and business?" Blackburn's gaze fixed on the brass between Marilyn's fingers. "Anyone who might have wanted to hurt her?"

Marilyn's shoulders tightened, but she held her ground, chin lifting deliberately. "No one would want to harm my mother." Her eyes flicked to the door, and she raised the key between them. "This probably fits that lock."

That lock. That door.

The tumblers surrendered with a whisper. Marilyn pushed, and the door swung inward. The air changed.

The shop's lavender sweetness died at the threshold. Beyond stretched a windowless chamber: burgundy walls drinking shadow, black leather gleaming under revealing lighting, restraints mounted with architectural precision. The room's purpose required no interpretation.

Blackburn crossed the boundary first. Her eyes catalogued: chairs positioned with mathematical precision, surfaces stripped of dust or fingerprints. The apple core had vanished. She traced her palm along a chair's spine, pressed fingertips against the table's edge.

Leave DNA, she calculated. Establish presence. Create plausible deniability.

Behind her, Reeves exhaled through his teeth. "What is this?" The words came flat, disgust bleeding through despite his control.

Blackburn's attention shifted to Marilyn. The woman remained frozen at the threshold, tendons visible in her neck, her gaze skittering across leather and steel as if the objects might rearrange themselves into something comprehensible.

So, this is your line, Blackburn noted. Interest sparked beneath her calm.

Marilyn's body locked. Her breathing hitched, then broke into something raw: half sob, half retch.

"My mother…" The words shattered mid-sentence. "She was sick." Her jaw clamped shut against rising bile.

Marilyn lurched backward through the doorway. She doubled over as her stomach emptied onto the polished oak, the sound harsh in the sudden quiet.

Blackburn remained motionless, observing. She tracked each spasm of Marilyn's shoulders until Reeves retreated past them both, collar pressed over his nose and mouth.

When the retching subsided into broken sobs, Blackburn moved. Her palm found the small of Marilyn's back, steady pressure, neither comfort nor coldness. "You're alright," she murmured, pitch calibrated for calm. But her eyes stayed sharp, dissecting every tremor and gasp. Was this a show for them?

If it was, she was good.

Marilyn's legs gave way. She collapsed against Blackburn, grief shaking through her frame like aftershocks. Her voice emerged threadbare: "I hate her." The confession disappeared into Black-burn's shoulder. "God, I hate her."

Blackburn supported the weight, one arm circling with cold efficiency, the hold of someone who understood leverage without yielding position. She let the silence stretch between them. This wasn't absolution or accusation. This was intelligence gathering.

Every detail mattered. The rhythm of anguish, the hesitation before hatred.

Marilyn hadn't known about the dungeon. That truth rang clear as struck crystal. Whatever else drove her feelings toward her mother, sexual proclivities hadn't been the trigger.

But innocence remained unproven. Hatred grew from many seeds, taking root in darkness.

After a calculated pause, Blackburn spoke, her voice threading between gentle and clinical. "It's difficult to love when we see things we don't want to." Neither judgment nor sympathy colored the words. "Secrets have a way of crossing boundaries you never meant to draw."

From the doorway, Reeves drew a sharp breath. He'd propped the door wide, letting the outside air dilute the acid stench. His stance, hands anchored on hips, a single nod when their eyes met, telegraphed his assessment.

Blackburn sealed the dungeon with a muted click that hung in the charged air. Reeves's stare bore into her, questioning. All she did was shake her head dismissively at him as she led Marilyn to a chair.

"She made me feel like I was the disappointment," Marilyn finally said.

Chapter 7

Marilyn stared into the room, the leather and steel, the sex toys laid out like a buffet. "This… She… I… What on earth am I supposed to do now?" The words spilled from her, raw and unfiltered. Tears carved channels through her foundation, leaving pale tracks against flushed skin. "She ruined so much," Marilyn said, her fingers gripping the arms until her knuckles reddened. "I have to fix this. Make it right again. Make it pure." Her voice thinned to a whisper, brittle as old paper. "Why couldn't she just be like everyone else? Why did she have to make things so hard?"

Blackburn moved closer, the floorboards creaking beneath her weight. She lowered herself until she was level with Marilyn's chair, maintaining a careful distance. The air between them was heavy with unspoken grief. "It's not always easy to understand why people do what they do," Blackburn said, her voice low and steady. She studied Marilyn's face, noting the tremor in her jaw, the way her eyes darted and wouldn't hold still. "Did you know about this?"

"Goodness, no. I thought she was up to something, always working late. In a candle shop, of all things." The words emerged on a shuddering exhale, Marilyn's chest hitching with the effort. "I thought she was a…"

Blackburn's eyes flicked to the dungeon door and back again to the teenager. "Drug dealer?" she said, completing Marilyn's thought for her.

"Yes," she said as she drew in a deep breath. "That's why I opened the door. I was expecting pot plants or a meth lab or something."

The shop's cramped space pressed in around them. The air felt syrupy, coating the back of Blackburn's throat with cloying sweetness. Reeves shifted his weight, floorboards groaning beneath him as he retrieved his notepad.

"Had you ever seen your mother use drugs? Anything at all?" His pen hovered over the blank paper.

"No, never." Marilyn's voice cracked. "She wouldn't even take aspirin without reading the bottle three times. Called it 'putting foreign chemicals in her temple.'" Her laugh rattled hollow against the low ceiling.

"But she drank?"

"Yes. Wine. Usually organic," Marilyn said. "What a hypocrite."

Blackburn studied the girl's face, marveling at how much she looked like her mother. She was grateful Jenna had no children. "What about here in the shop? Unusual visitors? People who didn't seem like typical customers?"

"Just regulars. Old ladies mostly, asking about lavender for arthritis. Some young couples were looking for romantic candles." Marilyn dragged her hand across her eyes, leaving a damp streak along her cheekbone. "I helped sometimes on weekends. It was always busy enough."

Silence pooled between them, broken only by the air conditioning unit's asthmatic wheeze as it battled the accumulated heat. Reeves turned a page, the paper's whisper sharp in the stillness.

"What about at home?" He kept his voice soft. "Anything out of place? Strange phone calls? People you didn't recognize?"

"Nothing." The word caught in her throat. Marilyn's fingers found a loose thread on her jeans, worrying it longer with each nervous pull. "She was boring. She made dinner at eight, watched the news, went to bed at ten. When she wasn't working late. The most exciting thing she did was buy different brands of tea and yell at politicians on TV."

"But you suspected something." Blackburn's words carried steel that drew Marilyn's shoulders tight.

"Started maybe two years ago. She'd stay late once or twice a week. Said she was doing inventory, reorganizing, cleaning." Marilyn's laugh scraped raw. "How much inventory does a candle shop need? How many times can you reorganize two hundred and fifty square feet?"

"Did the money situation change?" Reeves asked. "New car, expensive purchases?"

"No, that's what made it weird. We were doing okay, but not great. Same crappy house, same used Honda she'd driven since I was twelve." Desperation leaked into her rising voice. "If she were selling drugs, where was the money?"

Blackburn's steady steps creaked across worn wood. The girl drew back as she approached. "When did you first suspect something?"

"Last year. I came here once to see what was going on." Marilyn's whisper barely rose above the air conditioner's drone. "Sat in my car across the street for two hours. The lights were on, but I couldn't see what she was doing. Just shadows moving around."

"Did you confront her?"

"I tried. She said I was being paranoid, that I watched too many crime shows." Marilyn's control shattered, her voice careening off cluttered walls. "I thought she was breaking the law. I thought that's why she wouldn't tell me. I thought I was living with some criminal mastermind, and instead she was..."

Her trembling hand gestured toward the dungeon door. Blackburn followed the gesture, and she wondered, just briefly, what Marilyn would do with everything.

"Instead, she was what?" Blackburn said, snapping herself back into the conversation.

"A stranger," Marilyn breathed. "You think you know your mother, and now I find out she had this whole other life, and I..." Her voice dissolved. "I don't know who she was. I don't want to know."

Blackburn rose with grace and caught Reeves's eye with a subtle nod. No violence here, just a daughter adrift in grief's dark current, grasping at fragments of a mother she'd never truly known.

"We may have more questions later," Blackburn said, her professional armor sliding back into place. "Do you want a drive home?" she added, nodding toward Reeves.

Marilyn's palms found the mahogany counter as she rose, its grain worn smooth by years of transactions, now slick beneath her damp hands.

"I think I need to call my pastor. Figure out what to... Who can help me? Not him. Who can take all of this away?" Her voice fractured on the last word. She caught herself, fingers automatically smoothing the hem of her shirt, spine straightening into pretend composure.

Blackburn's hand moved to her pocket. "Here's my business card. That's my direct number. This card is for Victim Services. They can help you with a therapist or—"

"No." The word cracked like a slap. "That."

The room.

All that beautiful furniture. Everything.

Reeves shifted, leather holster creaking. His notebook lay closed between his fingers, pages pressed tight. The girl's distress filled the small space like another scent, sharp and acidic, impossible to ignore.

Blackburn knew it was all beautifully crafted, and she sensed her chance. With Reeves as a witness, she would have to be careful how she played it. This situation called for something more nuanced.

"What if..." She let the words emerge slowly, as if still forming. "What if I handled the removal personally? Not this weekend, but next weekend, when I have time. You keep the shop closed, give me the key. I could rent a truck, come through the back alley. No one would see anything."

Marilyn's chin jerked up, pupils dilating with sudden hope. "You would do that?"

"It's not standard procedure," Blackburn kept her tone clinical, professional. "But as you know, I'm not a standard detective. I understand your concerns about privacy. About respecting your mother's memory."

Reeves's frown carved deeper lines around his mouth. "Detective Blackburn, are you sure that's—"

"Sometimes we have to think of the family, not of ourselves, Detective Reeves." Just enough steel in her voice to remind him where they stood. "This isn't evidence in the case. Or do you think Kendria's room has something to do with her being hit by a car?"

His weight shifted from foot to foot, floorboards groaning beneath him. "No, boss, I was just thinking—"

"Detective. Kendria Chaplin's reputation doesn't need muddying. Her death has been a lightning rod for all the wrong reasons. Let's not stir things up. This was Kendria's personal property, and now it's Marilyn's. Personal property that has no bearing on our investigation."

The shop held them in its dusty embrace: wax and wick oil, old wood and new grief. Marilyn's knuckles had gone tight in the fist she formed at her side.

"I would be so grateful," she whispered. "I just need it all to disappear. I need to be able to remember my mother the way she was before I found... before I knew about any of this."

Blackburn inclined her head, features arranged in careful neutrality even as satisfaction uncurled in her chest. "I'll handle everything. You won't have to deal with any of it. But Detective Reeves, I need your word that this stays between us. The girl's been through enough."

"Of course, boss. Homicide detectives don't go shooting their mouths off. You have my word."

"Thank you." The relief in Marilyn's voice was almost painful. Her shoulders dropped, breath releasing in a long exhale. "Both of you. I don't know what I would have done."

As they prepared to leave, Blackburn permitted herself the smallest upturn of lips. Her basement waited. Not empty. Not eager. Just... ready. That weekend would prove quite productive indeed.

They left Marilyn in her car, settling into a silence thick enough to taste. Through the window's thin glass, Blackburn watched Marilyn fold into herself, shoulders curving inward like parentheses around an empty space.

Reeves held his tongue until they reached the car, gravel crunching beneath their feet. "She has so much motive to kill her mother."

"Embarrassment is not a strong motive," Blackburn said, watching the scene in the side mirror. Her fingers found her neck, tracing the pulse point there.

"Sex is. And that's what this is about," Reeves said, reaching for the car door.

"She didn't know, Reeves." Her certainty rang clear in the confined space of the car.

"Or she's an excellent actress," Reeves replied as the engine turned over with a reluctant growl. "We can't dismiss her yet."

He left it at that. Some truths didn't need elaboration.

Chapter 8

The light sliced through the precinct's grimy windows, cutting across open folders and coffee rings that had bled deep into the conference table's scarred wood.

Sinclair stood at the western windows, his silhouette sharp against the glass as he pressed his phone tight to his ear. His heart pounded. Tony Ricci's voice came through clear, low and familiar as old shoe leather. Ricci had been a cooperating informant for three years. He didn't embellish.

"It's him, Sinclair. Devon Malik. I'd stake my life on it."

Sinclair's fingers tightened around the phone. The name resonated like a struck bell. Devon Malik. His file had sat on Sinclair's desk for months: a warehouse homicide, Taylor Duvey found with two bullets in his chest. Cold until last week, when fresh evidence dragged Malik into focus. A witness, nervous after a federal sweep shattered Malik's crew, had finally given him up.

"Where?" Sinclair kept his voice level.

"St. Isidore's Chapel and Mortuary. North side. There's a funeral. Looks like he's planning to pay his respects. Keeping it low-key, but I know that face."

Sinclair checked his watch. If he could get this done before Blackburn showed up, he would be her hero. "When?"

"About five minutes ago," Ricci answered. "Service hasn't started. He just went in. Black suit, fresh shave, but I'm certain."

Sinclair knew St. Isidore's, a neighborhood funeral home where families gathered without ceremony or pretense. Not where you'd expect to find a fugitive, but that was likely the point.

"Alone?" Sinclair asked, already moving toward his desk.

"Didn't see anyone with him going in," Ricci said. "Could be muscle nearby. Parking lot or already inside. Don't assume he's solo."

Sinclair's pen scratched across paper: Devon Malik, 34, open warrant for homicide; assume armed; possible associates present. The Duvey case had shown how quickly Malik's people turned violent. No reason to think today would differ.

"Tony, get out of there," Sinclair said, voice dropping.

Ricci didn't argue. Their trust ran both ways. "I'm gone," he replied. The line went dead.

Sinclair steadied his breathing and dialed dispatch. He flagged Malik's presence and requested tactical support for containment. There was no margin for error inside a chapel packed with civilians. This was going to earn him a gold star from Blackburn.

Today, Blackburn was out on an interview with Reeves. Blackburn always chose Reeves. But this would make her think about *him* as a real detective. Get the attention he deserved.

He reached for his jacket just as Cooper materialized in the doorway, coffee steaming in his hand, sharp eyes following movement.

"You heading out?" Cooper asked from the threshold.

"Got Malik at St. Isidore's," Sinclair replied, checking his jacket for badge and keys. "My CI spotted him at a funeral."

Cooper's jaw tightened, a line creasing between his brows as he recalled details burned into memory from months chasing this case through dead ends.

"You think it's legit? Or cover?" Cooper asked.

"Either way, we treat it as real," Sinclair said. "I've got tactical rolling."

"That serious?" Cooper asked without surprise.

"If we don't control this scene, we risk a bloodbath." Sinclair gathered files as he spoke, a routine carved from necessity rather than comfort.

Cooper abandoned his coffee on a cluttered shelf. "You want backup here or remote?"

There was no way Sinclair was going to let Cooper in on his arrest.

"Monitor the tactical channel," Sinclair directed, not looking up from the files. "If this goes sideways before Blackburn returns, brief her immediately." He paused at the threshold. "And if we land Malik, make sure you have enough money to buy me drinks."

Cooper nodded. "You want that promotion, don't you?"

Sinclair gave him the finger. If he could pull this off, Blackburn would have to respect him, treat him like a partner instead of an inconvenience. And if he could do this while she was off with Reeves? Even sweeter.

The drive north took fifteen minutes through pitted streets lined with sagging brick buildings and battered storefronts. It gave way to rows of shotgun houses huddled near St. Isidore's modest sign and chain-link parking lot. Sinclair kept the radio locked on tactical frequency as the team relayed their approach. Ten minutes out and closing.

St. Isidore's emerged from the urban sprawl: red brick walls behind dying hedges, cars packed tight on cracked asphalt, mourners clustered at doorways and beneath shade trees in dark clothes, voices hushed.

All routine on its surface, a neighborhood funeral like any other. But inside waited a man who'd put two bullets in Taylor Duvey and vanished like smoke.

Sinclair positioned his unmarked cruiser across the street with clear sightlines on all exits but far enough to avoid attention from mourners stepping out for air or cigarettes beneath the pale morning sun filtered through exhaust haze.

Through his windshield he cataloged them: couples gripping each other along broken sidewalks; young men uncomfortable in borrowed suits; older women clutching worn purses against their ribs. None was aware their sanctuary harbored something far deadlier than grief.

His radio crackled: "Unit Seven to Detective Sinclair. We're establishing a perimeter." He pressed his damp palms against his thighs, fingers spreading wide.

"Copy," Sinclair responded, eyes locked on the chapel entrance. "Target is believed inside the main sanctuary. Stage accordingly, but maintain distance until my signal." His voice caught, breath hitching on the last word. Heat crept up his neck.

"Understood. All exits covered," came the clipped reply.

He watched the tactical choreography unfold, pulse quickening at each coordinated movement. Shadows flowing along fence lines in gear; an operator assembling surveillance equipment behind panel vans; team leaders coordinating coverage over encrypted channels. All invisible to those saying goodbye inside worn pews beyond stained glass dulled by decades of city grime.

The service began. Movement near the altar became visible through colored panes, catching dust motes in slanted light. Soon, people would drift out again. Their window was shrinking. Sinclair Sinclair's hands trembled as he gripped the wheel tighter, moving his hands roughly on the leather.

Across Chapel Road, mourners shifted restlessly, fumbling for keys, dabbing at eyes, preparing to leave while Malik moved somewhere among them, invisible except to those converging on his position.

The radio delivered its verdict: "All units. Execute entry."

Sinclair pressed back against his seat, breath coming shorter as anticipation built. The trap closed around St. Isidore's mortuary, where everything would change.

The breach unfolded with clinical precision.

"Devon Malik! Devon Malik! Police! Get down!"

The commands reached Sinclair in fragments, muffled by distance and stone walls. Hs heart pounded. His shirt clung to his chest, fabric damp with nervous heat.

"Keep your hands visible!"

Officers advanced person by person as Malik raised his hands. They moved the mourners aside, clearing them from danger.

His scalp prickled with perspiration, every nerve heightened as he watched Malik surrender. No protest. No scramble for escape. The man stood as if he'd been expecting this moment. Sinclair exhaled slowly, the tension leaving his body in waves.

Gloved hands encircled thin wrists. Metal cuffs ratcheted closed with a decisive click. They led him forward, chin level, face expressionless as marble, oblivious to the terror surrounding him.

"Target in custody."

Three minutes from start to capture. Clean efficiency without theatrics. Officers began their withdrawal, securing weapons and congratulating each other.

The suspect moved between them with deliberate steps, no resistance, no visible emotion. Even from this distance, Sinclair could read the emptiness in his posture: not defeat or defiance, just absence.

The transport van waited at the curb, rear doors open. Two officers patted him down, talking, verifying, searching. Then they stopped.

Stopped? Sinclair blinked, frowned, and exited the car. As he approached the scene, he saw it, and stumbled. He knew he had Elijah Malik, not Devon. His head fell back for a moment as he stared at the sky.

"Detective?" The tactical officer held up the driver's license, its laminated surface catching the harsh afternoon light. Sinclair's throat tightened as he read the name; the letters blurred momentarily before crystallizing into confirmation of his mistake.

"That's not our guy." His tone came out clipped, each word sharp against the humid air. "Wrong brother."

Sergeant Chang glanced between the license and Sinclair, his expression narrowing beneath the brim of his tactical helmet. "You sure about that, Detective?"

"I'm sure." Sinclair raked a hand through his hair, feeling the dampness at his scalp. "Elijah Malik, not Devon. I missed it."

Chang keyed his radio, the static crackling through the tense silence. "Control, subject is clear. Misidentification." Around them, tactical officers traded looks as their errors settled in. Twelve of them had just blocked off the street with their armored vehicles, stormed a funeral, and held an innocent man at gunpoint because some detective had failed to check the details.

Chang's boots scraped against the asphalt as he crossed to Elijah Malik, who waited in stillness with his hands secured behind him. "We're removing the cuffs, sir. You're free to go."

Elijah flexed his wrists as the metal restraints clicked open and fell away. "What was this about?" His gaze moved over the officers gathering their gear, the metallic clatter of equipment filling the space between his words.

"Mistaken identity," Chang said. He kept his response calculated, professional distance coating each syllable.

Elijah's stare settled on Sinclair. "Mistaken for what?" The question hung in the air. He knew this was about Devon. He wanted to hear them say it.

"Police matter," Chang replied. "We apologize for the error." The team had already started loading their equipment into the vehicles, doors slamming with finality.

Chang approached Sinclair again, his tone even but cool as steel. "Next time you call us out, be certain who you're after. My people don't need this kind of mistake."

Sinclair gave a short nod, watching Elijah Malik's careful steps as he walked back toward the church. He deserved the gesture sent his way by Elijah. His perfect arrest had dissolved into confusion and bad intelligence.

The disappointment of what just happened settled on him like lead. Not only had he screwed up spectacularly, but he'd done it in front of a full tactical team who would remember this. Word would get back to Blackburn within hours.

He was going to pay for this.

* * *

The paperwork told its own story of a transition from investigation to prosecution. Reeves arrived at his desk to find it still buried under forms. Incident reports requiring triplicate signatures, evidence transfer documents shifting custody from detective to attorney. The administrative finale to an investigation that had consumed three intense days.

After they returned from the interview, and startling revelation with Marilyn, Blackburn had retreated into her office. She promised to type up the notes, leaving Reeves with time.

He signed the final incident report three times. Blue ink bled into the white paper, his signature automatic after decades of repetition. The report would vanish into the vast archives of records storage, lying safely until some future attorney demanded its resurrection.

Evidence transfer required obsessive precision. Each item collected demanded its own detailed entry. The documentation had to be flawless. The chain of custody could not show the slightest gap. One careless error risked placing crucial evidence beyond legal reach forever. He unlocked his cabinet with his palm and retrieved the evidence.

Reeves stacked the signed forms with methodical care and carried them down to the Evidence Room. The windowless space carried a persistent chemical smell of preservatives and decay. Its rows of metal shelving were laden with catalogued violence.

Tommy Guerrero glanced up from his monitor as Reeves entered, fingers pausing mid-keystroke. Fifteen years in this vault of misery had given Tommy both efficiency and the necessary detachment. He processed evidence of human cruelty with the same careful attention he might give to filing tax returns.

"Scudamore case?" Tommy asked, already reaching for Reeves's paperwork.

"Everything's here," Reeves confirmed. "Weapon, photographs, witness statements. The complete package," Reeves said. "The DA needs everything transferred by Monday morning."

Back upstairs, Reeves noticed his message light blinking insistently. ADA Melanie Bowman had called while he was in Evidence. He settled into his chair and returned her call.

"Detective," Bowman greeted him, her voice carrying the slight strain of too many cases. "I've reviewed your file thoroughly. Excellent attention to detail throughout. We're proceeding with Murder One charges but keeping plea negotiations open."

"Has Mrs. Katt expressed any preferences?"

"We spoke at length this morning," Bowman said. "She'll accept a Murder Two plea if it guarantees real prison time and spares her from testifying about her daughter's abuse in open court. She wants closure more than vengeance."

It was an understandable position. Heather Katt would avoid reliving her daughter's suffering in public testimony. The state would secure a certain conviction without risking trial uncertainties. John Dala would serve decades behind concrete and steel walls.

The system would deliver what measure of justice it could.

"The arraignment is scheduled for next Tuesday," Bowman continued. "We'll present formal charges. The defense will request time to examine the evidence and explore their options."

"Anything else you need from me?"

"Just remain available in case plea negotiations fall through and we need testimony. But given the strength of evidence, I doubt this sees the inside of a courtroom."

Reeves hung up and completed the remaining transfer documents, officially shifting the Scudamore case from active investigation to pending prosecution. His direct involvement was finished now, save for potential court appearances or clarifying questions from attorneys who hadn't walked through the blood-stained kitchen.

He crossed to the case board. The room was quiet. Cooper and Sinclair were out. He uncapped a black marker, its chemical smell was sharp in the air. The red SCUDAMORE was erased, replaced with black, moving it to the closed column, pending trial.

The color change mattered in ways both practical and symbolic. Red meant active investigation requiring immediate attention. Black meant completed work awaiting the slow machinery of justice. The board mapped the entire squad's workload in this simple binary. What demanded action now versus what waited for courts to process.

The Scudamore file had followed a grimly familiar pattern. John Dala killed his wife during a breakfast argument, confessed without hesitation, left evidence that removed all doubt. No mysteries demanded solving. No hidden motives required excavation. Just violence, evidence, and consequences arranged in logical sequence.

After weeks drowning in autonomous vehicle algorithms and trying to understand emerging technologies, Reeves found unexpected satisfaction in this case's brutal clarity. A crime that made terrible sense, answered through proper procedure and careful documentation. Cases like this reminded him why he had joined the force.

Accountability didn't always require complexity. Sometimes a confession and a still-warm gun were enough. Evidence so overwhelming that even the most byzantine legal system couldn't distort it beyond recognition.

Chapter 9

Lilith Halperin walked down the corridor, heels announcing her arrival. Offices flanked her path: glass barriers containing employees who shifted at her approach, their posture and attention sharpening. She ignored the brief flickers of eye contact that darted away like startled birds. Her presence spoke for itself.

She had her every-Friday headache. Staff were too eager to let things slide until Monday. Get home, forget about the empire she had created.

Light from the east windows marked the floor ahead of her. Elongated shapes in neat geometric lines. She glanced at her watch without slowing, a vintage Hazzenale, its dial turned to the inside of her wrist. Nine-seventeen. The board meeting would start at eleven. She had over an hour to lock down the LightTime acquisition.

Charles kept pace just behind her. He held a tablet and a cup of coffee she had not requested. The ceramic warmed his palm at exactly the right temperature. He understood her patterns: the right time, the right temperature, no need to ask. Three years had taught him to deliver what mattered.

"The legal review came through at four this morning," he said, pitching his voice low enough for only her ears. No small talk. "LightTime's patents are clean. There are no licensing surprises."

She acknowledged him with a single nod and moved past marketing. Four people tightly clustered around a monitor filled with winter campaign drafts. The glow from the screen caught on their faces as they leaned in. As she glanced over, postures straightened, gazes fixed forward. She registered a color palette that was safe and uninspired but made no comment.

Charles pressed on: "Their distribution is North America and some European channels only. But Sunrise Blush has outsold our cheek line three-to-one in eighteen to twenty-fives."

She replied evenly, "One viral product doesn't justify their valuation, not from two chemists and an intern in a Portland warehouse."

The hall widened at a corner where indirect lighting softened the corporate edges. A junior copywriter scurried past them, his shoes squeaking on the marble as he stepped into an office that wasn't his before hurrying out again, avoiding eye contact. Lilith half-smiled.

Charles tapped through screens on his tablet, the soft clicks marking each new data point. "Azure's offer is forty million flat. Dream's up to forty-two with creative control for the founders. Markson adds equity that could push it beyond forty-five five if stocks hold."

Lilith paused at the window overlooking the city. Traffic thread slowly along distant streets like blood through veins, people reduced to motion without detail. Her reflection in the glass was composed. A sharp bob framed her face. Brown eyes scanned details even now.

Below her collarbone, a faint scar caught in the morning light. She'd made no move to hide it.

She considered each bidder in turn: "Azure can't merge their formulas with LightTime's. Their systems don't match up. Dream will gut innovation and bury what works; they'll kill half the line inside a year. Markson wants youth branding they haven't managed for ten years."

Charles accepted each point without argument. "Our position?"

She turned from the glass and continued forward, voice level and certain: "What LightTime needs isn't cash. It's reach, and someone who won't break what already works. Growth without dissolution. We keep their team together, extend their reach through our channels, and preserve the product's identity while increasing volume." The marble reflected her silhouette as she moved. Charles tapped every word she spoke into the tablet. "We're not just buying a popular rouge. We're securing innovation that we would spend years developing on our own."

Charles lowered his voice as they passed a group of designers bent over fabric swatches. "Their CEO is worried about culture shock," he said. "She called us a 'soul-sucking conglomerate' in her last message to the board."

Lilith smiled briefly and flatly. "If she doesn't want her soul to be sucked, she shouldn't be putting it up for sale. Integrity comes at a premium. I'll make sure she knows we're willing to pay."

They walked into the finance wing. Analysts worked silently at long tables, eyes fixed on shifting numbers and risk reports that flickered across multiple monitors. The air carried the faint scent of coffee and ozone from overworked electronics. One analyst glanced up, met Lilith's gaze, and nodded. She nodded in return, unable to recall his name.

"If we win this," Charles said, "we'll inherit their people. Fifty-eight staff, mostly creative and production."

"Redundancies?"

"Marketing overlaps. Their social media team outperforms ours."

Lilith considered the implications. "Build out integration plans, one for full absorption, one for selective retention. I want specifics."

"And the founder? Rachel Whiting says she wants to stay involved."

"With soul-suckers," Lilith said. "Offer her a two-year creative director contract with clear performance incentives. It's generous enough to show respect, structured enough to keep control."

They reached the double doors leading to the conference area. Through the glass, Lilith could see three executives arranged around the table. Papers were fanned out like playing cards, laptops open, a projector casting its blue standby glow. Jonathan would update her on the overdue app. The thought created a tightness in her chest. It was a familiar compression that wasn't fear so much as restrained irritation.

Charles read the change in her posture. "The revised LightTime offer will be on your desk when you finish with product development."

"Draft two," Lilith replied. "Forty-five million with rapid integration; forty-eight with a slower ramp-up. I'll decide after hearing their progress."

He made efficient notes on his tablet. "And the board meeting?"

"Move it up to eleven-thirty. I want the final numbers before I answer questions." She checked her watch: nine twenty-three. "Keep acquisition on standby for a ten-forty-five call."

Lilith adjusted her cuffs, the silk whispering against her skin. The weight was familiar to her skin. LightTime would wait exactly twenty-seven minutes. First, she would handle what needed correction.

Charles held the door for her, efficient and silent. She walked past him with a short nod, attention fixed on the executives inside. They straightened as she entered. Papers quieted mid-shuffle, coffee cups paused at lips, tension settling across polished glass and filtered air like morning frost.

Business resumed under her watchful eye: direct, contained, necessary.

"Nine twenty-four," she said. No glance at her watch. The words marked the hour, nothing more. A line was drawn before the reckoning began.

She sat at the head of the table, calm and direct. No fuss with her jacket, no idle gestures. The leather chair accepted her without protest. Charles closed the door behind her with a soft click that sealed the room. Across the table, Jonathan Koch, digital integration, tapped his stylus on his tablet in a nervous rhythm until her eyes stilled his hand.

Valerie McKee and Marcus Correa kept their expressions neutral, careful masks that revealed nothing. Product Development Director and CTO. Together responsible for an app now three weeks overdue.

"Halperin AI," Lilith said. Not a question. A demand for accountability.

Jonathan cleared his throat. "We've made progress since our last update."

She stayed silent. The air conditioning hummed overhead. He had space to explain or incriminate himself.

"The core features are working," he said, bringing his tablet to life with a swipe. Interface designs appeared on the wall: clean lines, Halperin's usual restraint rendered in pixels and gradients. "Camera works as promised. Facial recognition and color matching both exceed initial targets."

Lilith kept her gaze steady. "Then why isn't it ready to launch?"

Valerie leaned forward, her fingers laced together on the table's surface. "The AI recommendation engine still produces inconsistent results. We've expanded training data sets."

"Show me," Lilith said, flat and calm. "Skip the slides. I want to see it fail."

Jonathan adjusted his screen; new images filled the wall with harsh clarity. A young woman's face appeared. Brown skin catching the studio lights, round features softened by professional photography, followed by product suggestions scrolling below.

"The AI matched her with Alabaster foundation," Marcus said, pointing without meeting her eyes. "A mismatch for deep umber undertones. It recommended cool eyeshadows for a warm complexion, lip colors that won't suit."

Lilith's jaw moved once, almost imperceptibly. "And tutorials?"

Jonathan tapped again. An AI-generated video played of the same woman applying makeup with techniques that ignored both face shape and coloring. The brushstrokes were confident, but wrong.

"The personalization algorithms can't read nuance," Valerie said. "Basic features are fine, but the details get lost in translation, and tutorial generation—"

"Nuance?" Lilith cut in. Her voice was level but flat as glass over ice. "Is that what we call African American women's skin? I don't understand how an AI that can route cars through New Dresden traffic or predict quarterly variance within two percent cannot manage a foundation match."

The silence sharpened in its focus as workers outside did everything not to look into the room. Someone dropped a pen in the corridor; the sound carried through the glass.

"We're coordinating with the dev team nonstop," Jonathan protested. "The problem is specificity: not enough diverse beauty data in training. It's improving, but—"

"But learning." Lilith let him hear what she thought of that word. "Eighteen million dollars for a racist AI? That mixes up undertones and botches highlight placement? That confuses mascara formulas even after explicit prompts?"

No one replied. Tension settled between her shoulders in quiet knots, radiating up beneath controlled breath. She didn't move or break eye contact or let any anger show beyond the set of her spine and the icy edge of her silence.

"This application is our anchor for direct-to-consumer growth next year. It holds forty percent of our projected digital revenue." Lilith's tone was flat, almost bored. Dangerous. "The campaign launches in three weeks. The board wants answers today." She leaned forward, the movement minimal but deliberate, eyes on Marcus. "Explain why our damned AI can't process a basic color palette."

Marcus shifted in his seat, leather creaking beneath him. "It wasn't designed for aesthetic input. The network—"

"Basic. Color. Palette. I want solutions. Give me a timeline."

Jonathan spoke quietly, hands folded in front of him like a penitent. "We need four more weeks. New data, revised models—"

"Two." Lilith's voice made her meaning clear. "Two weeks until launch-ready. Not a concept, not a demo. Finished product."

"That isn't feasible," Jonathan said, face flushed with heat that crept up from his collar. "Doubling the team wouldn't close that gap. Continuous training would burn out the systems—"

"Then triple the team and run the cycles around the clock," she said. "Move engineers from other projects if you have to."

"The rec engine alone needs more—"

"Two weeks." She didn't blink. "Or we find people who can do it in two."

The silence pressed in like a physical weight. Valerie kept her eyes fixed on her screen, the blue light reflecting in her glasses. Marcus wrote something without looking up, his pen scratching across the paper.

"You're setting us up to fail," Jonathan said.

"I'm holding you to company standards," Lilith snapped. "The standards you agreed to when you took this job, and the pay that came with it."

"We've laid out the technical risks—"

"And I've clarified the business reality." She slid her tablet into her bag and stood, motion slow. "Two weeks: full launch functionality, accurate recommendations, proper onboarding guides. Otherwise, we replace leadership."

Jonathan pushed back from the table so hard his chair scraped across the floor with a sound like tearing paper. "You're asking for something impossible just to threaten us with termination when it doesn't happen."

Lilith didn't raise her voice or change her expression. She looked at him for three seconds, unblinking, counting each heartbeat.

"I know exactly what I'm asking for," she said with clinical detachment. "And you'll be getting a formal write-up from HR this afternoon for your conduct." She checked her watch, the metal cool against her wrist. "Nine forty-two AM. Two weeks from today."

She walked out without another word. Jonathan's breathing was uneven behind her, ragged at the edges; Valerie murmured something under her breath that might have been a prayer; Marcus was still writing, pen moving in tight, controlled strokes. "Fucking bitch," was the last thing Lilith heard.

Jonathan.

None of this required her attention now. The door closed quietly behind her, leaving them with their choices and consequences.

Two weeks remained: either they delivered or they would be gone. The market waited for neither excuses nor algorithms hung up on color theory basics. Lilith felt a warmth. Blood flowing, she felt alive.

Lilith moved down the corridor. Her presence cleared a path. Employees sensed her anger, sharp and cold beneath her restraint, like ice forming on still water. She reached her office and closed the door quietly. The soft click cut through the air with more finality than any slammed door could.

Inside, sunlight caught on crystal plaques set along mahogany shelves, scattering pale prismatic shapes across the white walls. This space was hers. Both a retreat and a front line.

She walked to her desk and sat, back straight in the black leather chair. The leather exhaled a muted sigh that echoed her own withheld breath. She pressed both palms to the desk's surface, fingers spread wide, holding steady while adrenaline pulsed beneath the thin skin at her wrists.

Jonathan's slur echoed in her mind: twelve years building this company, sixteen-hour days, hundreds of jobs relying on decisions only she could make, and still she was reduced to 'fucking bitch' when a man failed to deliver. The syllables hung in the air like smoke. She would not speak it aloud or let it show.

The laptop sat in perfect alignment before her. She flipped it open, logged in by rote muscle memory, and dismissed the avalanche of unread emails with a single click. In a new message, she entered "Sally Reinhardt."

Her message was terse:

Sally,

Jonathan Koch requires disciplinary documentation for insubordination and inappropriate language during this morning's product development meeting (9:24–9:42 a.m., Blue Conference Room). He used gender-based profanity directed at me personally, after questions regarding project timelines.

Level 2 write-up. File copy and notify personnel committee.

Lilith Halperin

CEO, Halperin Cosmetics

She sent it immediately. No revision nor hesitation. Details were sufficient; emotion was irrelevant. This was how she had built Halperin Cosmetics from nothing: exacting standards, clear responses.

The office phone glowed with an incoming call: Charles again. She left it unanswered and focused on her reflection flickering on the laptop screen. Calm and unreadable, every line of hair precisely arranged despite the morning's friction.

The old scar below her collarbone tugged at her attention. Two fingers pressed against it under silk. A thin ridge beneath fabric that carried warmth from her skin. An old lesson about power and vulnerability that lingered just under the surface.

Her eyes shifted to the window. Freedom beyond the confines of the office. She reached into her pocket to retrieve her personal phone.

Disconnected from company networks. Always separate, always private.

Her thumbprint woke the device: clean background, no photos or names on display. She tapped through labeled folders until she reached one marked "Finance Research." Inside lay an app with an understated black-and-white knot for an icon. Easy to miss unless you understood its meaning.

BDSMessages opened at her touch, a quiet world waiting behind all that control.

The app loaded her profile: sparse details, no photos, nothing revealing. *LH38. Professional. Discreet. Submissive (F4F only). Experienced. No permanent marks. Available weekends.*

She selected the search icon, filtered for "Dominants - Female," then narrowed to "Available Today." The list filled in, line by line, usernames appearing like promises. She recognized most of the names: women she had met before. Skilled enough, but never deep enough to reach the places that mattered. The need in her chest remained a constant, low-voltage urge for surrender and, for a short while, silence.

She scanned profiles: *CruelSummer.* Online now but wanting public play. Not her scene. Swipe past. *MistressD*: experienced, but with a focus on needles and blood; too clinical, too intense in a direction she did not crave. More profiles: wrong kinks, wrong signals. Each miss sharpened her frustration like a blade being honed.

The day's pressure lingered from the boardroom: two weeks left to fix the AI system already overdue. A pending acquisition at risk. The

Board meeting looming overhead. All of it pooled behind her eyes and pressed at her temples with familiar insistence.

She needed relief from everything. The order of submission in place of ceaseless decisions.

She changed the filter options, removing the 'Available Now' demand. At the bottom of the results, a new option appeared: *barbwire12*. Last active yesterday. The preview image showed hands, clean and strong, cupping bare breasts with confident possession; platinum hair fell over anonymous shoulders like water. The profile was brief: *Firm but fair. I see what you need before you ask. Experience with high-pressure professionals seeking release. No men.*

Lilith felt her pulse shift tempo, blood warming beneath her skin. She opened the profile fully and ran through the specifics with familiar scrutiny: location nearby, age listed as 42, dominant role confirmed. Interests: impact play, restraint, psychological edge. All compatible.

Her thumb hovered over "Message." Beyond her closed office door: phone calls, muffled voices filtering through glass, schedules in motion. Jonathan's careless remark still lingered. The reminder of another duty demanding poise and exactitude.

She typed:

>Professional woman, 38. Seeking same-day session; experienced submissive; hotel preferred. I can arrange a room if required. Strict rules expected; no permanent marks.

After a moment she added:

>I need clear correction.

Footsteps sounded beyond the glass wall; Charles neared with his tablet, the numbers she would soon have to review glowing on its surface. Behind him, her team gathered around Jonathan's anxiety like moths to a flame.

All of it waited for her leadership.

She hit send and tucked her phone away just as Charles arrived. Two taps against glass, precise as always.

"Come in," she said, voice quiet and ready.

On the surface: composed authority; every inch in control.

Beneath pressed fabric and old scar tissue, anticipation gathered in increments, for precise undoing by hands she hoped would know exactly what she needed.

Chapter 10

Blackburn cut the ignition and sat still. Across from Shelton & Sons Funeral Home, piano scales drifted through the Whittington Ballet School's windows. The notes were steady, repetitive, efficient. In the rearview mirror, her reflection looked back at her: controlled, the mask in place. No badge showing. Only the gun's steady press against her ribs confirmed her role.

Her eyes shifted. Behind the glass, young dancers in black leotards rehearsed under LED lights that buzzed faintly overhead. One girl adjusted herself at the barre, her spine lengthening as the instructor's eyes bore into her. The funeral home cast its pale shadow along the wall each afternoon. Discipline and mortality shared this block.

Blackburn stepped out of the car. Her heels struck the cement in even beats, each impact sending a small vibration up her calves. Warmth pressed against her skin; sunlight found no purchase on her charcoal suit. The fabric absorbed the heat, making her aware of every place it touched her body. It was a Saturday built for endings.

The walk was lined with cars parked clean and straight against the curb: black, silver, blue. A single red SUV caught her attention. Yellow toy ducks sat along its dash, their plastic smiles jarring against the somber code. Someone outside the choreography.

She catalogued license plates and makes. Reflexes unbroken by grief or ceremony.

To her left, children spun in slow circles behind studio windows while across the street adults gathered to mourn Kendria Chaplin. She wondered if repetition dulled the loss for those young dancers. Did grief seen daily become just background noise, or did every passing coffin leave a mark?

At the crosswalk, Blackburn waited for the green light and moved forward when it turned. Her posture was deliberate; cars paused as she stepped past. People looked up as she crossed. Her height, careful gait, and calm focus traced a path others noticed instinctively.

She paused for a moment mid-crossing, aware of being observed. A prickle at her periphery, but she saw no faces watching openly. She kept moving.

Outside Shelton & Sons, clusters formed quietly by the doors: hands clutching programs or balled tissues; small groups anchored by routine gestures of care. The habits of loss shaped their bodies and words.

Blackburn searched through them with organized purpose and found Marilyn immediately. She stood a head taller than Kendria had been, rigid beside Chaplain Mobel with her shoulders drawn tight. Blackburn recognized Mobel from previous funerals.

The girl saw Blackburn and her expression shifted, brightening. "Detective," she called out, slipping free from Mobel's touch. She approached with quick steps, her black dress swaying against her legs, energy breaking through the formality of the gathering.

Blackburn braced for condolences she didn't want to give. Instead, Marilyn's eyes found the silver cross at Blackburn's neck. "You're wearing it. The cross."

Blackburn's fingers closed over the cool metal. "I always do." It was easy to let people believe that.

Mobel made his way over, hand outstretched, as if he could catch Marilyn before she slipped further down.

"I told the Chaplain you had faith," Marilyn said. "That video, when you prayed with my mother. For that other woman? You were fighting for my mother's soul too, weren't you? Praying for her. You saw it too, right? The thing inside her. The succubus." Her voice dropped, each word deliberate. "It made her do things she couldn't stop. It took her away."

Blackburn looked quickly at Mobel, who only shook his head, and back at Marilyn.

Marilyn glanced upward, searching the sky as if an answer might materialize in the pale morning light. Blackburn followed her gaze, but saw nothing of consequence. Two women stood nearby, dressed in black. They leaned in to listen, exchanging wary glances.

"You knew it wouldn't go without a price," Marilyn continued, her voice softer now but unwavering. "The car was right there. Sudden. Absolute." She paused, waving her hand back and forth as if directing traffic. "You saved her. Sometimes God calls for what we can barely stand to give."

Mobel stepped closer, positioning himself between them with a hand on Marilyn's arm. "Marilyn, we should go in now."

"She needs to hear this," Marilyn insisted, her gaze holding Blackburn's. "You did what He asked. You brought the car when it was needed." She gave a slow nod that carried both gratitude and something sharper, more dangerous. "Thank you. For saving her soul."

Blackburn blinked, her mouth open. No sound. She waited.

Marilyn stepped forward, fingers twisting together. Her voice dropped to a whisper meant for Blackburn alone, the words barely stirring the air between them.

"You'll purify the store this weekend?"

Blackburn nodded, the movement considered. "As agreed." She would claim Kendria's furniture. Each piece promised its own particular pleasure.

Mobel shot her a questioning glance, his eyebrows drawing together. Blackburn offered only a slight smile, the corners of her mouth barely lifting, followed by the smallest lift of her shoulders. He couldn't grasp her meaning. She had no intention of enlightening him.

Mobel's grip tightened as he guided her toward the chapel doors, their footsteps echoing on the stone steps.

At the entrance, Marilyn turned back and held Blackburn's gaze one last time.

Mobel looked over his shoulder before leading her inside, his mouth forming a silent apology only Blackburn could read.

Blackburn watched her go. The girl bore watching. She hoped Marilyn could come back from this.

Shortly after, everyone began to head inside.

The room pressed close with heat, fabric clinging to skin. Blackburn turned to the entrance as those nearby eased aside for her without thinking. Something primal steered them clear.

Inside waited Kendria, or what remained. At Oak Street, she had held that body briefly, felt the warmth leaving it; here it was presented again, dressed and preserved but unmistakably altered by death.

The funeral parlor hid its purpose behind thick carpet that muffled footsteps and muted lights that softened edges. Lilies perfumed the air for mourning noses, their sweetness cloying, but did not erase the truth underneath.

Blackburn signed the guest book with a simple 'Detective Morgan Blackburn, NDPD.' No embellishments. The pen felt heavy in her fingers.

In the main room, conversation sank to whispers. She scanned faces quickly: employees from Coconut Glass Candles identified by glass pendants on leather cords catching the light; professional associates; clusters of friends filling seats out of love, not obligation.

At the center of attention stood Kendria's casket. Walnut polished to a high sheen by expense and finality.

Blackburn approached at a steady pace as space opened around her without request or effort.

She stopped at the casket and looked down.

Kendria looked assembled, not preserved. Makeup had been applied with clinical care: foundation a fraction too pale against her natural tone, blush exact and balanced. A composition more than a farewell. Her hair was styled in loose waves, unlike her usual curls.

Her hands rested over a cluster of white roses, their petals already beginning to curl at the edges.

She appeared peaceful. And somehow off.

The wrongness was in the absence of motion. Kendria alive had never held still; even seated, she had filled the air with small gestures and restless energy. Blackburn remembered first stepping into Coconut Glass Candles and seeing that vitality.

The bell above the shop door had chimed, its brass notes bright. Kendria hadn't turned right away, intent on arranging amber candles in sharp lines. Her body moved with efficiency. Weight forward, muscles prompting precise shifts beneath deep skin. Every inch under control.

"I'll be right with you," she had called out, her voice low and warm, inviting but limited. When she finally faced Blackburn's badge, her pupils flicked wide: curious, alert.

That curiosity deepened as they spoke. Through orderly answers about Jenna Langston and autonomous cars, something unspoken moved between them. An understanding formed in pauses and glances. Blackburn had closed the distance a fraction at a time. Kendria met her gaze without backing away.

One decisive moment: Blackburn undid the top button of Kendria's shirt during questioning. Testing a theory. The fabric parted easily under her fingers.

After that, boundaries shifted quickly but with consent. Dinner, where their knees touched under the table, a conversation about pleasure that led to the room Marilyn would later discover in disgust.

Then came authority. Simple and absolute. Kendria positioned on the massage table, body receptive, skin warm under Blackburn's palms, awaiting instruction. Blackburn traced commands along skin that shivered at contact; Kendria responded without hesitation to every word: "Stay still. Stay silent. Wait for my permission."

Obedience came easily to her. Fluid, graceful submission that triggered a possessive ache in Blackburn's chest. Mine, she thought each time Kendria arched beneath her touch. Mine to direct. Mine to shelter.

But shelter had failed.

Blackburn felt anger tighten inside her. Contained but fierce, as the scene on Oak Street replayed itself: burning asphalt searing her knees, squealing tires filling her ears, silver car ripping past. Kendria struck down; blood spread quickly, its metallic scent sharp in the air.

Something that belonged to her had been stolen. Removed systematically.

Her anger focused itself: cold resolve instead of heat now. She would find who did this and take them apart methodically. With no margin for error or leniency.

"You're angry."

Marilyn's tone was clear and direct at her side; Blackburn hadn't noticed her presence, hadn't heard her approach across the muffled carpet.

She turned back to Marilyn, schooling her face into kind calmness. "Anger fits."

Marilyn nodded, tapped her forehead, and turned to walk toward the exit. Chaplain Mobel quickly ushered her toward the front row seating.

"If everyone would please take their seats, we'll begin our remembrance of Kendria Chaplin." His authority was quiet, but absolute.

People filed toward their places in subdued lines. Grief packaged into small movements and uneasy silence, except for Marilyn. Marilyn appeared almost untouched in her fantasy. Blackburn retreated to the back wall, staying where she could watch the room without drawing attention. The plaster felt cool against her shoulder blades.

She took stock of each attendee with methodical focus. The candle shop employees sat close together. Two women and a man, leaning in for support. Four older women from neighboring shops filled a second-row bench, their presence steady, faces closed.

A tall man in an expensive suit stood apart along the side wall, unreadable. The fabric of his jacket caught the light differently than the others. Silk, not wool. Nearby, a woman hunched over a notepad, pen scratching softly, eyes everywhere but on Kendria's memorial. Reporter posture. Discreetly working even now. Blackburn made a mental note; she wondered if Brynn Cassidy was lurking elsewhere or if this was her mole.

At the edge of the crowd, a man in a baseball cap slipped in late, avoiding eye contact, posture tight with intent to blend in. Something about his manner set off Blackburn's instincts: sometimes killers returned to funerals to reassure themselves or savor what they had done.

She adjusted her stance, marking the distance between them. Close enough to intervene quickly if necessary but far enough to watch without alerting him. Her hand brushed her jacket, confirming the gun's presence.

Chaplain Mobel began speaking again, voice steady as he guided the mourners through ritual comfort. Blackburn stayed alert at the fringe of the ceremony. A watcher more than a mourner, tracking each sign of distress or self-consciousness in the crowd.

This was more than remembrance for Kendria; it was an opportunity. Every flinch, every tension in a jaw or hesitation at her name might yield something useful later. If she paid close enough attention.

Chapter 11

The weekend had passed well. Saturday morning, she ran along the riverfront until her lungs burned tight and her shirt clung damp between her shoulder blades. Then the funeral. Later, Willow moved through Blackburn's kitchen, the knife sliding clean through vegetables while oil hissed in the pan, preparing the meals she knew would please her. That evening, Willow knelt on the hardwood floor, her fingers working deep into the arches of her feet shaped by years on unforgiving pavement, feeling each knot release beneath her thumbs. Sunday offered solitude: time to examine the Deonte Mills file again, its pages already soft from handling. With Dawson out, the case had stalled like an engine losing compression. No one had built a proper record against the father. Either she would start over with new interviews and new witnesses, or she would find another angle entirely.

Now, Monday.

At headquarters, Blackburn stepped into the women's washroom. The air hit sharp with disinfectant trying to wrestle down the acrid bite of old urine. White tiles gleamed cold beneath LED strips, each footstep bouncing back at her from the walls.

She reached behind her neck, fingers finding the stiff tag that had been digging a raw line into her skin all morning. The buttons slipped free with a fluid motion. She shrugged the shirt off, the fabric still carrying the chemical smell of newness. Leaning over the sink, she caught the plastic fastener between her teeth, tasted bitter polymer before spitting it into her palm. Another tug freed the price tag. She flicked both toward the garbage can. One hit metal, the other whispered against linoleum.

The mirror threw back what she expected: shadows beneath eyes that had seen too much today, tension pulling her mouth into hard lines. Kendria's name pressed up through memory with shared laughter over soft wine, consequences that still tasted metallic, grief coiled and waiting. Her jaw locked tight enough to ache.

Guilt twisted as thoughts of Willow surfaced next. Those steady hands, that careful nervousness. Willow, who never spoke about wants, but followed every instruction with crystalline precision.

Blackburn bent to the tap. Cold water shocked her palms as she pumped soap from the dispenser. Rather than the usual astringent scent, this was... She held the foam to her nose. Lavender. A new company must have won the contract. She scrubbed hard, lather stinging where stress had worn her raw. The paper towel scraped like sandpaper, pulling away sweat and the morning's accumulated grime. She put the shirt back on, aligned the buttons, smoothed the cuffs flat. Each motion was sharp and automatic.

At the mirror again, her stare went flat. Then, a harsh buzz against porcelain. Her phone vibrated hard enough to walk across the sink's edge. Pure reflex made her snatch it before it fell.

The notification cut bright through the washroom's LED haze: BDSMessages app. The timing felt purposeful. Distraction or invitation, she'd know soon enough. She stared at the innocuous app icon, considering. People advertised niche services on the app. She was sure she could find someone to move the furniture and set up her basement for her.

She swiped the app and typed in her password.

The screen's blue glow caught her face as she read, pulse shifting from routine to something sharper than anything Chief Hayes could offer.

A message from a few days ago, missed, asking for correction. But today, a new one.

>*Hey. Lilith here. I like your style: confident, in control. Want to grab a drink? Looking for some intensity.*

Heat traced her lips into a smirk. Direct, appreciative, edged with challenge. Exactly what she needed right now. Blackburn's thumbs moved without hesitation.

Intensity is my thing. Maybe next week?<

The response landed immediate and sharp:

>*Works for me. I'll check in then. Try not to get arrested. Or at least bring the handcuffs with you.*

Laughter broke from her throat, ricocheting off tile and steel. The charge between words cut through the day's dull weight, leaving an afterimage that pulsed behind her eyes. Lilith materialized easily in her mind: dark confidence wrapped around the edges, hunger barely concealed beneath polish. The pull was immediate.

Handcuffs are a given. Question is whether you can handle what comes with them<

The phone slid into her pocket, its weight pressing warm against her thigh. A soft hiss overhead sprayed a gentle mist, the disinfectant poisoning her arousal.

At the mirror once more, she smoothed her shirt until it lay perfectly against her frame. Her reflection returned steady eyes and clean lines, composure masking the hum beneath her skin.

The phone jolted again. Hayes's assistant this time, words clipped as broken glass. *Office. Now.*

Blackburn's fingers found a button, freed it. Just enough. Then she turned toward his well-lit cage.

She filled his doorway. "Chief? You wanted to see me?"

Hayes glanced up, surprise flickering before professionalism locked down. His eyes tracked the loose strands framing her face, the way her shirt pulled across her breasts. He caught himself, refocused on paperwork.

She smiled, running fingers through her hair with precise slowness. Every gesture calculated. She knew that silence could speak louder than words in rooms like this. Let him remember who held control.

"Sit," Hayes said, indicating the chair.

Blackburn folded into it, spine straight but unhurried. His scrutiny pressed against her. She let it slide off.

"Sinclair's fuck up."

"Sir?"

Hayes gestured at the phone, as if that would explain everything. "Arrested the wrong person."

Blackburn rolled her eyes. "When? Who?"

"Friday morning, some guy named—"

"Friday morning? While Reeves and I were interviewing a Chaplin family member?"

Hayes's mustache trembled.

"I know nothing about this. I was in the office Friday. Not a word. This is on Sinclair, or whoever authorized him." Blackburn shrugged and gestured back toward the phone, knowing that would explain nothing.

"Fuck me, Blackburn. What is it with you and your team trying to destroy my life?" Hayes said, shaking his head. "Dawson faking my signature, you hitting a civilian, now Sinclair arresting someone at a damned funeral." Hayes grabbed a pen just to throw it across the room.

"I'll handle Sinclair. But you can't suspend your best detective and then act surprised when everything goes to hell," Blackburn said as she eyed the pen. It was jammed into the air vent, threatening to slip but not yet yielding. She waited a beat, and added, "Is that all, sir?"

"What's happening with this autonomous vehicle case? Chaplin? You interviewed someone?" The calm in his voice couldn't hide the tension vibrating underneath.

She checked her watch with theatrical precision. "Reeves and I. The daughter thought Kendria might be selling drugs out of the candle shop. We checked and found no evidence whatsoever."

The overhead lights carved harsh shadows into Hayes's face. Her attempt at lightness died against his silence. "None?"

She let the humor drain away. "We found a locked room in Kendria's shop. Private use, adult focus. Marilyn thought it might have been a drug lab."

Hayes shifted, leather creaking beneath him. "You think that's related to the murder?"

"Unlikely," Blackburn said, watching discomfort play across his features. "What matters is the daughter's attitude. Said she hated her mother. Said she was glad she was dead. But without the missing vehicle or a suspect, we just don't know. And we doubt it's Marilyn." She kept her tone clinical. "Right now, it's still a hit and run."

His fingers drummed on the desk, sharp raps filling the dead air. "The media's already circling. The governor won't stop calling."

Blackburn held his gaze steady. "That pressure wasn't mine to create, chief. You pulled your lead detective before the investigation even started. We lost critical hours. Days. I expected backup, chief. Instead, I got blindsided."

"You got blindsided? I wasn't expecting you to threaten to break that guy's jaw." Hayes straightened, shirt pulling taut across tense shoulders. "I'm protecting this department. The city."

"By throwing me under the bus?" Her laugh came out flat as old paint. "You're selling me out so nobody calls us reckless. The protests are coming regardless, chief."

He sagged then, the fight draining out like water. Fatigue replaced anger in the lines around his eyes.

"Damn it." His hand scraped over stubble, the silence stretching until it hummed. When he met her stare again, regret was naked on his face.

"You're going to hate this part," Hayes said.

Blackburn's hands found the desk edge, gripped hard. "What now?"

He exhaled like he was spitting out poison.

The word dropped between them. "Morgan."

Her spine went rigid. "You never call me that unless you are about to interfere with my investigation." No humor softened it.

"I have to pull you off Chaplin." His voice left no space for argument. "It's gotten too close."

The room contracted around them.

Blackburn's stare could have cut glass, but she kept the rage buried deep. "You know I get results." Level tone, pressing without begging. "Don't take me off the case. That's not what you want."

Silence stretched. When he answered, it wasn't an apology, just confirmation of the space between duty and trust.

Gray bristled in his mustache as he shook his head. Doubt clouded his eyes. "This isn't about your skills, Blackburn. It's about perspective. You're too close."

"Too close?" Her voice stayed as sharp as a scalpel. "Sir, when have I ever let personal involvement cloud judgment? I respect families, but my work speaks. I deliver a perfect clearance record. You know that."

She leaned forward just enough. Light caught the hollow of her throat where her shirt parted. Deliberate but deniable. Hayes shifted, uncertainty rippling across his features.

"There's scrutiny on every angle of this case."

She didn't pause. "I understand the stakes. But no one knows this case like I do. Remove me now, we lose critical ground. Details only I see because I've been inside from the start. You want answers. That's what I deliver. Not false arrests."

His posture shifted, leaning toward her, searching for cracks and finding none.

"No one but you knows my connections, sir. You lose more by sidelining me," she continued, voice dropping just enough to pull him closer. "Let me do my job."

Hayes pressed fingers to temples, the silence heavy while tension gathered in his shoulders. "Your dedication isn't in question," he said finally, authority fighting her presence. "But we need distance here."

Her gaze held steady, concentration etched in the set of her brow. She leaned in, voice going conversational, almost intimate. "Chief, consider the optics. If I'm removed now, the media will question your motives and your resolve. We both know this isn't simple."

Hayes stood up and walked over to the filing cabinet as if that held the answers. All it did was give him a moment to think, and Blackburn couldn't have that.

"Take me off the case because of a frankly justifiable overreaction. Stack that on the suspension and the fine? People will assume it's personal against me and what I did and the entire African American community of New Dresden. They'll turn this into something it's not. The public sees me as the lead on Kendria's case. Imagine the fallout if I'm sidelined now. It won't look decisive. It'll look like you're folding to politics."

Hayes turned, his gaze sharpened, crow's feet deepening as he weighed her argument. "I understand the optics, but..."

"We can't dismiss them," Blackburn replied, her voice carrying the easy neutrality of courtroom testimony. "You've made an arrest in Jenna Langston's case: negligence, not intent. There's nothing tying it to the other incident; no more than two random shootings linked only by caliber. Chief, please sit down."

She waited until he obeyed and then continued. "The circumstances don't match. Neither do the vehicles; both are different models of autonomous cars, best as we can tell. There's no credible link." She let the silence settle between them like dust before finishing, her words unyielding. "The team needs stability. Clear leadership."

Hayes's lips parted to respond, but she pressed forward.

"Sir. Looked what happened when I was gone for just a few days. You need a leader. You need someone who's survived that heat before."

"Schmidt managed the Stevens case." Hayes's fingers found his stapler, working the hinge in a familiar rhythm.

Blackburn didn't hesitate. "Schmidt can handle reporters. Can he manage the politics? The stares? The turned backs? You know I can." Blackburn wondered briefly if she would be fighting this hard if the victim weren't Kendria, hadn't been hers, just a little. She quickly dismissed the thought: every goddamn case was hers.

Hayes pressed his temples between thumb and forefinger, shoulders sagging. "You're forcing my hand here."

She shifted forward, the leather chair creaking beneath her, letting warmth seep into her tone. "Chief, we both remember how that anonymous complaint got twisted, accusing me of monopolizing Willow's time and resources while other units missed out." The LED lights hummed overhead, filling the pause. "Internal Affairs cleared me. Still cost me plenty. Schmidt wouldn't have survived what I'm still working through: new protocols, tighter oversight. Gossip."

A muscle twitched along his jawline.

"I took that hit," Blackburn said, her voice dropping to a register that made him lean closer. "I didn't complain about the selective scope of the entire process." Their eyes met across the cluttered desk. "Some partnerships get ignored."

Hayes's fingertips whitened against his temple. "That isn't the issue."

She kept her tone smooth as worn leather. "I know." Her gaze never wavered. "But I'm aware of how these things play. Loyalty counts. So does discretion." She angled forward, close enough to catch the bitter edge of his coffee. "If you pull me now, right after the press conference, it looks retaliatory. It looks personal."

The air conditioning clicked off, leaving them in thick silence.

She spoke softer now, each word placed as evidence. "The press would run with that story. If they started looking closely at our department, they wouldn't stop at one headline." She eased back, the professional mask sliding into place. "Let me stay on the case, chief. Let results speak for themselves. It's the simplest way forward."

Hayes studied her, the unspoken calculations visible in the set of his mouth. She could almost hear the gears turning, feel the moment when resistance gave way to pragmatism.

His exhale carried the sound of surrender. "You'll get one shot. One more. If this explodes, don't count on that desk being yours." The words came sharp and brittle.

Blackburn settled back, allowing only the ghost of satisfaction to touch her lips. "Understood."

He flicked his fingers toward the door. "Get moving."

She unfolded from the chair with grace. "Yes, sir," she said, crisp and assured.

Blackburn paused at the threshold. "I'll solve this. And I'll make it look routine."

She moved through the doorway without a backward glance, her heels marking a steady rhythm on worn linoleum. Behind her, she could feel Hayes's unease radiating like heat from office . Perfect.

The corridor walls pressed close, their institutional beige somehow energizing rather than oppressive. Colleagues lifted their heads briefly to register her pressed outfit and composed features before dismissing her. They could sense the electricity running beneath her skin, the careful calculations spinning behind her steady expression.

She pulled in a breath, tasting the familiar cocktail of floor wax and stale coffee that permeated every precinct she'd ever worked. It grounded her, this environment of controlled chaos and barely concealed ambition. Every solved case tightened her grip; every closed file carved another handhold in a cliff face others feared to climb.

Chapter 12

Passing the Homicide Division plaque, Blackburn's heels struck linoleum in uniform intervals. The nearby gazes pressed between her shoulder blades as she approached the bullpen. Her bullpen.

The LED lights overhead cast harsh shadows that made every face look drawn. Blackburn had walked this hallway hundreds of times, but today the distance felt infinite. Every step carried the weight of the chief's ultimatum, the governor's interference, the press breathing down their necks. She could feel the tension radiating from her shoulders, familiar armor that had served her well through fifteen years of climbing the department's ranks.

In the bullpen, Willow leaned close to Dawson's screen, her fingers striking keys in bursts. The rapid clicking filled the space between desks, punctuated by the distant ring of phones and indistinct murmur of conversations. Blackburn caught herself watching the fluid movement of Willow's hands, the way her brow furrowed in concentration. Those thick, strong fingers moved with precision across the keyboard, each keystroke sure.

Blackburn pushed aside distracting thoughts of those fingers and moved forward, though the image lingered at the edges of her awareness like smoke.

She opened the door and glanced back. "Morning," The single word carried enough authority to set them in motion.

"Boss." Sinclair's voice cut through the low hum of the bullpen. LED lights buzzed overhead while keyboards clicked in steady rhythm. He raised a hand, not quite meeting her eyes. Everyone stopped moving.

"In my office." Blackburn didn't wait. She opened the door and stepped inside, leaving it ajar behind her. The familiar scent of old coffee and leather filled the space.

Sinclair followed hesitantly. Once inside, Blackburn settled into her chair and fixed him with a level stare. He hesitated at the threshold, shoulders hunched beneath his wrinkled shirt, hands knotted together. The overhead light caught the sheen of sweat along his hairline. He looked like a man facing consequences he couldn't escape.

He spoke softly, his words barely carrying across the small space. "I have to tell you something."

Blackburn watched him in silence, letting expectation thicken the air between them.

He closed the door with a soft click and stood stiffly, jaw working as he searched for words. "I arrested Malik on Friday. From the Duvey murder. At St. Isidore's. There's a problem."

She waited, arms folded on the desk's worn surface.

Sinclair exhaled sharply in the quiet office. His voice dropped to barely audible. "Well, it wasn't him."

Blackburn didn't move. Her gaze remained steady. *Never ask a question you don't already know the answer to.* "Who did you bring in?"

"Elijah Malik," Sinclair said, the name hanging between them like smoke. "Devon's brother. Older by a few years. No violent record. He was at the funeral home for an actual funeral when we picked him up." His mouth worked, tongue darting across dry lips, searching for more explanation but finding none.

Blackburn let another moment stretch taut.

"Who authorized this?" Her tone was even, but she took a deep breath in.

"I acted alone," Sinclair admitted, his voice cracking. "My CI called it in. Said Devon would be there."

"Name."

"Tony Ricci. He's been solid before." A flush crept up Sinclair's neck, darkening his collar.

"And Friday?"

"I was wrong." The words came out raw.

Blackburn watched his posture crumble under the admission. The rigid line of his shoulders sagged with nowhere left to retreat.

"No fucking kidding."

Sinclair's eyes widened. *Swearing?* It meant she was furious.

"You know who told me? Chief Hayes. This morning. Chief Hayes called me into his office and told me. Not you. Him."

"I was going to call," Sinclair replied, barely above a whisper. "But I don't have your cell number."

Blackburn's fingertips pressed together so hard they turned red, then white. The leather chair groaned as she shot forward, her carefully maintained composure fracturing. He jolted backwards.

"You involved S.W.A.T. over a CI tip and arrested an uninvolved man at a funeral?" Her voice started low, deadly, then climbed. "At a *funeral*, Sinclair? And it had to be the chief to tell me first?"

Sinclair's face drained of color, his Adam's apple working frantically.

"Don't try to bullshit me. You have my number." She turned and picked up her desktop phone. "Left a voicemail. You could have just dropped by my house." She slammed the phone down. Heads in the bullpen snapped up. "Since you know where the fuck I live."

Sinclair's body tingled. First his hands, then his calves. It was working its way around his body. He took a deep breath, stumbling toward the door in his haste to leave.

"Sinclair." The name cracked like a whip.

He froze, hand trembling on the brass knob.

"I'll be sending you for retraining on identification procedures and arrest protocols."

His voice came out strangled: "Understood."

"You're on your own with this. Write your report. And get out of my sight."

The door shut with a decisive thud behind him, leaving Blackburn alone with the fallout already forming in her mind. The sun slanted through her blinds, casting sharp lines across her desk. She had no time for this.

* * *

Inside the meeting room, chair legs scraped against worn linoleum, and manila folders slapped onto scarred desktops. The conference room bore the accumulated power of countless briefings, its walls yellowed with age and stress. Coffee stains marked the table's surface like battle scars. Blackburn didn't need to prompt. Their routine was etched by habit and earned respect.

She noted how each team member arranged themselves. Sinclair, that asshole, to the right of her seat, always positioned himself close to her. Cooper directly across from her, notebook already open. Reeves slouched but alert, his eyes tracking movement with a detective's instincts. And Willow, laptop open, fingers already moving with that hypnotic rhythm, doing god-knows-what.

Once everyone had entered, she closed the door with a decisive snap. The latch caught with finality.

Blackburn studied each face as she walked to her chair. Sinclair's young features showed strain, as they should have. Cooper practically vibrated with nervous energy. Reeves had seen enough politics to know when the ground was shifting. He was ready for bad news. And Willow watched her with an intensity that made Blackburn's pulse quicken despite her professional composure.

"Listen up." Blackburn's tone sliced through the stale air, calm but absolute. "The chief wants us off Chaplin, but I convinced him to keep us on. Too political. Thinks we can't do it, can't stay professional. This stays between us. If you're in, I need your word. Nothing leaves this room except the person who wants off the case."

The silence that followed was pregnant with calculation. Blackburn could practically hear the gears turning in each detective's mind, weighing loyalty against career safety. She'd learned to read her team like a book, and she watched now as they processed the implications.

Her eyes met each of theirs: Sinclair, Cooper, Reeves, Willow. No one's gaze wavered.

"Why pull us off?" Sinclair's voice came rough at the edges. His fingers drummed against the table's surface.

"Optics. Politics. Even the governor's hand is in this now." Blackburn let the words hang, watching as understanding dawned on each face. The governor's involvement meant media attention, public scrutiny, careers potentially made or destroyed.

Reeves expelled a long breath, his chair creaking. "Great." The word carried volumes of frustration.

Blackburn's expression remained granite, though internally she felt the familiar burn of anger at the system's failures. She'd climbed through the ranks by being tougher, smarter, and more ruthless than her peers, but even she couldn't completely escape political machinations.

"This is your shot to make a name as a detective. The case gets statewide attention, maybe national, because I hit the guy. We crack it, everyone sees it happen. You're statewide heroes."

Cooper's jaw slackened before he nodded. "Understood." His voice was steady, but Blackburn could see the mix of excitement and terror in his eyes.

Sinclair's agreement came quickly. "We're with you." No hesitation. The response of a man who wanted to regain his status.

Willow nodded, unsure if any of this applied to her. She concentrated on her ever-present laptop, knowing that with an autonomous car involved, her skills were vital. The screen's glow cast light across her glasses, muscle memory guiding her fingers into the digital landscape where she felt most at home.

Blackburn nodded once, satisfied. The room's atmosphere shifted, tension dissolving into focus. She could feel the change like a physical thing: the way shoulders relaxed, how breathing deepened.

"What did you get on Kendria Chaplin?" She kept her tone level. She'd let Kendria down when it mattered most, but had to keep the anger from her voice.

Reeves spoke first, keeping to the facts. "Marilyn Chaplin is not a likely suspect based on our interview."

Blackburn nodded, the overhead LEDs casting sharp shadows across her desk. "We will keep her off the list unless something new comes up."

"I need to call Kendria's family and verify her boyfriend's status. Last I checked, he was still in lockup."

"Boyfriend?" Blackburn's voice carried neutrality. "Marilyn didn't mention one."

"Social media posts. He stole about one hundred fifty dollars in candles from Coconut Glass Candles. Kendria pressed charges. He was already in before any of this, but I want confirmation." Reeves traced his finger down his notes, the paper crinkling softly. "Marilyn mentioned Sandra Williams, a friend of her mother's. Marcus Williams supplies product to the shop."

"Any relation?" Sinclair asked.

"No," Reeves replied. "I will also draft warrants for phone records and pull the encrypted mesh network logs."

Blackburn glanced at him, one eyebrow lifting in a precise arc. "That is a full plate of work to be done." The underlying question was clear.

Reeves lifted his palms, the gesture catching the light. "I have also been on the Rhyanne Scudamore case. The husband who shot his wife over breakfast. I called you about it Monday morning. He was still at the scene when we arrived. Evidence was logged, ballistics checked out, the incident report was written, witness statements secured, and the DA notified. They will charge Murder One but expect a plea deal."

She allowed herself a faint smile, the corners of her mouth barely shifting. "All wrapped up except for a ribbon."

"That covers it," Reeves said, nodding at Cooper.

Cooper picked up from there, his voice filling the small conference room. "I reinterviewed both the cyclist and the truck driver from the Jenna Langston accident. Their stories remain unchanged. No driver, the doors never opened. Vehicle protocols state doors should have unlocked on impact, but that did not happen. Stan Raider gave me nothing useful."

"Not surprising," Willow murmured, the words barely disturbing the air.

Cooper's head snapped up. "Sorry?"

Willow straightened in her chair, the vinyl creaking beneath her. "I said it figures," she repeated, her voice thin as paper.

Blackburn addressed her without lifting her eyes from the files spread before her. "You should sign up for one of HR's assertiveness workshops, Willow. So we can hear you." She waved Cooper on with two fingers.

Willow's hands moved immediately to her keyboard, the soft clicking filling the momentary silence as she navigated to the personnel site and clicked through to Personal Growth courses.

Cooper resumed. "I would like to talk to Marla Sutton again. Maybe she recalls something new since your last interview, boss."

Blackburn's response came swift and certain. "No need. I will handle Marla myself." The finality hung in the air between them. She could not risk Marla telling Cooper that she knew Jenna.

"Sure." Cooper's pen scratched against paper as he checked his notes again. "That leaves follow-up on quantum computing angles, the van idea, and I might need Willow's help with that."

Willow nodded once, a precise movement. "What specifically do you need?"

"We can discuss offline," Cooper said, already gathering his papers. "I'm still waiting for a list of all autonomous car registrations in the city. Hopefully that's in my inbox by now."

"Willow, you are next," Blackburn said. Her fingernail tapped against the table's laminate surface in a steady rhythm.

"I checked the camera feeds that went offline before impact. At first it looked suspicious, but all those cameras run through a single ISP junction. A firmware update took them down at the same time. It is fixed now. There is no footage," Willow said. She adjusted her glasses, the frames catching the light.

"The visual glitches in what footage we do have line up with a power fluctuation at the substation," she added, her fingers hovering over her tablet.

"Nothing out of the ordinary?" Reeves asked, his pen tapping a counterpoint against his notebook.

"Nothing unexpected. I finished the technical report on Zhang's car and remote access, but there is no way to be certain since the car destroyed itself. I found nothing conclusive."

Blackburn leaned back, her chair protesting softly, and exhaled a breath that carried the case. "We are coming up empty. Sinclair?"

Sinclair cleared his throat, the sound rough in the quiet room. He had spent more time chasing dead ends than getting results.

"I have contacted local auto shops about Raider Straight Line service history, but have not found anything relevant," he said, the words coming slowly.

Blackburn's gaze found him, her expression carved from stone. "And the microwave tech?"

"Still working on it," he said, his eyes dropping to the scarred surface of his desk. "I am also checking databases for Cooper's Jane Doe."

"What do you have so far on her?" Blackburn asked, her body shifting forward, the movement subtle but unmistakable. She had helped Cooper with that case, and it mattered to her.

"Nothing yet," Sinclair admitted, the words bitter on his tongue.

He kept missing lately.

Blackburn leaned back, leather creaking beneath her as she planted both feet on the table's scarred surface. The meeting was not finished. "There are ways to locate the car we have not used yet," she said, her words cutting through the stale conference room air.

"If it's still out there, it will show obvious damage to the front end. It's visible."

"We reviewed the video feeds," Cooper replied, his voice tight as a piano wire.

"Are you scanning in real time? Using drones or aerial support?" Blackburn asked, tapping her heel against the table edge. "It's been days. The car could be parked anywhere. A body shop, a junkyard, a private driveway tucked out of sight. I want aerial views."

Reeves pushed his chair back, metal scraping against linoleum in a sharp protest. He stood, his gaze sliding past hers to fix on the water-stained ceiling tiles. "I'll get on it. I'll call Traffic." He left without another word.

Cooper got up, following Reeves.

Blackburn nodded at Sinclair, who shifted in his seat. "Check with Reeves for Marilyn's USB of security footage." She did not wait for a response.

Sinclair raked his eyes over Blackburn before leaving, his hands wiping the sweat onto his pants. She enjoyed seeing the pained, unrequited desire in his eyes.

Their exit left only Blackburn and Willow in the small conference room. The muffled hum of the bullpen beyond the door seemed miles away.

Blackburn could feel the change like electricity on her skin. Willow remained hunched over the table, her fingers drumming an irregular rhythm against the keyboard. The sound was hypnotic, almost musical.

Blackburn moved closer, her approach deliberate. Each step carried intention beyond the professional. She could smell Willow's shampoo, something light and floral that seemed incongruous with the harsh environment. The scent stirred something deep in her chest, a hunger she'd been suppressing for days.

She reached out with careful precision, fingers sliding through Willow's hair before withdrawing. The contact was brief but electric.

"You're staying away from autonomous cars, right?" she asked, her voice dropping to a register meant only for this space. "If you are out, walking on the street," she said as she stroked Willow's cheek, "keep your head about you." Her hand fell away, leaving coolness where warmth had been.

The silence stretched taut between them, both aware of what wasn't being said, both choosing focus over complication. Blackburn could feel her pulse in her throat, the way her body responded to Willow's proximity.

Willow looked up, vulnerability flickering in her eyes. "What if you were the target? Of the car?" Her words came softly. Concern shaped the question more than fear. "Maybe you need to keep a low profile. Stop going out so much?"

Blackburn's laugh was brief, dry as old paper. "I guess someone needs better aim." She kept it light, deflecting with casual ease. Still, something sharp pressed at the edges of her awareness, an irritation she refused to acknowledge.

The possibility had occurred to her, of course. She'd made enemies during her climb through the ranks. But showing weakness now, when her team needed her strength, was unthinkable.

She leaned in close enough that her breath warmed Willow's jaw. The room contracted to just their shared space. Blackburn's gaze held steady before she kissed Willow. A meeting of lips, controlled and unhurried. Her hand slipped against cotton fabric, fingers finding certainty. Blackburn pinched Willow's breast hard. Willow's sharp intake of breath melted into a soft sigh, her body relaxing under Blackburn's touch.

Drawing back, Blackburn searched Willow's face for any sign of hesitation. Her own expression shifted by degrees, professional armor cracking just enough to reveal something rawer beneath. "Are you free tomorrow night for some fun and games?" The words came low, heavy with desire.

Willow's pulse jumped visibly at her throat. "Yes," she managed, voice steady despite the sudden heat building beneath her skin.

"Good." Blackburn's smile was subtle, but its effect unmistakable. "Nine-thirty Tuesday night. Text me your fantasy before then."

Willow hesitated only a heartbeat before nodding. "Of course." Her eyes flickered past Blackburn to the bullpen, where she caught Sinclair's stare. Her skin prickled as she gave him a slight smile.

Blackburn straightened, composure settling back into place like a familiar coat. "Good girl," she said. It landed like a medal placed around Willow's neck: heavy, deliberate, deserved. Willow flushed and sat straighter, her shoulders back and her fingers finally stilled.

Willow watched Blackburn go, tracking the rhythm of her retreat. The moment stretched like a held breath, charged not by what had happened but by what might follow, leaving in its wake the electric awareness of boundaries tested and lines yet to be crossed.

Chapter 13

Cooper sat at his desk, watching the routine unfold. Sinclair's attention locked on Blackburn, his interest naked enough to make Cooper's skin crawl.

"Stop staring," he muttered, the glare from his monitor burning his retinas. "You're not subtle."

Sinclair's middle finger rose in response, casual and dismissive.

Cooper turned back to the spreadsheet sprawling across his screen. The database should have been straightforward; instead, rows of car registrations bled together into an indecipherable mass. His fingers found a rhythm against the desk's laminate edge: tap, tap, tap. "Spreadsheets," he breathed.

He solved murders, not parsed numbers.

Movement behind the conference room glass caught his eye. Blackburn leaned in and brushed her lips against Willow's: brief, controlled, somehow far too comfortable for fishbowl walls. Cooper's gaze slid away, filing the moment into memory.

He clicked to the Unregistered tab and winced at the chaos of cars that had their registrations canceled. Entries scattered like dropped papers, fields gaping empty. The moment Blackburn's office door clicked shut, Cooper called out: "Willow!"

She approached with even steps, fingertips pushing her glasses higher. "What is it?"

"I need a filter on this." Cooper gestured at the digital mess. "Just autonomous vehicles. Registered and unregistered, please."

A short laugh escaped her, relief cut with wariness. "Only that? I can handle it."

"I've heard you can handle a lot," Sinclair said. Willow stopped mid-stride.

"Huh?"

Cooper shot Sinclair a sharp look. "That you're a hard worker."

Willow frowned and nodded once, settling into the chair Sinclair pushed toward her with his foot. She worked at Cooper's desk in concentrated silence. Monitor light painted blue shadows across her lenses as she murmured, "Filter by manufacturer first. Stratix, Aeons, Vireos... Raiders too." Her voice remained flat, absorbed in the task. "Date, color..."

The spreadsheet transformed under her hands: color filling rows, columns resizing magically, data flowing into logical streams. She eased back in the chair and tapped a new dropdown menu. "You can select any manufacturer here now. This new tab? That puts your selection together into a clean sheet." Brief, efficient.

Cooper nodded once. "Appreciate it."

Alone again, he hunched forward, scanning the newly organized rows. A registered Raider model snagged his attention: dead stop in an intersection, no explanation. The incident log described swerving vehicles, Traffic Services' red flag for anomalous behavior.

He fired off a terse email to Reeves about the flagged entry. "Heads up," Cooper called across the bullpen's hum.

Sinclair's eyes flicked over, then away. Cooper returned to his screen, that stubborn anomaly refusing to make sense. Willow kept her eyes sharply on the computer monitor.

* * *

Reeves' computer chimed: "Raider Anomaly: Intersection Incident" from Cooper. He pushed his cooling coffee aside, focus sharpening as he absorbed the brief report. An autonomous vehicle had frozen dead center in an intersection, nearly triggering a pile-up. Traffic Services flagged it as unusual but offered no explanation. *Lazy jerks.*

He reached for the phone, fingers already dialing Traffic Services. Kilroy answered on the third ring, voice thick with boredom.

"Yeah, we saw that one," Kilroy drawled after Reeves explained. "Maple and Third. Car just seized up, right in the intersection's heart. Like someone parked it on an X. We hauled it out. Tried reaching Raider's people, but they ghosted us."

"Who owns it?" Reeves pressed the receiver closer.

"Stan Raider floor model." Kilroy's shrug was audible. "Still on company registration. Could've been a loaner, showroom piece. Maybe went rogue. Raider Group never called back, never claimed it. No injuries, no damage, so we filed it away. It's still in the garage if you want it."

"No need. Thanks." Reeves' pen scratched across the paper before he punched in Stan Raider Group's number. Joanne Kenin answered with her name, position, and department. Her voice was as crisp as fresh paper.

"That was a couple of weeks ago. I remember that case," she said. "Our data recorder confirmed the vehicle operated outside the expected parameters."

"If you never retrieved the car, how did you access that data?" Reeves' pen hovered, waiting.

"Floor models transmit event logs to our cloud servers," she replied smoothly.

"Do you track all your vehicles like that?" Reeves leaned forward. "I'm investigating one car that was involved in an accident."

"Remote uploads cease at the point of sale," Kenin stated. "Company policy."

Reeves let the silence stretch between them, thick as humidity before a storm. "Really?"

She remained silent.

"Nothing post-sale?"

The pause that followed carried substance, like air pressure dropping before bad weather.

"No, detective." Her words fell with the finality of a judge's gavel. "That's official policy," Joanne repeated, the phrase worn as smooth as a river stone from constant use.

"And unofficially?"

"Everything is official. That's all I can offer." The apology rang hollow as a cracked bell.

Reeves shifted tactics. "Traffic Services flagged it as an anomaly and tried contacting you. The car remains in NDPD possession." Across the bullpen, Cooper squinted at his monitor, blue light casting shadows under his eyes, while Sinclair's face shifted through a spectrum of colors from whatever screen held his attention. Willow now sat at Dawson's desk, working on her laptop.

Joanne's voice tightened like a wire under tension. "Yes, someone from your office left a message about a no-damage anomaly."

"Define 'anomaly' in this context?" Reeves' tone acquired an edge sharp enough to cut. He recognized her cadence now: polished chrome over rusted steel. The corporate firewall they trained people to become when something had gone wrong.

The LED tubes above hummed their monotonous song while his pen hovered above paper, the tip casting its small shadow, deliberately still.

She gave him three sentences of corporate fog, thick and impenetrable. Compliance this, escalation that. No identifiers, no ownership.

Reeves waited, then interrupted with flat certainty. "I'm switching to video." Willow's eyes flicked up, something sharp and evaluative crossing her features before settling back into professional detachment. She returned to her work, but her typing slowed just enough to track the exchange.

He pressed the button without asking. A moment later, her face materialized on screen. Perfectly composed against a neutral background that revealed nothing. But there was something in her eyes, the smallest flinch as she recognized the shifting ground beneath her feet.

"I find people are more precise when they're seen," Reeves said, his calm carrying weight.

"This wasn't agreed to."

"You're not under interrogation. Just a conversation with better lighting."

Joanne adjusted her collar with fingers that barely trembled. "I'm following company protocol."

"You're not. You're stalling. You told me there was an anomaly with an unauthorized vehicle on the road. Unauthorized. That moves this into criminal territory."

Her mouth opened, then closed. A quick dart of her eyes to something off-screen. Probably her legal pad. Or the empty chair where counsel should be sitting.

"I never—"

"You didn't need to, Ms. Kenin. We're talking about a showroom car, an unreliable car on the roads, driving by itself and almost killing people in a traffic accident," Reeves said as he leaned forward.

"The car isn't unreliable, detective."

"Apparently, yes, it is. Unless you are telling me it was deliberately stalled?"

Joanne closed her eyes and let a sigh escape from her lips. Her shoulders slumped, and Reeves knew he had her. She looked at him. Behind her eyes, calculations ran like ticker tape, but the numbers weren't adding up in her favor.

"I'm not trying to obstruct," she said, the words barely disturbing the air between them.

"Of course not," Reeves said. "You're just protecting a system that has already failed."

That landed hard. He watched the impact ripple through her shoulders, saw them tighten as if bracing for another blow. She glanced to the side again. Not at a person, but toward an escape route that wasn't there.

"I just run compliance."

"And I just ask questions. Let's not make this about hierarchy or responsibility. Let's make it about cooperation and anonymity."

Joanne exhaled slowly, the sound carrying inevitable surrender.

"There was a former employee," she said. "He accessed system architecture beyond his permissions."

"Name?" Reeves kept his pen motionless.

She hesitated, tasting the consequences.

"Joanne."

That cracked the dam.

"Kieran Mott. Senior systems engineer until immediately after the incident. We terminated him that day."

"Tell me about him."

Another hesitation. "Mr. Mott struggled in our corporate environment. His methods were... unorthodox. Since leaving, he's been vocal online, criticizing autonomous vehicles."

Reeves' chair creaked as he leaned back, pressing the phone harder against his ear. Joanne's corporate mask had slipped; irritation bled through the cracks.

"Kieran's actions were calculated." Her words came clipped now. "He programmed the car to stop at exact coordinates. Sending a message."

"Remotely?" Reeves' pen waited.

"No. Yes. Kind of." Joanne's voice dropped. "He stood at the intersection, twenty feet from the vehicle. Used a modified gaming controller. Security footage confirmed it during our review."

"Send it to me," he said.

The name gave Reeves his starting point. When the call ended, he bent over his keyboard. He searched Kieran Mott online, scanning through social media feeds dense with technical rants and public warnings about autonomous vehicles. Blue-white screen glare strained his eyes as technical diagrams, accusations of corporate negligence, and angry debates filled his monitor.

One name resurfaced frequently with his: Brynn Cassidy, the damned reporter from New Dresden Today. She'd been replying to Kieran's posts, amplifying his warnings, echoing his criticisms about safety failures. Reeves clicked through each exchange, collecting screenshots, his fingers quick on the keys as he summarized the pattern emerging before him.

Reeves scanned the bullpen, but Willow was gone. He composed an email, dragging images of Kieran from his profiles into the attachment field. "Can you check our surveillance footage for this face at the Chaplin scene?" he typed. "We may have overlooked him."

Willow's reply pinged back: "Checking now."

* * *

Willow sat hunched at her desk, the clinical brightness of multiple displays highlighted every line in her face. A crisp printout of Kieran Mott's photo rested beside the keyboard, its edges sharp against the chaos of sticky notes and pen caps surrounding it. She scrubbed surveillance footage, the timestamp blurring as she fast-forwarded through empty stretches, then slowed to examine frames when someone entered view near the site of Kendria's death.

Police facial recognition software had a success rate of just thirty-six percent with security footage. Far too unreliable for Willow to even bother using it.

The basement air pressed against her skin, cool and steady with hints of dust and old electronics. Willow barely registered it. Her gaze stayed locked on the passing crowds, searching for anyone who moved wrong, stood wrong, looked wrong. She wiped her glasses with her shirt hem and returned to scanning, blinking hard against the screen-burn threatening to blur her focus.

Time dissolved until a motion in frame 7817 made her lean forward. A lone figure drifted across the image, posture and build matching Mott's online profile. She zoomed closer: same height, same fall of hair catching a streetlight. The beard looked right too. Her breath caught in her throat.

She reached for her phone, thumb finding Blackburn's number by muscle memory.

"I've got him," Willow said, voice tight but controlled. "I spotted Mott on the footage."

Silence stretched across the line.

"Who?" Blackburn's tone stayed even.

"Reeves found him. An anti-autonomous car guy. He asked me to scan video near where Kendria Chaplin was hurt," Willow replied. "I think this guy is a suspect."

"Well done." Blackburn's answer came brisk, businesslike. "Bring everything to Homicide. The entire team needs to see this."

Willow exhaled and moved: clips transferred to the server with quick keystrokes, papers printed and stacked in rough order, laptop tucked under her arm. She took the stairs two at a time, rubber soles squeaking on concrete, energy carrying her forward. For once, she had hard evidence. Something that could shift the investigation and prove her worth beyond any doubt. Things were falling into place perfectly.

* * *

Blackburn stepped out of her office, headed toward the board room. Sinclair sat at his desk, shoulders hunched, hands gripping a stack of paperwork hard enough to crease the edges. He flipped pages with more force than necessary, paper snapping in the quiet.

"Trouble, Detective?" Blackburn asked, her tone matter-of-fact.

Sinclair's eyes dropped before meeting hers, heat crawling up his neck in blotchy patches. "You assigned me the security footage from that shop." He hesitated, jaw working. "I passed it to Willow. I thought I'd be on something bigger by now."

Blackburn watched him for a moment, arms folded across her chest, fabric of her jacket pulling taut. "I know what you can handle," she said. "And I saw you watching us earlier. Did you notice what I gave Willow?"

His gaze sharpened with recognition, pupils dilating. She didn't break eye contact, letting the silence thicken between them before she spoke again. "Board room," she said.

She turned and walked away, feeling Sinclair's stare trace the line of her spine. At the door she made a slight gesture: fingertips brushing the back of her slacks, smoothing invisible wrinkles. She heard his chair scrape behind her, footsteps uneven as he followed her inside.

* * *

The LED lights hummed overhead, casting harsh shadows as Willow connected her laptop to the projector, hands steady despite the slight tremor she felt in her chest. Her glasses caught the sharp reflection as she glanced at Reeves.

"Detective Reeves asked me to look for someone in particular," she said. Her voice came out quiet but even, carrying across the stale conference room air.

Reeves picked up the thread. "Kieran Mott. Ex-Stan Raider engineer. He lost his job after an incident with a Straight Line model: he overrode the vehicle systems while standing outside on the street. It was before Kendria Chaplin. Before Jenna Langston even. But I had

Willow check to see if he was near the Chaplin scene when the car struck."

Willow brought up the security video. The projected image flickered against the wall, washed out but clear enough to make out shapes and movement. She held up a printed photo of Mott beside it, paper crinkling. "He's here, in the background," she said, pointing to a blurred figure.

The team studied both images. Cooper leaned in, coffee breath preceding him, jaw set. "Build matches. Could be him."

"He's a Raider employee. Former. Stopped a Straight Line at an intersection using some kind of game controller. Proves he can control these things externally," Reeves said, his face scanning Blackburn for thoughts.

"Willow, how did Keiran pull this off?" Blackburn's voice cut through the conference room's recycled air.

"I don't know," Willow muttered, her gaze fixed on the laptop screen's blue glow.

"Nothing at all?"

She shrugged, the fabric of her blazer rustling against the leather chair. "Maybe something with their network. But honestly, I'm not sure."

Reeves shifted in his seat, the vinyl creaking as he studied his handwritten notes. "I spoke with Joanne Kenin at Raider Group. She told me their cars stay connected to the cloud until they're sold. Supposedly, they disconnect after sale." He paused, tapping his index finger against the paper. "But I got the impression those cars stay live longer than she admitted."

"What does that give us?" Sinclair's pen clicked against the polished table surface in a steady rhythm.

Willow's fingers hovered motionless above her keyboard, the cursor blinking on her screen. "If the cars are on the network, someone could access them remotely. You'd need senior credentials to update software or change important settings."

"Reeves, call Kenin again. Find out if Keiran Mott's access was truly revoked."

"It was." Reeves's jaw tightened. "They shut him out right after the incident."

Blackburn studied him for a moment, the LED lights casting shadows across her face, then turned back to Willow. Her voice dropped to a whisper. "She has lied before. Willow, can you reach the cloud these cars use?"

Willow's breath caught. "No. Their system is protected behind heavy security firewalls. And trying would be illegal."

Blackburn turned to Sinclair, who'd been tapping his pen against the table in an irregular rhythm. "Sinclair, bring Mott in for questioning." He wanted responsibility, he got it.

Sinclair straightened at once, chair rolling back, and gathered his coat with quick movements, focus sharpening around him like armor. "On it." He left without another word, door clicking shut behind him.

Blackburn surveyed the remaining detectives. "Good work. If Mott's involved, he brings known technical expertise, and a reason to use it."

Reeves smiled broadly, glowing in the faint praise from Blackburn.

Cooper nodded, his chair creaking under his weight. "He fits."

The meeting broke up quickly. Reeves lingered by the door with his coffee growing cold in the chipped mug, Cooper scrolling through new alerts on his phone, thumb moving in quick swipes. Willow packed her equipment with care, cables coiled just so, moving in deliberate silence, the last to leave except Blackburn.

Now alone in the conference room, Blackburn let her fingers rest against the cool laminate surface of the table, thoughts narrowing on what they knew: Kieran Mott, cut loose from Raider, had breached their autonomous controls using basic hardware. Just enough skill and grudge to matter.

She leaned back, vinyl chair protesting softly, eyes on the Mott photograph Willow had left. Wire-rimmed glasses caught the overhead light, sharp features beneath, hair gone untamed and greasy. The sort of face that belonged in blueprints and circuit labs: marked by neglect and a bitter edge. She flipped through the paperwork left behind.

Kieran's online rants made it clear: resentment, anger growing wild in all the places where discipline had once held him together. And that damned reporter. Brynn's handle appeared in the logs with suspicious frequency, her technical knowledge far exceeding what any reporter should possess.

Blackburn leaned back and looked at the ceiling as she thought. Her eyes roamed the cheap, pockmarked panels as she imagined how the conversation with Kieran might go.

The interviews of people like him tasted predictable. The clever ones believed their intellect gave them immunity; arrogance leaked from every answer, every guarded smirk. Kieran would walk in certain he understood the rules better than any cop at the table. She pictured him: posture rigid, arms tucked tight across his chest, lips curling into a false smile that never reached his eyes. He'd offer information by the teaspoon, his every word filtered and safe.

Patience was the only way through. She needed to let him feel superior, make him think she was another cop slogging through paperwork without understanding what mattered. Give him space to perform. In that comfort, he would underestimate her; maybe let arrogance seep into his answers like water through cracked concrete. That was when mistakes happened. Over-explanations, stray details meant to impress rather than conceal.

Blackburn's palm pressed flat against the table, feeling its grain through the finish. She would open with technical questions, let him expand on his specialty, inflate his ego just enough. Then shift back to the timeline: ask for a step-by-step of his day. His story would sound polished at first. But somewhere inside it, a seam would show.

She'd find it and pull until the whole thing came undone.

Chapter 14

The late afternoon heat pressed against the windshield, thick and unforgiving. Sweat gathered at Blackburn's hairline, trickling down her temple as she eased the unmarked sedan to the curb. The vinyl seat stuck to her back through her shirt.

She would have preferred interviewing Kieran Mott instead of trailing after wealthy car owners with Reeves. But Sinclair hadn't reached Kieran; Blackburn had made her disappointment clear. At least he promised to watch Mott's apartment until he surfaced.

Logic dictated that the suspect car would show damage. Cooper was working through luxury repair shops, taking over Sinclair's tasks. Blackburn found herself sealed in a hot car beside Reeves, the air conditioning struggling against the summer heat as they circled the city questioning owners of autonomous vehicles.

The estate rose ahead, all calculated spectacle: manicured lawns erupting with color, white columns thrusting from polished stone. Wealth announced itself in every detail, confident and unrestrained. She parked at the edge between this and the neighbor's house: non-committal enough to be visiting either address.

Reeves checked the address scrawled in his notebook, ink already smudging from humidity. He took in the mansion's gleaming facade with a look hovering between disbelief and resignation. "A place like this pays more in taxes than my entire salary," he muttered.

Blackburn's mouth quirked. "They could run our entire department on their landscaping budget." Her tone was dry, but her gaze lingered on the property, acknowledging the power displayed so openly.

They followed a crisp gravel path that crunched beneath their feet to the entry. Blackburn moved first, composed and assured despite perspiration dampening her collar. Reeves trailed a step behind. He straightened his tie, eyes meeting hers briefly before she raised her hand and knocked. The sound rang out, firm and sharp, echoing through the hush beyond.

A long moment passed before the door opened on silent hinges. Wilson Crutch stood framed by soaring ceilings and polished floors that threw back distorted reflections. He wore a salmon button-up shirt, sleeves rolled halfway to his elbows, the tan so even it had to be artificial. He looked out of place, a man weathered by bad habits rather than time.

"Mr. Wilson Crutch?" Blackburn asked, genuinely surprised a man of his wealth would deign to open his own door.

He blinked, uncertain. "Yes. Can I help you?" His voice wavered at the edges, cautious beneath civility's veneer.

Blackburn stepped forward and stopped just outside the entrance, eyes settling on Wilson with steady focus. "Detective Morgan Blackburn. Homicide," she said, voice even and professional. "My partner, Detective Victor Reeves." She gestured briefly to Reeves, who returned a slight nod, his attention sweeping across the ornate hallway behind Wilson, cataloging every gilded detail.

Blackburn leaned against the doorframe, posture casual yet commanding. It left Wilson nowhere to retreat but deeper into the house. "Mr. Crutch, do you own an autonomous vehicle?" Her tone gave nothing away: direct, unfazed.

Wilson hesitated, Adam's Apple bobbing as if searching for a safe answer. "Yes." The word came out tight. He watched both detectives, fingers drumming against his thigh. He cleared his throat. "How did you get past my security?"

Blackburn answered without pause. "We parked on the street and walked in. The gate is for vehicles only; people slip through."

Wilson nodded. He gripped the doorframe, uncertain.

Reeves stepped forward, scanning the driveway with detachment. "Where's your car?"

"In the garage," Wilson replied after a beat.

"We'll need to see it," Blackburn said.

Wilson shifted, weight moving between feet. "Do you need a warrant?"

Blackburn smiled, the expression not reaching her eyes. "Need one? No sir, not if you let us see the car. To check for damage. That's all. Significant front-end damage."

"My car is fine," he said, voice pitched higher.

"Let us see. Please lead the way," she directed. She waited, and then said what she did to every suspect who had something illegal to hide: "Sir, we're Homicide. We don't care about anything else."

He turned and moved ahead down the hall, their footsteps following, quiet but inescapable over marble that reflected more than surface wealth.

Family photographs lined the hallway, moments of happiness preserved behind glass that now felt distant. Their steps echoed against tile as they entered the garage. The scent of motor oil and leather polish hung distinctly, utilitarian.

Overhead lights clicked on with a soft hum, casting clinical brightness across four vehicles arranged in immaculate symmetry. The autonomous model drew focus. Sleek and understated, its glossy surface mirrored LED tubes above, but gave nothing away. The other three sports cars, brilliant reds and silvers, hinted at wealth and taste, but their presence faded against the business at hand.

"There it is." Wilson pointed to the autonomous car. His hand stayed steady, but a muscle jumped in his jaw.

Blackburn approached, eyes tracing every line of the vehicle. No visible scratches. No dents. Factory-perfect finish that smelled faintly of recent wax. She paused at the front bumper, running fingers along the edge, then circled to check for subtle impact points. Nothing.

Wilson shuffled closer, shoes scuffing concrete. "This is about that woman who died, isn't it?"

Blackburn turned and fixed him with a look. He took a cautious step back, shoulders hunching.

"Yes," Reeves answered, tone even. "Routine checks for all self-driving vehicles registered nearby."

Blackburn nodded once in acknowledgment before addressing Wilson, voice crisp: "Thank you for your cooperation, Mr. Crutch."

He lingered momentarily, mouth working silently before retreating toward the door.

On the driveway, gravel crunching underfoot, Reeves pulled out his notebook and crossed off Wilson's name with deliberate strokes.

"That's number three," Blackburn said as they walked back to her car, heat hitting them like a physical presence after the garage's cool interior.

"Twenty-two left," Reeves replied, already scanning down the list for their next stop.

As Reeves paged through his notes in the passenger seat, paper rustling with each turn, the crease between his eyebrows deepened. "Stan Raider's next on our list," he said, cutting a glance at Blackburn.

She didn't hide her annoyance, grip tightening on the steering wheel. "Perfect. He has avoided returning my calls. He's barricaded in his office, ringed by PR and legal."

Reeves snorted. "Guy's got a handler for every department. Meanwhile, we're left trying to get past reception."

He tapped a pen against his knee, the rhythm matching the thrum of tires on asphalt. His gaze fixed out the window. "You think his evasiveness is deliberate?"

Blackburn steered them onto the main road, merging into traffic with ease. The tires hummed beneath them. "Means he doesn't want trouble. Or accountability."

She picked up her phone without looking away from traffic, thumb finding Hayes's number by muscle memory, then tossed the device into Reeves's lap.

The chief answered on the second ring, voice flat and unmistakable through the speaker.

Without hesitation, Blackburn spoke. "Sir, one autonomous vehicle in question is registered to Stan Raider."

Hayes didn't pause. "Do not approach him until you've exhausted every other lead," he said, each word clipped. "Stan Raider Group is under contract with us for the Autonomous Project. We don't need friction."

"Understood." Blackburn's reply was crisp, though she couldn't keep the edge from creeping in. "I've done enough press photos for his rollout; I know how to play quietly." Her eyes flickered over Reeves before returning to the road.

"He stays off our radar until we're certain," Hayes reiterated.

"He'll be last on my list," Blackburn said. "We'll proceed carefully."

After the call ended, Reeves scoffed, shaking his head. "Special treatment much?"

"Fuck."

"What?"

"At that shoot, there must have been a hundred autonomous cars," Blackburn said. She pictured rows of polished metal beneath harsh studio lights, uniform and indistinguishable, the smell of new plastic and electronics thick in the air. "If a showroom model can be remotely controlled, any of those could have been."

"We'll need to check his inventory," Reeves replied, already tapping at her phone screen.

"And ours," Blackburn added.

He paused, finger hovering. "Ours?"

"Cooper skipped both the Raider Group and the department when he created the list. What if one of our vehicles was involved?" she said. "No NDPD decals on the car, but that guarantees nothing."

The police radio crackled to life, static cutting through the air like torn paper.

"Unit 22, come in. Unit 22, this is dispatch."

Reeves reached for the mic, plastic warm from the sun. "Unit 22, go ahead."

"10-4, Unit 22. Police drone eighteen reports a 10-33. Autonomous vehicle submerged in Lake Canada. Units are responding. Over."

The silence between them lingered, broken only by the steady engine thrum and distant sirens racing toward the lake.

Blackburn adjusted her grip on the wheel, leather begging beneath her palms, eyes straight ahead. Reeves closed his notebook with a soft snap and set it aside.

"10-4, dispatch. Unit 22 heading to Lake Canada. ETA twenty minutes." His voice stayed level, though anticipation tightened the corners of his mouth.

He met Blackburn's eyes as he replaced the mic. "This could be it," he said. "Our car."

Blackburn jerked the wheel hard, tires chirping against asphalt as Reeves braced against the sudden swerve. "Move," she said, voice clipped, anger coiled tight but not directed at him. He caught her tone, straightened in his seat, and kept silent while she navigated the snarl of evening commuters. In Blackburn's hands, speed felt inevitable: a force that pressed you back against worn leather and left no room for comfort.

The city flickered past: pedestrians moving like ants to and from their jobs, shopfronts flashing like dying neon in their peripheral vision. Blackburn drove with ruthless calculation, every lane change measured to the inch, each gap taken without hesitation. Traffic signals became suggestions. She ignored amber lights bleeding across intersections and pressed forward, her focus narrowed to one purpose: to arrive before anyone else could muddle the scene.

"Hang on," she warned, voice steady above the engine's growl as they threaded between slow-moving cars.

Reeves fumbled his phone free, fingers stiff with tension as he dialed Sinclair. The call connected just as another corner approached. Blackburn took it without slowing, tires squealing in protest. Sinclair's voice sounded unfazed through the speaker. "Yeah? What's up?"

"A drone picked up an autonomous on Lake Canada," Reeves said, checking Blackburn's expression: nostrils flared, a twitch in the jaw muscle. "We need you on-site now."

"You got it," Sinclair replied. "Willow's with me. Should I bring her?"

"Yes, we may need a tech on site," Blackburn said. She glanced at her watch. Why the hell was Willow with Sinclair?

Blackburn leaned toward Reeves's phone. "Willow: is the black box viable after submersion?"

A pause crackled between them, engine noise and wind rush filling the silence. Outside, the city thinned into an open road. Inside the car, resolve settled with their destination.

Willow's answer came clear and composed: "The event recorder won't be damaged by water. If it's intact, we'll get what we need."

Blackburn acknowledged with a brief nod, ending the call before tension could take root. "Move," she said. Her mind turned inward as she pressed the accelerator harder.

She kept both hands on the wheel, pulse steady but quickening as each mile carried them closer to Lake Canada. "Reeves," she said, eyes forward, "alert the garage. We'll need recovery gear on-site."

Reeves responded immediately. "Copy that." He relayed their needs to the garage.

The city gave way to stretches of pine and maple as they neared their destination. The asphalt curved through corridors of green, morning light filtering through branches in shifting patterns. Traffic thinned until only birdcall and engine noise remained.

Lake Canada appeared ahead: wide, mirror-calm, bordered by dense foliage that softened its perimeter. Weather-warped docks reached into the water like arthritic fingers. A handful of boats rocked against gentle swells, their hulls creaking. The setting appeared still, except for the undercurrent of official activity.

Two squad cars stood at odd angles near the lot's entrance, gravel scattered from hasty arrivals. Their lights flashed blue and red against long shadows. Blackburn parked near them. Overhead, a pair of drones traced slow spirals above the water, silent observers casting thin doppelgangers across mirrored blue.

Nothing about the scene betrayed urgency at first glance. But beneath the surface calm lingered her purpose: a metal body beneath water, evidence waiting in cold depths.

Blackburn stepped from the car and drew a slow breath, air cool and sharp with pine resin and lake water. She scanned the scene, gravel crunching beneath her shoes. The drones hovered above the water, rotors humming like mechanical wasps.

"You're done here," she called, raising one hand in an obvious gesture. Her voice cut across the clearing. She did not like the idea of being watched by hovering witnesses.

The drones lifted, their hum rising in pitch before fading into the sky. The lake's surface stilled to glass. Only the faint echo lingered in Blackburn's ears.

She and Reeves advanced to the water's edge, damp earth giving under their feet. Beneath the surface, the outline of an autonomous vehicle caught the light: a pale metallic shape distorted by ripples, more ghost than machine.

Reeves stared for a moment, then exhaled through his teeth. "Didn't think I'd see this today."

Blackburn took several photos with her phone, the shutter sound sharp in the quiet morning air. A crunch of tires on gravel drew her attention. Sinclair and Willow approached at a brisk pace, stopping just short of where wet sand darkened the shoreline. He parked near the growing collection of police vehicles.

Sinclair spoke first, breathless. "What's the situation?"

"Where's Kieran Mott?" Blackburn's voice carried an edge. She wanted that man, and Sinclair was supposed to be watching for him.

"No idea, boss. He's not home, and none of his neighbors know where he went."

Blackburn rolled her eyes and addressed Willow. "Do these cars float?"

Willow shook her head as she studied the submerged chassis. "Not really. They're too dense to stay up long."

"Then it's been under since it went in," Blackburn said.

She pocketed her phone and watched sunlight play along the lake's quiet surface, considering her next steps.

The group fell silent as heavy vehicles rumbled into the lot, diesel exhaust mixing with fresh air. All eyes fixed on the SCUBA divers as they suited up, neoprene squeaking. It was a sound Blackburn found alluring.

Reeves moved forward, ready to act, but Blackburn stopped him with a firm grip on his arm. "Let them work," she said, voice steady, frustration coiled beneath the surface.

Her hand closed into a fist at her side. She exhaled a clipped curse under her breath, capturing what they all felt as they watched the operation drag on.

The sun dropped low behind the trees, casting long shadows that complicated the divers' work. What was usually a quiet shoreline had become a hive of activity: rescue divers waded through the water, their movements mapped under harsh white beams from portable floodlights. The crowd behind the police tape pressed closer, their murmurs a constant backdrop to the mechanical whine of the winch.

Two divers emerged, wetsuits gleaming like sealskin in the light. One peeled off his mask with a wet snap and addressed Blackburn directly. "No body inside, Detective. The car is secured."

Blackburn gave a brief nod and gestured to the winch operator. The cables groaned and tightened, beginning to pull the submerged vehicle toward shore.

Sinclair approached without preamble. Willow waited near the truck, watching with professional fascination as the autonomous vehicle glistened in the spotlight. "Cooper's still at Mott's," he said. "Nothing to report."

Blackburn caught movement along the tape line: Brynn Cassidy had slipped past the first barrier with her cameraman, Joseph, following close behind. Both headed straight for the scene, equipment bouncing.

She addressed a nearby officer. "Keep the press back," she said evenly. "Double-check your perimeter."

The silver car breached the water's surface with a rush, sheets cascading from its sides like a metallic waterfall. The recovery team watched in silence as it rose above the lake, cables singing under the strain. Reeves and Sinclair positioned themselves for inspection as the car swung gently to settle on the flatbed with a hollow thud.

Under bright lights, water streamed from every joint and seam, pattering on the truck bed. The vehicle looked deceptively intact from a distance. Up close, the damage told its story: spider-webbed cracks across the windshield catching light like fractured ice, the front bumper hanging at a sickening angle, and a distinctive dent in the hood that spoke of terrible impact. The lake had washed it clean of blood but couldn't erase what it had done.

Chapter 15

They had been on scene for hours, watching the vehicle rescue crew work. Red and blue lights swept across the riverbank, painting the crowd and crime tape in alternating shadows. The water below lay black and still, having swallowed the car hours before without a ripple to mark its grave. Now it was found, and would soon end up in the police garage for a full analysis. Willow kept her focus tight, blocking out the spectacle as she adjusted her glasses against the bridge of her nose. Anticipation coiled cold in her chest.

She couldn't stop replaying the message she'd sent Blackburn yesterday, each word pressing harder against her thoughts:

> *Kidnap me because I am beautiful, sex=1, pain=2.*

She'd hesitated before sending it, typing, deleting, rephrasing, her thumb hovering over send. Simple on the surface, but Blackburn always preferred higher numbers.

Willow checked her phone. 9:25. Still early. She smoothed her t-shirt, fingers pressing out creases that weren't there. After a breath that tasted of river mud and diesel exhaust, she checked again: 9:25.

Blackburn cut through the scene with authority. Her hair hung loose around her face, blonde strands catching in the humid air as she spoke with patrol officers. In the harsh glare of floodlights, she looked carved from stone: no trace of distraction. All business.

When Blackburn glanced at her watch and then at her, Willow's pulse stuttered. She understood. Blackburn walked over, something predatory shifting behind her professional mask.

"You ready?" Blackburn's voice was low, controlled: a routine check-in for anyone listening. But her eyes held Willow's, and something electric passed between them.

"Yes." Willow surprised herself with how steady her answer sounded.

"Walk back to New Dresden," Blackburn said. Her words were ordinary but carried extra weight, subtle tension beneath the mundane. The instruction was both given and understood.

Willow nodded and stepped away from the yellow tape. The crowd's idle chatter faded as she picked her way through people to the road's edge, gravel shifting under her shoes, heart hammering against her ribs.

The night air bit sharper than expected. Out here beyond the crime scene's artificial day, the country road dissolved into walls of shadow. Each footfall rang against the asphalt. Willow listened to her own breathing despite the nerves twisting in her stomach.

She was alone now, slipping into the role she'd chosen.

Willow pictured herself from above as she walked: a drone's view of dark trees, a solitary figure threading through the night. Willow imagined ominous music swelling from nowhere, signaling the beginning.

But there was no music, just the scrape of her sneakers on the pavement.

She'd been walking for ten minutes when headlights swept the empty road behind her. The engine's rumble was familiar: Blackburn's car prowling closer. Still, Willow resisted turning. She kept her pace steady, shoulders straight.

The vehicle crept alongside her. The window hummed down. Blackburn's voice drifted out, transformed, lower now, silk wrapped around steel, a tone reserved for nights like this.

"Hey there gorgeous," Blackburn called. "It's a dangerous place to be walking alone." Her words hung in the air between them. "Something terrible might happen to a pretty woman like you."

Willow kept moving, eyes forward, glasses catching fragments of headlight glare. "I'm fine," she said, forcing steadiness into her voice.

Blackburn matched her pace at idle speed, the engine purring. "All alone out here," she said. "Not smart." Something dark threaded through her amusement. "You should get in. It's safer with me."

"No." Willow pushed the word out hard, quickening her steps, sneakers slapping faster against asphalt.

"You're stubborn," Blackburn replied, voice dropping to velvet. "You have gorgeous hair... shouldn't be wasted on the dark."

Willow didn't answer, but heat bloomed under her skin, spreading up her neck. The game tightened between them with each step, each word pulling the tension taut.

Her cheeks burned in the headlights' glare.

"Stop right there." Blackburn's voice sliced through the night, all warmth gone. Pure command.

Willow kept moving, breath catching. Each step was purposeful now. The cool air stung her flushed skin.

"I said stop." Blackburn's tone left no room for argument: velvet over iron. "Don't make me chase you."

But Willow heard the subtext beneath: *make me chase you.*

Her glasses slipped down her nose as she broke into a jog. Her heartbeat thundered, drowning thought. This was what she'd asked for, but reality made her legs unsteady. Blackburn behind her, relentlessly. The road was empty but for them and what would happen next.

"Please," Willow said. The word came out smaller than intended.

A dark laugh from behind. "You want me gone? You're not fooling anyone with that ass."

The crude words landed like a slap. Willow's run became desperate, sneakers scraping frantically. But Blackburn was faster. Much faster. Hands caught her arms, spinning her with experience, pulling her back, finally up against the car's cold metal.

Blackburn pressed close, pinning Willow's wrists overhead with one hand while the other cupped her jaw. In the half-light, Blackburn's eyes were all pupil, focused and predatory. Every movement was fluid.

"Trying to run from me?" Blackburn's thumb traced Willow's lower lip, deliberate and slow. Willow breathed in Blackburn's scent:

wood smoke and musk sharpened by adrenaline. She pulled it deep, hoping it might transform her from within.

"You have no idea how long I've been watching. How much I want this. How long I'm going to take with you."

Willow twisted against the grip, testing, but Blackburn's hold was iron. The closeness left room to struggle but not escape. Willow felt heat radiating through her clothes, Blackburn's body caging her.

Blackburn's breath warmed Willow's ear. "You hide behind those glasses. Bury yourself in your work. Did you think I wouldn't notice how beautiful you are?"

A metallic click split the silence. Cold steel circled Willow's wrists: handcuffs, final and unforgiving. Blackburn stepped back to survey her work, gaze traveling slowly, taking her time.

Willow drew a shaky breath, tasting the metallic edge of her own fear. Her protest emerged softly now, stripped of resistance. *Please don't let go. Please keep going.*

Blackburn's expression held steady, satisfaction flickering in her eyes as she reached past Willow to open the car door. The mechanism clicked, sounding like a chambered round. "Inside. Now."

Willow hesitated just long enough to feel Blackburn's hand tighten at her nape. The grip wasn't violent but impossible to ignore, fingers pressing into the tender hollow where skull met spine.

"I said get in." The words came low, edged with warning. "I'm not letting you leave me."

Awkward in the cuffs, metal biting her wrists, Willow climbed into the backseat. The leather was cool against her skin. Blackburn pushed her in roughly, climbing on top, pressing down, forcing.

Click.

The seatbelt engaged with finality. With her hands trapped behind her back, Willow had no way of releasing herself. The belt pressed across her chest with each breath.

Once Willow settled, Blackburn leaned close, voice level, breath warm against her neck, carrying mint and danger. "Look at you," she murmured. "Exactly where you're meant to be." Fingers traced along Willow's jawline, steady and proprietary, leaving trails of heat.

"I'm taking you," she said. "I'll take care of you."

The door shut with a powerful slam that reverberated through Willow's bones. She startled, pulse hammering as she watched Blackburn circle to the driver's side. Each movement was controlled, efficient. This was no longer a daydream bleeding into reality. This was reality, directed by the one woman who understood exactly how to unravel her.

Blackburn slid behind the wheel and caught Willow's gaze in the rearview mirror. Her eyes were steady, unreadable as polished stone.

"Settling in back there?" Her voice came low, almost clinical, as the engine purred to life. "We're just starting."

Heat crept along Willow's collar. Inside the car was the scent of leather and perfume and something electric. She could only watch Blackburn's gaze in the mirror, sharp and assessing. Her glasses slipped further down her nose, the frames catching sweat, but with her wrists locked behind her, she couldn't adjust them.

"Those glasses," Blackburn said, adjusting the mirror to study Willow's face more closely. "They keep you hidden." Her tone turned thoughtful. "Is that what you want? To disappear?"

Willow swallowed hard, throat clicking dry. "No," she said.

Blackburn's mouth curved, betraying interest rather than humor. "You fade into the background for everyone else," she said. "But I see you." She took a turn quickly, tires gripping the asphalt as momentum forced Willow to brace against the seatbelt. "Why cover up a beauty that is impossible to ignore?"

Flush rose on Willow's cheeks, spreading down her throat. She tried to answer, but stumbled over the words. Her toe found the seam on the back of the seat, tracing it compulsively. Up and down and back again. The repetitive motion grounded her.

"Beautiful," Blackburn pressed, voice even. "I've watched you walk the halls at work." She kept her eyes forward, hands steady on the wheel, grip relaxed. "Anyone paying attention would notice." The statement hung there, a fact more than a compliment.

Willow resisted the urge to respond. She felt the scrutiny, direct and unadorned. *Up. Down. Back.*

"Look up," Blackburn said.

Her foot stilled. She obeyed, angling her chin so their eyes met in the mirror. The silence stretched taut between them. Anticipation built not from what was said but what lingered unspoken, thick as smoke.

Blackburn's eyes lingered a moment longer. "Your lips," she said, tone dry and assured. "They give you away."

She smiled, small and involuntary. Even through the mirror, Blackburn saw the minute parts of her.

Outside, the city kept passing by in streaks of neon and shadow. Their world inside the car remained insulated from its motion. The vehicle slowed at a red light, engine idling. Blackburn finally turned to face Willow fully for the first time since they'd left the lake. "You're trembling," she observed quietly. "Is it nerves?"

"Yes," Willow murmured. The word emerged thin, uncertain. She knew it wasn't fear that made her muscles quiver. It was love. The word surfaced slowly, coolly, like a stone from deep water. She let it stay, a quiet warmth blooming in her chest. She knew it was hers alone. Real. Sustaining.

Blackburn's mouth almost curved into a smile. "Good." Her voice remained even, deliberate, a promise contained in restraint. "I told you I'd be thorough with you. I will be."

The traffic light blinked green, washing them in pale light. Blackburn turned her focus ahead, but she watched Willow's reflection in the rearview mirror. "Take off your glasses."

Willow hesitated, fingers flexing uselessly behind her. "I can't see without them."

"I know," Blackburn replied. "Do it."

Willow rubbed her face against the seat back, awkward and desperate, until the glasses slipped from her face, clattering down. The world blurred instantly. Shapes dissolved into one another, color and shadow merging at the edges like watercolors bleeding.

"Good," Blackburn said softly. "Nothing to hide behind now." She made a left onto a quieter street, tires whispering over damp pavement as they approached the familiar outline of her building. "We're home."

Willow felt herself pulled taut between anticipation and uncertainty. The word *home* edged into her awareness like a blade as Blackburn parked and killed the engine. Silence rushed in.

A quiet plea escaped Willow before she could stop herself: "Please..."

Blackburn reached over, her hand settling on Willow's knee, warm through fabric, a steadying touch or a restraint. "You'll have your turn to speak," she said, voice even but final. "But right now, I need you quiet."

The garage door rattled closed behind them, metal grinding on metal, shutting out the street and wrapping everything in amber light. Willow blinked against her own unsteadiness. Through blurred vision, she saw Blackburn's outline moving past the hood of the car. Deliberate, unhurried. Each footstep echoed.

In the thick silence between them, Willow listened for every sound: the cadence of heels on painted concrete, a single key scraping into a lock, and then her own breath settling as reality caught up to anticipation. Her heart thundered against her ribs.

"Inside," Blackburn said, tone level, free of ornament. She opened the back door. Cold air slipped in, raising goosebumps. "No trouble, or I'll make this difficult."

Willow felt Blackburn's grip on her arms, fingers pressing into muscle as she helped her out of the car. Metal clicked softly. The handcuffs shifted loose on one wrist. A detail that had escaped Willow until now. Intentional, maybe. It whispered possibility.

Blackburn's palm pressed to the small of Willow's back as they walked toward the interior. Heat radiated through the cloth. Willow squinted into the dark garage, shapes warping without her glasses. For a second, the edge of the door became a horizon. An opening.

At the threshold, Blackburn's hold eased fractionally.

Willow didn't remember deciding to move. Instinct took over. She twisted hard, shoulder dropping as she slid from both the loosened cuff and Blackburn's touch. Her shoes slapped against concrete, the sound sharp in the enclosed space. Behind her, Blackburn's footsteps followed, sustained and unhurried.

Blackburn's voice followed, low. "You shouldn't have done that." A note of warning threaded through with something else. Interest. "You're only making things interesting."

Willow kept moving, hands out as her fingers brushed past the cold metal tool racks. Oil and rust filled her nostrils. She circled the workbench, footsteps quiet against the concrete, trying to muffle her breathing. Behind her, Blackburn's approach was quieter still, unhurried and as certain as gravity.

"Where are you going?" Blackburn asked, voice close but indistinct in the shadows. "There's nowhere to run."

A noise cracked to Willow's left. She pivoted on instinct, but arms locked around her from behind.

Air rushed from her lungs as Blackburn drew her back tight, one arm banded across her waist, the other resting with deceptive lightness against her throat.

"Got you," Blackburn murmured. Her voice carried an undertone of anger, hot at Willow's ear yet unyielding beneath its calm. "Thought I'd let you slip away?"

Fingers found Willow's breast through her shirt: a pinch sharp enough to send electricity down her spine. Effective, provocative.

Another. Harder.

"Naughty girl."

Willow shuddered, nerve endings firing in confused signals. The sensation hovered between discomfort and invitation, arousal threading beneath restraint like smoke under a door. She exhaled slowly, tasting relief. Being caught gave her peace. This was why she'd come.

Blackburn held firm, control absolute without display, waiting for Willow's next move.

Willow's muscles uncoiled beneath Blackburn's hold, heat pooling low in her belly. Each point of contact sharpened her awareness. Pain and pleasure braided together until the distinction dissolved. The discipline in Blackburn's grip awakened something primal: a craving for boundaries drawn by a lover who understood the razor's edge between punishment and surrender.

Her breath quickened as Blackburn led her inside, past the shadowed hallway geometry to where lamplight pooled at the living room's edge.

"Kneel." The command felt cool and absolute. Blackburn's hands pressed down on Willow's shoulders, guiding her to the hardwood beside the couch. "Let's see how sorry you are for trying to run."

Willow folded forward, her cheek finding the warmth of Blackburn's thigh, seeking reassurance she barely understood. "I thought I was protecting myself," she murmured, words nearly swallowed by the room's hush. "But I understand now. I should have trusted you."

Blackburn's palm settled at Willow's nape, steady and deliberate. Willow's voice dropped to a breath. "Please. I won't do it again."

"I know." Blackburn's response came without pause. Her fingers traced Willow's jaw, tilting her chin upward. "Don't move, Fawn."

With a snap, Blackburn refastened the cuffs. Willow remained kneeling, almost blind, pulse hammering as she listened to Blackburn's footsteps retreat. The waiting pressed against every nerve. Her vision softened at the edges, choices peeling away in deliberate layers.

Time stretched and compressed. Willow floated, eyelids drifting shut, then opening to stare unfocused at the baseboards. She tracked Blackburn through sound alone: whispered fabric, a drawer sliding open, footsteps circling with careful control.

Willow held steady, anchored by Blackburn's invisible tether.

"So beautiful like this," Blackburn said from behind. Her hand returned to Willow's hair, fingers combing through with hypnotic rhythm.

Blackburn's grip tightened enough to spark awareness along Willow's scalp. "Should I trust you not to flee?"

"Yes." Willow's voice emerged soft but steady despite the heat climbing her neck.

"Why?"

"Because I'm yours."

Blackburn nodded once, her tone dropping to velvety depths. "That's right. All mine." She let the silence pool before continuing. "I think you're ready to understand what that means."

* * *

Willow lay on her back, wrists secured above her head by her robe's belt. The sheets were cool. One shoulder bare, a single breast partially exposed where the fabric opened. She stayed still. Her glasses sat folded on the nightstand, leaving the room blurred except for one clear point: Blackburn.

Blackburn moved around the bed with slow steps. Each floorboard gave quietly under her weight. Willow watched as she tied her hair back, and Willow's grip on the belt tightened.

Blackburn stopped at the bedside and let the silence grow. Then:

"Tell me why." Her tone was precise, almost impersonal.

Willow's lips parted before she found words. "Because I'm beautiful." The answer hung between them. Half assertion, half confession.

A pause stretched out. Blackburn's mouth softened. "Exactly." Her hand hovered above Willow's chest for a moment before she opened the robe with care, pulling it aside like she was examining a specimen under a clean light.

Cold air slipped across Willow's body. Goosebumps rose; muscles tensed under skin that wanted to shrink away. The restraint was tight enough to keep her in place but left no marks. It was a balance Blackburn always maintained.

For a while, there was only Blackburn's gaze: steady, analytical.

"Look at you," she said, neither kind nor cruel, just factual. She climbed onto the mattress beside Willow, denim rough against Willow's bare thigh.

Blackburn raised her hand again, tracing along Willow's jaw with careful fingers.

"Perfect symmetry," she murmured, as much an observation as a reassurance. Her thumb followed Willow's throat; skin shivered under it.

She waited before continuing:

"This neck." Her voice was low, more thought than speech. Fingers circled lightly over Willow's neck. Not squeezing, but pausing over tendon and hollow as if searching for some underlying pattern.

Willow swallowed; Blackburn felt it and held her hand there another second. "Responsive," she said.

The simple word left warmth behind.

When Willow finally relaxed a little, Blackburn trailed her knuckle along her collarbone and down. "There's structure here," she whispered, as if cataloguing artifacts in an archive after hours. "Light sits in these spaces."

Her gaze moved lower and settled on Willow's chest. She exhaled slowly; time widened between them until touch felt both near and unreachable.

"Open your eyes," Blackburn ordered suddenly.

Willow startled but obeyed quickly, a habit stronger than hesitation now.

"These breasts were made well," Blackburn said without flourish or apology. She weighed one in her hand; thumb brushed across a nipple drawn tight with chill and anticipation. "Substantial." It was an inventory: nothing more nor less than fact.

Her other hand traced three faint scars along pale skin, following their arc rather than meaning, until Willow felt bare beneath attention sharper than judgment.

"They fit my hands exactly." Blackburn spoke softer now; satisfaction flickered briefly across her face before discipline returned.

Willow breathed deeper as praise replaced anxiety wherever it landed. Her shoulders drew back, raising her body.

Blackburn withdrew her hand after a few seconds, a calculated absence where comfort had almost taken root.

She continued downwards without hurry.

"Your stomach." Her fingers spread against softened flesh shaped by time and survival rather than design. "Resilient." There was no hint of pity or disgust in her tone. "Adapted."

She didn't elaborate or embellish further. She waited to see if Willow would react, but neither flinch nor laughter came now.

Detachment was harder to push against than cruelty would have been.

Blackburn pressed lower still, her hands following hips broad enough for leverage but rarely admired outside this setting. "Support," she noted simply; thumbs finding bone beneath skin with enough pressure for certainty with a whisper of pain.

Willow shifted beneath the examination; thighs tensed together until one small shake of Blackburn's head prompted compliance without argument.

The next pause lasted longer; house sounds filtered in from elsewhere. Pipes ticking, wind tapping glass, cars distant beyond thick curtains blocking out time.

Blackburn moved past bent knees to where Willow's feet pressed flat into sheets. Every move was slow and deliberate, a methodical study rather than indulgence.

"These legs are strong," she said quietly as palms slid from calf to thigh with even pressure that neither hurried nor wavered when Willow trembled.

Then, both hands rested atop inner thighs, guiding them apart with gentle insistence until resistance disappeared completely.

"Open."

With no words left to offer protection, Willow complied. Vulnerability was not a secret anymore, but a fact made real under observation.

Blackburn looked at what was revealed with a formality that recalled laboratory work more than desire at first glance, but when her fingers finally touched wet skin, protocol dissolved at its edges.

"This is what I came for," Blackburn admitted, the first note of hunger threading through a composure otherwise held rigid by routine control.

Her fingertip traced the outer line slowly. There was no hurry toward a satisfaction neither offered nor yet sought out. "Full." A light press, a gathering of moisture marked Willow's readiness without drama or mythologizing it as something rare or holy.

Willow made a sound close to pleading; air swallowed it before it could echo far, but body arched closer regardless of the restraint overhead.

Blackburn found her clit easily. Her touch was steady, and she circled it once with deliberate slowness. "There you are." Her voice was soft now, but dense with intention that left nothing in its wake.

For a moment, only breath moved between them. Shallow, unsteady in the corners where time bent around need kept waiting, just past comfort's reach.

"Wet." The observation came clinically, but when fingers slipped lower, all detachment slipped too; want drove her fingers even when technique remained as careful and exacting as ever.

She didn't enter outright. Instead, she circled the entrance slowly enough that every nerve stretched under anticipation, nearly unbearable in its patience.

"You know what I see right now?" Words barely lapped at the surface tension where every inch waited for attention.

"I see no secrets," she continued. Her timbre was almost graveyard-low now, a truth spoken into skin that was flushed with exposure more intimate than any earlier touch had managed so far.

Finally, two fingers pressed inside, not deep but definite, and praise returned.

"You get wetter when I see you honestly instead of kindly." The words were whispered into an ear gone hot with want. Her other hand returned to tease one nipple until Willow's hips lifted off the bed in reflex. Synchronized to desire unhidden at last.

Willow blinked back tears she had not meant to display. The act itself bared her hunger rawer than any mapped anatomy revealed tonight. The rhythm pulled at her.

But then:

"Not yet," Blackburn cautioned softly; pressure vanished all at once, leaving Willow's nerves pitched high and unsatisfied by design. This was not denial, it was anticipation.

Silence stretched again; Blackburn's palm skated from Willow's ribcage across her waist and up once more. A litany she conducted by memory as much as measurement.

"I took you because your beauty belongs nowhere else," Blackburn finally said. "Yield to me." Not a question.

And Willow did, because yielding always ended here.

Blackburn leaned low enough that her words brushed Willow's cheek, already salt damp:

"Show me surrender."

Her fingers resumed their rhythm, neither rushed nor tentative. Each motion metered precisely until Willow's orgasm came swiftly but controlled: her muscles drew tight then fell loose all at once, tears quiet against the pillowcase.

Blackburn stayed close through aftercare, not offering comfort by name but present through the slow untangling of the restraints.

She checked wrists where cashmere had pressed faint lines, and asked only, "Good?"

Willow nodded once, the truth exceeding any words she could hope for.

Beauty arrived at last. Not showy but measured out with restraint that signaled experience rather than hesitation.

"You were perfect." Blackburn spoke plainly, and the compliment landed heavier in the aftermath than any fiction could carry.

Better than beautiful.

"Pick a number," Blackburn instructed, authority tempered with tenderness.

Willow's throat worked before producing a sound. "Twelve."

Blackburn settled beside her, radiating patient heat. "Twelve kisses to bring you back to me. Ready?"

Willow nodded. *I am here. I am wanted.*

Blackburn bent close. The first kiss pressed against Willow's temple, firm and grounding.

"One."

The second found the hollow behind Willow's ear, lips lingering to draw a shiver.

"Two. Still here?"

"Yes," Willow whispered.

A third kiss claimed the pulse at Willow's throat. Blackburn paused against the racing beat. "Your heart's flying. Let it settle."

The collarbone received its tribute next.

"Four. You're doing well."

The next two were reverent, one for each breast's curve.

"Halfway. Stay with me."

The seventh kiss pressed over Willow's heart. Blackburn's mouth lingered, breath warming her skin in a steady rhythm.

"Seven. Right here. Where you belong."

The next touch landed tenderly: lips meeting soft curls between Willow's thighs.

"Eight. Almost done."

Nine and ten blessed knee and ankle in turn. Each contact drew consciousness back into her body, anchoring her.

"Eleven." Blackburn's mouth found Willow's inner wrist, feeling the pulse flutter. "Last one."

Willow nodded. Tears tracked silent paths down her temples.

The twelfth kiss touched her forehead: weightless, complete.

"Twelve." Blackburn gathered her close, arms forming shelter. The charged air shifted; fantasy released its grip, leaving something solid behind.

Willow exhaled shakily, melting into the embrace as tremors ebbed. "Thank you," she whispered against Blackburn's throat.

Blackburn smoothed Willow's hair with steady strokes. "Our pleasure."

Willow softened further, defenses abandoned in the wake of their scene.

"My beautiful little Fawn," Blackburn said softly, pressing an unscripted kiss to Willow's hairline. "Go to sleep. I'll keep you safe."

Willow's eyes drifted closed, held secure by Blackburn's presence and unwavering voice. The fantasy had been exactly what she'd craved, but this quiet aftermath imprinted deepest: careful, grounded, real.

Chapter 16

Blackburn's fingertips still tingled from smoothing Willow's hair, the phantom warmth of skin contact lingering even as she gripped the steering wheel. Her throat felt tender, voice still pitched lower from their scene's quiet intimacy. She flexed her fingers once, dismissing the sensation with ease. She had work to do.

Blackburn eased her car into the slick lot outside headquarters, wipers beating their steady rhythm against the persistent drizzle. The vinyl seat creaked as she reached for her vibrating cell. The screen's blue glow cut through the gray morning: police garage.

"Detective Blackburn." Her voice scraped raw from the morning's first words.

"It's Jason Osterik, down in the garage. We've got the autonomous car from yesterday. The one pulled from Lake Canada. Water damage is extensive. Thought you'd want to see it before we start."

His tone carried a professional distance. She appreciated that.

"I'll be there in five." The phone clicked when she ended the call.

Her mind threatened to drift toward Willow's warmth still lingering on her skin, but she locked it away. Work came first.

She dialed Homicide. Three rings bled into the voicemail's mechanical greeting. Not surprising; dawn had barely cracked the horizon. The squad would stumble in soon enough. They met for bagels every Wednesday and were always ten minutes late.

"This is Blackburn. Meet me at the garage now. The car from Lake Canada. Need everyone here." The phone clattered onto the dash.

She shifted into reverse, tires hissing against wet asphalt as she headed for the garage service entrance. Her pulse quickened. Here, with evidence and procedure, the world made sense.

Inside, the garage's concrete throat swallowed her whole. LED tubes washed everything in sterile white, the taste of motor oil coated her tongue. Her heels struck notes across the floor, each step echoing through the cavernous space.

The autonomous car dangled from the hydraulic lift like a metal carcass, lake water still weeping from its wounds onto oil-stained concrete. Silver paint wore a shroud of mud and algae. Cattails wrapped around the quarter panels like dead fingers. Deep gouges scarred the bodywork.

Jason and Mohammed flanked the wreck, their faces etched with professional wariness. Jason's nod barely disturbed the air. "Detective. She took serious punishment before the water got her."

Blackburn circled the suspended vehicle, her shoes clicking with a clear cadence. The passenger door had collapsed inward. Metal peeled back like torn skin, safety glass transformed into crystalline teeth that caught the harsh light.

"Why is it still elevated?" She gestured upward.

Mohammed's voice carried steady competence. "We knew you'd want to observe the EDR extraction." He pointed at a panel beneath the chassis. "Exterior documentation's complete, top and bottom. Forensics will need her lowered for detail work."

They understood her methods. Blackburn's gaze dissected the undercarriage, tracking impact patterns and residue trails. Information threads began weaving together, though crucial connections remained elusive.

"Proceed," she said. "The event data recorder takes priority."

Blackburn stood with arms crossed, watching Mohammed's experienced hands guide the hoist controls with surgical precision.

"Bring her down slow," Jacob called out, authority earned through years of coaxing truth from twisted steel. "I need underneath access first."

Mohammed's fingers performed their dance across the controls. Hydraulics whined, lowering the vehicle in increments. "How low?"

"Waist height," Jacob replied, latex gloves snapping into place. "I need maneuvering room without wrestling on my back."

Blackburn tracked Jacob's movements with focused intensity. His hands moved with a purpose born of experience. She'd watched him extract evidence from other wrecks. Blood, hair, bodies. But this one carried a different weight.

The hoist shuddered still. Jacob approached the driver's door, features tightening. "Christ." He indicated the door seals where brackish water had pooled. "Complete cabin breach."

"Will that compromise the EDR?" Blackburn stepped closer, catching the lake's organic decay.

"Depends on module integrity. They're built tough, but..." His shrug spoke volumes before he gripped the handle. "Only one way to know."

The door opened with a wet, sucking protest. Murky water cascaded out, splashing across concrete and releasing a concentrated essence of algae and rot.

"Lovely," Mohammed muttered, retreating from the spreading pool.

Jacob waited for the flow to ebb, then leaned into the devastated cabin. Waterlogged upholstery sagged like dead flesh; electronics darkened beyond recognition. He reached beneath the dashboard, disappearing to his elbow.

"There," his muffled voice emerged. "I've got the bracket. Mohammed, drop her all the way. I need a better angle."

The vehicle descended further. Jacob folded himself into the footwell, contorting to fit the cramped space until only his legs remained visible.

Blackburn found her breathing syncing with his efforts as he navigated the maze of components by touch alone.

"Got it," Jacob's voice filtered from the cabin's depths. "EDR unit feels solid, but this mounting bracket's stubborn. Going to be delicate."

"How delicate?" Blackburn asked.

"Wiring connector's jammed. Barely reachable." A pause punctuated by effort. "Locking tab's seized, probably from impact. Working it loose."

Minutes stretched. She heard his controlled breathing, strained from the awkward angle. His legs shifted, seeking better leverage.

"Almost there." Strain threaded his voice. "Connector's fighting, but..."

A soft click, followed by a satisfied exhalation.

"Wiring's clear. Now the mounting bolts." Metal scraped metal, then a frustrated oath. "Metric, naturally. Mohammed, 10mm socket. Red toolbox."

Mohammed passed the tool to Jacob's briefly emergent hand.

The garage filled with careful sounds. Socket wrench ratcheting, Jacob's occasional repositioning, water's persistent drip marking time. Blackburn watched his visible legs tense and relax with each micro-movement with the patience of someone who knew haste bred mistakes.

Finally, Jacob began his careful extraction, backing out inch by measured inch. He emerged holding a scarred black rectangle the size of a paperback.

"The EDR unit," he announced, straightening with visible relief. "Housing took some hits, but it's intact. Data should be recoverable."

Blackburn nodded once, face neutral as the EDR disappeared into an evidence container.

Jason crouched beside the passenger side, gloved finger following a vicious scar from fender to door. "Here," he said softly, concentration absolute. "Deep impact. Whatever it hit was immovable."

Blackburn moved closer, cataloguing the deformation pattern. Mental gears engaged, clicking through scenarios. "Hit something solid before the water. Wall, maybe." Her tone stayed level, urgency lurking beneath.

Reeves entered with a brief whistle, acknowledging Blackburn with professional courtesy.

"Where's everyone else?" Her gaze swept the bay.

Before he could respond, Sinclair and Cooper materialized behind him, absorbing the scene.

Mohammed silenced the lift's motor.

"Why is it still wet?" Cooper asked. "Why so much water?"

"Seal integrity held pretty well. It'll drain through the floor grate to the catch basin," Mohammed explained, nodding toward the drainage system. He peered inside. "Interior's saturated. Most trace evidence is compromised, but we'll have VIN confirmation."

He located it efficiently: "JF1CZ8497VK482319."

Reeves transcribed quickly.

"Run it," Blackburn ordered. "I want registration immediately."

Reeves was already connecting the call.

"Ma'am?" Mohammed called, voice controlled but intent. "Found something under the back seat. Prescription bottle."

Blackburn leaned in, eyes narrowing on the small amber bottle on the back seat, reading the label with steady care. Cooper leaned past her, notebook ready.

His pen scratched across the paper without pause. "It's for Charles Roche."

Blackburn stilled. "Jesus Christ. He died on January twenty-third. Last year." She kept her tone flat, mind already moving ahead. "I'll call his estate lawyer. See if the car changed hands without registration." She glanced at Cooper. "Get Willow down here now. We need EDR data pulled and analyzed. She can work with Forensics."

Cooper nodded, phone pressed to his ear before she finished speaking.

Turning to the others, Blackburn let silence settle like dust before continuing. "We cover every angle. No mistakes."

Blackburn allowed herself a moment of stillness. The pieces were settling into position. The work was just beginning.

"Who is looking into any connection to Jenna Langston?" She waited a moment. She had dared not assign anyone. "I'll do it," she said.

She surveyed the garage one last time, concrete walls and oil stains blurring at the edges, then spoke quietly. "Keep me posted."

She exhaled and moved toward the exit. The next step would be the estate lawyer, Jacob Schwartz. They had crossed paths during Charlie's murder case, a meeting that left Blackburn wary. He seemed dodgy for an estate lawyer. She would have to stay sharp this time. First, though, she needed to submit her disclosure on possible conflicts of interest. Admin work always slowed down the real job.

She'd barely cleared the garage's stale air when her phone vibrated against her hip. Brynn Cassidy's name lit the display. Blackburn paused, eyes lifted for patience, then answered with a resolute tone.

"Detective Blackburn."

"Thanks for picking up," Brynn said, her energy crackling through the speaker.

Blackburn didn't respond to pleasantries.

"Detective," Brynn pressed on, voice cutting through the static. "You recovered the vehicle from the Chaplain case. That's another autonomous car death in three days, same street, same make and model. Are autonomous cars targeting people?"

Blackburn braced her shoulder against the rough wall, temper held in check. "That's Chaplin. There's no ongoing risk to the public. These cases are being handled."

"That's not enough," Brynn shot back. "Both incidents: Oak Street. Both Raider Straight Lines. You call that coincidence?"

"Correlation isn't causation," Blackburn replied, voice even but firm. "We're looking at all possibilities, but nothing connects these events except proximity and car type."

"So why did the Stan Raider Group start a voluntary recall? People have been filing navigation complaints for months." Brynn's tone sharpened further. "What are you holding back?"

Blackburn kept her tone even, the practice of professionalism smoothing any hint of irritation. She knew Brynn couldn't see her expression, but the effect would carry through her voice. Brynn had already spoken to Mott, at least online; the existence of the bugs was no longer in question.

"You just said the complaints started before the first incident. I can't comment on company actions. That's a question for them."

"They're not sharing everything with you?" Brynn pressed.

"Recalls happen routinely. This investigation is in its early stages. We're reviewing every angle."

"But this isn't just bad luck, is it? Two deaths. Both on Oak Street, both Raider Straight Line cars. That's a connection."

"They were both women. That's a connection. Both died in car accidents. That's a connection. Both were in New Dresden. You see where I am going? It doesn't make it meaningful. We're following valuable, factual, meaningful evidence. Right now, there's no reason to imply the streets are unsafe or that anyone should panic."

Brynn's voice sharpened, less curious and more demanding. "And the reports about navigation bugs? People complained before this happened. Now two are dead. Doesn't the public deserve answers?"

Blackburn felt frustration spark under her skin, heat rising despite the cool air, but she didn't let it show. She knew Brynn was trying to steer the investigation one way, and she steered back to protocol. Carefully and directly. "We're examining everything, including those reports. For specifics on their systems, you'll need to contact the Stan Raider Group. At this point, we have nothing suggesting a broader threat. The public can trust we're on this."

Brynn didn't yield. "You say there's no risk, but I've talked to sources. There's talk of these cars being hacked or compromised. Is that why the Stan Raider Group won't comment?"

"They're cooperating," Blackburn replied, voice cool and final. "Until we have new information, that's all I can say."

The silence stretched between them for a beat as Brynn considered her next move. When she spoke again, her words were clean, her intent unmistakable.

"Is it true Kendria Chaplin was holding your hand when she was struck?"

The question landed hard, but Blackburn let no reaction show. Her pulse jumped against her throat. Marilyn had been talking. She steadied her voice. "We were praying. You will not shame me over this, Ms. Cassidy. This interview is over. Direct any further questions to Media Services."

She ended the call, thumb pressing down until the screen went dark. For a moment, she stared at the phone in her hand, the device still warm from use, thoughts moving fast beneath a calm surface. Brynn was closing in. Too close. Letting anything slip was not an option. This was about keeping control of the narrative, of the investigation, and above all, of herself.

She slid into her sedan, leather seats cool against her back, mind grinding through possibilities as she left the garage. The city passed in streaks of neon and glass, but Blackburn registered none of it.

Chapter 17

The sandwich sat at the corner of Blackburn's desk, its crusts curling in the afternoon warmth that seeped through the blinds. She tapped her fingers against the cool glass surface: steady beats in the quiet office. The open Chaplin file stared back, its typed pages catching the slanted light. Her focus lingered on one fact: Marilyn had spoken to Brynn Cassidy. The reporter's smug rhythm during the call, the questions that pressed too close to sensitive details, left little doubt.

Blackburn lifted her coffee mug and sipped, the cold liquid bitter against her tongue. The taste carved a harsh path down her throat, lingering like regret. Across the bullpen, Reeves glanced over before lowering his eyes. It was a silent calculation she had seen a dozen times before. The division tracked Blackburn's moods with experienced caution. Today, the set of her shoulders and the stillness of her hands signaled danger.

She tried to recall if she had specifically told Marilyn to stay clear of the press. She replayed their last conversations: Marilyn's pale face with Kendria's eyes. No words formed clearly in her mind. She had not warned the girl. An oversight that tasted worse than the coffee.

She scanned through the file until she found Marilyn's number and dialed, each press of the keypad was deliberate, the electronic tones soft in the hushed office.

Ring after ring filled her ear.

"Detective Blackburn." Marilyn's voice came through clearly and steadily. There was no trace of reluctance or nerves threading through her words.

"Marilyn." Blackburn shifted in her chair, the leather creaking beneath her, and transferred the phone to her left hand. "I'm just checking in. How are you managing?"

A soft pause followed, then the gentle hush of fabric against fabric, someone settling in. "I'm at my grandparents' place in West Hamilton," Marilyn said. "Trying to get back into a routine."

Blackburn accepted this without comment for a moment, letting the words settle between them. "It's quiet there."

"Yes." The answer came crisp and concise. "My grandmother keeps everyone on a schedule. Meals at fixed times, early bed."

"Sounds like she knows what she's doing." Blackburn let the wall clock behind her tick through a full revolution before she spoke again. "I'm getting aggressive calls from the press. Is anyone harassing you? Bloggers, vloggers, reporters?"

"No." Immediate and firm, the word landing hard.

Blackburn tapped her pen once against the desktop, a sharp click in the silence. Either Marilyn was omitting something or Brynn had found another way in. Both options made her jaw tighten.

"All right," she said evenly, keeping her voice neutral. "If anyone approaches you, especially Brynn Cassidy from New Dresden Today, I'd advise you not to answer questions. She is agg—"

A shuffle sounded through the line, footsteps on hardwood, fabric rustling, and then an older voice took over, worn thin but determined.

"Detective Blackburn? Anastasia Chaplin. Kendria's mother."

Blackburn straightened in her seat, her free hand flattening against the desk's cool surface for balance.

"Hello, Mrs. Chaplin," she answered, matching the formality. "I'm sorry for your loss."

"I wanted to thank you." Anastasia's voice wavered like a candle flame but held steady enough for Blackburn to read the grief beneath the control. "For looking out for Marilyn, and for staying thorough."

Blackburn acknowledged it quietly, the praise sitting uneasily on her shoulders. Results justified thanks, not intentions. "We're doing everything we can, Mrs. Chaplin."

"She was my only child." Anastasia's voice cracked, splintering into a sob she couldn't contain. "I keep thinking I'll hear her laugh. That she'll call and tell me about some new candle scent she's working on."

Blackburn's gaze drifted to the crime scene photos spread across her desk: Kendria's body captured from every angle, measured and timestamped, each detail reduced to evidence under the harsh LED lights.

"I see," Blackburn said. She didn't. Empathy was a muscle she had let atrophy through years of similar calls.

"Do you have children, Detective?" Anastasia asked, her voice finding steadier ground.

"No."

"Then you can't possibly..." Another ragged breath scraped through the line. "I'm sorry. That was unfair."

Blackburn stayed quiet. Grief filled the silence between them, heavy and raw as an open wound. She offered nothing false: no platitudes about time healing, no empty promises of swift justice.

"We're moving as quickly as we can," she said at last. The words tasted dull and insufficient even as she spoke them.

There was a pause filled with shifting sounds, muffled voices, footsteps retreating. Marilyn returned to the phone. "Please excuse my grandmother," she said, her composure reassembled. "She's having a difficult time."

"That's all right." Blackburn rubbed her temple where a headache was beginning to bloom and felt something like relief at hearing Marilyn's even tone return.

"Did you need anything else, Detective?"

Blackburn considered pressing about Brynn Cassidy, asking directly if there had been contact between them. The question formed on her tongue, then dissolved. The girl's composure felt hard-earned; Blackburn recognized the effort thrumming beneath it.

"Detective Reeves will be in touch with your family members. Just checking in, standard procedure." She paused, weighing her next words. "If you need to reach me, you can, any hour."

"Thank you." Marilyn's voice had shed its last tremor. "Goodbye, Detective."

The line went dead with a soft click.

Blackburn set down her phone with deliberate care, as though it might shatter under careless hands.

The sky beyond her office window had deepened to indigo while she worked, night settling over the city unnoticed. She had searched for both women online, through her work computer, using standard protocols. Tracked and traced, nothing would seem amiss, nothing would suggest she knew of a secret connection between the women. If they had something in common, she had not found it.

Her own reflection stared back from the glass, ghostlike and merging with the murder board behind her: timelines mapped in red and black marker, Kendria Chaplin's photograph fixed at the center like a sun around which all other details orbited.

Across town, Brynn Cassidy would be piecing together her own constellation, facts bending into narrative, patience curdling into confrontation.

Blackburn leaned back, fingertips pressed together beneath her chin. Unease settled cold in her gut.

Two women were dead. Same block. Same type of car. Both deaths heeling nights she'd spent with them.

Was Willow next?

Her hand struck the keyboard. A sharp sound cracked the silence, eyes scanning staff reports for mention of a key tied to either the

Langston or Chaplin cases. Nothing surfaced. Each failed search tightened her frustration further.

If Willow was at risk, Blackburn had to ask herself: why now? Blackburn had always been very sexually active. If she was the connection, if sex was the connection, why now?

What if Willow was the killer? After everything she'd done for Willow, would her lover turn on her? But Willow had no reason to hate these women. Blackburn always returned to her. Someone else.

Brynn was already gunning. Hayes failed her multiple times. Reeves was dependable. But Cooper? No. Sinclair? He was outright suspicious.

Blackburn rose quickly, pacing her small office, the worn carpet muffling her steps, the tension in her shoulders mounting with each circuit. The walls pressed closer; the recycled air thickened.

She returned to her desk and sat with care. Blackburn disconnected her phone's handset, clipped an inline recorder in place with a soft click, then dialed.

"Chief Hayes," his voice crisp on the line.

"Sir, there are questions from the public about my involvement with Kendria Chaplin. For transparency, I want to clarify."

"Go ahead, Blackburn." Hayes's tone was neutral but wary.

"I'm recording this call for review." Her words dropped like stones into still water, steady and restrained. "Let's proceed. I understand this isn't comfortable, but you have my cooperation."

"Your cooperation? What is this about?"

"Kendria Chaplin, sir. I need to explain on the record."

A beat of static-filled silence passed before Hayes answered. "The department needs to keep everything clean." His reluctance bled through the professional veneer like ink through wet paper. "What do you need to explain?"

Blackburn kept her delivery clinical, each word careful. "For the record: I was present when Kendria Chaplin was hit. You know that. The whole world knows that. I was conducting a standard interview related to the case. Nothing more."

"Of course," Chief Hayes replied, his agreement coming too quickly. The rapid response betrayed his eagerness to move past this moment, exactly as Blackburn expected.

"I need to clarify a few details for the record."

"Absolutely." His tone clung to protocol like a lifeline. "What's your statement?"

Blackburn leaned back, her chair creaking softly. Through the office window, she tracked the steady rhythm of movement in the bullpen. Detectives crossed paths, phones rang, the machinery of justice ground forward. "I was with her on Oak Street, where her shop was, discussing the Langston incident. We saw a memorial nearby. She got emotional. We started praying."

"Praying?" The word lifted at the end, Hayes's surprise cutting through the line.

"Yes, for Jenna Langston. We held hands and prayed. I realize that's not standard conduct for a public servant, but it happened. Kendria was shaken by the first attack."

"First attack? Are you saying Chaplin was involved in another incident?"

"Yes, sir. She called 911 to report an autonomous car that mounted the curb and drove along the sidewalk toward her. Traffic Services responded first. I'd met her while canvassing shopkeepers. I left her my card, as I did with others. After Traffic wrapped up, she called me. I arrived maybe half an hour later."

Hayes paused, the silence heavy with calculation. "And you're pursuing that angle?"

"Sir?"

"This earlier attack. Does it connect? Why wasn't I informed?"

"I assumed Traffic Services updated you," Blackburn said, her fingertips finding the smooth edge of her desk. "It's their case. I just came from checking the garage myself. The car pulled from Lake Canada has heavy damage to the passenger side. I expect a match to the scene of the first incident. For now, I'm proceeding on the assumption it's the same vehicle." Her fingers tapped once against the recorder's plastic casing, a subtle reminder that every word was being preserved. "Better to chase a dead end than miss a lead."

"Right," Hayes acknowledged, the word landing flat. "Did you see the car before it hit?"

"No." Blackburn kept her answer unadorned. "We were focused on prayer. There was no warning. One moment she was speaking, and then." She let the silence paint what words could not. The sudden violence, the irrevocable shift from life to death.

The implication settled between them like dust after an explosion.

Blackburn recognized the quality of Hayes's silence now. He was weighing what to ask, measuring how far to push without stepping into territory best left unrecorded. She struck first.

"I don't think I was the target," she said, her tone level as a carpenter's rule. "But I can't rule it out."

Hayes's exhale crackled through the line. "What the hell?" It was not where he had intended to go, but it was where she had steered him.

"I doubt it." Blackburn kept her response clipped, professional. "But, sir, the car that apparently hit Kendria is registered to Charles Roche. I haven't spoken to Sadie Roche yet. Or her attorney. I'm not implying she was the driver or that she's connected. But it is Mr. Roche's car." The faintest trace of satisfaction warmed her voice. She knew how the wealthy and connected made Hayes's blood pressure spike.

"For God's sake, Blackburn. You know the first victim. Then, a woman prays with you, and she ends up dead. Killed by a car owned by a man whose murder you solved last year. Are you the target? Maybe the first Chaplin incident was just bait to get you there?"

"I'm not suggesting Ms. Chaplin set me up." The words hung in the air like smoke. She didn't need to elaborate. Hayes would fill in the blanks himself, his imagination doing her work for her. Every word made the case more labyrinthine, and she savored the complexity.

"Handle this," he said at last, his voice dropping an octave, stripped of official detachment. "Keep the media away from wild theories."

"Facts only," Blackburn replied, her tone crystallizing. "No speculation, no rumors circulating on my end. Brynn called about a supposed connection."

"Of course she did," Hayes muttered, weariness seeping through. "You took care of it?"

"Yes, sir."

"Good." Relief colored his voice like watercolor on wet paper. "Thanks for your cooperation, Blackburn. That covers what I need for the record."

Blackburn offered a smile that existed only in her voice, never touching her eyes. "Glad to be of help, chief. If you need anything further, you know where to reach me."

"I appreciate it." Hayes's goodbye carried the weight of a man backing away from a live wire.

She ended the call and let her gaze rest on the phone's dark screen before her thumb found the recorder's stop button. The small click echoed in the quiet office. These conversations had become routine. Calibrated disclosures designed to satisfy without exposing more than she chose to reveal. Mostly true. Always controlling what they learned. And what they never would.

Chapter 18

Blackburn stood at her window, the last of the daylight cutting a hard edge across the skyline. Orange and violet bled against the glass, sharp but distant. She watched only long enough to mark the day's end, then turned away.

She had reached out to Marla Sutton, who had nothing to add but the names of Jenna's parents. Blackburn called, expressed condolences, and summarized the calls for her notes.

Her office held the thrum of a department still grinding forward. Detectives hunched at their desks, faces lit pale by monitors. Keyboards clicked in an irregular rhythm, punctuated by clipped exchanges that punched through the hush without breaking it. The air carried the stale mix of coffee and sweat that marked long hours.

She leaned into the doorway, arms folded. "Sinclair." Her voice cut through the ambient noise, clear and unmistakable. Sinclair's head snapped up, surprise flickering before he masked it with an easy smile.

"Order food for everyone. My treat." The words were welcomed. "We're here a while longer. After that, you're all going home." She stepped back inside, leaving them to sort out details she didn't care to manage.

Sinclair's chair scraped as he pulled out his phone, thumb scrolling through delivery options. Cooper and Reeves drifted over, their voices carrying just enough to reach her office.

"Pizza?" Cooper said, rubbing the back of his neck.

Reeves grimaced. "Too heavy. Chinese might sit better."

Sinclair flashed them both a quick grin. "Burgers work for me."

The debate rolled on, each suggestion lobbed and batted down. Their laughter came easier now, cutting through fatigue. For these few minutes, the familiar ritual pushed everything else aside. Case files lay abandoned mid-sentence, reports blinked unfinished on screens. A brief pocket of normalcy in work that rarely offered any.

Sinclair pushed to his feet, pocketing his phone. His footsteps crossed the bullpen toward the amber glow spilling from Blackburn's office. He rapped once on the doorframe before stepping through.

"What do you need?" His tone stayed steady, though curiosity threaded underneath.

Blackburn let her head tilt, an invitation without promise. "What you have." The words hung between them, open to interpretation. "I mean, what have you. I'll have what you're having."

Sinclair's jaw tightened as he searched her face for something beneath the surface. After a beat, he gave a curt nod and excused himself to the washroom.

She watched him retreat, lips curving into a smile meant for no one. Some men required so little. A glance, a line drawn in empty air, and their resolve crumbled. She wondered if he'd remember basic hygiene.

Blackburn eased back in her chair as shadows stretched along the walls. She lifted the phone and dialed Jacob Schwartz's office. Each ring echoed against the quiet, unanswered, until voicemail clicked on with its flat, recorded greeting. She listened just long enough to confirm the empty office before cutting the connection.

Her fingers moved to his cell number. The line connected after two rings.

"Hello?" Jacob's voice came through unsteady, caught off-guard.

"Mr. Schwartz." Blackburn kept her voice level and direct. "This is Detective Blackburn, Homicide Division, New Dresden Police."

A pause. She caught the muffled sound of movement. A chair scraping, papers rustling.

"Detective?" His surprise sharpened into caution. "I wasn't expecting—is there a problem?"

"No immediate issue," she replied. "I need to clarify some details concerning Charles Roche's estate." Each word landed with deliberate weight. She heard the subtle shift as his surprise hardened into guarded professionalism. Death had made him busy. Now it was cutting into his evening.

"Of course," he said, steadier now but still wary. "I'm just in the kitchen. Let me get to my office."

Blackburn's gaze drifted to her team's personnel files splayed on her desk. She was already steeling herself for Sinclair's mediocrity.

Through the receiver came the soft shuffle of movement. Papers stacked, a door closing, a chair settling efficiently.

"I'm ready now," Jacob said, his voice sharpened to a lawyer's precision. "What do you need regarding Charles Roche's estate?"

Blackburn straightened, attention narrowing. "I'm interested in a specific asset. Did Mr. Roche own an autonomous vehicle?"

The line went quiet. Then: "He did. A Raider Straight Line model. Recent purchase. Maybe six months before he died."

"Current location?" Blackburn kept her tone flat while her pen hovered over her notebook.

"Should still be at the Roche residence," Jacob said. "Nothing's been moved or liquidated yet."

Blackburn's pen tapped three beats against the desk. "When did you last see it?"

A pause while he considered. "About a week ago. I met with Mrs. Roche, Sadie, about potentially selling Charles's vintage collection."

"And?" Blackburn let the question hang.

"Sadie wants to keep the classics. Sentimental value." His voice carried a note of understanding. "But the Straight Line? She made it clear she never cared for it. Was thinking about listing it."

Blackburn scratched a brief note. "Has she?"

"Not yet. She wanted more time to decide."

"Where is Mrs. Roche now?"

Jacob's tone warmed, relieved by safer ground. "She needed distance from all this. She's at their villa outside Rome. The estate matters have been draining."

Blackburn let the silence stretch until it pulled tight.

"Mr. Schwartz, there's something you need to know." She kept her voice even, letting the weight build naturally. "The Roche Raider Straight Line surfaced at a crime scene."

His sharp intake of breath carried clearly through the line. "That's not... what do you mean?" The lawyer's polish cracked, revealing raw confusion beneath.

"We pulled it from Lake Canada," Blackburn said. "Forensics indicates it was involved in a recent hit-and-run."

Jacob's voice dropped to barely above a whisper. "Was anyone hurt?"

"Yes." Blackburn didn't soften it. "Kendria Chaplin. You might have seen the coverage."

Only his breathing filled the line, shallow and uneven. When he finally spoke, disbelief edged with something like grief. "Christ. I had no idea. How? How did they steal his car?"

Blackburn could picture him clearly. Color draining from his face, knuckles white around the phone, the careful order of his evening shattered. She pressed forward. "Mr. Schwartz, I need to know who had access to that vehicle. We can't proceed without it."

"I'm not..." He stopped, gathered himself. "The car was bio-locked. Charles was particular about security, especially with his vehicles."

Blackburn's pen moved: bio-locked. Through her doorway, the scent of takeout invaded. Burgers and fries, hot grease cutting through the institutional air. The delivery man distributed bags while detectives gathered like moths to warmth.

"So only Charles and Mrs. Roche had access?" She kept her focus sharp. "I'll need Mrs. Roche's travel details. Departure time, airline, anything you have."

"No," he said. "I mean, yes. No, Sadie did not have bio access, only Charles. One more reason to sell. I'll send you her contact information, but she is going to take this very hard. How did it happen? The theft?"

No one but Charles, she wrote next to 'bio-locked'.

"We're looking into it. Thank you for your help," Blackburn replied, preparing to end the call. "You can contact our office later if you need details for an insurance claim. For now, we're holding the car as evidence."

She hung up and leaned back in her chair, the leather breathing beneath her weight. Movement in the bullpen caught her attention: her detectives circling the delivery bags with the restless energy of wolves around prey.

Blackburn stood and rolled her shoulders, vertebrae popping in sequence. Her footsteps struck the linoleum in calculated cadence, each click of her heels announcing her presence, though tonight no one looked up from their food.

She crossed to Dawson's vacant desk and claimed it without ceremony. The burger wrapper crinkled as she peeled it back, releasing steam that carried the scent of charred meat and onions. The first bite hit her tongue with salt and heat, something real and immediate after an hour spent navigating technicalities and impossibilities.

The bullpen settled into its feeding rhythm: paper rustled, ice rattled in cups, low voices haggled over sauce packets and missing napkins. For these few minutes, simple hunger eclipsed everything else. The day retreated to the edges, waiting.

"So," Cooper said, words muffled by food, "anyone else hate these new personal bio cabinet things?" In an effort to meet their own clean desk policy, small filing cabinets were given to each detective. They could be opened only by scanning your hand on the small scanner.

Reeves dragged a napkin across his chin, leaving a faint grease stain. "Hate. Three scans just to get mine calibrated. Clean hand, greasy hand, sweaty hand. Like I'm programming it for every possible disaster."

Sinclair leaned forward, eyes bright. "Mine worked first try. Maybe it's user error?"

Blackburn's mouth twitched at the corner. "Do we know what happens when someone is on vacation and we need the files?"

"Oh Jesus, I never thought of that," Cooper said. "Maybe we should scan all our palms on all the scanners?"

Willow's approach was nearly silent, her sneakers whispering against the floor. She stopped just outside their circle, arms wrapped tight across her middle as she calculated the cost of joining versus retreating to her basement sanctuary.

Blackburn's gaze found her. With a subtle tilt of her head, she summoned Willow forward. "Come on. You're part of this team too."

"Hey Willow, what about these bio scanners? How do we get to the files when someone is on vacation?" Reeves asked.

Willow settled at the periphery, surveying the graveyard of wrappers and empty cartons. The hollow sensation in her stomach sharpened.

"Freddie and I pre-scanned our palms as master keys," she said. "Either of us can unlock them. But it registers who does what, of course."

"Why not? They have access to everything on the servers," Sinclair said as he shook salt off a fry and popped it in his mouth.

Blackburn considered her options: share her food with Willow like a mother bird, or surrender it completely.

Blackburn pushed her fries across the desk and put her remaining burger down. "Take it. I'm done."

The unexpected kindness caught in Willow's throat. She blinked hard, swallowing the surge of emotion before it could betray her. Not here, not among these detectives who wore armor as naturally as skin.

She murmured thanks and rolled up a chair. The fries were still warm, salt crystals rough against her fingertips. Conversation flowed around her as she ate in small, deliberate bites. The others found reasons to look elsewhere while she ate, but Blackburn's gaze held no judgment.

Cooper drew her in eventually, asking about new cybersecurity protocols. Willow answered between mouthfuls: "The new NIST Post-Quantum Cryptography standards are being rolled out across most federal systems, plus there's the updated ISO 27001 framework with enhanced zero-trust requirements."

"Zero-trust?" Reeves asked.

The air shifted as Blackburn straightened, warmth draining from her expression like water through sand. "Let's get back to it," Blackburn said. Her attention fixed on Reeves. "Updates from your interviews?"

Reeve's humor evaporated. He cleared his throat, the sound rough in the sudden quiet.

"I called Kendria Chaplin's parents. They're in West Hamilton, so it had to be over the phone." His gaze drifted past Blackburn to some middle distance.

The pause stretched taut. No one filled it. Willow pressed her back against the chair back, feeling the curve on her spine as something tight holding her.

"It was difficult for them," Reeves continued, voice dropping low. "They hadn't seen her since Christmas. No known issues. No enemies. They insisted she stayed clear of trouble."

"Any recent contact? Texts, calls?" Blackburn kept her tone clinical. "Anything unusual?"

Reeves shook his head slowly. "Nothing. They said she was in good spirits last time they spoke, focused on her business." His throat worked as he swallowed. "They kept asking why this happened. I had nothing for them."

"And the others? The boyfriend?" Sinclair asked.

"Nothing. He was locked up, started crying when I told him. Nothing from either Sandra or Marcus Williams. Hoping to get the phone warrant tomorrow," Reeves said as he shoved the last of his burger into his mouth.

A muscle tightened along Blackburn's jaw, there and gone. Her gaze swept the room before landing on Willow with laser precision. "Willow, give us your findings from the event data recorder."

Willow adjusted her seat, the leather groaning. She wiped her fingers on her pants and reached across Blackburn to access Dawson's keyboard. Blackburn turned the monitor so others could also see.

Willow pulled up a report, its white glow washing across her face. Her voice emerged clear, if quiet, cutting through the recycled air. "This is the Charles Roche car. I've reviewed the data from the autonomous vehicle. There are anomalies. Big ones."

The room stilled. Every detective's gaze fixed on her.

"The car activated at 8:23 a.m.," Willow said, eyes tracking data streams across the screen.

Blackburn leaned forward. "Wait, how? It has a bio-lock."

"Yep. It was not activated. No doors opened before it started moving."

"How?"

"I don't know yet." Willow shrugged.

Blackburn waved her hand. "Go on."

"It drove directly to 483 Oak Street. The system logged an impact at 8:58 a.m."

Sinclair shifted, frowning. "That's not when Kendria was struck."

"Correct. That was an earlier attempt. Kendria called the police after that crash."

"Traffic Services responded," Blackburn added. "I've got their initial report."

"Afterward, GPS shows the vehicle circled the block five times, then parked and powered down."

The LED lights hummed in the heavy pause.

"That's around when Kendria called me. Traffic Services didn't think it was important enough, I suppose." Blackburn's voice barely disturbed the stillness.

"At 10:43 a.m., it powered on again. No doors opened. It returned to Oak Street and accelerated sharply at 10:46 a.m. That's when it struck Ms. Chaplin."

Silence suffocated the room. Cooper released a slow breath; Reeves stared across the table, brow furrowed. Sinclair's gaze darted between Willow and Blackburn, searching for answers none of them had yet found.

"She was the target," Willow said, gripping the tablet's edge.

"After the incident, the car left. It kept to the speed limit, never broke any traffic laws. The vehicle's destination was Lake Canada. It drove straight into the water."

She paused, holding Blackburn's gaze. "The EDR shows no doors opened at any time. No in-car interaction. There were technical anomalies. Chassis resonance, structural harmonics. But nothing that explains how this happened."

Blackburn studied her. "Just obvious outcomes."

"Exactly," Willow said with a small, satisfied smile.

"Put it in your report." Blackburn's tone sharpened, cutting through the room's thick atmosphere. She leaned forward, her forearms pressing into the desk's cool surface. Her question emerged quietly, each word precise: "How is that possible? Where did the command originate? The command to hit Kendria and then the command to drive to the lake?"

Willow's throat worked as she swallowed. She felt every eye in the room turn toward her, the weight pressing against her skin.

"It isn't clear," she admitted after a moment, the words tasting bitter. "I've checked the system repeatedly. The Integrity Map checksum failed. A recovery log was initiated but was incomplete. The core mobility AI continued operations in ghost redundancy mode. That's a last-resort behavior protocol not intended for extended use." She stopped, frustration tightening the muscles around her jaw.

Blackburn tapped a finger.

Willow cleared her throat. "It's like the car's brain glitched, so it used its emergency instincts to keep driving."

Silence settled like dust, its weight pressing down on the room. An autonomous car executed a killing and destroyed itself, all without violating a single rule of the road

Blackburn's gaze sharpened to a blade's edge, her voice low and direct. "Is a remote hack possible? Could Kieran Mott be involved? With his toy?"

Willow's fingers drummed once against the table before she shook her head. "No evidence points that way."

Blackburn pressed on, relentless. "What would we see if someone used an external device, something like a game controller?"

Willow angled forward, the laptop screen reflecting in her glasses as she chose her words. "If a console was used, the system would show odd entropy patterns. Synthetic Signature Fingerprints. Because of delays between an old USB interface and the CAN bus. The EDR shows nothing like that."

Reeves scratched his stubbled chin, the rasp audible in the quiet. "Translate?"

Willow kept it simple, her hands sketching invisible connections in the air. "There'd be a clear digital trace between the two different things. I didn't find one. I had Freddie double-check my findings. Nothing."

Blackburn's persistence filled the room like smoke. "What if they used digital gloves? I've seen those things before," she said, flexing her hand as if she was wearing one.

Willow met her eyes, the LED glare harsh between them, understanding the gravity now. "VR gloves? Depends on how they're interfacing. Gloves without advanced haptic feedback still create timing errors. Latency artifacts. Like sending Morse code through a straw."

Reeves's chair creaked as he leaned back. "So, yes or no?"

Willow allowed herself the briefest smile, a crack in her professional mask. "Possible in theory, but only with next-level custom hardware. Stuff you don't buy off the shelf."

Blackburn studied her a second longer, the silence stretching taut. "Sounds like you've run the scenario."

Willow's shoulder lifted in a minimal shrug. "Thinking in hypotheticals is part of my job."

Blackburn stood, her movement decisive, ending the discussion with a sharp nod. "Upload your draft reports and head home. We'll regroup in the morning."

Chairs scraped against the linoleum as the team cleaned up and filed out. Sinclair crammed his files into his cabinet and slipped away first, keeping his head down, his farewell mumbled into his collar. Willow followed, her footsteps silent on the worn floor as she exited behind him.

Cooper took his time, methodically tidying his notes, the paper rustling as he squared the edges. Paperwork safely stored in the cabinet by his desk. When he finished saving his report draft, the keyboard clicking softly, he gave a brief nod to the others and slipped out. The door shut with a quiet snick behind him.

Reeves pushed to his feet with tired stiffness, his joints protesting, lines of fatigue deepening around his eyes like cracks in old leather. Blackburn's voice halted him, smooth but unyielding. "Reeves, in my office." Her tone carried an easy calm, but steel lay beneath.

He stepped into the dim office, the air cooler here, tinged with the faint scent of old coffee. Blackburn sat at her desk, relaxed but commanding the space. She didn't waste words. "You had a look when Willow spoke in the meeting." Her gaze met his and held, unwavering. "What's on your mind?"

Reeves shifted, his shoes scuffing against the gray carpet's rough weave. "It's odd," he said slowly, tasting each word. "She spotted that exploit right away, the one for hiding prints. You ask about bypasses, and suddenly she has all the details."

Blackburn's expression remained neutral, giving nothing. "That's her job. She runs point on our digital issues. Nothing unusual in knowing how things break."

"Still," Reeves hesitated, his fingers working at a loose thread on his jacket cuff. His brow creased as he searched for firmer ground.

"You're uneasy because she answered too quickly." Blackburn let that settle between them like sediment in still water before continuing.

"I know you've been looking at the tech stuff," he said as he leaned back. "Your notes to us were pretty out there with hypotheticals. Did Willow help?"

Blackburn smiled and gave him a curt nod.

"I bet nothing comes of any of it. Microwave mesh bullshit. Like she is trying to waste our time."

Blackburn took in a deep breath. "She does seem to be holding back." Blackburn tapped her pen on her desk. "I want your concerns on record when you draft your report."

He looked up, surprise flickering across his weathered features. "Even if it's just instinct?"

"Especially then." Blackburn's reply emerged quiet but certain as bedrock. "I trust your instincts."

"It's unsettling to think."

"Do it anyway. Thinking is your job. If you have suspicions, act on them," Blackburn said.

He straightened, the doubt easing from his face like morning shadows. "We're not paid to like the answers, are we? I'll add it for review tomorrow."

"Good." She watched him leave, noting his step, the burden of new doubt pressing alongside fatigue.

Blackburn remained, the desk lamp's yellow light slicing through darkness, creating sharp boundaries between shadow and illumination. She worked through her team's reports, the pages whispering as she turned them. She read carefully, tracing not only what was stated but what lingered in the spaces between words.

Something important had been left out. Someone vital had been overlooked.

She needed to rip through this case, eviscerate it to get to the guts of the matter.

Blackburn pressed cool fingers to her temples, the persistent throb behind her eyes fighting her attempts at focus. The tension wound through her shoulders and neck like wire, making concentration difficult, but she forced herself to continue.

She could feel it in her bones: she stood at the center of this. Everything circled back to her like water finding its level.

Opening her leather notebook, the leather worn smooth from years of use, never the network, not yet, she found reassurance in its familiar weight. She uncapped her pen. The click broke the office's quiet like a snapped twig.

On a fresh page, the paper's texture rough beneath her palm, she wrote: "Cases CCTR-02412 / CCTR-02441." Beneath those numbers, the names Jenna and Kendria stood out in black ink. The codes felt as thin as tissue compared to who they represented.

She paused, pen poised above paper, before putting the pen down. She knew it was easy enough to read the information from the page below. Instead, she pulled out her personal phone and opened up a digital notepad.

SUSPECT LIST

Each line recorded suspicion, mapping a web that spread out from her.

Primaries

<u>Willow Adler</u>

Has access to systems and schedules

Possesses technical expertise

Knows my patterns with other women

Could be lying about technical evidence

<u>Kieran Mott</u>

Ex-employee of Stan Raider group, with grudge

Can manipulate autonomous vehicles

Was possibly near one crime scene (Chaplin)

Technical signature doesn't match (but maybe he has gotten better)

Need interview!

<u>Adam Sinclair</u>

Obsessed with me

Shows stalking behavior

Uses tech for tracking

Possible rejection motive

May have technical knowledge beyond what I know

Secondaries

<u>Unidentified Stan Raider employee, or competitor</u>

Business interests in autonomous vehicles

Possible sabotage, destroy company

Has any competitor advertised themselves as safer than Straight Line?

<u>Brynn Cassidy</u>

Reporter with inside information

Unusual access to confidential details

Possible involvement in creating incidents for story

Seems to hate the cars

Unikelys

<u>Charles or Sadie Roche</u>

Deceased but his car/bio-lock involved

Possible posthumous connection through compromised security

<u>Chief Hayes</u>

Political motivations

History of betrayal

<u>Unknown</u>

Any released murderers, friends, family, too fucking many!

Blackburn sat back, letting the silence settle in again like dust in an abandoned room, keeping her doubts where only she could see them.

She had one more name, and had to decide if he was secondary or primary. Blackburn hesitated, her fingers hovering over the keyboard, and made space under Willow's name.

<u>Mitch Dawson</u>

Accused me of murder – set me up to be arrested?

God, there are so many possibilities.

Doubt settled in her chest like a stone: any one of them could be involved. The possibility that it might be someone within her own circle, someone she'd counted on, lingered in the quiet room like an unwelcome guest.

She needed a distraction.

Blackburn looked at her phone's screen casting pale light across her knuckles as her thumb hovered over the familiar black-and-red icon: BDSMessages.

She tapped it open.

Lilith's avatar glowed green. She was online. A soft pulse at the edge of her digital presence.

Lilith had reached out first, eager and polite. But Blackburn had been busy and told her so with a brief, respectful message.

Now the urge to follow up pressed against her ribs like a held breath.

Well, well. Look who's back online<

The typing bubble flickered to life almost immediately, three dots dancing as if Lilith had been waiting.

>I was wondering if you'd notice

>Been thinking about our conversation

Have you now? And what exactly were you thinking about?<

The pause stretched thin as wire.

Then:

>*That you seem like someone who doesn't ask twice*

>*I like that in someone. Makes things simpler*

Blackburn sank back in her chair, releasing a small, satisfied breath. She kept her body still and focused on someone across the city.

Simpler how?<

No reply at first. The silence hummed with possibility, then:

>*I know what I want*

>*And I'm pretty sure you know what you want too*

>*No games, no pretending I don't want it*

Blackburn's smile curved slowly into something firmer, more possessive. That familiar tension between command and patience settled into her bones like muscle memory, returning after a rest. She savored the game: the give and take built on trust and anticipation. It wasn't simply about denial; it was about a negotiated pleasure.

Enlighten me then. What is it you want?<

The pause stretched longer this time, taut as a held note, but when Lilith answered, her submission poured through:

>*Someone who takes charge*

>*Someone who isn't afraid to leave marks*

>*The kinds that remind me later what happened*

Blackburn picked up her edge, heightened now by anticipation and bravado. She savored that suggestion.

Marks? You sound like you can handle more than most<

Another pause, the kind that felt like someone gathering courage. When Lilith's response came through, it arrived all at once:

>*Try me*

>*I'm not fragile and I'm definitely not vanilla*

Blackburn's gaze traced the last word like fingertips mapping her skin. That kind of offer stirred something low in her belly, a tight, warm coil of power more intoxicating than pleasure itself.

But she did not want another Jenna, another woman who stretched the truth. She answered carefully:

Bold words. Easy to say behind a screen<

Lilith responded quickly this time, messages firing as rapidly as heartbeats:

>*Then don't keep me behind it*

>*I told you I'm not looking for gentle. I meant it*

Blackburn rewarded good manners when they deserved it. And right now, Lilith was being very good indeed beneath that vulnerable hunger. She crossed her right leg over her left, squeezed, and kept typing:

What if I told you I was thinking about<
bending you over my knee<

A beat passed, her thumb hovering over the keys before she added:

until you forgot how to be so confident?<

There was no delay in Lilith's response now:

>*I'd ask when and where*

>*And I'd probably show up early*

A clink came from the hallway. Cleaners. Blackburn held her breath until silence settled completely, then continued:

Good answer. You might actually be worth my time<

Lilith took longer this time. Whether nerves or honesty slowed her response, Blackburn couldn't tell. But eventually:

>I don't disappoint

That raw truth struck deeper than most sexted fantasies ever managed. It wasn't just desire anymore. It was an admission. Blackburn's tongue swept slowly across her bottom lip before she softened what came next just enough:

We'll see about that. Would tomorrow afternoon work for you?<

>Absolutely

>Fair warning though

>I bruise beautifully

>Just in case you were wondering

Good girl. Beg me when you are ready<

Her ending line came without flourish, but weighted enough to linger on her screen long after her phone darkened.

Chapter 19

The morning light sliced through the blinds, cutting pale bars across Blackburn's desk. She sat rigid, exhaustion carved into the hollows beneath her eyes. Her spine ached from the office couch's unforgiving springs. The metallic aftertaste of vending machine cheese coated her tongue. Coffee had turned bitter and cold beside her elbow, useless against the fog clouding her thoughts.

Her gaze remained fixed on the computer screen. Evidence summaries, time-stamped videos, and half-formed timelines bled together in the monitor's harsh glow. She worked methodically, searching for the thread that would unravel everything: a pattern buried in the noise. So far, nothing had emerged. Details circled back on themselves, motive hidden behind routine and contradiction.

Her chair groaned as she shifted, muscles locked from hours of stillness. She ignored the protest. Comfort was a luxury she couldn't afford, not with this case closing in and the chief expecting answers.

A notification pulsed on her phone, cutting through the quiet: BDSMessages. Her thumb hovered over the screen. The app had been her sanctuary, an escape from precinct politics and crime scene photos. Now that boundary felt paper-thin. Personal and professional worlds threatened to merge like watercolors in rain. No one knew who anyone was online, anyway.

A knock rattled her door.

She swiped the app closed. "What is it now?" The words came out flat and guarded. Her hand drifted to her holster by instinct.

Sinclair shouldered through before she could say more. "I finished my report, boss." His shoulders curved inward as he extended the file, fingers pale against manila. His gaze slid past her face.

"Which report? The false arrest report?"

"The tracker report, boss."

Blackburn gestured to the chair. He dropped into the seat across from her, staring at the bookshelf on the wall behind her head. The silence stretched taut between them. His recent use of a police-issued GPS tracker on her personal vehicle crossed every professional line. She had ordered him to document his actions, to explain himself on paper. She doubted she'd find "reckless" or "invasive" anywhere in his prose.

Blackburn studied him, spine straight but relaxed. She weighed her options: make an example now or let him dig himself deeper. She let the silence work on him, watching for cracks in his facade.

He placed the report on her desk with deliberate care. Paper whispered against wood. His hands retreated to his lap, fingers laced tight, shoulders braced.

Blackburn leaned forward. Her eyes tracked across the document, mouth quirking as she read aloud: "Out of genuine concern for the health and safety of Detective First Class Morgan Blackburn." She lifted her gaze to his, voice neutral except for the razor's edge beneath. "Thoughtful."

Before Sinclair could respond, movement caught Blackburn's peripheral vision. Willow lingered at the bullpen entrance, poised between retreat and advance, absorbing every gesture in the office. Blackburn catalogued the new variable and adjusted her approach.

She tapped her ear twice and flicked her eyes toward the door. *Listen.* She wanted witnesses.

She turned back to Sinclair, voice dropping low. "Tell me. Was it you outside my home a few weeks ago?"

Sinclair's jaw flexed; air hissed through his nostrils. Willow went still just inside the doorframe, gaze darting between them like a spectator at a tennis match.

The fool hadn't noticed her. Hadn't noticed the entire bullpen tracking Willow tracking Sinclair tracking Blackburn.

The question hung in dead air, demanding truth while the precinct watched.

"Yes." The admission leaked out defenseless. "I was watching your home." Words tumbled faster, uneven. "But I never looked into your bedroom or bathroom. I wouldn't cross that line."

Willow's face shifted from surprise into something raw. Her fingers curled into fists at her sides. She held herself like glass about to shatter.

Blackburn kept her eyes on Sinclair while cataloguing Willow's every micro-expression: the tension in her shoulders, the white of her knuckles, the carefulness of her breathing. The office walls pressed closer, air thick with unspoken accusations.

"I almost shot you," Blackburn said finally.

"I know. I nearly shit myself when I saw you pull your gun out. I ran so fast." Relief colored his voice, as if he'd escaped again just by remembering.

Blackburn settled back, regarding him with the detachment of a scientist studying a specimen. "How long?" Her tone gave nothing away.

Sinclair's eyes skittered across the room, landing nowhere. His shoulders hunched as if expecting a blow. "About three months." The words barely disturbed the air.

"Three months." She let it sit between them. "That's dedication for simple concern. My neighbor watched you plant the tracker a few weeks back."

"I... it kept falling off somehow. But I didn't know anyone saw. I'm sorry." His head dropped forward.

"You will be."

Willow's breath caught. That phrase belonged to Blackburn's darker moments, to heat and surrender. Why here? Why now?

"I'm not obsessed." Color flooded Sinclair's face; the protest came out raw and too loud. "I just worry sometimes. You take on too much, these cases..."

Blackburn cut him off. "Bullshit." She let the diagnosis hang, giving him time to feel its weight.

Then she shifted her attention to the doorway, eyes landing on Willow with manufactured surprise. "Willow. How long have you been standing there?"

Sinclair twisted in his chair. Seeing Willow stripped his last pretense. His mouth worked without sound.

"That'll be all, Sinclair," Blackburn said, dismissing him with a gesture. "Go."

He lurched upright and fled, sliding past Willow without making eye contact. She tracked his retreat, expression locked behind her glasses like a closed door.

Blackburn's focus snapped to her. She indicated the vacant chair. "Close the door. Sit."

Willow complied, the click of the latch sealing them in together.

"What just happened?" The question came softly but urgently.

Blackburn reclined, professional mask firmly in place. "Sinclair's developed a hobby. Following me." Her tone stayed conversational, revealing nothing. "For my health and safety, apparently."

She pushed Sinclair's report across the desk. Willow's eyes swept the first lines; her mouth compressed into a thin line before her attention returned to Blackburn.

"Maybe he saw us," Blackburn continued, voice clinical as a coroner's notes. "Maybe he watched us the other night." She let the possibility settle between them like a loaded gun.

Heat crept up Willow's neck, but she held her silence. Her hands lay still in her lap, fingers flexing once before freezing. Blackburn observed without reaction.

"Don't let Sinclair distract you," Blackburn said finally. "I'll handle him." The promise carried weight.

Willow paused, concern etched on every line of her face. "Watch your back," she said.

Blackburn exhaled, a short, brittle sound that might have been laughter if warmth hadn't abandoned it entirely. "Everyone seems to have an opinion about my safety lately."

The sarcasm cut through the office air like a blade through paper. Willow sat motionless, uncertainty shifting across her features as the words settled between them.

Blackburn leaned forward, her voice dropping to something softer. "Don't trouble yourself over Sinclair. You'll protect me, won't you, little Fawn?" She let the nickname slip free, intimate as a whispered secret. The word landed gently, and something shifted behind Willow's carefully maintained guard.

Willow broke into a wide smile and nodded happily, almost giggling. "I will."

"If you're feeling bold," Blackburn continued, her gaze unwavering, "there's an opportunity to unsettle him. Subtle work, nothing permanent. Your skills make it simple enough to place something on his computer. An image where it shouldn't be. A questionable search term in his history. Just enough to make him sweat. Nothing more."

Willow's eyes searched Blackburn's face, reading the angles and shadows there. "You want me to?" The question hung in the air, barely voiced.

A smile ghosted across Blackburn's mouth. "I do."

The resistance melted from Willow's frame, replaced by something brighter: anticipation mixed with relief. She nodded, confidence seeping back into her posture. "I'll take care of it." Her laugh escaped, sudden and genuine. "Sometimes it helps to be a little bad."

"A little bad," Blackburn echoed, punctuating the words with a quick wink. She settled back in her chair, amusement softening the hard lines of her expression. She tracked the transformation in Willow's bearing as spine straightened and shoulders squared, the shift both subtle and magnetic.

Willow moved toward the door. At the threshold, she hesitated, throwing a glance over her shoulder. Their eyes met and held. Admiration flickered there, shadowed by something harder to name.

The door clicked shut, leaving Blackburn wrapped in the white noise of LED hum and distant keyboard clatter from the bullpen.

She sat motionless, letting the silence pool around her. Then, a soft chime split the quiet.

Her phone screen lit up with the BDSMessages notification.

She didn't smile. But her thumb moved faster than intended as she unlocked it.

>*Today*

>*I've made a three-hour break in my day*

>*Please don't make me wait any longer*

Ah, Lilith. Three lines. Raw, unvarnished enough to make Blackburn's fingers tighten around the device. Her breath caught quickly, while her expression remained perfectly composed at her desk.

Lilith's profile photo filled the screen. No face, just pale skin, a black lace bra showing off her décolletage, a red choker with a black onyx stone around her throat.

Blackburn pressed her knuckles against the desk's cool surface before typing.

Good. Meet me at Merlot's on Fifth<

1 PM<

Table under the name Parker<

She knew it was close to a QuickStay.

The response landed instantly:

>Perfect

>Parker

Blackburn exhaled through pursed lips, quiet enough to escape notice beyond her glass walls. The thought of her hand on Lilith's ass made her fingers tingle.

Wear that red choker<

A soft notification, then the image loaded: Lilith's shadowed décolletage, a white shirt against pale skin, a sheen of perspiration catching light at her collarbone. Her hand held a red choker up against her throat. Behind her, a large window and nothing but sky.

>This one?

Blackburn pressed two fingers to the hollow of her own throat as she responded:

Yes<

Beautiful<

You are dressed like you have somewhere important to be<

Something that comes off easily<

Blackburn shifted, crossing her legs tighter beneath the desk. A sound threatened to escape. She caught it, held it, let composure settle over her features like a mask. This one wasn't like Jenna: no games, no pretense. More like Kendria: direct, certain, unashamed of her hunger.

> Understood

>Anything else I should know?

Her fingers traced the forgotten file on her desk, movements deliberate and unhurried.

We'll talk limits over lunch<
Come prepared to be honest about<
what you can and can't handle<

Lilith's reply hit instantly:

>In the name of honesty

>I wasn't kidding about the spanking

>Just so you know what you're working with

She released a breath through barely parted lips. Her fingers found their rhythm on the keypad:

Don't be late<

Blackburn signed off BDSMessages and quickly booked a four-hour room at the QuickStay, and a table at Merlot's.

* * *

The monitor's clock glowed: 9:47 AM. The hours would stretch between now and one o'clock, each minute weighted with mundane tasks that couldn't quite suppress the electric current running beneath her skin.

Blackburn's pen scratched across the paper in tight, controlled strokes. The Deonte Mills file spread before her: autopsy photographs, witness statements typed on coffee-stained forms, timelines that refused to align. Each detail catalogued itself in her mind's filing system. A child's death demanded her full attention; the facts arranged themselves like evidence tags, emotion held at arm's length.

The squad room's familiar sounds created white noise against her concentration: keyboards clicking, phones trilling, the gurgle of the ancient coffee maker. Yet something disrupted the pattern. Dawson's desk sat too quiet, his absence stretching backward through memory. Last week? The week before? The gap widened with each passing hour.

Her phone felt cool against her palm as she dialed.

"Hayes."

"It's Blackburn." The words emerged clipped, professional. "Dawson hasn't been in contact for some time."

Silence stretched across the line before Hayes spoke. "You're worried about him?"

"Me? No. But I want a welfare check done. Matter of protocol. Not one of my team. Uniform please."

"All right. I'll assign someone now and update you when I have news."

"Thank you." The call ended with a soft click.

Finally, just a half hour longer. Her desk drawer slid open on well-oiled tracks. Inside, cheap toys in crinkled plastic caught the overhead LEDs. She selected the compact vibrator, its weight negligible as it disappeared into her leather satchel. The bag settled against her hip as she rose.

The washroom's harsh lighting revealed every detail in the mirror. Blackburn's fingers worked through her hair, coaxing waves that softened her usual severity. She studied her reflection: the resolute expression, the steady gaze that gave nothing away. Her fingers found the top button of her blouse, releasing it with deliberate slowness. Cool air touched newly exposed skin.

The squad room's atmosphere shifted when she returned. Sinclair stood frozen beside his desk, pupils dilated, chest rising and falling with barely controlled breaths. Blackburn's gaze swept over him, acknowledging, dismissing, one eyebrow lifting in silent question.

She positioned herself where only he could enjoy the show. The second button came undone with theatrical precision, revealing the delicate edge of lace beneath starched cotton. Then the third. The sound of Sinclair's sharp intake of breath cut through the ambient noise.

Her smile remained minimal, a cat's satisfaction. Each button returned to its place with the same deliberate care, her fingers moving like a conductor's through familiar music. Sinclair tracked every movement as she left, jaw tight with poorly concealed hunger.

Fun and games.

The stairwell echoed. Coffee-bitter air mixed with the sharp bite of industrial disinfectant, scents so familiar they barely registered anymore. Each footfall counted down the minutes until escape.

The lobby opened before her, afternoon light slanting through tall windows. Her trained eye swept the space automatically. Willow stood near reception, tablet glowing in her hands, data scrolling in endless streams as the receptionist sat idly by. Their eyes met in a moment of mutual assessment, nothing given or taken. The slight dip of Willow's chin acknowledged what went unspoken.

Blackburn felt Willow's gaze track the details: the artfully loosened hair, the collar that suggested rather than revealed. She maintained her pace, heels striking tile in a steady rhythm, each step carrying her toward the door and away from scrutiny.

The lobby door swung shut with a pneumatic hiss, sealing away the station's familiar chaos. Behind her, Willow remained motionless except for the subtle turn of her head, the only evidence of thoughts left unvoiced.

Blackburn arrived at Merlot's with several minutes to spare. The restaurant's quiet refinement spoke for itself: amber light pooled across mahogany surfaces, conversation drifted in waves, and somewhere beneath it all, porcelain touched porcelain with quiet restraint. The maître d' acknowledged her with a brief nod, familiar enough to remember her preferences, professional enough not to linger, and guided her to the corner booth.

She slid into leather that held the warmth of the atmosphere, fingertips finding the tablecloth's crisp fold. The space felt familiar, its geography mapped in her mind: the service corridor angling left past the kitchen, the alley door's heavy bolt, which servers moved and which merely drifted. She filed each detail away without conscious thought.

Her gaze swept the dining room in arcs. She registered the businessman who'd ordered his third martini, the couple whose silence stretched too thin, the server who kept touching his pocket, checking tips or something else. The movements around her created patterns, and patterns told stories.

She adjusted her position through micro-movements that kept her back to the wall and her sightlines clear. The tension lived in small places: the set of her shoulders, the angle at which she held her water glass, how her breathing stayed deliberately even. Anyone watching would see composure. Anyone trained might notice the readiness beneath.

Time moved in restaurant rhythms through the soft percussion of service, candlelight wavering across white linen. Then Lilith entered.

Blackburn caught her silhouette before the hostess reached her: red choker with a black onyx stone, crisp white shirt, tan slacks, sensible shoes, hair dark as ink. The hostess motioned, Lilith nodded and walked as Blackburn looked at her watch, and back to Lilith.

Lilith moved through the dining room like smoke through still air. Her shoes made no sound on the polished wood, but conversations stuttered in her wake. She didn't acknowledge the attention; she simply existed within it, separate and self-contained.

As Lilith approached, Blackburn rose and extended her hand. Their grips met firm and cool. "Nice to meet you. I'm Morgan." Her voice carried just far enough, pitched low beneath the ambient noise.

Lilith's fingers pressed back with equal pressure. Something like amusement touched her mouth as she said, "I'm Lilith. Nice to meet you." Her gaze dropped deliberately to where Blackburn's top parted, revealing the edge of black lace, then lifted without hurry.

"Beautiful choker." Blackburn released Lilith's hand, vertebrae aligning as she reclaimed her composure.

They settled into their seats, the space between them charged but contained. Blackburn sat with geometric precision, spine straight, hands visible, every gesture deliberate. Lilith leaned forward, elbows claiming table space, her posture a study in controlled provocation. Where Blackburn offered restraint, Lilith promised something sharper.

The restaurant's soundtrack continued around them: silver against china, ice settling in glasses, fragments of other lives playing out at other tables. But their booth had become its own territory, separate from the larger performance.

"So, Morgan," Lilith said, testing the name's weight. "What brings us here?"

Blackburn's finger traced her water glass rim, casual motion masking assessment. "It's private enough for conversation. I have booked a QuickStay at Fifth and Front." A pause, calculated. "It works for me. What do you think?"

Lilith's laugh came low and certain. "I like a woman who handles all the details." Her attention never wavered from Blackburn's face.

The server materialized at their periphery, notepad ready. "Anything to drink?"

Lilith's fingers touched the wine list but waited.

"Water for me," Blackburn said definitively.

Lilith's head tilted, interest sharpening. "No interest in loosening up?"

"I do my best work clear-headed." The words carried weight beyond their surface.

Understanding flickered between them.

"Vodka cranberry," Lilith told the server.

Once alone again, Lilith shifted into a posture both relaxed and alert, a cat considering whether to play.

"You were a little late," Blackburn said. "You told me you'd be early."

"A woman who remembers," she observed, approval threading through her tone. "I admire that."

"A long memory." Blackburn's voice remained level. "You also said you'd be honest."

Lilith's laugh cut warm through the air, but with edges. "Honestly, I got here as quickly as I could. But if it concerns you, make me regret it." Her smile sharpened.

Blackburn leaned in, elbows claiming table space, matching Lilith's earlier posture. "Be careful what you wish for." Her voice dropped, intimate despite the public setting.

The server's return interrupted the building charge. He brought the drinks and took their orders.

Alone again, the air between them settled into something denser, more focused. Their questions circled closer to the truth with each exchange.

Blackburn's attention found Lilith's choker again, red leather pressed against her pale throat. A stunning statement. "It stands out in person," she observed, voice neutral as water. "Looks sturdy."

Lilith's smile bloomed slowly and knowingly. She angled her neck just enough to catch the light. "It is. Custom made." A beat. "Built for pleasure."

The words hung between them, weighted with invitation. Blackburn's stillness deepened, her pulse betraying what her face wouldn't. She studied Lilith with the focus of someone recalculating odds.

"Are you open on the first date? To take things to your limit?" The question came quietly, privately. "You're comfortable with pressure?"

Lilith met her gaze straight on, her answer written in the steady rise and fall of her breath, the deliberate placement of her hands on the table, the way she held herself open to scrutiny while keeping her secrets close.

"I am," Lilith said, her tone like water finding its level. "I've been there before with people I trust." Her confidence settled between them, unforced. "There's a certain draw to it. To letting go for a moment." The words hung in the air like smoke, inviting but restrained.

Blackburn listened, the clink of cutlery on china marking time around them. She considered the edges of risk that Lilith represented, the appeal familiar from her own work: danger and thrill running parallel tracks. "Do you have to trust your partner completely?" she asked, voice quiet enough to slip beneath the restaurant's ambient hum.

"I know where my boundaries are," Lilith replied. She held Blackburn's gaze, pupils dark in the warm light. "And I know how to yield when I want to."

Blackburn allowed a pause. The air between them tightened like a drawn bowstring, but neither moved to fill it with excess. "I understand," she said, each word deliberate. "Letting someone else take control has its own kind of power."

The server approached, setting dishes down with care. Steam rose from the plates. For a moment, attention shifted to the simple act of eating. Only after the server's footsteps faded did they exchange another glance, weighted by everything left unsaid.

Blackburn focused on Lilith instead of her cooling food. She kept her tone even, practical: "What about specifics? What works best for you?"

Lilith's response came quickly. "Pull my pants down," she said, voice dropping to match Blackburn's volume. "Bend me over your knee. Start soft, work up from there. Use a little restraint, clear signals. Sometimes a hand over my mouth as a reminder not to scream." Her smile was small, contained.

"Good. Clear communication." She paused, considering. "I prefer to set the pace myself. You'll let me know if it's too much?" Blackburn asked, intent on clarity.

"Yes," Lilith answered, raising a piece of cauliflower to her lips. "I'll keep my eyes closed. Makes every reaction more intense." She paused before adding, "I've made the usual preparations, if the opportunity arises."

Blackburn smiled broadly. Approval and lust flickered behind her eyes. "Good to know. I have the room from two until six."

Lilith nodded once, steady as stone. "I'm excited." Then she leaned in, lowering her voice to thread private meaning through the lunch service din. "And you, Morgan, what do you want?"

Blackburn set her glass down with precision, the base meeting the table without a sound. She met Lilith's eyes without wavering. "Control." Her voice softened, each word clipped and quiet. "I like to have a woman under my hand. To hold her so she feels the edge: right there, just shy of too far." She watched Lilith's pupils dilate, noted the subtle shift in her breathing. "You'll beg me for more before I'm finished."

Silence settled over their table. The restaurant noise receded until only their breathing remained audible.

Lilith's fingers curled against her glass. "I hope you'll prove it," she said, voice almost lost in the space between them.

A faint smile crossed Blackburn's lips. Sunlight stretched across the table and caught on Lilith's cheekbones, illuminating each line of anticipation.

Blackburn signaled for the check with a tilt of her chin, never breaking eye contact.

"How long do you think you'll last?" she asked, her fingers flexing around imagined flesh.

Lilith straightened in her seat, spine finding steel. "Longer than you expect."

"Ah, a tough woman? I like it. You'll need to be thoroughly tenderized."

Lilith laughed, her head back, the choker bobbing, drawing Blackburn's gaze.

Blackburn catalogued details she'd revisit later: the way Lilith's fingers drummed against the table, the slight flush at her collarbone. "Ready when you are," Lilith said, and the casual words carried a weight that made Blackburn's breath catch.

Their bill settled, the two women left their table. The restaurant's din faded as they stepped onto the city sidewalk, swept into the flow of foot traffic. Blackburn took the lead. When Lilith drifted ahead by half a step, Blackburn pulled her back with a sharp gesture.

"Stay beside or behind me when we walk," she said, her voice sharp and commanding.

Lilith adjusted her pace, falling in line. "Sorry," she murmured.

"You'll answer for that later," Blackburn replied with a wink.

The afternoon sunlight slanted between buildings, warming patches of sidewalk. Lilith's fingers found the cool stone at her throat, tracing the leather choker as her eyes swept the street.

"Which way?" Lilith asked, nodding toward the intersection where a delivery truck straddled two lanes, its hazard lights pulsing amber against the pavement.

"Madison. It's quieter," Blackburn said.

They fell into step together, matching each other's unhurried pace. Near the crosswalk, tourists huddled around a city map, their German rising and falling as they gestured in opposite directions.

The light changed with a musical click. They crossed amid office workers clutching paper coffee cups, students with backpacks sagging from their shoulders, and an older man whose terrier strained against its leash to investigate a fire hydrant.

Lilith slowed at a narrow storefront squeezed between a dry cleaner's chemical smell and a phone repair shop's neon glow. Behind the window, mannequins posed in chain mail dresses beneath hand-painted lettering: "Valkyrie Vintage—Armor for the Modern Warrior."

Blackburn tilted her head, studying the metallic shimmer. "Is that real chain mail?"

"I hope so," Lilith replied, her mouth curving. "I bet their reviews are entertaining."

An autonomous cab beeped behind them, weaving around a double-parked sedan. The sedan's driver gestured wildly at her phone while a traffic cop approached, his shoulders already slumped with afternoon fatigue.

"You drive an autonomous car?" Blackburn asked as she eyed the cab.

"No. I prefer the control of a plain old oil and gas car. Haven't even moved to electric," Lilith said.

Three teenagers carved through the foot traffic on skateboards, their wheels clicking over sidewalk cracks. A businessman pulled his briefcase closer as they whizzed by. A bus thundered past, diesel fumes mixing with the scent of nearby food carts. Its side displayed a glossy advertisement for a courtroom series that Blackburn had dismissed as pure fiction.

Lilith stopped abruptly and turned to face her fully. "That's why you looked familiar. You're…"

Blackburn maintained the space between them. "That's why I need discretion."

Lilith's gaze held hers, unwavering and direct. "You'll get it from me."

A bike messenger shot past in a blur of chrome and neon as they stepped off the curb toward the QuickStay. He vanished into the gap between a cab and a steaming food truck before either could blink.

"I booked online," Blackburn said, retrieving her phone from her pocket. "No check-in desk needed."

"Do you use your work phone for this? I keep two: personal and professional."

"Same here," Blackburn replied, her thumb sliding across the screen. "My phone's been subpoenaed more than I have." The app confirmed: Room 210, rear entrance.

At the doorway, Lilith hesitated, her pulse visible at her throat. "My safe word is 'window'. And if I can't talk, I'll snap my fingers until you stop," she offered quietly. Blackburn put her hand on the small of Lilith's back and urged her in.

Chapter 20

"All good?" Blackburn asked, turning the lock behind them with a soft click.

Lilith glanced back, lips curving into a small smile. "Perfect."

The room held the clean scent of fresh linen mixed with lavender sachets. Lilith crossed to the window and opened it a crack, cool air threading through the curtains as she drew them aside. "Fresh air," she said.

Blackburn switched on the bedside lamp. Soft amber light pooled across Lilith's shoulder and caught the curve of her cheek, casting gentle shadows along the wall.

Lilith leaned back against the desk, arms crossed, her gaze steady and direct. "What now, Morgan?"

"Come here."

The space between them collapsed slowly, deliberately. Blackburn had learned that anticipation was its own kind of violence. The exquisite cruelty of delay. When their mouths finally met, it was with the careful hunger of two people who understood that real power lay not in taking, but in making someone desperate to give.

Lilith's breathing changed first, a subtle hitch that Blackburn catalogued. She deepened the kiss gradually, her fingertips finding the hollow of Lilith's throat where pulse met skin. The choker there, black velvet against pale flesh, reminded Blackburn of something she couldn't name. Ownership, perhaps. Or surrender disguised as decoration.

"You arrived empty-handed?" Lilith's voice carried the faintest tremor, though her hands remained steady as they traced the curve of Blackburn's hips.

"I improvise well." Blackburn caught Lilith's lower lip between her teeth, applying just enough pressure to blur the line between pleasure and warning.

She worked Lilith's shirt open with methodical patience, each button a small conquest. The fabric whispered against skin as it fell away, leaving Lilith exposed in the amber lamplight. Blackburn had always found something profoundly honest about nakedness. It stripped away pretense along with clothing, revealed who people truly were when they thought no one was looking.

"Beautiful," she murmured, though the word felt inadequate. Lilith's body told stories Blackburn wanted to read with her hands, her mouth, her teeth. She pressed her lips to the sensitive skin just below the choker, feeling Lilith's pulse quicken against her tongue.

"Okay?"

"More than okay." The words came out breathless, strained with want.

Blackburn shed her own shirt, then reached behind Lilith to unhook her bra. No ceremony, no false reverence, just the quiet authority of someone who knew exactly what she wanted and how to take it.

"You have perfect breasts," she said, stooping to take a nipple between her lips. Lilith's sharp intake of breath was better than applause. Blackburn bit down gently, then harder when Lilith arched into the pain.

"Please—"

"Please what?" Blackburn straightened, meeting Lilith's eyes. "Use your words."

"Bite me. Mark me." The confession spilled out raw and desperate, and Blackburn felt something predatory unfurl in her chest. This was what she lived for, the moment someone stopped pretending they didn't want to be consumed.

She pushed Lilith down onto the bed and followed, trailing kisses and carefully placed teeth down her torso. Each mark she left was deliberate, a signature written in sensation that would linger long after they'd dressed and returned to their separate lives.

"Harder," Lilith gasped, fingers twisting in the sheets.

Blackburn stopped abruptly. The sudden absence of sensation was more brutal than any slap. "Undress me," she commanded, her voice carrying the quiet authority that made hardened detectives scramble to obey.

Lilith sat up, pupils blown wide with need, and reached for Blackburn's remaining clothes. But when her thumbs brushed across Blackburn's nipples, Blackburn seized both wrists in a grip that would leave finger-shaped bruises.

"I didn't say you could touch."

"What'll you do about it?" Lilith's grin was pure challenge, the kind of defiance that begged for correction.

"Strip me," Blackburn repeated, releasing her wrists with a slight push. "With your mouth."

The order hung between them like a dare. Lilith sank to her knees without hesitation, and Blackburn felt the familiar thrill of watching someone choose their own subjugation. It was never about force. Real dominance came from making people want to kneel.

Lilith worked at the buttons with lips and teeth, fumbling with determined persistence until Blackburn's pants gaped open. The zipper proved more challenging, but she persevered with the single-minded focus of someone performing an act of worship.

"Clever girl." Blackburn stepped back, shedding the rest of her clothes with deliberate slowness. "Though you could work faster." She placed one foot on the bed, the position both invitation and command. "Earn your pleasure."

Lilith leaned forward without hesitation, pressing her mouth to the soft skin of Blackburn's inner thigh. Her tongue traced lazy patterns upward, teasing until Blackburn's patience frayed. When that skilled mouth finally found its target, Blackburn's control cracked just enough to let out a quiet groan.

The sound emboldened Lilith. She worked with increasing confidence, her tongue finding that perfect pressure, the ideal rhythm. Blackburn tangled her fingers in Lilith's hair, not to guide, but to anchor herself against the sensation building in her core.

Then Lilith's mouth moved lower, exploring with careful reverence. The first tentative touch made Blackburn's hips jerk involuntarily. Such an intimate violation, and yet Lilith approached it like a sacrament, tongue circling and teasing until Blackburn forgot why she'd ever thought she needed to maintain distance from anyone.

"That's it," she breathed, her voice rougher than intended. "Don't stop."

Lilith's fingers joined her tongue, stroking Blackburn's clit with maddening lightness while her mouth worked with increasing boldness. The dual stimulation built toward something that felt less like pleasure and more like dissolution. The terrifying, exhilarating loss of self that came with truly letting go.

When the orgasm finally crashed over her, it was with a violence that surprised them both. Blackburn's grip on Lilith's hair tightened to the point of pain as waves of sensation rolled through her, each one threatening to unmoor her completely. She rode Lilith's mouth until the aftershocks faded, then looked down into eyes that shone with something deeper than satisfaction.

"You did beautifully," Blackburn murmured, the praise carrying weight beyond mere words. "Very beautifully."

Lilith smiled, wiping her mouth with the back of her hand before leaning up for a kiss that tasted like salt and surrender. Blackburn returned it without hesitation, recognizing something of herself in Lilith's hunger.

"Your turn," she said simply, guiding Lilith back onto the bed.

"Yes," Lilith whispered. "Please."

Blackburn positioned herself behind Lilith, hands mapping the geography of hip and thigh with the thoroughness of someone conducting an investigation. Every touch was catalogued, every response noted and filed away for future reference.

She found the small tube of lubricant in her discarded jacket pocket: preparation disguised as spontaneity. The sound of foil tearing seemed unnaturally loud in the quiet room.

"What's your favorite number?" she asked, coating her fingers with clinical efficiency.

"Seven."

"Seven minutes, then." Blackburn's smile held promise and threat in equal measure. She positioned Lilith across her lap, admiring the way lamplight caught the curves and hollows of her body. "Count them for me."

The first slap was almost gentle, a warm-up that made Lilith gasp more from surprise than pain. Blackburn calibrated her response, watching for the subtle tells that would guide her hand. The arch of Lilith's back, the way her breathing changed, the flush that spread across her skin like watercolor on wet paper.

Each strike built on the last, intensity climbing in careful increments. Blackburn's free hand traced soothing circles between impacts, easing the sting just enough to keep Lilith floating in that perfect space between pleasure and pain.

By the fourth minute, Lilith was undone, her cries raw and desperate. The careful composure she wore in daylight had been stripped away, leaving only honest need. Blackburn found herself mesmerized by the transformation. This was who Lilith truly was beneath all her careful masks.

"Time," Blackburn announced when seven minutes had elapsed, though part of her wanted to continue indefinitely. Lilith's skin glowed crimson where her palm had landed, each mark a testament to boundaries crossed and trust earned.

She soothed the heated flesh with gentle strokes, grounding them both in the aftermath. "You took that beautifully," she murmured, letting genuine admiration color her voice. "Are you ready for your reward?"

Lilith's answer was wordless. A shift of hips that spoke louder than any plea.

Blackburn reached for more lubricant, warming it between her fingers before trailing them along the cleft of Lilith's ass. The first touch made Lilith shiver, muscles tensing with anticipation.

"Breathe," Blackburn commanded gently, circling that tight entrance with infinite patience. "Let me in."

The initial penetration was careful, controlled. Just enough to stretch without overwhelming. Blackburn watched Lilith's face in the lamplight, reading every micro-expression for signs of discomfort or desire.

"More," Lilith gasped when she'd adjusted to the intrusion. "Please, I need more."

Blackburn added lubricant and pressure in equal measure, working deeper with methodical thoroughness. Each millimeter was earned, claimed through patience rather than force. When she was fully seated inside Lilith's body, they both went still, overwhelmed by the intimacy of the connection.

Then Blackburn moved, establishing a rhythm that was both dirty and reverent. Her other hand found Lilith's clit, adding another layer of stimulation that made her victim writhe and beg incoherently.

"Perfect," Blackburn murmured into Lilith's hair as they moved together. "You're absolutely perfect like this."

The praise unlocked something in Lilith. Her orgasm, when it finally arrived, was volcanic. A complete surrender that left her shaking and spent across Blackburn's lap. Blackburn worked her through every aftershock, drawing out the pleasure until Lilith could take no more.

In the quiet aftermath, they rearranged themselves under the hotel blanket, bodies fitting together with surprising ease. Blackburn found herself stroking Lilith's hair, a gesture that felt dangerously close to tenderness.

"You gave yourself to me completely," she said eventually, the words carrying more weight than she'd intended. "That takes real courage."

Lilith turned in her arms, eyes still glazed with satisfaction. "It felt like coming home."

The confession hung between them, too honest for the careful boundaries they'd established. But neither moved to take it back.

Later, they shared a shower that was both practical and intimate, washing away the evidence of their encounter while creating new memories. When they finally dressed and prepared to leave, Blackburn found herself reluctant to break the spell they'd woven.

"We'll do this again," she said, the promise carrying certainty that surprised them both.

At the door, they shared one final kiss, softer than what had come before, but no less charged with meaning. Then they stepped back into the world outside, carrying the secret of what they'd shared like a brand beneath their skin.

Chapter 21

Blackburn tilted her face toward the late afternoon sun. Its amber glare pierced through her eyelashes, forcing her eyes into slits and leaving phosphorescent spots dancing across her vision. She checked her watch. The metal band felt warm against her wrist. Nearly five o'clock. The day had dissolved like sugar in hot coffee.

Lilith had been a welcome distraction, but now the case pressed against her consciousness like a persistent headache. Kendria Chaplin.

Blackburn's mind shifted gears as she walked, compartmentalizing the morning's catastrophe, the afternoon's activities while the moans of Lilith still lingered. She turned her attention back to her murder investigation.

She settled into her chair and booted up her computer. The fan whirred to life, pushing stale office air across her desk. An email notification from Chief Hayes blinked on screen. She opened it, tracking the words with amusement. Two beat cops had conducted a welfare check on Dawson, finding him "intoxicated and agitated" but otherwise unharmed. Chief Hayes had instructed HR to force Dawson into a week's vacation.

Blackburn leaned back. The chair's springs groaned in protest. Her mind churned through possibilities. She could still see Dawson's mottled face after she'd humiliated him over his solve record. His jowls had trembled, spittle catching the LED lights as he'd hissed his threats. The memory tugged a smile from her lips, brief as a struck match.

She closed the email, tension gathering between her shoulder blades. Dawson's sudden "vacation" added another knot to an already tangled case. Her fingers found their familiar rhythm against the desk's worn surface, tapping out her frustration as she considered his open cases and his monumental failure with Ira Malone. Far worse than Sinclair's screw-up. The arrest warrant had crumbled like wet paper because Dawson claimed to have a phone contract linking Malone to the cell found at the Cole Chandworth murder scene. But the idiot had fabricated it. When the extradition request demanded evidence, he'd conveniently "lost" it. The damned case was becoming cold.

"One hundred percent," Blackburn muttered. The words tasted like copper pennies. Everyone else was failing, but not her. Her solve rate was one hundred percent. Everyone else, less. Dawson? Pathetic at just thirty-eight percent.

Leather groaned as she shifted forward, mind still churning. A ding. She pulled out her phone. The screen's blue glow felt harsh in the dimming office. Messages scrolled past like a river of obligations.

There.

The subject line sparked electricity through her nerves: *Bringing in Kieran Mott. 30 min.*

Just enough time to grab some protein.

The city's pulse thrummed around her as she exited the building, its rhythm indifferent to the calculations spinning behind her eyes. A red autonomous car glided past, silent as a shark. Through the window, an elderly woman's knitting needles clicked in steady counterpoint to the vehicle's progress.

Blackburn lengthened her stride. The investigation settled across her shoulders like an old coat. Shadows stretched like dark fingers across the pavement, and the day's accumulated heat radiated up through her shoe soles. Two and a half hours at lunch. When had she last stolen time like that? Sex had a way of making hours evaporate like morning dew.

The sidewalk grew thick with bodies as she neared the deli. The early exodus had begun. Ties hung loose like nooses slipped, jackets transformed into burdens. Blackburn threaded through the human current, her thoughts already racing ahead to Kieran Mott and what secrets his arrest might spill about Kendria Chaplin's death.

"Excuse me," a voice cut through the urban white noise. "Hey, excuse me!"

Blackburn pivoted to see a man in paint-stained coveralls closing the distance between them. His work boots slapped concrete. Construction or maintenance. His hands bore the honest dirt of manual labor. Sweat beaded his earnest, anxious face.

"Are you that cop who hit that guy?" The words came between gulps of air.

Blackburn's jaw locked like a triggered trap. She'd been bracing for this confrontation with civilians. "I was suspended and fined," she said, each word flat as pressed steel. "I've already paid for that."

His hands rose in surrender. "No, no. You don't understand. I just wanted to say thanks."

"Thanks?"

"Look, cops hit people all the time, right? Usually, it's some kid who zigged when he should've zagged, or somebody having the worst day of their life. But you? You hit Clyde Mullen. That piece of garbage had it coming for years." His expression hardened like setting cement. "He terrorized my sister's family for months. Restraining orders, police calls. Nothing stuck. Then he opens his fucking mouth about that dead woman, and you were there."

Blackburn stared, words dying in her throat.

"What I'm saying is," he pressed on, "sometimes the right person gets hit by the right cop at the right time. Just wanted you to know not everybody thinks you're the bad guy here."

Before she could formulate a response, he gave her a sharp nod and dissolved back into the crowd. He left Blackburn frozen as the human river flowed around her like water around a stone.

She remained anchored there, processing the unexpected absolution, then resumed her march toward the precinct. *Of course she was the right cop. Of course it was the right thing.* The scorching sun painted everything in shades of honey and rust. Ahead, the deli. Then, Keiran Mott.

Blackburn's mind shifted to Mott as she threw the sandwich wrapper in the garbage. The evening sunlight caught the sharp edge of his corporate portrait: another tech engineer, confident in his own cleverness. She scanned his employment history, noting six years at Stan Raider's autonomous vehicle division with solid evaluations until the last entry. "Unauthorized system manipulation. Demonstrated security vulnerability outside approved protocols." The bureaucratic language barely masked the truth: Mott had exposed something they wanted hidden, and they'd made him pay for it.

She opened a browser tab and lowered the volume as Mott's face filled the YouTube frame. Low subscriber count, active comments scrolling beneath. He sat before a cluttered bookshelf, hands cutting through the air as he spoke.

"They don't want you to understand what these cars are," he said, voice tinny through her speakers. "It's not just about driving. It's surveillance and control. And yes, they can be turned into weapons."

Blackburn couldn't argue with that: she was the poster girl for the Raider partnership with NDPD and she was grateful that everyone had forgotten.

Blackburn studied him: fervor burning in his eyes, shoulders rigid with conviction or resentment. Anger ended and performance began. She'd met enough true believers to recognize when someone had swallowed their own myth.

Behind her, Willow's sneakers squeaked against the floor as she pinned recent evidence to the board, movements brisk. Since Kendria's death, Willow's habits had sharpened. Blackburn noted it, then dismissed it.

"These EDR pulls confirm the car accelerated toward Kendria," Willow said without turning. "Langston incident matches. Manual override of safety interlocks."

"Would the car have killed her if it decelerated?"

Willow froze, turned. "No."

"Then of course it accelerated." Blackburn rolled her neck until vertebrae popped and faced the evidence wall. She was there, she knew the car accelerated. There were rows of photos connected by red string and paper-clipped reports. Two faces dominated the display. Jenna Langston, Kendria Chaplin. Different stories with identical endings.

"Footage from First National?" Blackburn asked.

Willow pressed a grainy printout against the corkboard. "Bank camera caught this figure thirteen minutes before impact."

A hooded shape crossed a rain-slicked sidewalk. Approximate height and build matched Mott, though the cap shadowed most features. A partial profile, at best.

"Might be him," Blackburn said. "Could also be any guy working in this neighborhood."

"Facial recognition came back at twenty-three percent confidence." Willow pushed her glasses higher. "No sign of anything in his hands, though."

Blackburn caught the implication: not him unless he felt so guilty, he would point himself out. She absorbed the timestamp. 1:23 PM on tape, Kendria struck at 1:36 PM. Thirteen minutes to position himself, execute whatever breach was required, then disappear.

Doable for someone like Mott? Seemed possible.

Her phone vibrated against the desk's laminate surface. Sinclair's name flashed across the display.

Mott's arrived. Five minutes out.

She thumbed a brief reply and slipped the phone into her pocket. Blackburn straightened her blazer out of habit more than necessity. Since returning from her suspension, she favored severity. Let anyone questioning her composure find reassurance or intimidation in the precision of her appearance.

"Profile suggests he'll respond best to direct challenge," Blackburn said, more to herself than Willow. "He sees himself as wronged. A victim seeking acknowledgment."

"They're always writing themselves as heroes," Willow murmured.

Blackburn closed both file and tablet with deliberate care. The man possessed skills, means, and clear grievances against his former employer. A volatile combination for someone seeking payback disguised as ideology. But there was a crucial difference between an engineer showing off and one willing to kill.

"He'll want to explain things," Blackburn said. "Men who think they're smarter than everyone else can't resist correcting you."

Willow nodded once. "I've prepared technical prompts that should provoke him. If he hacked these vehicles himself, he'll take the bait." She handed over a sheet of information that Blackburn barely glanced at.

"The ego snare." Blackburn allowed herself a brief smile before letting it dissolve.

"Here's your earpiece," Willow said, pushing a black box along the desk. "I'll let you know if he says anything technically misleading, or if one of my questions is wrong or something," she said.

Blackburn smiled as she put the tiny speaker in her ear. "If one of your questions is wrong, I'll be sure to let you know." Willow's toes curled.

The office air stilled around them. Blackburn let herself sink into the familiar alertness, part instinct, part cultivated skill, of an interrogation. Reading micro-expressions beneath every denial.

"If he did this," Willow said after a beat, "he covered his digital footprints well."

Blackburn's gaze found Kendria's picture again. Caught mid-laugh outside her shop window, oblivious to how little time remained.

"No one erases everything," she said. "We only need one mistake."

She turned from the board. The shift from analysis to confrontation demanded discipline she'd refined through hundreds of interviews. In all those sterile rooms, she'd learned that danger came not from monsters but from men convinced by their own justifications. People like Mott, who were ready to cross lines when principle demanded it.

At her door, she paused, centering herself. "Let's see what Mr. Mott thinks we know."

Willow collected her laptop without comment and fell into step half a pace behind as they moved down the corridor toward interrogation rooms bathed in unforgiving LED light. Nothing was hidden here, every flaw exposed beneath its glare. Perfect conditions for dragging the truth into the open where it couldn't hide.

The interrogation room waited, stripped of comfort: LED panels buzzing overhead, recycled air sharp with disinfectant that couldn't mask the sweat of countless suspects who'd sat here before. Blackburn settled into her chair. The metal legs scraped concrete as she positioned herself, squaring her shoulders to the empty seat across the table. She centered Mott's file on the stainless-steel surface with a deliberate placement.

At the corner workstation in the viewing room, safe from the monster, Willow arranged her tools. Her laptop screen cast a pale light across her hands as she aligned evidence folders by priority, positioning her water bottle beyond the reach of any sudden gesture. The overhead lights caught her lenses when she glanced at Blackburn through the one-way window.

The door released with a pneumatic sigh. Kieran Mott entered ahead of Sinclair, who lingered at the threshold, assessing, realizing he would not be welcome, and withdrawing. Mott's body telegraphed defiance: shoulders hunched forward, arms locked across his chest, chin lifted in studied resistance. His eyes tracked the cameras, measured distances to exits, catalogued every detail before he dropped into the chair opposite Blackburn. A smirk ghosted across his face, there and gone.

"Mr. Mott." Blackburn kept her tone neutral. "Thank you for coming."

The chair groaned as Mott shifted his weight. "Wasn't really a choice."

"There's always a choice." Blackburn opened his file with slowness. "You could have refused."

His fingers tapped once against his bicep. "Why would I? Haven't broken any law. Besides, it's fodder."

Blackburn acknowledged this with a fractional nod and pressed forward. "Let's discuss your employment at Stan Raider's autonomous vehicle division." She slid a document across the table: his termination paperwork, edges crisp. "You were let go for unauthorized system manipulation. Walk me through it."

Heat flashed across Mott's expression. Familiar territory, but the wound was still fresh. "I exposed a vulnerability they wanted buried. One that could kill people." He leaned forward, arms uncrossing, as conviction replaced caution. "I used a modified controller to hijack a showroom car during an investor demo."

"In active traffic," Blackburn noted, her finger marking the relevant line.

"That was the point." His voice edged higher, urgency bleeding through. "Proved their security was theater. It had to be public, or they'd ignore it." His fingers carved quotes around 'security.'

Blackburn studied the flush creeping up his neck, the quickened rhythm of his breathing now that indignation had overtaken wariness.

"You bypassed disclosure protocol," she observed.

"They stonewalled me." His palm struck the table, not hard, but emphatically. "Three reports filed and buried. I found another way to make them listen."

She let the silence stretch taut between them.

"You've built quite a following from this," Blackburn said finally, gaze steady on his face. "Your channel has an audience."

The smirk returned, fuller now. "Twenty-three thousand subscribers who deserve the truth."

"Which is?"

The words came rapid-fire: "That these cars are deathtraps. Hackable. Built by companies who value stock prices over human lives."

Blackburn shifted forward, closing the distance without aggression.

"Did you hack the vehicles that killed Jenna Langston and Kendria Chaplin?"

The air compressed. Mott went rigid, shoulders pulling back, palms pressing flat against the table. A muscle jumped in his jaw.

"No." Clipped. "I didn't kill anyone."

Blackburn remained clinical. "That wasn't my question. Did you hack *those* vehicles?"

Mott's gaze flicked to the mirror he knew someone hid behind, then back. "No. I hacked a different car. Not to hurt anyone."

"When?"

"Three weeks ago." His index finger drummed once on metal. "Before anyone died. A Raider Straight Line at Maple and Third. Check the traffic cameras. No injuries, just a two-minute stop. Hazards on."

"Why there?" Blackburn turned her attention from him to the file. It sent a message: his answer was not important.

"Maximum visibility." The words came tight. "Witnesses, attention, zero risk." He inched forward. "If I wanted bodies, there would have been bodies."

"Why did you leave it in the intersection?"

"What else was I going to do with it?" he asked, squirming in his chair. "If I kept it, that would be theft."

Willow's voice cut in. "Prompt 3."

Blackburn's eyes flickered to Willow's prepared prompts. Number three. "Your demonstration used a modified gaming controller running custom firmware." She looked up, holding Keiran's gaze. "That creates a specific signature. It was brute force targeting the emergency brake subsystem."

Mott gave a reluctant nod.

Blackburn decided to wing it. "But the Chaplin vehicle," she continued, tapping her folder as if it held much more information than it truly did, showed something completely different. "They got in deep, made it look like the commands were coming straight from the Stan Raider group. Slipped past every layer of security without raising a single flag." She tapped her fingernails on the folder. "As far as the car knew, it was just doing what it was told."

Mott's mask slipped, professional pride snagged on her analysis. "That's not..." He caught himself.

"Not what?" Blackburn let the question hang.

"Not how I'd do it," he finished, subdued.

"But you understand the method," Blackburn stated.

A pause, then a single nod. "Theoretically." He leaned in now, defensiveness giving way to genuine interest.

"Explain."

He exhaled slowly. "This level requires either physical access to the diagnostic port or..." The sentence died.

"Or?" Blackburn prompted.

His eyes stayed on the folder. "Backend privileges. Command server access. Senior engineers, administrators only."

"Access you had before termination."

His head jerked up, irritation sparking. "I didn't do this."

"You were spotted one block from Kendria Chaplin's death scene. Thirteen minutes before impact." She pulled a photo out of the folder and pushed the grainy image across the table.

He studied it, jaw tightening. "You can't identify anyone from this."

"Our system flagged a partial match." Behind the mirror, Willow smiled.

A sharp exhale came from Keiran. "Partial means nothing."

Blackburn let silence work for her.

His frustration sharpened each word: "I don't need to hack those cars to know the method. Anyone who understands the architecture could do it."

"They fired you," Blackburn said softly, waiting.

He met her gaze directly, color flooding his face. "Making me the perfect fall guy." His voice rose, trembling with indignation. "You think being fired would turn me into some kind of monster? That I'd murder an innocent woman just to, what? Prove some point about technology?" He shook his head violently. "I already proved my point on Maple Street."

His eyes slipped over to the mirror again, where he saw what was *really* happening. Mott met Blackburn's eyes, his face coloring. "I'm the convenient scapegoat." His tone was sharp, restrained but simmering. "You think losing a job turns someone into a murderer? That I would snap because I got pushed out?" His fingers dug into his palms. "I built my life making these vehicles safer. The thought that I would turn one into a weapon, that I would embrace what I hate most, is offensive."

Blackburn held her smile: this would not be the first time she offended a suspect.

He shifted toward the one-way glass, his posture stiffening as realization struck. "Someone's watching from back there." He kept his focus on the glass, his voice flat now. "It's all very neat. Make the engineer look volatile. Meanwhile, those autonomous cars are already mapping people's movements, quietly deciding where and when anyone can travel. Freedom isn't yours anymore. It belongs to their systems."

He turned back to Blackburn. "You're helping them, Detective. Chasing the obvious story instead of seeing how deep this reaches. They're not just designing transportation. They're drawing boundaries. And you've become part of the mechanism that keeps everyone confined. I can tell you this: whoever stands behind that glass was involved."

Blackburn absorbed the accusation as it landed: whoever stands behind that glass.

"All right, Mr. Mott," Blackburn said evenly, her voice cutting through the stale air of the interview room. "You admitted to the company that you hacked a Raider Straight Line three weeks ago using a modified gamepad. You described it as a controlled, nonviolent demonstration: two minutes stopped in traffic, hazards blinking, no injuries. You claimed it was meant to draw attention, not cause harm."

Keiran nodded and leaned back in his chair, the metal frame creaking with his movement. "That's right. No harm."

"Then we discussed the more advanced breach used in the Langston and Chaplin cases. Deep system infiltration, commands disguised to look like they originated from Stan Raider headquarters, no security alerts triggered." She paused, watching his face tighten. "You said that. You recognized the method and said you understood how it could work, but only theoretically. You explained it would require either physical access to the diagnostic port or backend server access. Those are credentials reserved for senior engineers. You confirmed you had that level of clearance before your termination, but you denied using it. You insisted that someone else with similar access and knowledge could have executed this. And that could be the person behind the glass."

Keiran wiped a damp hand down his face, his palm rasping against day-old stubble. "Yes, that's correct. But I didn't have backend server access when that woman died. And it remains theoretical. It can't actually happen."

Blackburn turned to another page in her folder, the paper whispering against her fingers, revealing a diagnostic printout dense with code she couldn't interpret. "You don't think the theory move into practice?"

"Look, I..." His voice caught. He looked at his hands, at the ceiling, at the hole someone had tried to carve into the wall. "Fuck. If someone hacked those cars, and I have no way of knowing if that's true, then they found a way to bypass everything I designed." The word came out like a punctured tire. "They circumvented my work. Were they actually hacked? Not driven by someone?"

"According to you, Mr. Mott, it's only theoretical. Yet here we are discussing it." Blackburn smiled, though it never reached her eyes. "According to you, if someone controlled them remotely, they're smarter than you." She closed her notebook with quiet finality and stood.

"You're a bitch," he snapped.

Yes, I am.

"You're free to go, Mr. Mott."

Surprise flickered across his features before satisfaction settled in. "Is that it?"

Blackburn did not look at him. "You cannot further help us. We'll contact you if we have further questions. Stay available."

Mott rose, straightening his shirt. "You're chasing shadows, Detective." The title dripped with condescension. "The actual killer isn't some outsider. They're on the inside. Finding out who got my job will tell you everything you need."

She watched him leave, his stride lengthening with each step, convinced he'd emerged victorious, with a hint of doubt. He had no idea he'd just handed them their strongest lead. Not as a suspect, but as someone who understood the system intimately enough to illuminate how another could weaponize it.

Blackburn walked into the viewing room, slapping the folder onto the desk beside Willow. They were all there: Sinclair, Cooper, and Reeves. Even Hayes had watched. The room felt sharper, a space scraped clean of pretense.

"He's not our killer," Blackburn said, her voice low.

Willow's typing never slowed. "His approach is crude compared to what we're seeing in the logs. He's swinging a hammer. This is scalpel work."

Blackburn sat on the desk and rolled her shoulders, vertebrae popping softly as she worked out the knots from sitting too rigid for too long. She circled one ankle, sorting through impressions: Mott's clipped answers, the quick flash of indignation in his eyes, the outrage of someone wrongly accused but not entirely clean.

"Thoughts?"

"He said something useful," Cooper noted. "He doesn't have to hack these cars himself to know how it's done."

"That caught my attention too." Willow adjusted her glasses, lenses catching the overhead LEDs. "He understands the mechanics but can't execute at that level. Whoever breached those vehicles knew backend architecture, internal protocols. This went deeper than surface exploits."

Blackburn gripped the steel frame of Willow's chair. "If you had that kind of access, you wouldn't need theatrics. Wouldn't need visibility."

"Exactly." Reeves said as his eyes flicked briefly to Willow's laptop. "You could keep it silent, make it look accidental."

Blackburn completed the thought: "But the killer chose not to. The killer made it obvious."

The silence stretched taut while everyone turned this new angle over.

"Someone is sending a message." It was Sinclair.

Blackburn studied her reflection in Willow's glasses: suit still crisp despite the long hours, posture blade-straight, shadows pooled beneath her eyes.

A full audience today, but she was good.

"Who is the message for? The Stan Raider group? Online technophobes?" Reeves asked, turning away from the laptop. Too many numbers, not enough letters.

Willow's fingers stilled on the keys. "You?"

A bitter smile flickered across Blackburn's face, there and gone like static. She straightened, creating a deliberate distance between them.

"That's reaching," she said, voice dropping to that careful neutral tone she used when closing doors on unwanted possibilities. "Two victims with no connection to me beyond coincidence." The lie settled between them, smooth as a river stone. Even Hayes remained silent. Accepting.

Blackburn turned away, grabbing the folder. "Let's focus on what we know, not what we imagine. Publicity, chaos, maybe market disruption." She tapped her index finger, three sharp clicks. "They're performing. Making a spectacle."

She glanced back at Willow, her expression now perfectly composed. "And I don't have time for theater," she said as she walked out of the room.

Chapter 22

Blackburn exited the station's gym, letting the heavy door swing shut behind her. The evening heat pressed against her damp skin, mingling with the salt tang of cooling sweat. Her muscles uncoiled from exertion, still warm and loose beneath her street clothes. She wore dark jeans and a charcoal henley, the soft cotton a relief after days trapped in business attire.

Her footsteps whispered against the concrete parking lot. She moved through pools of shadow and LED glare, her gaze sweeping familiar corners. Her sedan waited in its usual spot: third row, northwest edge, the routine of it as comforting as a locked door. Inside, the leather seats released the day's trapped heat. She adjusted the rearview mirror by reflex, though nothing had shifted.

Friday traffic crawled through New Dresden's surface streets. Blackburn kept to side roads, steering clear of the interstate's red river of taillights, following routes carved by years of work and avoidance. She pulled into the strip mall's lot without hurry. Grocery trip. Weekly, automatic. Three years running this circuit. She knew which checkout lanes cleared fastest and when to use the self-checkout instead.

She let the engine tick and settle before getting out. Through the windshield, she watched people navigate painted lines and cart corrals. Movements measured, intent on ordinary tasks. A mother's hands moved with care as she buckled a toddler into a car seat. An old man smoothed crumpled bills against his thigh beside a rust-spotted trunk.

She pocketed her keys and crossed the sunbaked asphalt toward the grocery entrance. Halfway there, she stopped. Something restless coiled at the base of her ribs. Not hunger or thirst exactly. Just the sameness pressing against her chest. So predictable.

The coffee shop caught her eye from across the lot, green umbrellas throwing shade against the late sunlight. Without thinking it through, she changed course, passing storefronts with sun-bleached lettering and dust-filmed windows.

Inside, the afternoon noise enveloped her: the sharp crack of grinders, steam hissing from chrome nozzles, voices calling orders in rhythm. The air tasted of roasted beans and burned sugar. Blackburn studied the menu board before stepping forward.

The barista waited. A young woman with silver rings climbing the curve of one ear.

"Large latte," Blackburn said. Her usual order was simple: black coffee or straight espresso. Nothing to soften the bite. Blackburn paid and moved down the counter to wait.

Behind glass and steel, the staff moved in synchronized precision: tamping grounds with exact pressure, wiping steam wands between each pour. The espresso machine released controlled bursts of steam.

Each hiss was a reminder that pressure contained is often more dangerous than pressure released.

When her drink arrived, an intricate fern pattern floated in white foam atop caramel-colored crema. She carried it outside to a metal table pressed against warm brick. Back protected, sight lines clear out of habit more than concern.

Sun heated the metal chair beneath her thighs as she tasted coffee mellowed with steamed milk. The unexpected sweetness coating her tongue like a confession.

She set the cup aside and drew her phone from her pocket.

QueryQuanta loaded quickly, its interface stark black and white, every pixel serving function over form. Willow had mentioned the app weeks ago: "No content filters," she had said, her tone neutral but her eyes sharp. Information offered without judgment.

Blackburn opened it, her thumb suspended over the empty search bar while patio conversations blurred into white noise around her.

The cursor blinked against white. Blackburn's finger swiped steadily across the screen, each letter a wave in the river: "How do autonomous vehicles receive remote commands?"

The reply appeared in clean segments. Vehicle-to-infrastructure links, wireless protocols for speed and route control. Protocol stacks layered with encryption and authentication, automated checks at each step.

She lifted her latte. The foam atop her coffee had dissolved to thin rings clinging to the porcelain edges. Another question formed beneath her fingers: "What physical access is required to compromise an autonomous vehicle?"

The response unfurled across her screen. A catalog of ports and hatches, locations set by regulation but interpreted differently by manufacturers. Diagnostic connectors tucked under dash panels or concealed behind sealed covers, not always obvious. Fleet management held remote keys for routine updates and monitoring. Multiple entry points in every car, some tangible, others abstract. All supposedly secure. None impervious.

The ceramic had cooled against her palm, the liquid inside tepid. She typed again: "Can autonomous vehicles be controlled remotely without manufacturer authorization?"

QueryQuanta answered with stark clarity. It cited research on cellular vulnerabilities, outlined how network traffic could be intercepted or rerouted when protections failed. Security teams patched known exploits, but patching demanded downtime and coordination. Never universal, never instant.

Blackburn read slowly, the words settling into memory. Vulnerability lurked in the margins. Every connection carried risk. Every added feature became another hinge ready to snap under pressure. Vehicles promised fortress-level safety, but each layer of complexity carved new gaps no code could fully seal.

She set her phone aside, gaze lingering on the final reply. Light slanted across the table, warming the wood grain beneath her fingers. The cars that killed Jenna and Kendria had not been isolated vaults. They were networks bound together by code and trust. Trust easily misplaced. Kendria had even predicted autonomous vehicles talking to each other.

Her fingers hovered above the keyboard again but stilled. No more questions for now. Sunlight traced a warm line across her forearm as she drained what remained of her coffee. The liquid had gone flat, its richness faded. Through the café's glass walls, shadows stretched longer across the patio tiles.

A child's voice cut through the murmur of conversation around her.

Blackburn looked up as a boy near the grocery store entrance bounced against his mother's hip, one small hand wrapped tight around her sleeve while the other jabbed skyward.

"Mom! Look!" His voice pitched high with urgency, the kind that demanded an immediate response. The woman juggled grocery bags in one hand while her keys jangled in the other.

"Yes, honey, I see." Distraction dulled her words even as she tried to match his excitement.

"It's hovering!" He tugged harder at her sleeve, the fabric bunching beneath his grip. "Right there! It's watching us!"

Blackburn's attention sharpened at that word. Watching. She followed his pointing finger upward and raised her hand to block the sharp summer sun.

The sky stretched clean and blue except for faint vapor trails dissipating above the city skyline.

She spotted it quickly. A drone suspended above the parking lot, perhaps two hundred feet overhead. From this distance, it appeared no larger than a dinner plate, four arms forming a rigid cross as it hung motionless despite the breeze that rustled umbrellas at the café tables.

Blackburn studied both machine and boy. Each fixed on their target with singular focus. She waited to see what would happen next.

The mother finally looked up, keys nestled in her palm. "Oh, someone's drone. Maybe they're taking pictures of the mall."

"Can we get one?" The boy's voice held steady wonder, neck craned at a sharp angle. "I want to fly it over our house and look in Tommy's yard."

"We'll see." Noncommittal. She hefted the grocery bags into the trunk while the boy kept watching, palms pressed flat against his brow to block the sun, gaze locked on the hovering machine.

Blackburn settled deeper into her chair, the wood groaning beneath her weight. She kept her muscles slack. Eyes on the drone. The machine hung motionless above the lot, rotors whispering, camera angled down. The coffee shop patio gave her a clear view across the sea of windshields and the mall's angular roofline.

Drones cluttered the sky these days. Her department operated a fleet for documentation and searches. This one prickled against her instincts. It wasn't mapping or running patterns. It watched. The gimbal twitched in micro-adjustments, holding something specific in frame.

She recalled the specifications from recent briefings. Commercial drones could capture individual pores from a hundred feet up. Their cameras perched on slender stabilized arms, some equipped with thermal overlays or night vision. A few models could isolate conversations through ambient noise, software stripping away engine hum and wind until only voices remained.

The woman pressed her trunk closed with a solid thunk and pivoted toward her son. "Come on. We need to get that ice cream home."

"But Mom."

"In." Steel threaded through the word. He stole one last glance skyward before ducking into the car.

Blackburn held still, peripheral vision tracking their departure while the drone dominated her focus. The machine made no move to follow. The camera stayed fixed on its original target as the car backed out and merged into traffic.

She lifted her phone from the table's sticky surface, tilted it as if checking messages but activated the camera instead. At maximum zoom, the image dissolved into blocky pixels, yet enough detail survived: a consumer model with four rotors in standard configuration. Nothing military or law enforcement grade. Thirty minutes of battery if the operator was conservative. Two miles range at the outside.

The instant her lens found it, the drone reacted.

No gradual drift or casual repositioning. The machine snapped left, rotors tilting hard, body rolling into the turn. It sliced away from the mall's airspace and disappeared behind the store's concrete edge in three seconds flat.

Blackburn set her phone down and released a breath. The drone had hovered there throughout her coffee break, likely longer. Yet it bolted the moment she showed interest.

That meant active monitoring. Someone sat behind a screen somewhere, watching the feed, alert for signs of detection. Her mind sorted possibilities: investigator, reporter, stalker, or perhaps a nervous hobbyist who recognized her scrutiny and chose flight over confrontation.

Who was watching her?

She considered Brynn. The reporter liked to work close, prizing immediate reactions over distance. Drone surveillance didn't fit Brynn's preferred strategy. She thrived on confrontation, on watching the first ripple of discomfort cross a subject's face.

The coffee shop patio had emptied out, the after work lull leaving only scattered cups and the steady thrum of refrigeration units bleeding through the open door. Blackburn sat motionless, her gaze soft but encompassing, taking in the entire parking lot without focusing on any single point. If someone was flying that drone manually, they needed visual contact. They needed elevation, an obvious vantage point within blocks.

Her fingers touched the table's surface once, then stilled. The safest assumption was active surveillance. The drone's precise hover, its swift retreat when she had lifted her eyes, marked it as deliberate. Not random flight.

She had two vehicle deaths with all signs pointing to remote interference; now someone watched her with a drone that vanished the moment she noticed. Patterns mattered more than coincidence.

Blackburn pushed her empty cup aside and rose from her chair. Metal scraped against concrete in a brief, sharp note. Dried foam traced pale veins down the ceramic's interior, evidence of her momentary lapse into leisure. She left it for the staff and crossed the patio onto asphalt that radiated stored heat through her shoes.

Her pace slowed as she catalogued angles: windows above storefronts catching the glare, the parking garage's stacked levels, a cell tower wrapped in faded plastic greenery at the lot's far edge. Dozens of sight lines, none perfect but all sufficient for a dedicated watcher.

She had covered half the distance to her car when movement caught her peripheral vision. A white compact idled near the fourth row back from the store entrance, positioned at an angle that commanded clear views of both coffee shop and grocery doors. Sunlight exposed the left taillight's damage: red plastic fractured and bound with yellowing tape.

Blackburn shifted her path, letting a row of tall SUVs shield her while maintaining her view of the white car. One driver sat alone inside. No shopping bags visible on seats, hands still on the wheel rather than occupied with phone or food. Engine running.

The set of his shoulders triggered recognition before she could see his face clearly. That particular slouch belonged to someone who had spent too many hours in cars, waiting for something to happen.

She stopped beside a pickup truck several spots away and studied him through its tinted rear window. He wasn't here for errands. Just sitting in an idling car, attention fixed on his rearview mirror, searching for what he had just lost sight of.

The profile told her what she already knew. Even behind glass, through parking lot glare, Sinclair betrayed himself with the tilt of his head. Too casual on purpose, chin dipping forward at the edge of a slouch. A rookie's tell. He had picked his spot well: simple lines of sight while facing in the opposite direction, appearing not to look.

First the drone, now Sinclair in person. Blackburn's irritation sharpened. Two tactics so close together didn't happen by chance. Sinclair still hadn't learned his lesson. The GPS tracker humiliation had meant nothing. She remembered making him beg last time, his voice cracking as sweat beaded on his forehead. Apparently, it wasn't sufficient discipline.

The decision came fast and clean. She pivoted away from the truck and broke into a jog straight toward him. Not sprinting. That would draw attention. Instead, she moved steadily and unhurriedly, as if out for morning laps, her footfalls rhythmic against the pavement.

The gap narrowed. Forty yards. Thirty. Through the windshield, she watched Sinclair stiffen when he finally registered her approach. His posture snapped rigid, knuckles tightened on the wheel. The car's reverse lights blazed to life as he fumbled into gear.

Blackburn kept pace, pulse stable, stride efficient from an hour in the gym. Tires squealed when Sinclair jerked backward, the acrid smell of burned rubber drifting across the lot. She shifted her angle, closing in until their eyes met through tinted glass.

Sinclair's panic showed in every feature: slack jaw, pupils dilated wide. He yanked the wheel hard and shot into drive, the engine roaring as he raced toward the exit lane. Blackburn slowed to a walk as he pulled away, letting the numbers burn into memory: 1ADAM1ADAM. The damaged taillight blinked erratically through the midday sun while the car tore around a pedestrian and vanished onto Riverside.

She stood in the abandoned parking space, heat radiating from the asphalt where his tires had been. Shoppers rubbernecked at the odd spectacle. A woman running down a car that fled in retreat. Blackburn didn't acknowledge them. She unlocked her phone and dialed the station direct.

"NDPD, Officer Cross."

"Detective Blackburn, badge two-five-nine. Pull up a license plate for me." Her tone stayed flat and official.

"Go ahead."

"One-Adam-One-Adam, custom plate. White four-door Diplo sedan."

Keyboard clatter filled two seconds of silence. "Registered to Adam Sinclair, apartment twenty-three B on Mova Street."

"Copy." She ended the call without thanks or explanation. Consequences weren't her concern today. Let Sinclair wonder how soon until she showed up at his desk.

Phone pocketed, she pushed on to the automatic doors, which slid apart with a pneumatic hiss, washing her in cold air that prickled against sweat-damp skin. Grabbing a cart from the corral felt routine, ordinary. The metal handle was cool beneath her palms. The only anchor left some days.

Aisle after aisle: milk first, in the cart's corner, then eggs cradled carefully and bread that gave under her fingers. Every motion pared back to function. Precise hands choosing food as if building evidence one item at a time. Her mind stayed locked on surveillance and its implications, the questions turning over beneath the LED hum and distant muzak.

She scanned the produce with a trained eye, choosing apples by weight and firmness. Each selection was measured, exact. Kendria surfaced in her mind for a moment, an echo triggered by bruised red skin and the crisp snap beneath her thumb. She let the memory slip away unfinished. Focus on what mattered now.

Sinclair's surveillance had shifted from clumsy GPS trackers to direct observation. A refusal to accept consequences or limits. His attention was personal and petulant. The drone, though. Its pattern had been colder, more methodical. Two separate sets of eyes, or Sinclair paired with someone who knew how to watch without being seen?

She had seen him and Willow arrive together at Lake Canada. Unusual, but not a first.

The checkout line crawled forward, each delay pressed flat by routine. Blackburn studied the slow-moving cashier and calculated responses. She'd miscalculated the speed she thought the line would move.

She could escalate through official channels, file stalking charges, force Sinclair into a corner he couldn't wriggle out of. Or she could address it herself with a clear message that she did not tolerate this. And yet, Willow, tasked to help her, had yet to sabotage his computer.

Her groceries moved across the scanner one by one. The electronic beep marked each item with finality. Normalcy dressed in the thin skin of habit. But nothing about this was normal anymore. The watchers had revealed themselves through their mistakes; competent ones would have remained shadows.

Blackburn carried the bags to her car, twisted rope handles cutting thin grooves into her palms. She paused behind the wheel, eyes scanning reflected faces and idling engines in the lot. Any of them could belong to someone watching for her misstep. Her badge might be on ice, but she had not gone soft.

The route home skirted Sinclair's building. She considered taking it slow past his windows. Let him see her and wonder. But she dismissed the thought as indulgence. Better to let tension build on his side instead. The apples shifted quietly in their bag with every turn, their weight rolling against paper. Predictable habits were weaknesses; today had made that plain.

She would not give them another chance to follow her pattern.

Chapter 23

Reeves set his pint on the table, foam clinging to his upper lip. The pub carried its usual Friday night noise: glasses chiming against wood, laughter cutting through conversations, a steady layer of voices that made private talk possible even at close range. The smell of hops and fried food hung thick in the air. For the two detectives, the commotion was a disturbance to the usual quiet of their office.

Sinclair joined them a little late. "Sorry, I had a thing," he offered lamely as he set his drink down. He was becoming vaguer every day.

Cooper looked at Reeves and rolled his eyes.

"Sarah has this practice test tomorrow," Reeves said. He traced a line through the condensation on his glass. "She keeps telling me she's not ready. Like Princeton's going to turn her away if she doesn't break 1550."

Cooper nodded. His gaze wandered over the crowd, eyes glazed with fatigue rather than drink. His scotch sat neglected, the amber liquid catching a dull shine from the bar lights overhead.

"You tell her Princeton doesn't care about one number?" Cooper asked. The words sounded practiced: a phrase used enough times it no longer belonged to any listener.

Sinclair's attention was locked on his phone, thumb moving in short strokes across the screen. Blue light flattened the lines of his face, casting shadows beneath his eyes. His whiskey sat untouched, ice slowly melting.

"I told her," Reeves said. His voice carried the drag of too many interviews in a single week. "Linda says I go too easy on her. Wants more prep classes. But Sarah's up half the night already, working through calculus problems."

Cooper gave a soft sound in reply, just enough to maintain presence without offering an opinion.

Reeves drank again, the sharp bitterness coating his tongue before he continued. "The damn sink keeps dripping. Three weeks and counting. Linda brings it up every morning like I forgot, like I don't hear every drop echoing through the pipes while I'm supposed to be sleeping."

Cooper's mouth twitched toward a smile. "Call a plumber."

"Eighty an hour? On our pay? No thanks." Reeves massaged his forehead with his fingertips, the pressure of exhaustion settling into the gesture.

Sinclair set his phone down just long enough to speak. "You can find tutorials online." Another alert buzzed against the table; he drifted back to the screen.

"My son said that too." Reeves finished most of his beer in one long pull. "He called yesterday. Didn't say he's drowning in Econ 201, but you can hear it in his voice when someone is."

Sinclair flagged the bartender for another round with two fingers raised in the air. "Is it supply and demand tripping him up?" That was the only economic phrase he knew, aside from 'bankrupt'.

"The whole nine yards. Interest rates, inflation curves. Fucking tariffs." Reeves shrugged. "He's smart enough; just doesn't care unless it grabs him right away." He glanced toward Sinclair, who had already retreated behind his phone's glow again.

"You thinking of going up?" Cooper asked.

"That's what I'm weighing." Reeves leaned in, elbows pressed against the sticky table edge. "Sarah has college visits next month. She's wound so tight she could snap if I'm not there. But Justin? He'd never ask for help directly, that's not how we raised him."

Cooper made a quiet sound that might have meant understanding. He knew the pattern: pride passed from parent to child through habit or silence more than intent.

"Linda says I should go. Says Sarah will understand." Reeves' voice thinned, nearly lost beneath the steady drone of bar conversation. "But will she? Seventeen isn't simple."

"Seventeen is a war zone," Cooper said, finally giving the conversation his full attention. "My niece had a breakdown because her eyebrows didn't match."

Reeves managed a real laugh, tension slipping from his shoulders. "Sarah cried last week when her AP Bio teacher called her lab report 'adequate.'"

Reeves turned his glass slowly, watching the beer settle against the sides. "Justin's considering changing majors. Economics isn't working for him. Brought up criminal justice."

Sinclair looked up from his phone, suddenly focused. He slid the device into his pocket. "Criminal justice at State's solid."

Reeves caught the shift but continued. "He wants internships. Real work experience. Says he'll be ahead of the game if he starts now."

"Smart," Cooper said, nodding as a fresh drink landed in front of him with a soft thud.

"There is no replacement for time in the field," Sinclair added, his posture straightening by degrees. "Textbooks don't show you how this job actually works."

Reeves kept his expression carefully neutral. "We don't run intern programs these days. Budget slashed, liability stacked too high."

Sinclair was already moving ahead. "Has Blackburn ever taken students? For homicide?" His fingers began tapping a quiet rhythm against the table: impatient energy seeking outlet.

Cooper's eyes narrowed at Sinclair's tone. The tension wrapped around Blackburn's name, the slight flush creeping up his jawline. It wasn't subtle, and it wasn't new.

"Blackburn?" Reeves echoed with mild disbelief. "Haven't seen it happen. She's not big on teaching." He could not imagine putting his son within a hundred feet of the woman. If Justin couldn't handle pressure now, he'd be crushed under Blackburn's demands in a day.

Cooper snorted into his glass. "She can barely handle us, no way would she want an undergrad shadowing her every move." Cooper shook his head. "Although, if he could pick up some of her intuition..."

"She might if the right person asked," Sinclair pushed, his voice tight and earnest now. "Especially for someone tied to her own team." The offer hung in the air, transparent as glass. He thought he and Blackburn had a special connection that he could use.

Reeves regarded Sinclair quietly over the rim of his drink. "You volunteering to get Blackburn to say yes?"

"I could mention it," Sinclair said, failing at casual, intensity betraying him. "I'll see her next week about the Hargrove case."

Cooper glanced at Reeves, a silent message passing between them: here comes another round of this.

"Thanks." Reeves kept his tone even. "But Justin's still on the fence about everything right now."

Sinclair nodded quickly. Too quickly. "Sure. But if he decides, let me know." He reached for his untouched whiskey; the ice had softened its color to pale straw.

"I'll keep that in mind," Reeves replied, his tone taking on the same flat register he used when suspects' stories veered off course.

The air shifted as Cooper seizes an opening for distraction: "Did either of you catch that press conference? Chief looked ready to chew glass when reporters grilled him about those Chinese restaurant fires today."

Sinclair's brief spark faded; he checked his phone again, thumb hovering over the dark glass, waiting for something that wouldn't arrive tonight.

"At least no one has died. I'm glad Major Crimes has that shit." Reeves chose not to comment on the tension settling over their table like smoke. He had watched Sinclair orbit Blackburn too many times. The rigid posture when she entered a room, quoting her offhandedly in conversations, angling for a spot on any case she touched. This was only another chapter in the same worn pattern: persistent and obvious, if you bothered to look.

"I could coordinate with Major Crimes. Keep us in the loop. That way, when it becomes our case, we're not starting from zero," Sinclair said as he downed his drink. "You think it would work?" Sinclair asked, his voice low and abrupt. "If I brought it up with her?"

Reeves weighed the question carefully. "With Blackburn, you can't predict. She doesn't always give you what you expect."

Sinclair caught an edge in Reeves's tone, turning defensive. "She values initiative."

"Sometimes," Cooper said. He set down his glass with a soft click. "Other times, she calls it overstepping."

Sinclair looked unsettled, uncertainty creeping in where confidence had been moments before. The rules were never clear with Blackburn, and he felt it keenly now.

Reeves shrugged. "Think on it. No need to rush. Justin's not going anywhere."

Sinclair nodded, but his focus had already shifted inward. Calculations flickered behind his eyes: options, approaches, contingencies all cycling through.

Cooper shot Reeves a quick look: concern mixed with resignation. They wouldn't interfere; some lessons needed to be lived through.

Reeves nudged Sinclair's shoulder. "What are you doing?" Sinclair didn't answer at first, still locked on his phone's screen.

"Just checking the score."

Reeves shook his head and looked at Cooper. It was his turn to talk.

Cooper leaned in, elbows braced against the varnished table. His posture shifted, voice carrying more energy than usual. "Tournament's coming up." He looked between them, animation quickening his words. "Big stakes this round. SoccerStrike 23 patched yesterday. The whole defensive meta changed overnight."

Sinclair slipped his phone away, picking up on Cooper's shift. It was a rare spark from someone usually so focused. Reeves nursed his beer, listening without quite following the thread.

"The update changed everything." Cooper traced rough patterns on the table with his fingertip, sketching plays only he could see. "Everyone used to run 4-3-3 attacks with wingbacks pressing high. Now inverted fullbacks and false nines are everywhere. It's all new systems overnight."

Reeves blinked, trying to parse the jargon. "You play this on your computer?"

"Console. Zip Console." Cooper mimed holding a controller, thumbs working invisible buttons. "Guild coordinates through Echo chat. Tuesday night strategy sessions."

"Guild?" Reeves echoed.

Cooper grinned at that, the question landing well for once. "Yeah. Not fantasy stuff though. SoccerStrike just uses 'guilds' for teams because of its whole medieval stadium theme." He sat straighter, pride seeping through his modest posture. "My squad, Midnight Tacklers, climbed from Silver III to Diamond I over two seasons."

Sinclair perked up, leaning closer across the table. "Diamond I? Is that top tier?"

"Second highest." Cooper sipped his scotch without showiness. "Grandmaster sits above that. Only twenty-six Grandmaster teams worldwide. Why?"

Reeves tried another angle, wanting to connect. "People watch you play?"

"Thousands," Cooper said simply. For a second, even he seemed surprised by the interest Sinclair was showing. "Last final brought in sixty-eight thousand live viewers." He paused, a flicker of self-consciousness surfacing, then added: "Not like League or anything huge yet, but for SoccerStrike it means something."

Sinclair's fingers resumed their quiet tapping against the wood. "Big purse?"

Cooper reined himself back. Of course. The money angle. "Twenty-ty thousand to the first-place team. Five for second." He shrugged once, matter-of-fact rather than boastful this time. "But most of us aren't there for the prize money."

"How many split that?" Sinclair kept pushing.

"Eight starters," Cooper replied tightly, eyes steady now. "Two alternates and a coach, plus the guild takes their cut."

Reeves caught the shift in atmosphere and moved things along. "These online matches. You all log in from different places?"

Cooper latched onto the question gratefully. "Yeah, remote play. Our striker's in Seattle, midfielders are in Toronto and Chicago. Defense is anchored by a kid in Stuttgart. He reads the game like nobody else." His hands carved passing lanes and formations through the air. "For finals, though, everyone flies out. LAN event. We play together on stage."

"LAN?" Reeves asked.

"Local Area Network," Cooper said, his tone patient. "No lag. Keeps everything fair."

Sinclair leaned in, attention sharpened to a point. "Do people bet on these tournaments? Legally?"

Cooper's response came measured. "Some sites set odds." He made it clear he didn't want to dwell there.

"But you're ranked up there," Sinclair persisted. "You'd know which teams are strong. Which players aren't showing up?"

"It's not about that," Cooper said, his grip tightening on his glass. "It's about teamwork and execution."

Reeves shifted focus back to safer ground. "What changed with this update? That's got you looking forward to it?"

Cooper let out a breath, grateful for the redirect. "They changed how player stats work. Used to be all about speed. Just outrun defenders. Now, technical skill matters more: positioning, awareness, decision-making." He straightened, confidence returning to his voice. "That's always been my game."

Reeves looked genuinely interested now. "What's your spot on the team?"

"Defensive midfielder," Cooper replied. When neither detective reacted, he added, "I don't score goals. I break up plays, keep shape, make passes to the guys who create chances."

Reeves nodded thoughtfully. "Sounds like detective work."

Cooper considered that for a beat and nodded back. "Right. You read what's coming next."

Sinclair still circled the earlier angle. "These matches go out live? Anyone can tune in?"

"That's the whole draw," Cooper said, his tone sharpening again.

"And betting lines, those shift before games start? News comes in, odds move?"

Carefully setting his glass down, Cooper replied with deliberate restraint. "That's not my concern. We train and play; nothing else matters."

Sinclair started again, but Cooper cut him off quietly, but definitely: "I'm here for the competition and my team."

The table fell silent for a moment; Sinclair got the message and looked away toward the bar.

He shrugged, voice turning casual again. "Just making conversation."

Reeves stepped in smoothly. "So when's this big match?"

"Three weeks from Saturday," Cooper said, his shoulders relaxing a fraction. "Semis on Friday night; finals Saturday afternoon."

"You going to stream?" Reeves asked.

A trace of surprise flickered across Cooper's face before he nodded once. "Yeah. I'll send you the link."

Sinclair's phone disappeared into his pocket, his attention flickering out as quickly as it had appeared.

Cooper observed the change with relief. Sinclair's interest always felt conditional: sharp when there was something to gain, absent the moment he sensed resistance.

"The new update added weather effects," Cooper said, turning to Reeves. "Rain changes how the ball moves across the pitch. Wind makes long passes harder to judge."

Reeves nodded. "Tech gets better every year." He hesitated. "Does Blackburn know you play with controllers?"

Cooper shook his head, a brief look of understanding crossing his features. "I just know how to play games, not hacking. But I'll keep her in the loop."

"Good call," Reeves said. He shot a meaningful look toward Sinclair. "Better she hears it from you."

Sinclair set his phone aside with deliberate care, as if proving he was present again. A third whiskey had smoothed out his edges; his movements were less crisp, his voice carrying a liquored calm. "Got my own plans this weekend," he said, inviting himself back into their conversation. "Looking at the Hargrove file again. Something's off about the wife's timeline."

Reeves and Cooper exchanged a brief glance across the table.

"Hargrove?" Reeves asked as he finished his beer. "Thought Dawson was handling that one."

Sinclair nodded, tracing his glass rim with one finger. "He was. Case hasn't been reassigned yet, so someone needs to keep an eye on it." He straightened up at the mention of her name. Not lost on either man. "Figured I'd get ahead before anyone else does."

"On a Saturday?" Cooper asked.

"Just the morning," Sinclair replied too quickly. "People notice follow-through." The line sounded rehearsed; something he had told himself more than once before. He lowered his voice conspiratorially. "Been thinking about the spatter analysis. Brain matter on the dumpster goes down at the wrong angle."

Reeves gave a polite nod, eyes unfocused. He had heard this theory already. Cooper took another drink, remaining silent.

Sinclair pressed on, his tone shifting as he let his guard down further. "That's just to start off the day. Saturday night's what I'm looking forward to." His posture relaxed; hands moved with more energy now. "Bright Star has a high-stakes hold'em tournament. A ten grand buy-in."

Reeves placed his empty glass on the table with deliberate care. "Ten thousand?"

"Yeah," Sinclair said. The hint of a smile surfaced. Part challenge, part pride. "Private table in the back room. Invite only."

"You have ten grand lying around?" Cooper asked, his voice carefully steady.

Sinclair shook his head with a casual flourish. "Been lucky lately. I'm up thirty-two grand since March." His tone left no room for doubt; this was meant to impress. "Besides, this isn't just any game. Harris is showing up, the developer? Can't bluff without pulling his ear every time." He leaned in, voice dropping to confidential. "And Richardson from city planning? Guy holds his breath when he's got something strong."

The noise of the pub faded as Sinclair spoke, his focus shifting to the casino with a clarity absent from most case discussions.

"Bright Star revamped the VIP lounge last month. Italian marble on the bar, new felt for the tables. It's deep green, so you can see every card like it's under studio lights. They hired a bartender out of Vegas who's got this old-fashioned down to a science. He crushes the sugar cube with a wooden muddler, uses orange bitters custom-bottled in Portland."

Reeves adjusted in his chair, discomfort sharpening his gaze. "Must cost a fortune."

"It's worth it," Sinclair said, brushing past the skepticism. "But the real draw is the players. People with too much cash and no impulse control."

He lowered his voice further. "There's Whitfield, a hedge fund guy who thinks he's clever but always goes too hard after the flop.

Overplays suited connectors every time. Then there's Dr. Menken, an orthodontist. Never bluffs. If he raises, you only stay if you've got something solid."

Cooper paused mid-drink, weighing details against motive. He had seen this side of Sinclair before; energized, sharp-eyed, cataloguing every detail with methodical pleasure: an intensity rarely brought to paperwork or witness interviews.

"How often do you play there?" Reeves asked evenly.

Sinclair met his eyes, tone casual but clearly rehearsed. "Few times a month. When it makes sense."

"Every weekend?" Cooper pressed.

Sinclair hesitated, then: "Not every weekend."

"Most," Reeves said flatly.

A trace of defensiveness crept into Sinclair's voice. "It's professional networking. The tables are full of talkers. Bartenders, retirees, people who say everything when they're up or losing bad."

Reeves didn't argue. "If you say so."

"Look, two months back I was at the table with Jenkins, the day bartender here. He starts venting after a few drinks about some guy who walks tabs all over town. Says he'll wind up dead someday." Sinclair leaned in, energy rising again. "If he does, I have a suspect lined up already."

Cooper gave him a noncommittal nod. "Could be useful."

Sinclair caught none of the reservation. "Blackburn always says informants turn up where you least expect." Her name surfaced again. A touchstone for justification and authority.

Reeves glanced at his watch. It was a clear signal to wrap up. "If you want Blackburn impressed, she'll want progress on Hargrove more than theories."

"That's what I'm aiming for," Sinclair said, but his attention was already drifting, calculating hands or probabilities rather than facts.

"Before or after you blow ten grand at Bright Star?" Cooper asked quietly.

Sinclair's expression tightened before smoothing into neutrality. "Preferably both."

Reeves stood, pulling his jacket from the back of his chair. "Better call it. Linda's expecting me."

"Tell her I said hi," Cooper said, finishing his drink.

"And good luck to Sarah on the SATs," Sinclair added. He was making an effort.

Reeves gave a brief nod, looked like he might say something else, but let it go. He left cash on the table and threaded through the growing Friday night crowd.

Cooper and Sinclair sat without speaking, the table feeling larger now. Without Reeves, there was less reason to linger.

"I should head out," Cooper said, reaching for his wallet.

"I'll cover this." Sinclair put down his card. Maybe he owed it; maybe it made him feel generous.

Cooper didn't protest. He stood, zipping his jacket. "Good luck with Hargrove."

"Thanks." Sinclair stayed seated, already signaling for another whiskey. "Early night anyway. Still need to go over those files."

Cooper's posture shifted, just enough to register disappointment or resignation. One more drink meant Sinclair would be here a while longer, telling himself it served a purpose.

"See you Monday," Cooper said, pulling up his collar.

Sinclair lifted his glass in acknowledgment, already turning back to his phone. The blue screen lit his face with its harsh glow. His expression tightened as he scrolled: calculations running behind a blank mask.

At the door, Cooper glanced back once. Sinclair remained at the table, alone but unbothered by it. It was a familiar scene, routine enough that Cooper knew not to interfere.

Outside, the air felt cleaner. The cool wind cut against his skin after hours in the stuffy pub. Cooper pulled his collar higher and started toward the subway, leaving Sinclair with his drink and whatever consolation he found in routine or distraction.

The pub door swung shut softly behind him.

Chapter 24

The New Dresden PD Straight Line rolled down Oak Street as Blackburn hit her stride, breath steady and even. The city's early heat pressed against her skin like a damp cloth, promising another long, suffocating day.

Cops called them Justice Jalopies. Civilians preferred PigBots.

Blackburn just saw quarry, and she closed the gap.

She cut through the park where heat hung thick in the air, green leaves and dry earth. Birds chattered somewhere behind the rumble of traffic. Ahead, the Straight Line glided past low shops setting out chalkboard signs, obstacles she sidestepped without breaking rhythm. Above, glass towers caught the sun and threw it back in sharp angles that made her squint.

She gave a sidelong glance to a sign in her path, leaped over it cleanly, landing softly on the balls of her feet.

The Straight Line slowed at a light. Blackburn caught up just as red and blue strobes painted the intersection and the siren split the morning stillness. Without warning, the vehicle rolled forward through red, leaving other cars behind.

Inside, two officers twisted in their seats as their ride took command, alarm written plain across their faces. The police car swept left across lanes and snapped into a tight corner, tires squealing faintly. Blackburn watched their panic with cool interest; the corner of her mouth twitched.

She moved after it, weaving between idling cars and hoods edging into crosswalks. Horns blared in sharp, angry sounds, which she let wash over her. Pulse tight in her throat, legs sure beneath her, she kept pace with the machine.

Whatever had triggered the Straight Line's emergency response would draw attention fast; Blackburn intended to reach it with them. She focused on her breathing and kept her stride even as the car darted unpredictably ahead.

Five minutes of riding adrenaline got her there: The Straight Line braked hard in front of an old thrift shop, its windows dark behind iron grating. It stopped mid-lane; inside, both officers jolted against their belts.

Blackburn slowed as she neared them, eyes scanning for threat or detail. One officer looked green and wide-eyed as he looked up and from side to side.

The senior officer reached down to reset the controls. The lights died out; silence replaced the siren's whine as Blackburn drew level with the back quarter-panel before rapping it twice with her knuckles. Sharp knocks rang hollow against metal.

The Straight Line sat quietly. Blackburn waited on the curb, pulse slowing, sweat cooling on her neck as she sized up the two officers inside.

The passenger finally managed the window, cheeks still flushed pink. He looked young with fresh academy polish, nervous energy radiating from his shoulders.

"Detective Blackburn, Homicide," she said. "What prompted your call?"

He glanced at his partner, fingers brushing his nameplate: Wyatt. "Yes ma'am. Saw you on the Raider Group flyer. Hey Robies, it's her." His attempt at confidence cracked at the edges.

Blackburn flashed a noncommittal smile. Her mind flicked briefly to Willow and that photo shoot at Raider Group, Willow half-hidden among the vehicles, obedient and eagerly licking a tire. Blackburn blinked it away.

The autonomous cruiser had stopped them at an empty storefront. Wyatt fumbled with the door before stepping out.

"And the magic dash says..." Robies muttered, leaning back into the vehicle. The screen displayed: PRIORITY CALL - 10-70 IN PROGRESS - THRIFT SHOP PROWLER. Robies looked up at the faded thrift store sign. It was the empty store.

Wyatt scanned the quiet street, hand resting on his radio. "I don't see anything."

Robies straightened from the car, shaking his head. "System shows an active break-in, but..." He gestured at the darkened shop windows, the undisturbed alley, the complete absence of any disturbance.

Both officers moved cautiously toward the thrift shop. Wyatt tested the front door. It was locked. Robies circled around back, returning with a shrug.

"Clear," Wyatt called into his radio. "False alarm at the thrift shop location."

"False alarm?" Blackburn asked, keeping her tone neutral. "Walk me through your call, officers. I'm interested in how the car works."

"Standard prowler report," Robies said, glancing back at the cruiser uncertainly. "Came in as a 10-70, but there's nobody here."

Blackburn studied their faces, then looked back at the cruiser's dashboard still glowing soft blue. "How does it feel to let the car lead?"

Wyatt hesitated before answering. "Strange," he admitted. "But I guess we're supposed to trust it."

Blackburn didn't respond immediately. She marked the time, too early for anything clean or accidental about this call, and brushed at her top, the fabric rough under her fingers. "Since you're here," she said evenly, "give me a lift to headquarters."

Relief flickered across their faces; compliance came quickly. Blackburn slid into the back seat, a first for her. The seatbelt locked across her chest with a mechanical click, instantly bringing up an image of a woman—Harley? Carol?—strapped into her harness, buckles gleaming and clicking as she moved. She made a note to look the woman up.

As the Straight Line pulled away from the curb, she took in every detail: synthetic upholstery that squeaked under her weight, the silent engine humming beneath them, air thick with that new-car, chemical smell. She made mental notes about how little control even the uniformed men held inside these machines and watched the city slide past through tinted glass.

"Tell me about the safety features," Blackburn said. Her tone stayed smooth, more interested than probing. "Are these as advanced as everyone says?"

Wyatt turned in his seat, vinyl creaking. He brightened at the invitation to explain. "They're impressive, Detective. The seatbelts, for example, are automatic. They calibrate to each passenger's size and weight for best protection."

Blackburn absorbed this, eyes steady. She weighed the responsibility of those designing such systems: safety should outrank profit or praise. She expected nothing less on her streets.

"Any problems with the seatbelts?" she asked.

Wyatt hesitated, voice dropping lower. "Not perfect for very short people. In those cases, we buckle them in manually."

She considered what that meant. Missed details always carried risks, sometimes fatal ones.

Before she could press further, Robies interjected, eager to impress. "Watch this." He flicked a switch on the dash.

A metallic hum vibrated through the seat. A partition began sliding into place, dividing the front from the back seats. Metal panels snapped across Blackburn's line of sight, closing off the open space with a muted click that felt final.

Her body tensed automatically; old reflexes fired before thought could intervene. The sensation of being shut in, walls closing where there should be none, triggered something sharp and immediate in her chest, a tightness that spread to her throat.

She couldn't breathe.

And she couldn't have this.

Blackburn kicked hard at the thin metal door. The impact jarred up her leg; each strike left a new dent, the barrier buckling under vicious blows that rang through the cramped space.

With a crack, one panel derailed and flopped onto her lap. The other sagged, loose and rattling, as the vehicle slowed.

Relief came gradually as light and air returned to her corner of the car. She exhaled sharply, tasting metal on her tongue, and reset her posture by force of habit.

The car halted; the broken barrier swayed in place.

Robies and Wyatt turned around, faces tight with alarm.

Blackburn gave a short cough and brushed the fabric tight on her thighs. "Testing structural integrity under stress," she said, measured now, tone almost dry. "Looks like there's room for improvement."

Robies released a shaky breath and wiped damp palms across his knees. "I... yeah, I guess," he said.

A silence filled the car, sharp and brief, dispersing the fear that had pressed thickly into the cabin moments before. Blackburn let out a breath. Relief steadied her; embarrassment flickered beneath, hot on her cheeks, but she let it pass.

"I'll report it," she said, her tone precise. She turned to Wyatt. "Document the damage. Record how it happened. The Raider Group will want details."

Wyatt nodded, already taking his own notes as the car rolled forward again. Blackburn leaned back against the seat and dialed Willow's work number.

"It's me," Blackburn said to the voicemail. "Contact the Raider maintenance liaison. Their number should be in our paperwork. I need a full list of recent repairs on all Straight Line models. Let's go with the last month."

A loud click came from the dashboard, and a red light flickered on and then off.

"If it's long, print it and leave it on my desk. Otherwise, email is fine."

Blackburn hung up without another word; it felt routine, necessary.

She looked to Robies. "How's this one handle?" She put the piece of metal on the floor behind the driver's side.

Robies shrugged. "It does most of the work for you, ma'am, but the build quality's not great." He gestured toward the battered security door.

Wyatt chimed in from the passenger seat, "The potholes are the worst part. It tries to avoid them so aggressively it can jerk across lanes. You don't always see why until you're halfway over the line."

Blackburn narrowed her eyes. "So to dodge a pothole, it'll veer into oncoming traffic?"

She thought of Jenna Langston: surveillance footage replayed behind her eyes. The car pursuing Jenna, striking her down with a sickening thud, reversing over her body before driving off and flames consumed everything inside.

"They say an update is coming," Wyatt added quietly.

Robies spoke up: "The programming favors pedestrian safety above all else, even if it costs the car itself."

"This is our second Straight Line this month," Wyatt said.

Guilt pried at her ribs for an instant; she forced it aside.

The Straight Line moved through New Dresden with quiet efficiency, its electric hum barely audible beneath the city's morning sounds. Without warning, the Straight Line jerked right. The motion pressed her shoulder into the door. Wyatt swore, hands darting over the dashboard controls.

The car's acceleration pushed them deep into their seats. Exterior noise faded to a muffled rush. Robies' hands grabbed the dash.

"Situation?" Blackburn kept her tone even.

Robies scanned a notification on his terminal and answered without looking up. "Pursuit mode. Detected a priority alert nearby."

Blackburn watched, impassive, as the city slipped past in streaks of color and motion. "Let it handle it." She noted the lack of lights or sirens; spoke it aloud.

Wyatt read from the console: "Suspect vehicle is a blue 2020 Supido Frenzy, four-door." His voice pulled tight.

Blackburn's eyes tracked traffic ahead as the Straight Line maneuvered with clinical aggression, threading lanes and adjusting speed in sharp increments. Each movement felt calculated, nothing wasted.

Wyatt's voice cut through: "Visual, three cars up."

"Details?" Blackburn asked.

Wyatt skimmed an update. "Armed robbery at a variety store, two nights back."

Robies lifted the radio, plastic warm in his grip. "Unit 217 to dispatch. Active pursuit of blue '20 Supido Frenzy eastbound Main." He waited for confirmation but barely acknowledged the reply, attention locked forward as tension built like static in the air.

The gap closed rapidly. The Straight Line aligned itself beside the Supido Frenzy. With a calculated swerve that made Blackburn's stomach lift, it edged the suspect toward parked cars ahead, a beautiful trap. Using the rear passenger side. Her side.

The Supido's driver fought the wheel, but physics won. Metal scraped against metal as the Straight Line pressed its advantage. The Supido bucked and resisted, its driver yanking the wheel left, then right, but the Straight Line's mass and momentum were relentless. With a final metallic shriek, the smaller vehicle wedged itself between two parked cars, trapped like prey in the jaws of a patient predator.

Doors released with soft clicks when they stopped, including Blackburn's rear exit. It just released whomever was in the back seat. A security issue she marked for later review.

Wyatt and Robies were out in an instant.

Blackburn released her seatbelt and stepped out quickly, cool air hitting her face as her shoes met hot pavement.

Robies and Wyatt moved fast. They had their guns up, metal gleaming dully in the morning light, sights fixed on the Supido Frenzy. Their commands cut through the air like blades.

"Driver, hands out the window," Robies said.

"Step out, slowly," Wyatt added, voice steady as stone.

The suspect, late twenties with sweat beading on his forehead, did as he was told. His hands trembled visibly. When he stepped from the car, denim catching on the door frame, Wyatt kept him moving.

"Back up to me. Keep your hands high."

The man followed instructions, unsteady but compliant. Wyatt holstered his sidearm with ease, searched him with quick efficiency, then snapped cuffs over his wrists. The sound was crisp and final as a closing door.

Robies kept the weapon trained as he asked, "Name?"

Blackburn lingered at the edge of the action. She observed with cool approval, procedures followed to the letter, but it was time to go. The chase had broken up her day, left her blood singing, but she was restless now.

She's seen enough. She turned and jogged away, shoes hitting concrete in a steady rhythm that echoed off buildings as she left Robies and Wyatt to finish up.

To hell with the office. There was other work waiting. A room full of furniture needed her attention.

* * *

Blackburn did not return to her home after her run but instead, headed to Oak Street, skin slick with sweat, salt on her lips, focus sharpened to a fine edge. Her breathing came steady and deep. The early morning sky pressed low over New Dresden, heavy with a coming rain that scented the air with ozone. Good. It kept everyone inside.

The white cube van, an online rental with no markings, waited for her in the public parking lot where the KarShark app had promised. She spotted the branded lockbox, pressed in the code, and retrieved the van keys.

It was a five minute drive to the Coconut Glass Candles store. In the alley behind the store, her hired muscle was already waiting. *Physical labor service play. Fetish furniture. Silence and latex gloves required. Payment negotiable.*

Two men took the offer. They would handle everything by hand from the van into her basement without the benefit of the ramp. They had agreed to meet in the alley. Both wore black shirts and jeans with matching black latex gloves. The tall one rolled his shoulders as she cracked open the back door.

She unlocked the door and let them follow her in. The scents of wax, lavender sharp, bergamot citrus-bright, vanilla sweet, wrapped around her, unable to soften what waited deeper in the building.

Blackburn led them straight to Kendria's room.

Close burgundy walls pressed close, the color of old blood in the dim light. The massage table dominated the space, its black leather surface cool and undisturbed under the flat LEDs. Metal rings lined the wall above it, catching glints of light; floggers and paddles hung organized and still as sleeping bats.

"Okay, boys. Table first. Then the chair," she instructed, her voice cutting clean through the thick air. "Boxes after." She ran her hand along the vase, new since she was there. "Make sure this goes last," she said.

They lifted and maneuvered each piece with surprising efficiency, muscles working smoothly under their shirts. The wide leather chair followed next, its weight making them grunt softly; oil bottles and sex toys clinked as they boxed them with care. One man took his t-shirt off and wrapped the kintsugi vase before boxing it. Two crates from the shelves stacked quickly, wood scraping against their gloves.

She made them ride in the back as she drove to her home. Blackburn had told the men she would make them sweat. It was hot. Ramp up. One trip. Down the basement stairs. Don't touch the walls. No complaints.

Her own basement felt cold by comparison, concrete rough underfoot, pipes groaning overhead. Her equipment waited: the treadmill was dark and silent, the free weights were lined precisely, a punching bag was hanging near one wall like a body. The men placed Kendria's belongings along bare cinderblocks in silence, their breathing the only sound.

The massage table now sat beneath a single bulb, shadows pooling beneath it, its presence altered by the new setting.

Blackburn reached into the box of toys, letting her fingers roam until they found what she wanted. She traced the edge of the leather tawse: worn, supple, softened by years of use.

Behind her, she heard them. Latex squeaked softly as it stretched over their knuckles.

She lifted the tawse, feeling its balanced weight in her palm. No flourish, just authority.

Their breathing quickened.

"Three each," she said simply. "You earned it."

The larger man, the one already shirtless, licked his lips.

She tapped the tawse once against her thigh. The slap was flat and businesslike, echoing in the concrete room. No music. No audience. Only purpose.

"Hands out," she ordered. "Gloves off, unless you want me to do it for you."

They obeyed, gloved hands out, elbows tucked. The smaller one trembled. Blackburn stepped closer, matching his height as she met his eyes. She peeled off his gloves, one after the other, and tucked them into his shirt.

For the taller man, she pressed his wrist with her thumb before peeling away the glove. It snapped free from his fingers. The second followed, both tossed to the floor beside his shirt, near the vase.

She adjusted their wrists with expertise, noting the flex of tendons, the breath held tight in their chests.

Then she got to work.

Chapter 25

Sunday morning arrived without expectation. Blackburn took her coffee outside and lingered on the porch. The ceramic was warm against her palms. Birds scattered their calls through the trees, sharp chirps and long trills cutting through the morning quiet. Down the block, two kids darted along their driveway on bikes, wheels clicking over concrete cracks. Their laughter broke through the air, bright and sudden.

She tightened her grip on the mug, feeling heat seep through. Deonte Mills should have sounded like that, riding battered training wheels with arms spread like wings, chasing friends under the open sky. He was five. Only five.

Sandy was five when she died.

His father found him: a small limp boy laid out on a towel instead of a bed. The 911 call came in frantically, choked with half-finished sentences and unasked questions. The case landed on Dawson's desk; he barely touched it before taking leave three weeks ago. Now it waited in a drawer somewhere. Almost forgotten.

Another ring of bicycle bells drifted up the street, metallic and clear. Blackburn stepped back inside, the screen door clicking shut behind her. Deonte's memory shadowed her steps.

The case file had become part of her now, every detail cata-logued and sharp. A child, twenty-three pounds with ribs visible through tissue-thin skin, dead in a dirty apartment littered with heroin residue. Syringes. Cotton balls darkened with use. A rubber tourniquet tossed on carpet stained brown and yellow. His father said he had tried to cool a fever with ice, but the evidence spoke for itself. And in the background of the 911 call, a woman's voice. Dawson hadn't traced her.

Blackburn set her coffee aside with a clipped motion, the mug meeting the counter harder than intended. No toys in those photos, no sign a child had ever lived there. Only scorch marks from burned spoons and beer cans crushed against sagging furniture.

Sunday morning or not, this couldn't wait. She couldn't wait.

Sunlight pressed between city buildings as she steered her black sedan through New Dresden's streets. Downtown pulsed with week-end traffic: churchgoers in church, crowds drifting toward brunch spots and open patios. The smell of grilled meat and coffee drifted through her cracked window.

She drove easily, attention narrowed to what mattered. Just a con-versation with Caleb Mills, nothing more. She didn't bother slowing her speed for stop signs; red lights merited abrupt halts at best, fingers drumming impatience along the leather-wrapped steering wheel.

The waterfront rose ahead: bricks faded to dull orange, paint peel-ing from sun-bleached walls in long strips. The apartment complex hunched over cracked sidewalks, a relic clinging to its own neglect.

Just one quick stop at a nearby corner store for cigarettes, and she was ready. Blackburn parked and cut the engine. For a moment she sat still, watching sunlight stretch across concrete and garbage-strewn grass. The car ticked as it cooled. Then she stepped out into the day, ready to see Caleb Mills for herself.

Blackburn checked her notes. Apartment 1703. She had no intention of confronting him where Deonte had died. Nor would he want a cop in his home. Caleb Mills would come down.

She walked to the entry phone, heels steady on cracked concrete. The receiver was sticky with grime; she held it away from her face, scanning the faded name list. C. Mills, code 1501. She keyed it in and listened to the electronic buzz.

When Caleb answered, her voice shifted, even and measured. "Mr. Mills, this is Detective Morgan Blackburn with New Dresden police, here about Deonte. I'm new on the case. Mind coming down for a quick word?" Her tone balanced command and reassurance.

A pause, static crackling, then what sounded like relief on the other end.

"Yeah. Main door?"

"That's right." She hung up before he could add anything else. She wiped her palm on her coat, feeling the residue still clinging.

Waiting, she slipped back to her car and took the sanitizer from the glove box. The gel was cold on her skin. She used more than needed, rubbing hands until they stung from the alcohol, the sharp scent cutting through stale air and old garbage.

She watched the sidewalk: two men loitered by the wall, both tense and alert like animals sizing her up. The taller one had a sharp jaw and jittery movements; his companion was heavier-set, clothes loose and stained, eyes darting as if expecting trouble.

Blackburn kept her posture straight, hand near her sidearm but not quite touching the textured grip.

"NDPD Homicide," she called out, voice flat and clear. "You two hear about the little—?"

That broke their confidence fast enough; neither waited for follow-up. Their footsteps scraped against the pavement as they faded into shadow without argument or glance back.

A door groaned open behind her; she turned toward the entrance just as Caleb emerged.

Caleb Mills was a gaunt, disheveled man in his mid-thirties, with hollow cheeks and sunken, bloodshot eyes that spoke of sleepless nights and relentless drug use. Thin, unkempt hair. Sallow skin marked with sores and a deathly pallor.

He moved with effort, thin to the edge of collapse, clothes barely hanging on him, hands deep in pockets to hide their shaking. Each step looked rehearsed for someone who rarely left his apartment. The soles of his shoes scraped with each movement.

He was ready to break. Blackburn kept her expression neutral as he approached, letting silence do its work between them.

"You the cop? Investigating Deonte?" His voice was rough, like sandpaper on wood.

"Yes." Blackburn approached, her tone neutral, softer at the edges. "I'm sorry for your loss."

He nodded but watched her warily, eyes bloodshot and restless. "What about him?"

"Would you like to sit? We can talk here." Blackburn nodded toward the concrete steps, stained dark in patches, cracked where weeds pushed through.

Caleb hesitated. His weight shifted from foot to foot.

Blackburn glanced over the steps and chose a spot where old stains had faded. She lowered herself onto the concrete, feeling the cold seep through her pants. The surface was rough beneath her palm.

After a moment, Caleb sat beside her, keeping his distance. His body was rigid, fingers making restless circles against worn denim. He avoided her eyes.

A faded cross marked the webbed skin between his thumb and index finger, old work with ink blurred at the edges. A teenage impulse, most likely, done with a needle and India ink in someone's garage. His forearm carried a rose whose petals had lost their definition, and beside it, an uncertain tiger with stripes that wavered like heat mirages. Between them, 'mom' sprawled in basic script, the letters uneven. Barbed wire wrapped around one bicep, the metal thorns breaking apart into birds that took flight toward his shoulder.

Blackburn scanned the empty lot around them, then the quiet street beyond. The day was mostly silent except for distant traffic, a low rumble like waves, and occasional gusts pushing empty dry food wrappers along the sidewalk with skittering sounds.

Thin weeds pushed through cracks in the steps, stems bent but persistent. They looked out of place among broken bottles that caught light and crumpled wrappers faded to gray. The building's paint had almost surrendered, peeling in long strips, exposing concrete beneath like exposed bone. Windows were patched with cardboard or cloth, corners lifting and flapping in the wind.

Blackburn cataloged these details: this was not a home. She noted Caleb's twitching fingers, a slight tremor hinting at nerves or something else he needed. His knee bounced in a steady rhythm.

Across a paved courtyard sat a playground: motionless slides and warped swings hung from chains that creaked softly in the breeze. Grass had thinned to hard-packed dirt; trash collected around the sagging fence like driftwood.

Somewhere far off, sirens wailed, a constant presence here but muted by distance into something almost melodic.

Caleb watched her take in the scene. Her expression gave nothing away. He felt nothing at all.

"I didn't call ahead," she said, voice steady. "Hope that's all right."

Caleb shifted weight, shoes scraping concrete. "It's fine. I lost track of time. Where's that other guy?"

"Detective Dawson? On another case. How are you managing?" She looked over at him, expression neutral. Her eyes gave away nothing.

He rubbed his sleeve across his chin, the fabric sounding rough. "I don't know. Some days are worse than others."

She let a moment stretch between them, counting her own breaths, before speaking again. "Will there be a funeral for Deonte? I'd like to come."

He hesitated, shoulders caving in on themselves. "I'm not sure I can afford one." His voice carried exhaustion in every syllable.

"The county has programs." Blackburn kept her tone even, reassuring. "Once everything's resolved, they'll cover the arrangements directly with the funeral home."

Caleb glanced at her, uncertainty flickering across features. "They pay them straight? Not through me?"

"It's their policy," she said.

She pulled the cigarette pack from her pocket, cellophane crinkling as she peeled it back. Caleb watched her hands, but said nothing.

She offered him the pack with a nod, cigarettes neat in their rows.

"Yeah, thanks." He took one, fingers brushing hers briefly, his skin cold and dry.

She tapped out another for herself, holding it without lighting it.

"Need this?" She produced a silver lighter, metal smooth in her palm.

"Yeah." His answer barely reached above the ambient noise.

They sat side by side in the sunlight. She flicked the lighter open and held it steady for Caleb as he hunched forward, cupping his hands to protect the flame from the faint wind.

A brief glow caught his face: hollow cheeks, tired eyes, stubble dark against pale skin. He drew on the cigarette, ember brightening, showing every nervous tick. Tobacco crackled softly. Blackburn studied him, noting a slight tremor in his hand, the way his lips pressed tightly between drags. The guilt was already there; she just had to give it permission to surface.

He exhaled slowly. Smoke drifted upward, blue-gray and thinning into thin air. His shoulders lowered as if the cigarette let some tension bleed out.

"You not having one?" His voice rasped, dry as old leaves.

She shook her head. "No. Trying to quit." A half-smile touched her lips. She often used new packs for suspects who needed a hint of kindness.

A car passed by, tires rolling over cracked pavement and scattered glass before vanishing down the block. The engine faded to nothing. "Ever try quitting?" she asked.

Caleb let out a dry laugh that caught in his throat and took another drag. "Nah. Too much hassle." He blew smoke at nothing in particular, watching it dissipate. "Child Services used to ride me about that."

"Smoking?"

He nodded. "Yeah. Said I was messing up Deonte's lungs or whatever." Another long pull from his cigarette, the ember glowing bright.

"Kids are tough," Blackburn said, voice flat. Her gaze never left him. She could feel him breaking, the fissures spreading with each carefully chosen word.

Caleb went quiet. He stared at the ground, at a crack running through concrete like a dark vein. "Sometimes they don't come back from it," he muttered.

Blackburn waited, letting the silence settle between them, heavy but not oppressive, before answering. "You never know what can happen," she said.

The only sound was his cigarette burning down, paper curling black; ash clung to his fingers before falling.

Caleb turned to her, uncertainty clouding features. "You got kids?"

She watched him a second longer before answering. "Yeah, two." Her tone was soft. "With their grandparents now." She gave a small shrug, shoulders barely moving. "Some things you just can't fix."

Caleb's eyes narrowed to slits. "Child services?" His voice barely carried over the distant hum of traffic.

Blackburn nodded, steady. "You care about your kids, then somebody shows up. Doesn't matter what you do, they tell you it's not enough. Or it's too much." Her tone stayed calm, but she shaved words down, letting frustration creep in at the edges like rust.

Caleb flicked his cigarette away. The ember traced a brief arc, sparks scattering as it hit the broken asphalt with a soft hiss. He let out a long breath that disappeared into the warm air. "They never get it." His words dropped between them, weighted with old anger.

He stared at his hands, knuckles split and scabbed, skin roughened by years he couldn't name. Blackburn noted the contrast: her own nails clean, trimmed neat; his ragged and bitten down.

She kept her eyes on him, weighing each micro-expression. "I'm not narcotics," she said, tilting her chin toward sores on his hands, red and angry against pale skin. "I've seen things too. I know you have."

His fingers twitched involuntarily; gaze settled on a new scab bright against old scars. He picked at it once, a bead of blood welling, before stopping. "Yeah," he muttered.

Something shifted behind his eyes, it was exactly what she'd been waiting for. She brushed dust from her knee deliberately, unhurriedly, feeling grit beneath her fingers. "Getting by isn't easy," she said. "Some nights just don't let up. Makes a person do things they never thought they would."

Caleb looked up quickly; red-rimmed eyes met hers and just as quickly skittered away like startled birds. "Never thought of it like that," he said, his shoulders tightening, pulling inward. Defiant but hollow.

A slight curve touched Blackburn's lips, there and gone like a shadow. "Not everyone holds up," she replied quietly. "You do." Her voice stayed even, letting respect and observation stand without cushioning.

Silence pressed in until only distant sirens cut through, wailing high and thin, a reminder of everything beyond this patch of concrete and shadow. Caleb's hands fidgeted, fingers drumming against his thigh as his eyes tracked aimlessly across the sidewalk, following cracks and stains.

Minutes slipped past without a word, marked only by their breathing.

At last Caleb spoke again, voice taut as wire. "Got another cigarette?"

Blackburn opened the pack and offered one without comment, motion smooth. She held the lighter close, thumb on the wheel. Their faces caught its brief flare, orange light dancing across skin, before settling back under the sun's steady glow.

Caleb inhaled deeply; smoke rose around him as he exhaled, wreathing sharp cheeks and tired eyes that narrowed when they found Blackburn watching him.

"You hunt killers?" He drew on the cigarette again, ember pulsing, and waited for her answer.

"Sometimes," Blackburn said. Her tone stayed level, almost distant. "But most of the time, they turn themselves in. Killing changes you, if there's anything left to change." She saw the emptiness in his eyes. "If you have a soul."

Caleb frowned, confusion tightening the corners of his mouth. "Doesn't everyone have a soul?"

Blackburn's smile was small and as cold as winter air. "Not even close. That's a story people tell themselves, churchmen especially, so you'll pay them to 'save' something you never had. Tithes, donations, whatever helps the cause. It does nothing real for anyone. Some of the most faithful are the worst killers I know." She looked at him directly, unblinking. "Just my opinion. I couldn't say for sure. I've never killed anyone."

The silence that followed hung between them, dense but not dramatic. Caleb kept eyes on his cigarette, rolling it between nicotine-stained fingers, ash building, letting seconds stretch like pulled taffy.

"So," he said after a while, steady but uncertain. "Killers don't have souls?"

Blackburn met his look without blinking. "Some do. You'll notice them. They're the ones who can't live with it. They confess or turn themselves in after a while. Their conscience eats away at them piece by piece until there's nothing left but guilt and the need for relief." She paused, letting the words settle. "Confession's the only cure."

"The churchmen got that right, huh?" Caleb said with a dry laugh.

She stretched one leg, feeling the stiffness in her knee, then drew it back in, barely shifting on cold concrete. There was no threat in her posture, a quiet readiness instead, but she didn't break eye contact.

"The rest, the ones I hunt, they don't confess because there's nothing inside them to punish or forgive." Her words came clipped, businesslike. "No soul means no cost."

She studied Caleb's eyes, reading whatever flickered behind them: fear, doubt, something else swimming in the depths.

"You pray much?" she asked him quietly. "Did your mother make you?"

He hesitated, cigarette trembling between fingers, silent long enough that it became its own answer. Blackburn didn't rush him.

Finally, he spoke, his voice as rough as gravel. "If you pray, does that mean you have a soul?" He sounded like he was testing words, rolling them around like foreign objects.

Blackburn shook her head once, not unkindly. "There are plenty who pray, hoping to get one," she said simply.

Caleb looked lost for a moment, mouth working silently before he found words. "Does that work?"

"Sometimes." Blackburn watched him closely, cataloging each twitch and tell. "It's called the dark night of the soul. Ever heard of that? Maybe from your mother in church?"

Caleb blinked as if smoke stung his eyes; cigarette smoke drifted between them, a gray veil, while he considered her words and what might be true about himself after all. "I think maybe in a song?"

A figure stepped from the building, footsteps sharp against concrete. For a moment, the movement divided Blackburn and Caleb, a dark shape blocking each from the other's view. The presence hovered, leather jacket creaking, keys jangling, then fading. Silence returned deeper than before.

Caleb broke it. "Yeah. Maybe I've heard of that," he said, voice clearer in the emptiness. He straightened, vertebrae popping, then let himself slump back down. "Not sure."

Blackburn watched him, expression carved from stone, her study methodical as a surgeon's. She tracked small shifts in his face: fear pulling at the corners of his eyes, exhaustion in the downward curve of his mouth, something like shame coloring his cheeks. She caught herself responding to his discomfort, a softening around her eyes, before making herself still again.

"It's what comes next," she offered. "When you're sure everything's done. That's when things change. Sometimes, hitting bottom is when you can start over. Start breathing again, you know?"

Caleb took a drag, the ember flaring orange-bright against his face. Smoke hung near his skin, clinging, before dissolving. He glanced at Blackburn, voice rough as torn paper. "You really think that?"

Her gaze stayed fixed on him, unwavering. "A lot of people do," she replied evenly. "And yeah, I do too. You only know who you are once you hit bottom. That's when you see if there's anything left worth saving."

He hesitated, Adam's apple bobbing, then asked, "But not everyone has that, right?" His tone faltered, cracking on the last word.

Blackburn noted the way he asked, the desperate edge beneath casual words; she could sense doubt pressing his chest.

"No. Not everyone does." She let it sit for a heartbeat, two, before continuing: "But if you're worried, if pain like that keeps you up at three in the morning, you've got it. It's your soul talking to you, pushing you toward something better."

Caleb looked away and drew deeply on his cigarette, the ember eating toward his fingers, his hands unsteady.

Blackburn rose without hurry, knees fluid, movement graceful. She brushed dust from her coat with a sweep of hand, feeling grit fall away. Caleb watched her movements as if they held a meaning he could decode if he tried hard enough.

"In my experience, Mr. Mills," she said, as level as still water, "your soul knows how to survive the worst night you'll ever have." She paused, counting three beats of his rapid pulse visible at his throat. "If you wake up in the morning ready to start over, that's how you can tell."

Blackburn's fingertip traced a path along her own neck. "Ever thought about a swallow? The old sailors got them. It stands for freedom. Loyalty to family."

Caleb's hand drifted upward, unconsciously mirroring her gesture. "Maybe."

Blackburn's fingers closed around the lighter, metal warm now from her palm, and slipped it into her pocket. She took out the cigarettes, her business card sliding into the pack with a soft whisper, a quiet signal of intent. She tossed it to Caleb; it landed in his lap with a light plop. His gaze darted from the pack to Blackburn, searching for meaning in her blank expression.

She turned and walked to her car. Each step was steady, heels tapping out an even rhythm on the cracked pavement. She knew he was watching her. She got in, the door closing with a solid thunk. The leather seat felt cold. As she drove off, she glanced in the mirror: Caleb was reaching into the cigarette package as he stood on the curb, shoulders hunched against more than her words.

Out of sight, Blackburn allowed herself a quick burst of satisfaction, a low exhale that was almost a laugh. The air through the cracked window sharpened her focus. She knew he would call in the morning. The certainty settled in her chest like a stone.

Chapter 26

Blackburn stared at the kintsugi vase she had taken from Kendria's back room. It was beautiful. Gold filled the fractured lines, a striking contrast to the black porcelain. She picked it up, rotated it in her hands. It felt smooth and cool. She flipped it over. It was branded with a maker's mark.

The phone rang, its shrill tone cutting through the bullpen's murmur. She answered, recognizing Sergeant Beckett's clipped cadence immediately.

"Detective Blackburn. There's been an accident with an anonymous car. Details coming in. Ten and Progressive Drive. Units en route. Figured you'd want the heads-up."

She kept her voice even, her fingers tightening on the receiver. "Appreciate it, Sergeant." She hung up. The idiot still didn't understand 'autonomous'.

She quickly typed a message:

You okay?

Blackburn rose and called through her open door, "Reeves. Let's go."

Reeves stood from his desk, grabbed his jacket, and followed without a word.

They took the stairs to the garage in silence, their footsteps echoing in the concrete stairwell. Blackburn didn't want to think about Lilith or the persistent knot tightening in her stomach. She focused on the nearest professional step: get to the scene, assess, report.

Reeves slid into the passenger seat as Blackburn started the car. The exit ramp was slick and tight. She pushed through traffic, every stoplight an irritation burning behind her eyes.

"What's going on?" Reeves asked.

"Autonomous vehicle accident," she replied, the words tasting metallic. "That's all we've got."

She didn't share more. Not about the fear crawling cold at the back of her mind. She increased speed along each straightaway, tires humming against wet asphalt.

Her phone buzzed. She could not answer, but knew it was Lilith. She was okay.

At Tenth and Progressive, emergency lights painted the night in strobing blue and red. Uniformed officers cordoned off the intersection while bystanders pressed against the yellow tape, phones raised like offerings to the chaos. A twisted electric vehicle sat in the center of it all, its smooth lines now warped metal. Paramedics were already closing up their gear.

Blackburn stepped out into a gust of wind carrying burned rubber and the sharp chemical tang of coolant mixing with battery acid.

Reeves surveyed the scene, jaw set hard. "Damn," he said under his breath.

A uniform officer approached, his skin washed pale under the flashing lights. "Detective Blackburn? Sergeant said you'd be here." He hesitated, swallowing before continuing. "One fatality. The driver. No one else was hurt."

Relief flickered through her chest, almost instantly replaced by sour guilt. Blackburn closed both away behind procedure. "Show me," she said.

They walked to the vehicle together. Paramedics pulled a black sheet over the shape in the driver's seat, the fabric settling with terrible finality.

Blackburn glanced inside, confirmed no passengers, then stepped back. This was not their case. This car was electric, not autonomous. No sign of anything tying this to her ongoing investigation.

She turned to Reeves. "Not ours after all. We're leaving." She nodded to the officer. "This one is yours."

Brynn Cassidy cut through the crowd, the reporter's hair snapping around her face as cameras tracked her every move. She was already closing the distance, recording equipment catching the light like weapons.

Blackburn exhaled and muttered to Reeves without looking at him. "You'll want to see this."

Reeves gave a quick nod and leaned against an unmarked cruiser to watch.

Brynn reached them first, voice pitched for maximum reach over the crowd chatter. "Detective Blackburn. Is this linked to your ongoing hit-and-run investigations?"

The cameras waited for Blackburn's answer as Brynn's gaze pressed in on her, a constant test for weakness that Blackburn refused to show.

She let a small smile settle on her mouth but kept things brief. "Early indications are that this is a straightforward car accident." She turned away, but Brynn pressed forward with another question before she could leave.

"Detective, given New Dresden's history with autonomous vehicles killing civilians, what steps are you taking to rule out connections? What details are you investigating for crossover?"

Blackburn felt pressure building beneath her ribs but showed nothing outwardly. "This is a manual electric vehicle. There is no evidence at this time linking this incident to the autonomous vehicle case," she stated evenly.

Brynn didn't back down. Her microphone extended further, tone sharpened by persistence. "Can you comment on whether navigation or autopilot features might be involved, like with Jenna Langston or Kendria Chaplin?"

The names hit harder than any physical blow. Memory gave a flash of violence and loss, but she held steady. Her reply came cool and measured. "This crash will be investigated thoroughly, like any other traffic fatality. By Traffic Services. I have nothing further to add."

She turned away from the cameras and walked back toward Reeves. Scene assessed, interview managed, control restored, almost.

Brynn pressed forward, eyes steady and voice sharp as metal. "Witnesses say the EV driver acted strangely before the crash. Are you considering possible tampering or a hijacked navigation system, like in prior cases? How does that factor into your current investigation?"

Joseph Henderson adjusted his camera, pushing in close. The lens picked up every shift in Blackburn's face, the slight tightening at her jaw, the deliberate stillness of her eyes.

Blackburn allowed herself a moment at the center of attention. The heat from the television lights pressed against her skin. She recognized Brynn's ambition. This story could make the reporter's career. Blackburn waited, letting more cameras crowd in until Brynn's shoulders dropped, realizing she'd lost her exclusive. The reporter's mouth tightened.

"The investigation is reviewing all statements about the vehicle's behavior," Blackburn said, her words thoughtful. "You need to speak to the investigating officers."

Brynn didn't back down. "Given these recent fatalities involving autonomous tech, what measures is the department taking to safeguard public trust and safety? Is this the same system used by Straight Line cars?"

Blackburn addressed the full press line, feeling their collective gaze. "No, clearly not. This is an *electric* vehicle. The NDPD treats all events with the utmost seriousness."

Reporters pressed closer, their breath and body heat creating a wall of humanity under the glare of camera lights. The smell of coffee and sweat hung in the air. Blackburn stood still, shoulders back, letting the intensity break around her without comment.

A red-haired reporter forced his way forward, his elbow catching another journalist. "Detective Blackburn, why are homicide detectives here if this was just an accident?"

She looked out over the group, noting the hunger on their faces. "It's early in the process, and while it appears to be a single-car accident, standard procedure sends our best investigators to major incidents like this."

Before he could speak again, a short woman with close-cropped blonde hair stepped up, her voice cutting through the murmur. "After these unexplained problems with autonomous vehicles, do you believe the police are prepared for the complications these technologies bring to public safety? Even the fire trucks are moving to autonomous now."

Blackburn answered without pause, the words flowing smooth. "Our department sees value in new technology but knows it comes with challenges we're still learning to manage. We're working with specialists to adapt our investigative approach as these systems evolve. The goal is always a complete investigation and clear accountability."

The blonde reporter started a follow-up but was cut off by a heavy-set man with a thick beard who pushed past her. His tone carried an edge of skepticism. "Some say reliance on autonomous vehicles could hurt policing. Less human contact means less community trust. Where do you stand?"

Blackburn didn't flinch, though she felt the shift in the crowd's mood. "People worry about technology overshadowing human interaction. That's fair. But tools don't replace people; they support us when used right. For homicide detectives especially, most encounters aren't wanted. No one is happy when we arrive at their door, regardless of tech."

Brynn leaned in again, her face flushed with frustration at losing command of the story. Her question came quickly and directly, words clipped: "With Jenna Langston and Kendria Chaplin both dead, is there evidence this crash is part of a pattern targeting people connected to autonomous vehicles?"

Blackburn kept her tone even, though she could taste the tension in the crowd. The hunger for something sensational showed clearly on every face, in every forward-leaning body.

"I can't discuss this accident," she said, firm but measured. "Traffic Services will pursue all possibilities until the facts are certain. It's too soon for speculation."

She shifted focus away from Brynn, glancing at Reeves, who watched from a distance, his figure a steady presence against the chaos.

But Brynn broke in again, her voice carrying a different quality now: "Is it true you have someone new in your life? Should they be worried for their safety?"

For a moment everything contracted. The crowd stilled. Even the ambient street noise faded.

Bitch.

Blackburn turned back to Brynn, voice steady but cold now, each word precise. "Pardon me?"

The energy shifted. Curiosity soured into something darker, suggestion and threat beneath Brynn's words while the assembly waited, breath held, for Blackburn's next move.

Brynn didn't move. Her voice remained even, though something coiled beneath the surface. "Doesn't this all seem suspect? After what's happened, you want to risk someone else?"

Blackburn kept her face still, letting the moment stretch like pulled wire. She evaluated Brynn's tone, the pointed glance, the subtle shift of weight that betrayed calculation. The line between professional curiosity and something sharper wavered in the air between them. For a second, Lilith's face flickered behind her eyes. How close was this? Was Brynn guessing, or did she know?

"Detective, what's she talking about?"

"I have no idea."

Brynn smiled without warmth, her eyes fixed on Blackburn like pinpoints of ice. "There's a pattern here with these victims. You might want to be more careful about your relationships. Someone could say you're at the center of all this."

Blackburn studied her. No flash of anger crossed her face, just a calculation that ticked behind her eyes. She stepped in, close enough to catch the faint scent of Brynn's perfume, close enough to force her back a fraction. Her voice dropped low and quiet.

"If you have evidence, bring it forward."

Blackburn leaned in further. Her lips nearly brushed Brynn's ear, her breath barely stirring the air between them, her voice flat and cold.

"If you keep this up, I will shoot you in the face."

Brynn stiffened. For a breath, her mask slipped. Confusion cut across her features before she recovered. Behind them, the press kept shouting questions, their voices blending into white noise.

"What did you say?" Brynn's voice wavered, the shock bleeding through despite her effort to contain it.

Blackburn straightened, her tone clear and carrying for the crowd. "If there's documentation about either incident, vehicle data or otherwise, you can send it directly to me."

Anger flared in Brynn now. Heat rose in her cheeks as she snapped back. "That was a threat! You just threatened to shoot me in public!"

The noise dimmed as attention shifted to their exchange. Blackburn remained relaxed, hands visible at her sides, posture open but unreadable as Brynn raged.

"Are you going to shoot me in the face?"

"I what?" Blackburn leaned back. A small, puzzled smile played at the corners of her mouth. "I'm not sure what you think you heard, but threatening a member of the press would end my career. Why would I do something so self-destructive? Of course I did not."

"You did! She did. She just said she would shoot me!" Brynn looked at the surrounding reporters. "Everyone heard that! You threatened my life on camera!"

Blackburn shook her head, then she suddenly turned and called out, "EMS! Over here." She waved an EMT toward them from the edge of the crash scene, a sharp pivot that refocused every camera and microphone in range like iron filings to a magnet.

"I dare you to say it again!" Brynn shouted, her voice becoming tight and shrill.

"If you have information about either incident, vehicle data or otherwise, you can send it directly to me. Or you can send it to anyone at the NDPD," Blackburn said as she held Brynn's gaze.

"You didn't! You said you'd shoot me!" Brynn screamed. She shook, her face flushing. "You'll pay for this, Blackburn."

The EMT jogged over, his equipment bag bouncing against his hip, scanning them both for visible injuries. Reporters murmured among themselves as photographers reset their focus on Brynn and the medic beside her. Brynn shot Blackburn a glare edged with uncertainty.

"Why are you calling EMS?" she demanded.

Blackburn didn't blink. "You just said something about being shot in the face." Then, to the EMT, "She claims she was shot in the face."

"Ma'am? Where are you hurt?" he asked as he plopped his bag down.

The medic moved toward Brynn automatically, latex gloves already half-pulled from his pocket, but she shoved his hands away and snapped, "I wasn't shot! I said she threatened to shoot me!" Her words rang out above the commotion, but only brought more attention from every angle. Lenses turned in a coordinated wave of curiosity and confusion as more EMTs appeared behind her.

Blackburn stayed where she was, almost sympathetic, almost concerned, but not quite either one. "Nobody threatened anybody," she said softly to the EMT, then addressed Brynn again without looking directly at her. "Why would I do that?"

Brynn insisted anyway, her voice rising above the renewed chaos. "She said it! She threatened me!" Reporters now shouted over each other for clarification, their questions overlapping into a cacophony.

"Did Detective Blackburn make a violent threat?" one called out from behind a camera tripod.

"Was anyone shot here?" another demanded. "Detective? Did you shoot someone?"

"Of course not." Blackburn simply shook her head once, her expression neutral as morning fog, as the growing disorder of crisis pressed around them all.

Blackburn raised her hand for silence. "I've never fired my weapon in the line of duty, or for any other reason," she said, her voice cutting cleanly through the ambient chatter. "I have no idea what Ms. Cassidy means."

She moved toward the EMT, dropping her tone to something that was *almost* too soft for the other reporters to hear. "You should know that Brynn Cassidy is acting erratically. She seems fixated on threats. Maybe check if she's all right, for everyone's safety. Make sure she's stable." She delivered it like a fact, nothing more.

The EMT nodded and approached Brynn cautiously, hands visible and open. "Ms. Cassidy? Brynn? I'm just going to check in with you. How are you feeling right now?"

Brynn's arm whipped out, fast and sharp. "Get away from me!" The slap cracked against his hand, loud enough to turn every head in the crowd. Camera shutters fired in rapid bursts, the sound like insects swarming as bodies pressed closer.

Blackburn caught Reeves watching her, one eyebrow lifted in something that might have been awe.

She pitched her voice to carry: "Brynn, if you strike an EMT again, you'll be arrested for assault." Each word landed. "If he's hurt, felony assault is on the table: up to two years and a four-thousand-dollar fine."

The reporters' eyes gleamed, hungry and attentive.

"Oh, don't worry about me," he said. "I'm concerned about Brynn here."

Blackburn turned back to Brynn, letting the temperature drop from her voice. "The EMT is here to make sure you're safe. Let him do his job."

Under the harsh glare of lights and lenses, Brynn's face shifted from fury to bewilderment, then to something rawer as understanding dawned. The cameras kept rolling while she stood exposed, her colleagues' expressions no longer friendly or familiar.

"I'm fine," she managed, the words barely carrying. She caught Joseph's eye, her cameraman, and retreated through the crowd with quick, uneven steps.

As Brynn's figure receded, Blackburn thanked the EMT and drifted to where Reeves waited at the crowd's edge, allowing herself the briefest smile.

Reeves shook his head, disbelief coloring his quiet words. "That was a hell of a play. Did you actually threaten to shoot her?"

A short laugh escaped Blackburn. "Me? Not even close."

They walked to Blackburn's car, the crowd noise fading behind them. Inside the quiet cabin, she dialed Sergeant Beckett.

"It's Blackburn," she said when his voice came through. "The incident is outside my usual jurisdiction because of the vehicle class, but it's good I was there. A reporter, Brynn Cassidy, made a scene. EMTs cleared her before letting her go."

Beckett's relief carried clearly through the speaker. "Appreciate it. The less I deal with reporters, the better."

After ending the call, Reeves regarded Blackburn from the passenger seat, skepticism playing at the corners of his mouth.

"You improvise well," he said.

Blackburn turned the key, the engine purring to life beneath them. She offered only a small, satisfied curve of her lips. "Imagination is Brynn's department."

They eased away from the curb into the deepening dusk, Blackburn's hands steady on the wheel as the city swallowed them up, leaving whatever chaos they'd sparked to burn itself out in their wake.

Chapter 27

Blackburn walked down the hallway in her usual uniform: crisp white shirt, black pants, sensible shoes. The play on Brynn was picture perfect. It was a pleasant power that grounded her while her mind sharpened for the day ahead. The message from Lilith was cute.

>*Yes, okay. Thank you for following up.*

The weekend had been productive. The back room at the candle shop was emptied. Her basement workspace was coming together, new tools at her disposal and payments left their marks on willing men. The welts would fade by week's end. She'd pressed a suspect to his edge; his voice had cracked during their last conversation.

And now, down the hall, Blackburn could see possibilities. She paused outside Willow's office. The familiar scent of coffee and electronics drifted through the doorway. Her lips twitched as she slipped inside, leaving the door deliberately open behind her. LED lights washed the space in cold white, bleaching color from everything they touched. Willow looked up from her computer, surprise flickering across her features before she smoothed her expression into something neutral.

"Hi," Willow said evenly. "Something I can help you with?"

Blackburn eased into the chair near Willow's desk, the vinyl creaking softly as she crossed her legs. "Just checking on Sinclair," she said. "Any movement on those files? His photos, browser history?"

Sinclair had confessed to watching her. That called for consequences. Blackburn preferred hers personal. A folder of explicit material loaded onto his station would end him if needed.

Willow shook her head, continuing to type without looking away from the screen. "Nothing yet. I have the photos, but I haven't installed them."

"That's fine." Blackburn let her gaze wander over the tangle of cables and stacks of hardware that cluttered every surface. "I rode one of those Straight Lines this weekend. Standard activation protocol." Her voice carried the tone of casual conversation. "Strange how routine it felt."

Willow's fingers stilled, suspended above the keys. "You did?" She kept her tone carefully neutral.

Blackburn nodded, eyes narrowing as she tracked every micro-expression on Willow's face. "Had me thinking about Jenna and Kendria again."

Silence stretched between them. Willow remained motionless, face blank except for the slight tightening around her eyes.

"I'm still working on the video from the candle store," Willow said.

Blackburn offered a faint smile. "You don't use autonomous cars, do you?"

"Uh, no. Well, cabs. It's hard to avoid that now. Why?"

"As long as there are no cars chasing you," Blackburn said as she ran her fingers through Willow's hair. "Not Lilith either. Not so far."

Willow stiffened. Her throat worked as she swallowed, glancing at the open door before she spoke again. Her words barely disturbed the air: "Lilith? Who is that?"

Blackburn met Willow's look with something close to satisfaction. "Don't worry about that," she said simply. "As long as you are safe." She kept her tone clinical, matter-of-fact.

The effect was immediate. Willow's gaze dropped to her desk, jaw muscles tightening visibly. Blackburn watched emotions ripple across her features. A flash of private anger or hurt, then nothing.

"Don't get anxious," Blackburn said. She reached forward and brushed a strand of hair from Willow's forehead with careful precision. The gesture was calculated more than affectionate. "You have your place with me." She let the words hang between them long enough to wound, then scab over. "Maybe Lilith could join us sometime. She might even give you orders while I watch." Her suggestion landed without warmth. An experiment more than an invitation.

Willow's response was slow in coming. She glanced down at the stack of files on her desk, voice low but steady. "Can I ask you something personal?" She hesitated just long enough for the silence to stretch between them. "Is there a reason... why what we have isn't enough for you?" Her hands lightly tapped the space bar on her keyboard, nervous energy bleeding into the motion. "I keep wondering if there's something missing, or if it's me, somehow."

Blackburn leaned forward and ran a tender hand down Willow's cheek.

"There are lines you won't cross," Blackburn continued, voice level now, almost clinical in its detachment. "You've made them clear. No blood, no whipping. You have a very long list." She gave a fractional nod that might have been compassion, but didn't reach her eyes. "Lilith doesn't draw those lines."

She let the words settle into the space between them and waited, measuring as much as reassuring. Always observing how much each person could carry before they broke or bent toward use.

A mild tremor moved through Willow's shoulders. Her glasses slipped down the bridge of her nose, catching the harsh light. She left them where they were.

"I'd never ask you to cross your hard boundaries," Blackburn said. "Keep them. I expect honesty about what you need. Wanting is not betrayal unless you hide it."

Willow gave a single nod. Reserved, deliberate. Not quite surrender. Blackburn reached out again and brushed Willow's hair through her fingers like silk on a loom. The motion was careful, fingertips barely grazing skin. Willow stayed perfectly still.

"You're still mine," Blackburn said, voice dropping low. "But no one is everything. You know that?"

Another nod from Willow. Blackburn let it stand.

Outside the office, the lights buzzed softly. Not different from before.

Blackburn eased back in her chair, the vinyl protesting softly as she studied Willow's expression. The air in the room shifted. Private became procedural.

"Speaking of everything." Her tone snapped into command. "Did you finish reviewing the maintenance reports on the department's Straight Lines?"

Willow turned to her monitor, shoulders dropping fractionally as she shifted into work mode. "Yes, there's nothing wrong with our maintenance records. But there's something else off." She scrolled through the document, a frown deepening at the numbers on the screen. "We contracted for and bought fifteen."

Blackburn leaned forward, interest sharpening her features as she scanned the screen beside Willow.

"Confirmed?" Her voice was quiet but direct.

Willow pulled up a second file and compared entries, jaw tight with concentration. "Triple-checked."

"I've also reviewed the Coconut Glass footage Detective Sinclair gave me," Willow said as she pulled up a folder of video files. "I don't see anything suspicious. Do you want me to give it back to him, to double-check?"

Blackburn stood, smoothing the wrinkles from her shirt sleeves. Her posture shifted from intimate to brisk professionalism. "He's an idiot. I can't trust him anymore."

Willow took in a sharp breath and sat straighter. Blackburn noticed.

"What?"

Willow swallowed hard, her hand rising unconsciously to her chest. "I think he's still following you," she said.

A softer look flickered across her face as she passed behind Willow's chair. Her hand brushed across Willow's shoulder. Brief contact through fabric.

"Of course he is," Blackburn said simply. "Tell me if anything else comes up."

She walked out, leaving Willow shaking her head.

* * *

In the bullpen, Blackburn's gaze found Sinclair hunched over his paperwork across the room. She paused, assessing him with an unreadable expression. She recalled his presence in the grocery store parking lot, his fixation too obvious to ignore.

Sinclair noticed her watching and looked up, his face caught between anxiety and hopeful defiance. Blackburn held his stare until he dropped his eyes to his desk. She allowed herself a cool half-smile before approaching.

"Shop there often?" she asked, her finger tapping on the desk. Cooper's eyes flickered up, then down.

"I was following up on a lead," he said.

"No, you weren't," she said before disappearing into her office, leaving Sinclair unsettled in her wake.

There was a message on her desk phone.

"Detective Blackburn, this is Marilyn Chaplin. Thank you for clearing out the room. The silence feels different now. Lighter somehow. You kept your word. I am an only child, and my father is long dead. Settling the estate should be simple. I plan to liquidate the store soon and sell the house. The brass doorknobs are already losing their warmth. The proceeds will cover university, just as my mother wanted. Her... her voice still echoes in the empty hallways sometimes. It's still early, but I wanted to thank you. For everything."

Blackburn deleted the message.

Within moments, Reeves called, requesting her presence at Interview Two.

"Caleb Mills wants to talk to you," Reeves said, nodding toward the interview room. The LED lights cast harsh shadows across his face. "Didn't sleep last night. Kept replaying what you told him. Maybe he has a soul?"

Blackburn allowed herself a thin smile, the corners of her mouth barely lifting. Predictable. She passed Dawson's desk on the way to Interview Two. The corridor was lined with frosted glass and peeling paint.

"He admitted it. Said he gave his son heroin to keep him quiet. Claims it was too much, that it wasn't intentional." Reeves' voice carried the weight of too many similar confessions. He trailed behind Blackburn past three more offices until they got to the viewing room for Interview Two.

"On video?" Blackburn asked.

"Yes. And a signed, handwritten confession."

"He decided to do it." She glanced at her nails, examining the neat French manicure while remaining indifferent to the muffled sounds of sobbing that filtered through the mirrored glass.

The confession spoke for itself: possession, use, and administration of a Schedule I narcotic. No ambiguity lingered in the sterile air between them.

"I'll talk to him in an hour. Charges so far are felony murder. Felony child abuse. Class One Dangerous Felony." She turned from the viewing window without hesitation, her heels clicking against the linoleum floor. "Typical. Another father who chose his high over his child's life."

Chapter 28

Blackburn waited outside Interview Room C, watching the clock's minute hand shudder forward in mechanical increments. The corridor stretched, empty except for a telephone ringing somewhere distant, already ignored by someone with better things to do. She checked the file one last time, then smoothed her jacket. Forty-three minutes of isolation should have softened him nicely. The anticipation thrummed beneath her professional mask. That familiar hunger before psychological combat.

Her heels struck the linoleum with deliberate precision as she entered.

The room throbbed under LED lights that bleached everything white and unforgiving. The table hunched between them, scarred metal bearing countless confessions. No color survived here except the cold gleam of steel and the sheen of nervous sweat. The recycled air hung thick and motionless.

Caleb Mills had become all angles and anxiety, his body sagging against the metal chair while his wrists pulled at the cuffs with every nervous twitch. Perfect. Blackburn cataloged each tell with precision. The gray hollows beneath his eyes, the film of perspiration making his skin gleam, the rigid set of his jaw that spoke of teeth clenched too long. He was already breaking himself. She just needed to guide the collapse.

A flicker crossed his face when she entered. Hope perhaps, or simple relief at any interruption. Textbook trauma bonding response. Leverage she intended to use.

"Mr. Mills." Her voice carried a neutrality, professional but not unkind. Let him think she was his salvation. It worked once already. She lowered herself into the opposite chair with unhurried movements, placing the casefile where he could see it. A deliberate reminder that he'd confessed to killing his son.

He wet his lips, already flinching from questions not yet asked. "Deonte. I need to talk about what happened to my son." The words came out brittle, drained of resistance.

He wanted his confessor again. Tell him that now his soul was saved. Predictable. She nodded once. No warmth, but no judgment either. "We'll get there." A pause stretched between them, flat as glass. Make him wait. Make him want her approval. "Let's start with Rosie. You were the last person to see her. When did you last talk to her?"

"What?" Unexpected. Excellent. His gaze fixed on a water stain climbing the wall behind her shoulder, mining either memory or guilt from its irregular pattern. "Don't know exactly," he muttered, the words barely disturbing the air.

Lie number one. Blackburn let silence pool between them. Four seconds was as long as most people could handle. She watched his nervous system betray him. The slight tremor in his left eyelid, the way his breathing went shallow. He knew exactly when. He was just not ready to admit it.

"It's been a while," he added, the chair creaking beneath his shifting weight.

She leaned forward, just enough to increase her presence, and dropped her voice so he had to strain to hear. Force engagement. Make him work for every word. "When you two talked, what came up?"

His cuffed hands worried at the raw skin around his wrists, the gesture more habit than response to pain. "Mostly Deonte," he managed after a beat too long. "Said I'd get clean. Tried to tell her that."

Another lie, wrapped in partial truth. He was following the script. Minimize his role, emphasize good intentions. She absorbed this with calculating silence, her attention becoming a weight he couldn't escape.

"You said you wanted to fix things," she reminded him, her tone soft but precise at the edges. "Come clean. You said that." He hadn't, but it didn't matter.

His breathing hitched, quick shallow pulls that failed to fill his lungs. The first crack in his composure.

She continued as if the room's atmosphere hadn't shifted: "Rosie needs honesty. Like Deonte needed honesty. Now more than anything else."

His lips pressed together until they lost their color. He was wrestling with it. Part of him wanted to tell everything. She sensed wounded prey.

Silence accumulated between them. No clock marked time here, only the electrical hum overhead and Caleb's uneven breathing breaking against the stillness. Let the pressure build. Let him fill the void with his own guilt.

The first real fracture came when he dragged both hands across the table's edge, chains whispering against steel.

"I don't. Can't." The words crumbled before forming into excuses.

Beautiful. Blackburn felt a familiar satisfaction watching his defenses disintegrate. She reached for the tissue box with precise movements, sliding it across the table. A calculated kindness that would bind him further to her authority.

He pulled one free and pressed it beneath his nose, eyes rimmed red but tearless. Still holding back authentic emotions. But not for long.

When he finally drew a breath deep enough to meet her gaze again, she began her methodical return to Rosie. Each question was a scalpel, designed to separate truth from self-preservation.

They both knew what had happened.

"How did it start?"

"What triggered it?"

"Which words?"

Everything Caleb offered came ragged at the edges. Imprecise times, half-formed images that shifted under scrutiny. He edited in real-time, keeping the worst details locked away. But she could see them lurking beneath his evasions like shadows beneath ice.

Each time he drifted from an answer, she curved back toward it from another angle. Never urgent but never releasing him, either. Like working a knot. Pressure from multiple directions loosened the hold until it gave way completely.

"You told me you wanted something different," she said after another deflection. "Did you mean it?"

The wire of silence stretched taut between them until it vibrated with tension. He decided right now. Whether confession might bring the relief he had been craving. It was why he asked to speak with her.

She allowed him to feel it before continuing: "Is Rosie with Deonte?"

Perspiration beaded along his hairline. He wiped it away with a shaking fist before dropping his gaze to the fingerprints worn deep into the table's surface. Shame response. Excellent. Shame was an honest emotion.

She remained steady through each shift, cataloging his disintegration with precision. Every fact accounted for. Every twitch observed. He was almost there. Just needed one more push.

"Walk me through it again," Blackburn said at last, her chair groaning softly as she shifted forward. "Last time you saw Rosie."

He launched into familiar evasion, voice thin enough to tear under pressure. This time she navigated quietly around each gap until only specifics remained unexplained. Corner him with his own inconsistencies.

"You say she seemed upset." Her voice dropped low, barely enough for the recording equipment. "Earlier, you said otherwise."

Contradiction noted. Filed. Weaponized.

"What was she carrying?" She let curiosity flatten into routine. A question asked from duty rather than empathy but sharp, nonetheless.

Caleb crushed the tissue in his fist until it shredded against his palm, knuckles blanching above the cold metal surface. Physical displacement of guilt. He was reliving it now.

Her questions found their rhythm.

Where did you go after you last spoke with her? Did you reach for her again? Why did her phone go dark?

Each one landed softly but left its mark. Death by a thousand cuts. Each question removed another layer of protection.

The air thickened with unspoken truths. The LED hum grew louder against his thinning breath as Mills contracted into himself by degrees under the harsh light. He was drowning in his own silence. Time to throw him a rope, one that lead exactly where she wanted him to go.

Finally, Blackburn simply watched him tremble against the steel chair. Her own stillness remained absolute except when necessary: a slight lean forward, forearms braced wide on the scarred metal barrier between them.

"Caleb," she said, his name spoken flat, without judgment or sympathy. Make it personal. Use his humanity against him. "I've seen secrets eat people alive. Sometimes all anyone wants is someone willing to see what's underneath."

For one second, he met her eyes directly before dropping his gaze below the horizon again. There. That flash of desperate hope. He wants absolution. Wants someone to understand.

"Rosie's been missing long enough," Blackburn added simply. Her meaning clear in what remained unspoken. The world will find its own villain if you don't speak soon.

Nothing filled that pause except sweat gathering at Caleb's temples and guilt etching itself into every line of his face. He was calculating. Weighing the cost of silence against the relief of truth.

"Was Rosie afraid?" Her tone stripped bare. "Did you go after her?"

He stared into his hands as if they might explain how things had gone so wrong. Sweat trickled past broken nails pressed together hard enough to shake against their restraints. She looked at his hands. They remembered what they had done.

Blackburn let silence grow roots in the concrete. Let him feel.

"Did you fight again?" No anger. Just curiosity honed by repetition.

Caleb flinched hard. Direct hit.

"Where is she?" Still no inflection beyond necessity.

His throat worked twice before he could swallow. The kind of gulp that signaled surrender rather than thirst. And there it was. The moment of collapse. Blackburn felt the familiar thrill of total psychological dominance, the intoxicating rush of watching a mind surrender completely to her will.

His hands flexed open then closed over empty air, grasping for something lost.

"She wouldn't stop," he managed finally. A whisper aimed more at the concrete floor than any human listener.

The first real truth. Finally. His voice wavered toward ruin. "I just." The chain rattled beneath trembling fists.

Blackburn waited through another long moment without moving, savoring the inevitability she had so carefully orchestrated. This was the moment when denial died and truth took its place.

Then, with no drama left, Caleb let the words fall free. "I killed her." It landed dull against metal. Not admission so much as exhaustion finally released.

There. The confession hit her like a drug. Pure, concentrated satisfaction. She had systematically dismantled his defenses, stripped away his lies, and extracted the truth like poison from a wound. Beautiful work.

A hollow rattle escaped him. Breath scraping against his throat while shame compressed each rib inward.

"Hit her," barely audible now. "More than once." His eyes squeezed shut against the merciless light. "Put her in my car. Drove past the lake. She's in the forest."

He stopped there. Voice failing as his body folded tighter around the truth finally spoken.

And there was the whole ugly picture. Blackburn felt a complex mixture of triumph and distaste. The satisfaction of a job perfectly executed, layered with revulsion at the pathetic creature before her.

Another broken man who couldn't control himself. Another victim who deserved better.

She acknowledged this with only a small nod. "Thank you for being honest."

He slipped out of his chair, hands still cuffed. On his knees. Praying. "Do I have a soul?" he asked.

"You do, Caleb," she said as she reached toward him, hands stopping just before reaching his. "Will you work with my colleague? Victor Reeves? You met him earlier."

Caleb nodded. "Okay, back in the seat. Sit up. That's what men with souls do, Caleb. Victor will need details of where she is. Okay?"

"Can't I talk to you?"

Her hands tingled. He was begging for her. "I think things are getting too personal between us," she said. The smooth lie felt good. "It has to be Victor."

She rose smoothly, the chair scraping against concrete. She opened the door without looking back at the wreckage of Caleb Mills. Reeves waited ready in the hallway.

"You're amazing," Reeves said, shaking his head. Blackburn gave him a small wink and walked away.

Another predator caged. Another family that might find peace. Her expression remained professionally blank beneath the corridor's glare, though beneath that mask, Detective Blackburn allowed herself a moment of cold satisfaction. The air felt cooler here, cleaner. Free from the stench of guilt and broken promises she'd left behind those walls.

Now, time to celebrate.

Chapter 29

Willow's eyes tracked the message on her phone.

Where are you?<

Direct and to the point. But nothing was ever simple with Blackburn. Her thumb hovered above the screen before she typed her response, explaining that she was heading north from Maple and would return to the site soon.

Blackburn's reply came after a pause that stretched thin and put Willow on edge. She waited with her muscles coiled.

Midtown Boutique. Tell the clerk: 'I am Blackburn's pet.' They'll give it to you<

She stopped walking. Heat bloomed up her neck as she reread the words: 'I am Blackburn's pet. They'll give it to you.'

Her stomach clenched. She opened her maps app and found the Midtown Boutique two blocks away. It was a sex shop. Dread mixed with something sharper beneath her skin. She imagined speaking those words to a stranger, the moment stretching out, impossible to picture without a furious rush of embarrassment that left her pulse jumping.

Her phone buzzed against her palm.

Text when you turn it on<

Willow hesitated, part of her wishing for another task, something less exposed. But she knew she would not truly be exposed in public. She could already see Blackburn's expression: calm, clinical approval threaded with warning. The fear came from within.

>*On my way.*

Good girl. I'm watching<

Willow's gaze swept the street as her skin prickled. She saw no sign of Blackburn, but that meant nothing. The pressure built as she moved forward with her fingers tight around her phone.

She quickened her pace with her nerves pulled taut as she pictured each step: the shop clerk's face, how they might react when she spoke the phrase, how small she might feel in that moment, and how precisely Blackburn wanted it that way.

The boutique appeared ahead with its red and silver sign catching the streetlight's glare. Her heart thudded against her ribs as she reached the door. Her legs locked briefly before carrying her forward. She paused just outside with her eyes fixed on the lettering, gathering herself.

Blackburn's instructions looped through her mind: 'I am Blackburn's pet.' Willow pushed herself forward. She pulled air deep into her lungs as her fists tightened until blood rushed back to her fingertips.

Inside, a soft chime marked the door's closing. Willow stood frozen for a heartbeat, taking in the space. The floors gleamed beneath her feet while shelves displayed their contents in meticulous rows under lighting that left every corner exposed.

She knew there was no practical reason for shame here. Still, warmth spread across her skin and pooled in her ears, betraying her despite every rational thought.

At the counter across the room stood a young woman with flame-bright hair. She shifted forward, watching Willow enter with the mild interest of someone marking another customer's arrival.

The clerk met Willow's eyes with a restrained, knowing smile. Willow recognized the assessment in that look and kept her pace steady as she crossed the polished floor to the counter. Her pulse thrummed against her throat, but she didn't let it show.

She pushed her glasses up the bridge of her nose and spoke quietly.

The words landed with a faint tremor, heavy but controlled.

"I, um, I'm Blackburn's pet."

The clerk's smile turned sly, her fingers drumming once against the glass countertop. "Of course you are." Her tone was light, almost teasing. "You're lucky. She's one of our best clients. Keeps things interesting, I imagine."

Heat crept up Willow's neck as her gaze dropped to the smooth countertop. The clerk didn't wait for a reply. She knelt behind the counter, fabric rustling, and returned with a small black box.

She set it down between them with a soft thud. "Everything's here," she said, her voice businesslike now. "Blackburn has the remote already." She tilted her chin toward the side door. "The changing room's there."

Willow nodded once and lifted the box. It settled in her barely trembling hands.

"Enjoy," the clerk added, her gaze steady and unblinking.

Willow gave a brief nod and walked to the changing room. The door clicked shut behind her before she opened the box. Inside, nestled in velvet, lay the Viola's Passion Panty Vibrator, its silicone surface catching the overhead light, along with a folded instruction sheet and a packet of lubricant. She checked the diagrams. Simple and clear.

She unzipped her jeans with brisk movements, the metal teeth parting smoothly. In one motion, she detached the magnet from the device, slid it into place against her skin, and snapped on the outer piece through the cotton of her underwear. She added a drop of cool lubricant as directed, just enough. She pressed the power button, felt the brief hum of activation, then zipped up and straightened.

No hesitation marked her exit from the room. She caught only a flash of approval in the clerk's eyes as she stepped out into the afternoon air.

On the sidewalk, Willow pulled out her phone and typed:

>*It's in place. Where next?*

She hit send and kept moving, her boots clicking against concrete. Blackburn's name appeared almost instantly above a terse message:

Porterhouse Restaurant. Wait outside<

Willow spotted its sign ahead with gold letters gleaming against polished wood. She slipped her phone away and squared her shoulders as she approached, steady now. Steadier, anyway.

Her gaze locked on the restaurant's entrance as her feet carried her forward, each step light with anticipation. Excitement fluttered beneath her ribs, her thoughts already racing ahead to the moment she'd see the woman she loved. Yet with every step, she noticed the almost imperceptible pressure shifting against her most sensitive skin.

The glowing sign drew closer, its amber flicker reflected in the darkened windows, matching the quickened rhythm of her pulse.

Ten feet away.

Her focus narrowed to the brass door handle gleaming ahead until a soft buzz pressed against her clitoris, sharp and electric, sending shockwaves through every nerve. Her knees buckled, and she pitched forward, her palm slapping against the rough brick wall.

Air punched from her lungs in ragged gasps. Her fingers splayed against the coarse mortar, legs trembling as her glasses slid down the bridge of her nose. Her chest heaved, each inhale catching in her throat as her mind scrambled to process the sudden assault of sensation.

She blinked hard, the sidewalk tilting beneath her feet. Heat bloomed from her core, radiating outward in pulsing waves that left her skin tingling.

Distant laughter drifted from behind. Then fingers, cool and precise, wrapped around her throat and yanked her from her daze.

Blackburn's manicured nails pressed into the soft flesh beneath Willow's jaw, compressing her windpipe just enough to send adrenaline flooding through her veins. Before she could react, Blackburn spun her around and crushed their mouths together.

Her heart hammered against her ribs as Blackburn's tongue swept past her lips, commanding and insistent. She felt herself dissolving into the embrace, her body transforming its initial shock into something else entirely. The grip on her throat loosened but remained, fingers resting against her racing pulse.

As the panic ebbed, an unexpected warmth spread through her limbs. She knew she should feel frightened, violated perhaps, but instead she felt anchored. She knew what to expect. In Blackburn's arms, the bustling street faded to nothing. The world compressed to just this: lips and teeth and the faint taste of mint.

When Blackburn finally pulled back, Willow's cheeks burned hot and her breath came in shallow pants. She looked up through her askew glasses, still reeling. Blackburn's mouth curved into a knowing smirk as she threaded her fingers through Willow's hair.

Blackburn knew Willow disliked public displays. "People are watching us," Blackburn murmured, tracing a finger along Willow's jaw. She savored how Willow's eyes darted sideways, scanning the faces of passersby. Blackburn claimed her mouth again.

"They're watching you being kissed by a beautiful woman." Blackburn's breath warmed her ear. "They know you must be extraordinary to have a woman like me want you."

Willow's knees went weak. "I'm so lucky," she breathed. The words 'to have you' caught in her throat. She didn't dare presume ownership of Blackburn.

Blackburn tipped Willow's chin and looked her directly in the eyes. "Do you want this?"

Willow swallowed. "A lot."

Blackburn's hand slipped into her pocket and pressed the remote. The vibrator hummed to life again, teasing against Willow's swollen flesh. "I was going to take you out for dinner, but then I thought, why not dinner and an orgasm for my little Fawn?"

She released Willow's throat and pressed a kiss to her flushed cheek. With a low chuckle, Blackburn laced their fingers together and led her through the Porterhouse's heavy doors.

The dining room glowed with warm amber light from crystal chandeliers, casting shadows across dark wood paneling and burgundy leather banquettes. Heavy white tablecloths draped each table, set with gleaming silverware and thick-stemmed wine glasses that caught the flicker of votive candles. The smell of cooking meat filled the air.

Once settled in their booth, Blackburn tapped the remote again. The vibrations intensified, pressing insistently against Willow's clit.

"How's that?" Blackburn asked. Before Willow could answer, she added a sharp pulse to the steady thrum.

Willow jolted, her water glass rattling against the table. "Perfect."

The early evening light filtered through the Porterhouse's windows, casting warm shadows across their table. Blackburn ordered for them: a hamburger for Willow, steak for herself, no asparagus.

They chatted about the warm weather, their words drifting among the clink of silverware and the indistinct murmur of other diners. All the while, Willow shifted minutely in her seat, acutely aware of the secret pulsing between her thighs. Soft jazz spilled from hidden speakers, mixing with conversation and the periodic scrape of knife against porcelain.

Blackburn reclined in her chair, one hand disappearing into her pocket as she swirled her wine. Their corner table offered just enough seclusion without feeling isolated from the restaurant's energy.

Willow adjusted her position, ice rattling in her glass as she drew a sharp breath. Her palm pressed flat against her thigh, fingers digging into the fabric as if anchoring herself against invisible waves. The hamburger before her, juices seeping onto the pristine plate, sat half-forgotten despite its obvious quality.

"Good choice?" Blackburn's voice carried *that* pitch: casual to anyone listening, loaded with meaning for its intended audience.

Willow nodded too quickly, reaching for her napkin. "Amazing," she managed, dabbing at her lips before taking another unsteady bite. A breathy laugh escaped her, contrasting with how her thighs pressed together beneath the tablecloth.

Blackburn's smile sharpened as she sliced into her steak, the blood-red center exposed beneath perfect char marks. "And the toy?" The question hung between them, deceptively innocent.

Willow struggled with her next bite. "Perfect, the toy is perfect," she finally answered, her voice catching.

Blackburn's gaze never wavered, cataloging every flush of color, every involuntary twitch that rippled through Willow's body in predictable intervals. She raised her glass for a sip, savoring both the wine and the exquisite tension radiating from across the table.

Blackburn's fingers found the remote.

"Don't come."

A simple command, nearly impossible if she calibrated the controls correctly. She knew Willow's responses intimately, could read every micro-expression that signaled the approaching climax.

Click.

Click.

Cl—

Perfect. Willow's pupils blown wide, irises catching the soft restaurant lighting like wet stone. Her lips parted in a silent gasp, breath catching in her throat. Her lashes fluttered rapidly while her gaze went unfocused, seeing nothing. The delicate muscles along her jaw clenched and released in a stuttering rhythm. Moisture gathered at the corners of her eyes, threatening to spill but holding steady. Her nostrils flared with each shallow breath, chest rising in desperate little hitches.

Willow recognized the inevitable approach, fighting against the tide. "I'm coming, Lioness. I, uh, I can't stop, yes…" Her voice emerged rough and broken.

"Not until I tell you," Blackburn leaned forward, dismissing an approaching server with a subtle gesture.

"Please Lioness. Please let me come. I, ow, oh, please. Let me c-come." The words scraped from Willow's throat, raw with need. She clung to decency by threads, seconds from snapping. She needed Blackburn's permission like air.

"Please. Please."

"Now."

The command shot through Willow like lightning, releasing the coiled tension she'd barely contained. Her spine arched, body seeking the pleasure Blackburn had so expertly withheld. The restaurant dissolved into a meaningless blur, leaving only her need and Blackburn's penetrating gaze.

"Good girl," Blackburn purred, the words wrapping around Willow like silk. "Let it all go."

With a muffled gasp, Willow shattered. Light burst behind her eyelids as she clenched rhythmically in her seat, waves of release crashing through her limbs. Heat that had pooled low in her belly erupted outward, molten and overwhelming.

Blackburn observed with predatory satisfaction as Willow came apart. The sight intoxicated her: submission and power balanced on a knife's edge, each second reinforcing their dynamic. Willow's face transformed in those moments, vulnerability melting into transcendent bliss tinged with beautiful desperation.

As the aftershocks faded and Willow's breathing steadied, Blackburn relaxed into her chair with deep satisfaction. "You did well, little Fawn," she said conversationally, sipping her wine as if they hadn't just performed an exquisite ritual of control and surrender. She eased the vibrations gradually, matching Willow's descent.

Willow's eyes shimmered, feeling stripped bare yet gloriously complete under Blackburn's steady regard. "I...that was amazing," she whispered, still floating.

"Beautiful," Blackburn murmured, leaning in for a searing kiss. Her fingers found Willow's wrist, stroking gently before tightening just enough to remind her exactly who held the power.

Chapter 30

The overhead lights hummed as Willow scanned her monitors. Her fingers moved across the keys in a steady pattern. The noise of the squad room seeped through the walls: distant voices, an occasional siren, footsteps echoing down the hall. Her office was cramped, cluttered with loose files and empty wrappers from takeout meals that left a sour taste in the stale air.

She'd spent the evening with Blackburn: dinner, sex, and then that bitter moment on the curb as Blackburn left her behind. Afterward, need drove her back to the precinct. She told herself it was for the quiet, though it was less lonely than her apartment.

She pushed back from her desk, the chair wheels grating over worn carpet squares. Her glasses slid down the bridge of her nose; she nudged them up as she started to organize her office. The narrow aisle between desk and cabinet forced her sideways, her hips bumping against the filing cabinet.

The contact made her pause. Metal. Cold. Unyielding.

Like the restaurant booth's edge pressing against her back when Blackburn had leaned over her, close enough that she could smell her shampoo. The memory surfaced unbidden. How her body had gone completely still on the outside, but wild on the inside. The way her breath had caught when she had spoken just loud enough for the neighboring tables to hear, her voice carrying that enticing tone that made her spine straighten involuntarily.

She pressed her palm flat against the filing cabinet, steadying herself. The dinner had been a performance, she understood. But what unsettled her wasn't the public nature of it, but how completely she had surrendered to it. How, for those excruciating minutes, she'd felt both utterly exposed and strangely safe. Protected by the very person who denied her.

And now, hours later, she could still feel the phantom weight of her attention, the way it had pressed down on her like gravity itself had shifted.

What did that make her? What did it mean that part of her loved it?

Sweat formed along her hairline by the time she fished a crumpled napkin from behind the tower. When she straightened, one elbow caught a stack of folders; they slid across the floor in a loose fan of paperwork, pages whispering against linoleum.

"Damn it," Willow muttered. Alone or not, she winced at the sound. She crouched down, her knees creaking in protest, and gathered the folders into a messy stack against her chest.

A stale smell lingered in her office: old fries, cheese gone cold and congealed. It reminded her how bad things had gotten after the last breakup with Blackburn, how easy it was to let things slide when nobody was watching. When no one cared.

In the mirror hanging by the door, she caught sight of herself: hair messy and damp at the temples, cheeks blotched red from exertion and shame. She straightened her glasses and patted down the flyaways out of habit.

Her cellphone rang, a sharp tone that filled the small room. She wasn't ready for conversation.

"Willow Adler," she said, her voice clipped.

"It's me."

Willow braced herself. It was just after nine pm. Something always happened when Blackburn called. Her heart picked up its pace as if getting ready for orders.

"What do you need?" Her words came out calmer than she felt.

"I want everything you can find on Brynn Cassidy and autonomous cars." Blackburn didn't wait for confirmation. "All of it."

Willow's jaw tightened at the mention of Brynn. The reporter had tormented her and then barely acknowledged her existence, making it clear Willow was an afterthought, a means to an end. "What specifically?" she asked, keeping her tone clipped.

"I need everything we can find," Blackburn said. "Background, connections to any victim or suspect, any patterns. Look at the chat rooms, check for personal ties to the case. I want to know if she's got a thing for cars, a problem with women, or a habit of bending facts." She paused. "Anything that connects her to the autonomous deaths."

Willow nodded once. "I'll have something by morning." She forced herself into motion, channeling the frustration into focus. There was work to do.

* * *

Willow waited by the printer, watching as the Eccel 7300 processed her latest request. The store was empty except for her and Walter's quiet presence behind the counter. The machine operated with muted efficiency; she heard only a steady mechanical hum and an occasional click as it shifted tracks. She pressed her palm against its metal edge and felt a faint chill seep through her skin.

Walter's BizNezz was open all night, a rare thing in New Dresden, and its equipment was reliable. It was nearly dawn, but here she could work undisturbed with a printer wide enough for departmental flowcharts and durable enough for grommet reinforcement.

She had designed this chart to span nearly eleven feet: a visual map to anchor their briefing room, every connection color-coded and clean. At the top sat Brynn Cassidy's headshot, pulled from her new station's website. Everything radiated outward from that point, like a spider's web.

Red lines linked to Brynn's recent articles: "The Not-So-Smooth Ride," "Caught in the Crossfire," and "Road to the Future." Willow had boxed them separately. These three captured Brynn's focus on autonomous vehicles and risk. Dozens of other articles existed, but these fit the department's narrative best.

Orange lines trailed into Brynn's audio appearances: Future Tech Today and Gadget Geekery flagged tech credentials; The Allusion Illusion veered into fringe territory. On that show, Brynn had debated global ship tracking conspiracies with Goatman, their host. It was a stretch beyond her usual scope, but worth noting all the same.

Willow let herself look over what she'd built so far: precise, objective, unadorned except for the coded links. Order imposed on chaos. She watched as more connections printed line by line, the vinyl unfurling with a soft whisper, ready to bring back to Homicide when the sun rose.

Surveillance stills from Jenna's final minutes went under yellow. One frame caught a woman resembling Brynn, tagged simply: "On Scene?"

Green marked social media posts hostile to autonomous vehicles. Brynn's posts stood out, their words sharp against the screen, calling the tech an "ethical vacuum." One read: "Autonomous cars with automated cops for the automaton mayor." Willow had enlarged that one for emphasis.

Indigo highlighted an anonymous forum post signed RepGrrl-NewDresden: "A lenticular sign exploits how cars see the world. Printed to change appearance depending on angle, it can show a human one message and the car another. Say, speed limit from one view, stop sign from another. The car misreads and reacts." Underneath, Willow had mapped Brynn's known online handle to RepGrrlNew-Dresden in a short, clean chart.

Violet traced back to Brynn's JournaPro profile. One quote was circled: "Winning the New Dresden Excellence in Investigative Journalism Award is my top goal. It would validate everything I've put into this work." It was circumstantial at best; Willow left it to others to decide if ambition counted as motive.

Pink boxes came last, sharp and glaring in dark boxes. Willow disliked pink. Her adoptive mother had insisted on it for years, convinced it would soften her into someone more acceptable. By thirteen, Willow's life had matched most other girls' stories. Trauma layered over trauma. But she never became what was expected.

She reserved pink for the least substantial evidence: half a dozen wild online comments between Brynn about PhilosophyGrad793 about secret government plots and vanished planes. "MH370 was rebranded as MH17 and shot down to hide HIV cures," "It's not the birds that watch us, but the cats," and Willow's favorite: "If you hear the horn, it's already too late!!!" The triple exclamation points made her smile.

If Brynn truly believed these things, she might take drastic action against autonomous cars used by city police. Or so Willow reasoned.

The Eccel 7300's cutter finished its run, slicing through the vinyl with clean precision. As the finished flow chart spooled into her hands, smooth and warm from the printer, Willow imagined Blackburn's reaction. A silent nod of approval.

* * *

Blackburn entered the Homicide Division just after sunrise. The corridors felt empty, the air flat with last night's industrial cleaner burning faintly in her nostrils. She walked to her desk, her muscles still warm from her morning run, sweat cooling beneath her shirt, her thoughts circling the day Kendria died.

The car had passed by so closely.

Kendria's death pressed at Blackburn from beneath every quiet moment. The screech of tires, the flash of movement, Kendria's hand in hers for an instant, warm and alive, then gone. These memories lingered, sharp and unyielding. Blackburn flexed her hands, studying the faint creases on her palms as though they might still hold some trace of what she had lost.

What if *she* had been the target?

She set the thought aside and surveyed the office. Something new caught her attention: an enormous banner stretched across the meeting room wall, its colors vivid even in the morning light. It hadn't been there yesterday. She rose and crossed to the doorway.

Willow was curled up asleep on the carpet. Her hair was tangled across her face, glasses tucked beside her, one lens catching the light. Blackburn watched her for a moment before kneeling and resting a hand on Willow's shoulder, feeling the warmth through the thin fabric. She leaned in and kissed her.

"Willow," she said.

Willow's eyes flickered open. Recognition surfaced with a sudden energy. She pushed herself upright, eager and wide awake, carpet marks pressed into her cheek.

"Oh! You're here." Her voice was hoarse, but alive with excitement as she slapped her glasses on. "I've been working all night. Look." She motioned at the banner, nearly stumbling as she stood, ready to explain everything all at once.

Chapter 31

Willow stepped forward, gesturing to her eleven-foot chart spanning the wall. "Brynn Cassidy is our strongest lead. I made it last night," she said with pride.

"Only you would work that hard on a Monday night," Cooper said. Despite his intent, the comment landed dully.

Willow nodded, smiled, and continued. "Brynn has technical expertise from her autonomous vehicle articles and podcast appearances, public hostility toward the technology, calling it an 'ethical vacuum'. More importantly, I traced her online handle RepGrrl-NewDresden to forum posts explaining exactly how lenticular signs could fool autonomous vehicles. They can show one message to humans, another to the car's sensors. She understands the attack vector."

Willow's finger traced the connections. "She's desperate for the New Dresden Excellence in Investigative Journalism Award, sees it as career validation. Three victims would certainly make headlines. The conspiracy theories about FEMA camps and missing planes suggest someone willing to act on extreme beliefs. Everything points to her having a strong motive."

Blackburn sighed. "For as much as I would like to be rid of that cockroach, I do not think talking about missing planes means she is willing to act on anything. She stays on the list."

Blackburn leaned against the wall, arms crossed. LED lights cast their unforgiving glare across the conference table, where case files lay scattered in methodical chaos. The room carried the acrid bite of coffee left too long on the burner, with undertones of stale sweat that clung to every surface.

Cooper sorted crime scene photos into sequence, his fingers precise against the glossy paper. Reeves slouched in a metal chair nearby, watching Blackburn with the wariness of a man who had learned to read her moods like weather patterns.

"Is this all?" she asked, her voice carrying a stillness that made suspects confess.

Cooper nodded without lifting his gaze from the photos. "Photos, statements, tech reports. Everything we have on Mott."

Reeves unfolded himself from the chair with deliberate care and crossed to the coffeemaker. The glass carafe scraped against the warming plate as he lifted it. "Fresh batch," he mumbled, though the bitter smell suggested otherwise as he filled three mugs with the dark liquid.

The door clicked open. Sinclair entered, his shoulders rigid beneath the tailored jacket. His eyes locked onto Blackburn immediately. She snatched Kieran Mott's file from the table and sent it sliding across the laminate surface. It whispered to a stop precisely at his fingertips.

"Updates." Blackburn gestured to Cooper.

He straightened in his seat, the leather creaking beneath him. "I checked the quantum computing angle. Short version: it's not possible. Current quantum computers are confined to labs under extreme cooling. Nothing portable, nothing anyone could run out of a van. They are error-prone and limited. We are a decade way from useful."

Blackburn kept her tone flat. "We're not hunting a mobile supercomputer?"

"No, it's a dead end."

Blackburn turned to Willow. "Status on the bio-lock for Roche's vehicle?"

Willow spun her laptop around, projecting data onto the wall. "Straight Line KX-9C, Level Four biometric lock registered to Charles Roche." Her fingers flew across the keys. "System logs show no unlocks for over a year. No breaches, no spoofing attempts, nothing since Roche died thirteen months ago."

"Not even system checks?" Reeves leaned forward.

"Just routine battery maintenance." Willow faced them, screen light catching her features. "The KX-9C requires live biometric matching. That's pulse, temperature, conductivity. It can't be fooled by synthetic prints or molds."

Sinclair tapped his pen against the table. "What about lifted prints? I saw that on TV once."

"Obsolete attack vector. Every attempt would be logged." Willow shook her head. "Nothing here suggests tampering."

Blackburn folded her arms across her chest, the fabric of her jacket rustling. "Then how did someone drive it?"

Willow offered a small shrug. "They didn't use any conventional entry point. So, external control."

Reeves slid his printouts into view, paper whispering against the table as conversation quieted again.

"Phone warrants came in earlier," he said, voice steady but subdued. "Mesh network logs for Kendria and Jenna cover six months of encrypted traffic." He set one page down for all to see.

"I focused on device signals within twenty feet. Signal bleed only."

"Can you decrypt it?"

Reeves shook his head. "No. Not the message contents. Mesh logs only give proximity, timestamps, device IDs. That's what I checked."

Blackburn motioned him forward. "What did you find?"

"Five hits," Reeves said. "All short. Under ten seconds each."

Sinclair frowned. "Just the two passing by?"

"Exactly," Reeves said. "The signals look like someone walking past at street speed. Jenna walked past the store, didn't even glance in the window."

Willow set her pen down with a soft click. "Nothing else? No overlap in buildings or neighborhoods?"

Reeves shook his head again. "Nothing close enough to matter. Besides those five sidewalk passes, their phones never came within fifty feet of each other. No co-location, no recurring pattern. If they were talking, they kept it analog. No trace in the data."

Blackburn nodded, eyes narrowing a fraction. She glanced at Sinclair, who dropped his gaze.

"Update?" she asked. "Sinclair."

He straightened in his chair, the movement sharp. "Right. Auto shops statewide, service centers for Raider Straight Lines and recent repairs. Nothing stood out. No records matching what we're looking for." Blackburn stared at him until he shifted in his seat, smile fading.

"We have the car now, Sinclair," she said. "Why chase old repair logs?"

He hesitated, voice cautious. "Covering bases, boss. Maybe someone tampered with it during an earlier test drive and left a trace. Just being thorough."

Blackburn gave a slow nod, barely patient. "Microwave interference theory?"

Sinclair leaned back from the table, his tablet's screen dimming in front of him. "I ran down every angle: defense research papers, energy labs, even federal procurement lists for off-book tech acquisitions. Nothing local and nothing in private hands that fits the bill. The closest anyone gets is three states away, and they're not mobile yet, just fixed systems under controlled conditions." He paused to let it settle in before continuing. "And even if someone managed to get a focused microwave array set up? You'd still need a truck's worth of batteries and a clear shot for half a minute at least. Not discreet."

Reeves raised an eyebrow but stayed silent.

Sinclair shook his head once more for emphasis. "You'd set off every frequency monitor for blocks and fry half the cellphones nearby too."

Blackburn leaned forward, her shadow shifting on the table, tone final. "It's not feasible."

"Not remotely," Sinclair said. "We can rule out microwave attacks."

"All right," Blackburn said, putting her feet on the table without ceremony, the thud resonating through the wood. She scanned the room. Both Sinclair and Willow watched not her, but her feet.

"I contacted Marla Sutton, Jenna's friend. She had nothing useful and I said to call me if anything comes to her. Jenna's parents too. Nothing new. After Zhang's arrest, everything quieted down. Like Reeves, I couldn't find any online connection between Jenna and Kendria. They had nothing in common."

She glanced at Willow, who studied her boots, expression unreadable. If she had heard the lie, she gave no sign.

"I heard from Sadie Roche. She's still in Italy." Blackburn checked her notes, paper crinkling. "Kieran Mott's position was eliminated. It had been scheduled for redundancy for three months. If some co-worker wanted to set him up, they got nothing."

"Uh, boss? I reviewed every Straight Line model on the street," Sinclair reported, his eyes flicking away from Blackburn's steady gaze. Cooper and Reeves glanced at each other across the cluttered table, tired but attentive.

"There are three versions. The PD-2A Police Fleet is basic: instant door unlocks after collision, no biometrics because multiple officers use it, stripped-down comms for cost. Emergency responders' special codes, human driver required." He laid out the facts without embellishment, his voice carrying the hours spent poring over technical specifications.

Blackburn tapped her fingers against her thigh in a slow rhythm. "Go on."

Sinclair gained momentum, straightening in his chair. "Jenna Langston was killed by a Zip model. That's the standard consumer version with mid-range features. No biometrics, not built for emergency situations, though maybe it should be. It runs driverless. Stan Raider designed it for passengers. A person *should* be in the car, but it's not a technical requirement."

He paused, clearing his throat while all eyes remained fixed on him, the LED lights humming overhead.

"Kendria Chaplin's car was a KX-9C luxury model. Ten-second delay on door unlocks to prevent bump-and-jack carjacking. It gives the driver time to keep the doors locked if they're attacked. Full biometric security, superior networking, tamper-resistant EDR, and administrative backend privileges."

He spread his hands as if presenting the information for inspection, his palms catching the harsh office light.

Blackburn crossed her ankles and glanced at the water-stained ceiling tiles. "Each victim was killed by a different model. Sounds like whoever did this changed methods to match the car. That suggests sophistication growing over time." She shifted her gaze to Willow and then to Reeves, her eyes sharp despite the late hour. "Willow, how likely is it that someone could ramp up their skills that fast?"

Willow's attention went to her computer screen for an instant, the blue glow reflecting off her glasses before she answered. "Unlikely, but not impossible. If you can hack the KX-9C, you could easily handle the simpler Zip model."

"Like knowing how to crack a vault means you can open a desk drawer," Cooper said, rubbing the bridge of his nose.

"Right," Willow replied.

Reeves broke in, his chair creaking as he leaned forward. "It would have to be an engineer, then?"

Willow shook her head, her fingers still poised over the keyboard. "Not just engineers anymore. There are plenty of online courses, even dark web shortcuts for people who want results without learning anything. With AI tools and stolen code, you could get into much bigger systems than these cars. You could get into nuclear facility control systems. Some of those places are still running 1990s software."

"Sweet Jesus, I did not need to hear that." Reeves grimaced and leaned back in his chair, brushing files aside with a weary hand.

Blackburn let out a brief laugh that cut through the tension. "The technology isn't what narrows our suspect pool anymore. Anyone could figure it out with enough time or desperation." She uncrossed her legs and set both feet flat on the worn carpet. "Let's focus on motive and opportunity instead. Get to it, people."

She stood up from the table, her movement signaling the end of the discussion.

Sinclair and Cooper gathered their folders, papers rustling.

"Uh, boss?" Cooper paused next to Blackburn. "That Jane Doe case? We finally got a call. Anonymous tip said she was Dallas Bautista."

Blackburn nodded. "You looked her up?"

"I found a social media page for that name. Looks like her. Here in New Dresden. She works at Gearlokz."

"Good man," Blackburn said. Over his shoulder, she caught a flicker of jealousy on Sinclair's face as he gawked.

"There are only a few employees there. Seven staff. She's listed on their website," Cooper said as he leaned against the table. Blackburn leaned back so she could keep an eye on Sinclair's growing envy.

"Let me know when you go. If you'd like some company, that is." She knew Cooper would miss the tone that hit Sinclair hard.

"Yeah! Sounds great. I'll come get you," Cooper said as he hopped up. He swatted Sinclair on the way past.

Reeves lingered over his paperwork, pretending to think.

Willow left after him, trundling out with her laptop and tablet under her arm, followed by Sinclair.

Reeves looked up to see Blackburn and he were alone, and she was watching him. He rose slowly, tucking his paperwork under his arm.

"Told you so," Reeves said quietly as he exited behind them, his voice barely audible over the hum of the ventilation system.

Blackburn picked up a pen from the table, its plastic surface cool against her fingers. He had told her. Told her that Willow's ideas would take them nowhere. She took a position against the wall, pen spinning between her fingers. The clarity she craved remained elusive.

The questions lingered as the sunlight slanted lower across the table. Beyond the windows, the city's pulse continued. Ordinary life flowing past while they hunted a killer who might be almost anyone. And all the work led nowhere.

Blackburn's pen rotated between her fingers as she thought of her list of suspects. First on the list was Willow. The plastic clicked against her thumb with each turn. Her thoughts meandered from one theory to another, each overlapping the last.

The pen spun faster. Anyone could do it technically, according to the tech geek. Willow had motive, though she'd never been this jealous before. Not like Sinclair. He had no technical skills, but that was not a requirement anymore. And he also had jealousy as a motive, regardless of how delusional it was.

The pen became a blur between Blackburn's fingers. No longer spinning, she simply flicked it back and forth, back and forth. Frustrated, she grabbed the pen in both hands and twisted. The plastic gave way with a sharp crack. Blue fragments scattered across the floor at her feet, the broken pieces hitting the linoleum with tiny, hollow sounds.

Dusk painted the windows purple while LED tubes hummed their indifferent tune overhead. She had moved past easy suspects. Now came the harder truths.

Chapter 32

The break room at Gearlokz Manufacturing carried a stale chill, the kind that settled into concrete and never left. Seven employees were expected; six sat scattered in vinyl chairs, each one conscious of the empty seat. The LED panels above cast a flat, clinical light across the battered tables and faded linoleum, turning skin sallow and shadows sharp.

Blackburn pulled out a chair with a scraping sound that drew silent glances. She took her place at the table, spine straight, shoulders set.

Grant Schroeder sat opposite her, his navy shirt darkened at the underarms despite the air conditioning. His hands pressed flat against the tabletop, knuckles white, a tremor running through his fingertips. Years on the line had carved deep grooves beside his eyes.

Detective Cooper waited near the door. His body camera blinked steadily, a rhythmic red pulse. The low vibration of machinery bled through cinderblock walls, a constant thrumming that rose from the floor itself.

Blackburn spoke without preamble. "Tell me about Dallas Bautista."

Grant met her eyes for an instant before fixing his gaze on the wall behind her shoulder. "She was quiet. Came in, did her job." The words came out flat, rehearsed.

"When was the last time you saw her?"

His jaw worked silently. "I'm not sure. Maybe May? We didn't share shifts." His fingers drummed once against the table before he crossed his arms tight against his chest.

Blackburn shifted her weight. The vinyl creaked beneath her. "What are Gearlokz hours?"

"We're ten to seven." His eyes skittered away from hers.

She let the lie sit between them, untouched. There were no shifts here. Everyone worked the same hours straight through. Grant offered nothing else.

Blackburn watched his throat work, the Adam's apple bobbing in small, nervous swallows.

"Dallas was found dead on May third," she said. "She spent weeks in our morgue before anyone put a name to her."

Grant's eyes dropped to his hands as if they might supply an alibi he didn't possess. The overhead lights caught the sheen of sweat along his hairline, making the fake wood grain of the table gleam like plastic.

He cleared his throat, a rough sound in the stillness. "So how did you know it was her?"

"An anonymous tip." Blackburn kept her tone even. "A man called in with her name. His voice was low. Sounded familiar." She watched for any crack in his composure. At 'familiar,' his eyelids fluttered like moth wings.

She waited. The machinery hummed its indifferent song through the walls.

"Must have been difficult for him," she continued, "watching those reports about an unidentified woman while knowing exactly who she was."

Grant's leg started bouncing beneath the table, his boot heel tapping an uneven rhythm against the cracked linoleum. His breathing shortened, chest rising and falling in quick, shallow movements.

"Tell me what you know about how she died."

His shoulders tensed, voice suddenly harder. "Just what I saw on TV. That she turned up in some alley downtown."

"What else?"

Grant shifted again. Fresh patches of sweat bloomed dark across his back and under his arms. The plastic chair groaned with each restless movement.

"I heard she was killed somewhere else first. Polson Park. Then moved," he said finally, still studying his hands as if they held answers.

Blackburn let the silence stretch until it grew heavy before speaking again.

"Where did you hear that, Grant?" Her voice remained level, patient, while she watched every micro-expression that crossed his face.

Grant stiffened, his posture strained and unnatural. The color drained from his face, leaving him the gray of old newsprint. "The news. Or maybe online," he answered, his voice thin as wire.

"Yes, she was killed in a park and moved later. How did you know it was Polson Park?"

His hands trembled as they gripped the table's edge. The metal legs groaned beneath his tightening hold. In the background, machinery kept its rhythm. Hiss, clank, hiss, clank. The sound pressed against the walls but failed to fill the growing silence.

Blackburn let him sit with it. The pause stretched between them, weighted by the scent of machine oil seeping through the walls. Sweat beaded at Grant's hairline, droplets catching the LED glare before sliding down to mark the table's scarred surface.

"How did you know she died in Polson Park, Grant?"

"I heard it somewhere." The words crumbled as he forced them out.

"Where was that? This matters."

"I said I don't know." His voice cracked on the last word.

Blackburn shifted her approach, trading accusations for something quieter. "All right. I've heard you were caught looking through her purse. Is that true?"

"No." The denial came too fast, too sharp.

"And she threatened to tell your supervisor."

"She didn't say anything. My boss never brought it up." Grant's breathing had gone shallow, each inhale catching in his throat.

"Maybe she died before she had the chance," Blackburn said.

"Maybe." His knee bounced faster beneath the table, his boot striking an uneven rhythm against the concrete floor.

"She seemed decent," Blackburn observed.

Grant's composure shattered. "She was a bitch."

The shift from brittle control to raw anger took only a heartbeat.

"What makes you say that?"

"She would have told on me." Heat flushed his cheeks while muscles twitched along his jaw.

"For going through her purse," Blackburn clarified. She kept her tone unhurried. "I don't have the purse myself. Just curious what was inside."

"Usual stuff. Wallet, makeup, phone."

"We haven't recovered her purse."

Grant jerked one shoulder upward in a rigid shrug. His fingers tapped against the table, then flicked toward Cooper at the door. The camera's red light pulsed steadily in the corner.

"Maybe she left it here," Blackburn said lightly. "Cooper, note that we'll need a warrant to search for her purse."

"I'll take care of it," Cooper answered without shifting his gaze from Grant.

"What does her purse have to do with anything?" Grant's voice frayed at the edges.

"We won't know until we find it," Blackburn replied evenly. "You said her phone was there. Maybe there are messages."

He crossed his arms tight against his chest and fixed his glare on a point past Blackburn's shoulder. "I don't know where it is."

"No problem. We'll track it down."

Grant's eyes darted to the door, restless and wary. He looked less like a suspect and more like a man bracing for escape. Or searching for something he had lost.

Blackburn kept her tone measured. "Killing someone over a purse doesn't add up," she said. "If she had it on her and someone tried to rob her, maybe. But if the purse was left here? What would be the point?"

Grant only shook his head.

"Doesn't make sense to me either." Blackburn let the silence stretch, the hum of LED lights filling the space between them. "Maybe she was worried you went through her things. Maybe she planned to report you."

"She didn't," Grant protested.

"She didn't get the chance."

Grant's leg bounced faster, the metal chair creaking with each nervous movement. His gaze swept the room, measuring distances, cataloging exits.

Blackburn's expression shifted, adopting a thin veneer of sympathy that never reached her eyes. "That must have felt threatening," she said. "Having a new hire threaten your job. Plenty of men have lost their careers for less than that. Where pretty girls are involved."

"I didn't take anything," Grant said, his voice hollowing out.

"Twenty years on the job and you let some kid intimidate you?" Blackburn leaned forward, her voice dropping low enough that Grant had to strain to hear. "Bet that stung."

"She didn't intimidate me."

"No? Sounds like you were afraid of her. Rifling through her purse. Childish move." Blackburn's words came out flat, each syllable precise. "Not exactly brave."

Grant's shoulders tensed, tendons standing out along his neck. The effort to contain himself shattered. His fist cracked against the table, sending vibrations through the metal surface. "She was going to ruin my life! I just wanted to borrow a pen, then she said she'd tell the boss! I've worked here twenty years, and she was ready to destroy all of it over nothing!"

The words tumbled out hot and ragged, pride crumbling at the edges.

"You followed Dallas after work?" Blackburn asked. Her voice remained steady, untouched by Grant's eruption.

Grant shot up from his chair, the legs scraping against concrete. Red blotched across his face, veins bulging at his temples. "She kept walking away, calling me a creep! Said she wanted me gone! I grabbed her by the throat so she'd stop running her mouth, and she fought back! I wasn't trying to kill her! She just wouldn't stop!"

The confession hung in the recycled air between them.

He lunged toward Blackburn but barely covered half the distance before she was up and Cooper intercepted him. Cooper caught him mid-stride and drove him down, Grant's cheek meeting the table with a dull thud.

Blackburn stepped in close while Cooper wrenched Grant's arms behind his back. She delivered two sharp strikes to Grant's kidney as Cooper dragged him to the floor.

The steady drone of machinery swallowed any remaining sounds as Grant's world collapsed around him.

"Grant Schroeder, you have the right to remain silent," Cooper recited, his breath coming hard as he pressed his knee between Grant's shoulder blades. "Anything you say can and will be used against you in a court of law. You have the right to an attorney..."

Grant's sobs leaked onto the grimy linoleum as Cooper continued the familiar litany, each word cementing the ruins of Grant's existence with mechanical precision.

Chapter 33

>*I see you're online.*

>*How are your hands?*

Tingling. How is your ass?<

>*Still a delicate sting when I move just right*

Ready for more so soon?<

>*Not that. But I would like to thank your hands*

How?<

>*I will take your fingers one by one*

>*slowly kiss each one, pull, rub*

>*let them feel my lips and tongue*

My hands are ready<

>*A quick meet in the dark?*

>*Private and convenient?*

>*I need to stroke them*

>*Please*

Meet me in the New Dresden Foods parking lot<

11 pm<

>*Thank you.*

Now admit it. You will do anything for my touch<

>*I confess: I crave your gaze, your hands, your attention*

>*It sets every nerve alight. I'd do anything to please you*

That's my good girl<

* * *

Lilith moved the length of her bedroom, fingertips tracing the dresser's polished edge as she weighed how Blackburn might respond tonight. The silk robe shifted against her skin, a delicate tickle. Streetlight sliced through the blinds, painting amber bars across the floorboards. She caught her reflection in the standing mirror: hair disheveled, makeup worn thin, faint indentations from her glasses marking tired eyes. Unacceptable. Nowhere near what Blackburn expected.

Her thoughts drifted to work, settling on the stony silence that followed Dream's announcement about LightTime. The deal was supposed to be hers after weeks of grinding negotiation and expensive design prototypes. Instead, she had watched it evaporate, and she had to face the board.

Worse was Wentworth checking his watch as she began her report. Voice steady but low, she had asked if he was hoping someone else would step in.

He did not look at her. "Just waiting for this to be over," he said.

Her palm flattened against the cool glass as the bedside clock clicked over: 9:48 PM. She had promised Blackburn she would arrive by eleven. Lateness was not negotiable; Blackburn maintained standards that Lilith found anchoring through expectation, structure, resolution.

Tonight would not be about endurance or pain since her body needed recovery. Faint yellow/green remnants of bruising from last week still dotted across her thighs, a sharpness whenever she pressed. This evening demanded something different. Blackburn managed her aftercare well, grounding Lilith when self-doubt threatened to consume everything else.

Aftercare sounded clinical but felt vital, a protected space where failure loosened its hold. She wanted to let Blackburn know her work was appreciated.

She let the robe slip from her shoulders and pool beside her feet. At the dresser, she selected black lace lingerie: bra first, quick fingers adjusting straps until they sat perfectly; then matching panties, smoothed into place. The ritual steadied her racing thoughts.

From the closet she drew a black dress, tailored but flexible enough for movement. She had chosen it deliberately; kneeling in this dress would reveal exactly what Blackburn appreciated. Details mattered.

Perched on the bed's edge, Lilith extended one leg and rolled a silk stocking over foot and calf with care, no bunching or twisting allowed. She repeated the process with its mate before stepping into black pumps that lifted her stance just enough to remind her who she belonged to tonight.

Each minor discomfort was intentional, a signal and a promise that discipline began long before she reached Blackburn's car.

She settled at the vanity, leaning into the mirror's steady glow. Makeup went on with quiet precision: foundation smoothing her complexion, contouring adding subtle definition, eyes enhanced but understated. She finished with her signature red lipstick, Command. It was her own brand. The name still needled her, a private irony from her last breakup.

Lilith studied herself in the full-length mirror. The dress hugged her hips, ending just above her knees, polished enough for any board-room. From behind, it revealed a clean expanse of skin between her shoulder blades. Her hair sat in its precise bob, no trace of disorder despite the day's chaos. The last thing. Her red choker. She would hold it for the trip and ask Blackburn to fix it around her neck. She appeared composed. In control. A necessary performance.

The clock showed 10:00 PM. The drive to the store would take twenty minutes; her phone's navigation confirmed it. She preferred arriving early. The time alone in the car allowed her to transition from executive authority to something softer, more receptive. It was a shift she never rushed.

She collected her essentials: keys, phone, card, ID, bag secured on her shoulder. She locked the condo, registering the solid thud as the door sealed. The elevator arrived immediately; penthouse privileges had their advantages. She kept her gaze straight ahead, ignoring her reflection scattered across brass panels.

The descent took twenty-eight breaths until the doors revealed P1.

In the parking garage, the air hung cool, tinged with concrete dust and motor oil. Her heels clicked a steady rhythm toward the red sports car gleaming under harsh LEDs, still new enough to feel like a prize rather than routine transport. She pressed the key fob and heard the locks release. The interior glowed with pale leather as she settled in and pulled the door closed.

The car enveloped her in familiar quiet. Phone nestled into the charger, seatbelt secured, ignition pressed.

Nothing.

Dashboard lights stuttered briefly, the battery warning flashed crimson, then died. Lilith took a slow breath and tried again, holding the button longer.

"Not tonight," she murmured when the silence persisted.

She pressed repeatedly, each attempt more insistent, until even optimism felt exhausted. The dash remained black. Tension coiled through her shoulders as if everything capable of failing had chosen tonight, when timing mattered.

Lilith checked her watch. 10:12 PM. She calculated the remaining time, noting how narrow the window had become. Being late for Blackburn was not negotiable. If she cited car trouble now, Blackburn would reschedule without warmth or understanding. Lilith would have only silence and her own disappointment for company.

She exited the car, closing the door with a sharp crack. The sound ricocheted through the empty garage. Lilith stood beside the vehicle, fists tight, regulating her breath in short intervals. She uncurled her fingers, straightened her spine, and strode toward the elevator.

Inside, she retrieved her phone and opened a rideshare app. The nearest car showed seven minutes away, impossible. She closed it and switched to her regular taxi service. Booked. Ahmed was three minutes out. She exhaled softly as the knot between her shoulders loosened.

The elevator doors parted at the lobby. The night doorman lifted his gaze from his desk, caught her eye, and offered a single nod of recognition.

>*I will arrive in a cab*

She waited, watching for a response.

With a driver?<

>*Yes, New Dresden City cab. Ahmed.*

Good girl<
How long is the ride?<

>*20 minutes*

Keep me apprised<

She released a slow breath. Smiled at the screen.

Outside, city air cooled her flushed skin. She scanned the street until she spotted it: a silver autonomous cab at the curb, its angular lines catching stray light from passing traffic. She looked at Ahmed. According to his photo, he was a man about sixty years old with tired eyes and an amiable smile. She held it up and compared it to the driver. It matched.

Ahmed waved as she approached and pressed a button. The door lifted open, silently and smoothly. When he spoke, he was soft and clear. "Ahlan, Miss Lilith," he said, smiling. "Car should be cool enough for you inside."

Lilith nodded back, pleased by the calm friendliness. "Thank you."

She slid in quickly, bag on her lap, wrapping the choker around her hand, watchful but composed, as the cab sealed itself from the night beyond.

"New Dresden Foods?" he asked. Ahmed's voice carried the steady reassurance of someone who had driven these streets for years. It eased some of Lilith's tension, though recent news kept her alert.

"Yes, thank you." She met his glance in the mirror, her response unhurried.

Ahmed nodded. "That place is usually locked up tight this late. You sure that's your stop?"

Lilith allowed a small smile. "It's the right place. I'm meeting a friend."

The cab merged into traffic with mechanical precision. Lilith relaxed into the seat, eyes tracking the city sliding past her window, a blur of amber streetlights and darkened storefronts. Ahmed sat ready, hands hovering near the steering wheel despite the car's quiet autonomy.

She hoped for a message, but nothing came.

The ride flowed through silent streets, New Dresden's night pressing close against the glass. She ran a finger thoughtfully along the choker in her hand for a few moments, hoping Blackburn would be pleased. Lilith reached for distraction and touched the display screen before her.

Driver icon: Ahmed's profile appeared first. A photo, ten years with the company, consistently high ratings. Even a shot of his family, smiling at some beach.

Car icon: Raider Straight Line Zip. Single charge range 540 miles. Efficient, updated automatically every month. Manual override available if needed.

Routine details.

Map icon: The car's marker traced their route across New Dresden in real time. No surprises.

Lilith leaned forward to catch Ahmed's eyes in the mirror.

"Do you enjoy driving these autonomous cars?" she asked.

Ahmed smiled faintly, crow's feet deepening. "Not especially." His hand drifted near the controls as if drawn there. "Been driving for real most of my life. It feels strange letting the car run itself."

She nodded, understanding that sense of surrendered control. "But you can take over whenever?"

He looked at her again, voice warming. "I can." He seemed grateful for that option, however seldom it mattered these days.

Lilith reclined, restless energy coursing through her. Conversation felt thin compared to what waited ahead.

She watched the map as they turned right. The red indicator tracked their movement, then vanished. The screen went black. Lilith frowned and typed quickly.

>*The map just disappeared*

>*Not sure*

The car continued forward, undisturbed. "Does this map in the back control the car?" she asked.

Ahmed shook his head. "No, miss. That's just for passengers. The real navigation is up front, in the dashboard. Secure." He tapped the plastic panel between them. "We turn left here. Watch."

The turn came as smooth as water, then a right. The car followed its route with silent efficiency: corrections barely perceptible, speed constant, every movement calibrated.

Her phone vibrated against her thigh. She was disappointed to see the text:

Message not sent.

She tucked her phone back in her bag as the vehicle eased off the accelerator. She peered outside, searching for a reason: a crossing animal, construction, something to justify the slowdown, but she saw only darkness pooling beyond the glass.

"Why are we stopping?" Her tone remained level, though her fingers pressed into the seat's edge.

A shape drifted across the street ahead: a person, hood pulled up, invisible except for a brief interruption in shadow. Lilith's muscles tightened as they passed through the car's headlight beam, almost ghostlike.

"How did it notice that?" she asked quietly. "I couldn't see anyone out there."

Ahmed glanced over his shoulder. His eyes crinkled at the corners. "Radar picks up more than human eyes," he said matter-of-factly. "It reads through fog and dark much faster than us. No worries."

Lilith nodded once. The car glided forward again without hesitation.

She fixed her gaze on the passing lights outside. Distant apartments clicked by one after another, anticipation and nerves braided together in her chest. Blackburn waited for her ahead: a secret separate from everything ordinary, hidden beneath all this order and automation.

Chapter 34

Blackburn killed the engine and let silence settle into the cabin. The New Dresden Foods sign flickered overhead, washing half the lot in a sickly green pulse. The other half sank into shadow. She had chosen her space deliberately: wedged between a hulking pickup and a concrete barrier, visible but not exposed, with lines of sight clear to the parking lot entrance. The dash clock cast its glow: ten-thirty.

She didn't move. Stillness was its own tactic. Patience revealed things that motion buried; she let her vision adjust, mapping outlines and weighing their relevance. Two cars hunched by the loading dock: a sedan with windows fogged from within, and another with headlights burning, carving a wedge of cracked pavement from the darkness. Someone shifted inside the lit car. A deliberate movement, nothing was rushed.

A stray shopping cart caught the wind and clattered across the asphalt. Its wheels struck a seam in the blacktop, veered left, then collided with a bollard. The hollow clang dying too quickly in the quiet air. Blackburn watched it rock to stillness without reaction.

After business hours, this lot transformed. Groceries by day, anonymous meetings by night. She understood both purposes and their rhythms.

Her attention returned to the lit car. Two figures pressed together, parted briefly, then merged again. Likely kissing, judging by their posture and timing. She observed them as she would any evidence: detached, collecting details. People left traces even when they believed themselves invisible.

The driver's window descended a few inches, and a hand flicked out something that sparked as it hit the ground. A cigarette stub died on the pavement. The window sealed again. Inside, shadows converged with renewed urgency; movements quickened, heads disappearing below the window line. The car rocked once, twice, then stilled.

Near the loading dock, condensation cleared from the sedan's windows. Sex warped time differently; minutes stretched or compressed depending on which side you occupied. For Blackburn, control meant owning every second; here she simply counted them.

She lowered the sun visor and opened the mirror. The weak interior light carved her features in sharp relief.

Her hair was undisturbed, her face was composed: not a smudge displaced or detail overlooked. She examined her reflection without affection or criticism, just confirmation that she was beautiful.

She closed the mirror and let darkness reclaim the space. Her fingertips drummed once against the wheel—four beats—then stopped as focus returned.

The lit car's engine finally turned over. A door opened; someone emerged and crossed to a nearby compact, her gait marked by familiarity rather than haste or shame. Both cars departed within two minutes. No pause for words or backward glances.

Blackburn wondered briefly which one had suggested New Dresden Foods as their meeting point. Probably him. Women rarely chose grocery store parking lots for sex. Too exposed. Too many associations with domestic routines. Men thought differently about these spaces. They saw only convenience, not context.

Her phone vibrated once against the console: a text, not a call. She let it lie facedown. Control mattered, even in insignificant gestures. Then, finally, she looked.

Willow. *Are you awake?*

Three words. Simple on the surface, but weighted with everything unspoken: 'Are you awake?' Mentally, physically, with possibility.

Another message followed: *Need company?*

Deleted.

Willow would come if summoned. But Lilith was already en route. She locked the phone and set it aside. The body doesn't switch modes as quickly as the mind does. Her thoughts cleared; her skin didn't. Not yet.

Headlights swept through the darkness. Cold white beams sliced across the rows. A police cruiser eased in, the engine rumbling low. The anticipation in Blackburn's chest flattened; routine intruded.

She watched two officers emerge, their uniforms sharp under the green light, movements casual but cautious. The driver, Watson, according to his name tag, was broad-shouldered and thick. He approached at a pace that broadcast wariness more than threat.

He stopped several feet away, his gaze traveling from her car to her face. "Everything alright here?" His tone stayed neutral, but taut.

Blackburn swallowed the exhale meant to dispel irritation and answered evenly: "Detective Blackburn, homicide." She held her badge at eye level for a beat before returning it to her pocket.

The younger officer, DeForest, lingered half a step behind but maintained eye contact. Recognition flickered across his features as he matched her badge number to memory. "You're with NDPD? Saw you on Channel Six last week."

"Hope they got my good side," she said, her voice offering no warmth.

Watson surveyed the mostly empty lot again, eyes narrowing as he assessed the scene. "Are you meeting someone?"

The question hung in the cool air; professional plausible deniability. Blackburn held his gaze a moment too long before responding. "Just sitting," she said.

The night pressed in around them, with routine colliding with something less defined, held steady by restraint and expectation rather than threat or spectacle.

"Working a case," she added, voice level. The words carried more truth than deflection. Watson's gaze lingered, assembling whatever he could from her presence here. "Needed a break from the flood of calls and paperwork at headquarters. I picked somewhere close, somewhere quiet."

The silence that followed felt dense, but not hostile. DeForest glanced at her, uncertain. Watson looked uneasy, but curious.

"What brings you two to the parking lot?"

Watson shifted his weight, rubbing the back of his neck before answering. "Car system flagged four unauthorized vehicles in the lot. Protocol says we check it out."

Blackburn raised an eyebrow. "Four? Unauthorized? Here?" She scanned the area. The couple were no longer visible. Smart. "I didn't realize this spot was off-limits. I just needed quiet to review my notes. But it's not as peaceful as I'd hoped."

DeForest shuffled, hands hooked into his vest. "No harm done, ma'am. Night's decent enough for some air."

"True," Blackburn replied, eyes tracking the city's edge where lights pulsed steadily and distant. "How's patrol tonight?"

Watson shrugged, looking out toward the street. "Unremarkable so far. Trying to keep it that way."

DeForest nodded toward the street. "We've got company."

They turned as a silver autonomous cab slowed across the street and stopped opposite the lot entrance. Blackburn caught Lilith's profile through the window. The recognition was instant and poorly timed. She kept her reaction contained; Lilith wouldn't approach with officers present.

Blackburn spoke, already crafting an excuse. "Looks like—"

Her words died as every interior light in the cab blazed to life at once, flooding the cabin with a harsh white glare and exposing both occupants completely: Lilith seated rigidly behind the driver partition, the driver startled, both faces turned upward toward the lights.

"What's happening there?" Watson asked, frowning.

Before anyone could answer, three sharp beeps pierced the quiet lot. The lights extinguished and shadows reclaimed the car's interior as abruptly as they had fled. The headlights flickered off, then on again, casting an empty light across the asphalt.

The cab lurched away from the curb, taillights dissolving into night traffic. Through the rear window, Lilith's eyes found Blackburn's for an instant: wide, afraid.

Watson exhaled slowly. "That wasn't normal."

Blackburn muttered a low curse and reached for her phone.

A single text waited on the screen:

>20 minutes

Lilith's last message to her. She tapped the call button and lifted the phone to her ear.

We're sorry, the number you have called is temporarily unavailable.

"Damned autonomous car," Blackburn snarled. "We should follow it."

"Oh, like those other cases? Shit." Watson and DeForest moved quickly, sliding into their cruiser. Watson hit the red emergency button on the dash.

Blackburn started the car and pulled out, following the wailing siren that had ignited in front of her. The cruiser pulled onto the street, lights painting blue and red across empty storefronts.

Blackburn accelerated, gravel scattering beneath her tires as she followed them out of the lot.

Her mind sharpened on the chase. Not on Lilith or what she had just abandoned, but on control: reclaiming it, wielding it. Her fingers gripped the wheel. Measured, but not dry. Beneath the discipline ran something hotter, uglier. Not just urgency. Not just fear. The body's thrill at having a target, a task, a thing to catch and dominate.

The night pressed against the glass while she maintained pace behind DeForest's taillights.

The city blurred past in cold slashes of neon and shadow as they pursued the taxi through New Dresden's main artery. The siren sliced across the quiet blocks, announcing their presence to sleeping apartments above.

She clawed at the glovebox, grabbed the handheld, and toggled the radio on.

DeForest's clipped voice came through. "Dispatch, Car 54 in pursuit. Eastbound Main Street. Occupants in distress, vehicle non-responsive to traffic stops. Requesting additional units."

"Copy, Car 54," Dispatch replied without hesitation. "Maintain pursuit and update."

The airwaves crackled again: "All units, be advised: two 911 callers report being trapped inside the target vehicle." More units checked into the pursuit in rapid succession; each voice tighter than the last.

Blackburn grabbed her radio. "Detective Blackburn, badge two-five-nine, following Car 54 in pursuit. Suspect vehicle is an autonomous car."

Adrenaline kept her focused and steady at the wheel. The city came at her in stark relief, every movement calculated. She ignored her phone buzzing on the seat beside her; priority was clear and singular now.

Storefronts and bar signs streaked past in alternating flashes of blue, red, and sodium-yellow as Blackburn closed in behind DeForest's cruiser, both cars carving a path east through late-night traffic. Ahead, the cab threaded between vehicles with mechanical precision: no wasted motion, never holding a lane marker for more than seconds at a time.

She tracked its taillights through gaps in traffic, an unbroken line to follow, each moment extending this contest between order and chaos another block deeper into the city night.

"Car 54 to dispatch, we're in pursuit of the autonomous vehicle heading north on Moore," Watson reported. His voice came tight, clipped, but urgent.

"Copy, Car 54. Other units responding. Monitor your speed," the dispatcher replied.

Blackburn gripped the wheel, eyes locked on the flash of taillights ahead. She did not have to monitor her speed. Police cruisers converged around her, their sirens shredding the night. The city's grid dissolved beneath motion and noise; familiar turns became a series of split-second calculations.

She slipped past Car 54 when they slowed at an intersection. She knew it was clear, their car did not.

In the runaway cab, Lilith braced herself with one hand and shouted into her phone for help. Ahmed, behind the wheel, stabbed at the dash in desperation. "I can't stop it!" he yelled into his phone, filling the space between them and their loss of control. His own phone screen flickered. A lost connection.

Blackburn kept her eyes on the cab ahead. Her radio crackled, but Lilith's screams were all she heard. She pressed the gas, closing the gap.

The cab slammed on its brakes, red taillights flashing. Blackburn braked hard, tires shrieking. It accelerated again, and she stayed tight behind.

The car jerked right, then left, blocking her path and shifting between lanes just enough to trap her behind traffic. Every time she drew even, it cut her off. Ahead, Lilith pounded the rear window. It was the only signal Blackburn needed to keep pushing.

She tried for a PIT maneuver, lining up as the cab swung wide. The impact was shallow; metal scraped against metal, but the autonomous cab recovered and sped forward. Blackburn fought for control, steadied the wheel, and forced herself to breathe.

She darted between cars stopped at green lights, the city blurring past. Streetlights flickered across her windshield in sharp intervals as she narrowed the distance.

At the next intersection, the cab ignored a red light. Horns blared as cars slammed to a halt inches from collision. Blackburn followed without pause; her own turn was precise. Reflex over fear.

Blackburn adjusted her grip on the wheel. She tracked every swerve of the cab and shifted lanes before it could pull away again.

Traffic peeled away around them as they crossed into deeper night. Blackburn closed in. Methodical and silent despite her heart hammering against restraint.

She kept her focus tight: hands steady, body aligned with every move. The chase narrowed to seconds and angles, a controlled pursuit through emptying streets.

Every choice narrowed down to this: match its moves and get close enough to end it before anyone else got hurt.

She kept her breathing measured. Eyes forward. Nothing wasted, every action counted now.

They climbed toward Dunbar Bluffs. The dispatcher's voice, which had been buzzing the entire time, cut through the haze.

"Two-five-nine, do you have visual?"

Blackburn finally looked in the rearview mirror and saw a dozen police cars behind her, driving like snails.

"Still on it," she said. Her focus narrowed on the silver vehicle ahead, the speedometer climbing as the road curved toward the cliffs.

"All units, Air Seven overhead."

The helicopter reported in, tone even. "Vehicle is approaching Dunbar Bluffs at speed. Proceed with caution; sharp turn incoming."

Blackburn gripped the wheel, attention locked on the winding ribbon of asphalt and the void beyond. Her breath was ragged, her mind was racing. Sweat trickled down the back of her neck. She had never felt more alive. Or more trapped inside that awareness.

She pressed harder on the accelerator. The engine responded with a controlled surge, not reckless but calculated. Blackburn swung into the opposite lane for a better angle. Oncoming headlights flashed past too close. Tires screamed behind her in protest, horns cutting through the dark.

The city dropped away to one side; cliff side shadows flickered past her window. Blackburn kept her line tight, pursuit locked and silent but for her hitching breaths.

Chapter 35

The cab's brake lights blazed red against the jagged horizon. Blackburn watched it lurch to a stop, teetering half over the bluff as gravel scattered into the void below. The police helicopter's spotlight pinned both vehicles in harsh white light.

Through the rear window, Lilith's palms slapped frantically at the glass. Ahmed sat frozen at the wheel, tears streaming down his face as he gripped the unresponsive controls.

Blackburn killed her engine and stepped out, legs unsteady on the uneven ground.

The helicopter pounded above, but the sound felt distant, muffled by adrenaline and the wind cutting across the bluffs.

The autonomous cab rocked in the breeze.

The vehicle inched closer to open air as Ahmed squeezed his eyes shut, the remnants of hope draining away. Backup arrived fast. Car 54 skidded in behind her, and more cars behind that. Blackburn ignored them all, her attention fixed on Lilith's trembling silhouette inside the cab.

Shouts rose behind her, but Blackburn let them recede into empty sound. Her feet stuttered when she tried to move.

Then, she ran. Gravel bit through her shoes. At the car, her hand closed on the door handle. The metal refused to move. A second hand, a foot against the car for purchase. The handle did not give.

The car's rear tires found empty space. Gravity won. Gravel groaned, the edge collapsed, and the vehicle tipped fully into space.

As it dropped, the rear passenger door juddered loose. Not wide, just enough to shift. To reveal.

For one breathless instant, Lilith's arm was visible. Fingers splayed into nothing. The fall was silent. Just air rushing past. Then the body, the car, the night swallowed it whole.

Blackburn felt the ground crumble under her feet. For a second, she hung suspended between the collapsing road and open air.

Then the moment shattered. The car hit earth then air again, metal shrieking as it fell. Steel twisted on its way down, smashing against the rocks below. The echo carried up from the gorge, a clean rupture in the night.

Blackburn landed hard on the road, dust coating her tongue. She choked and spat out grit as hands grabbed her shoulders. DeForest was pulling her back just before the edge gave way completely.

Her chest heaved. She tasted copper and earth. A laugh slipped through anyway, sharp and thin.

Lilith was gone now. No survival was possible. Far below, fire licked the wrecked cab's frame as the battery lit white-hot against the black rock. Flames hissed in the updraft, pushed sideways by wind that tunneled along the gorge. Metal gaped where the rear passenger door hung loose, torn open during descent.

Blackburn didn't rise. She didn't look over the edge. She didn't need to.

Her Lilith was dead. The only one who hadn't flinched under Blackburn's hands, who had worn every mark with pride and made Blackburn want to leave more. That body was a ruin now, somewhere below in fire and twisted metal, reduced to whatever trace survived the impact.

It wasn't grief that filled her. It was anger at being denied what was hers to keep or end as she chose. Lilith had belonged to her, a perfect fit for needs Blackburn could never name aloud. Now, someone else had taken even that choice away.

But already she saw how it would play: the rogue cab, the detective nearly lost in the attempt to save lives, the young officer's timely rescue. The press would eat it up. She would set the terms of loss and heroism herself.

Around her, officers called out orders and swept flashlights over empty space. Radios crackled at their belts. EMTs reached for her shoulders, helping steady her as she got to her feet.

She steadied herself, her gaze moving over the scattered gravel and the torn guardrail at the cliff's edge. The place where Lilith's story ended because someone else wanted control. Down below, fire marked where Lilith lay.

I've been there before with people I trust. Lilith had said those words early in their relationship. Blackburn twisted violently, shaking off the EMT's grip.

"I can walk by myself," she snarled.

The EMT motioned for her to sit on the ambulance's rear step and began his evaluation. "Your name?" he asked, his penlight tracking across her eyes. The light was hypnotic, calming.

"Morgan Blackburn. Detective, New Dresden Police Department," she answered, her voice even.

"What day is it?"

"Thursday, very early morning."

"Dizziness? Nausea?"

"No. I'm clear," Blackburn said, her focus shifting back to the scene.

The EMT finished his work in silence. Across the cordon, DeForest watched her, uncertain and waiting for direction, congratulations, something.

Blackburn gave him a small nod. "Thank you. Call heavy rescue." Her words were measured and calm. "I'll let the chief know."

Underneath the composure, something pressed up, sharp and unfinished. She closed it off. There was no room for more.

She would write the ending, yes, but she couldn't un-feel what it had cost her to arrive here.